# Linda – As in the Linda Murder

## Leif G.W. Persson

*Translated from the Swedish by Neil Smith*

**Doubleday**

LONDON · TORONTO · SYDNEY · AUCKLAND · JOHANNESBURG

TRANSWORLD PUBLISHERS
61–63 Uxbridge Road, London W5 5SA
A Random House Group Company
www.transworldbooks.co.uk

First published in Great Britain
in 2013 by Doubleday
an imprint of Transworld Publishers

Originally published in Sweden
as *Linda – som i Lindamordet*
in 2005 by Piratförlaget

Copyright © Leif G.W. Persson 2005
Translation copyright © Neil Smith 2013

Leif G.W. Persson has asserted his right under the Copyright, Designs
and Patents Act 1988 to be identified as the author of this work.

This book is a work of fiction and, except in the case of historical fact,
any resemblance to actual persons, living or dead, is purely coincidental.

A CIP catalogue record for this book
is available from the British Library.

ISBN 9780857520869 (cased)
9780857520876 (tpb)

Addresses for Random House Group Ltd companies outside the UK
can be found at: www.randomhouse.co.uk
The Random House Group Ltd Reg. No. 954009

The Random House Group Limited supports the Forest Stewardship Council (FSC®), the
leading international forest-certification organization. Our books carrying the FSC label are
printed on FSC®-certified paper. FSC is the only forest-certification scheme endorsed by
the leading environmental organizations, including Greenpeace. Our paper procurement
policy can be found at www.randomhouse.co.uk/environment

Typeset in 11.5/15pt Dante by
Falcon Oast Graphic Art Ltd.
Printed and bound in Great Britain by
Clays Ltd, Bungay, Suffolk

2 4 6 8 10 9 7 5 3 1

*For Maj Sjöwall and Per Wahlöö –*
*who did it better than almost anyone*

# 1

*Växjö, Friday 4 July*

It was a neighbour who found Linda, and, all things considered, that was far better than her mother finding her. It also prevented the police from losing a great deal of time. Her mother hadn't planned to come back from the country until Sunday evening, and she and her daughter were the only ones living in the flat. The earlier the better, as far as the police were concerned, especially regarding a murder investigation.

The alarm had reached the regional communication centre of Växjö Police at five minutes past eight in the morning, and a patrol car in the vicinity had responded. Just three minutes later they had reported back. They were at the scene, the woman who had sounded the alarm was safely installed in the rear seat of the patrol car, and they were about to enter the building to check the situation.

The duty officer himself had taken the call. The two younger men who had picked up the request had already managed to acquire something of a reputation in the local force. Sadly it was not a wholly positive one, and, since the duty officer was twice their age, had thirty years in the force, and reckoned that he spent far too much time up to his neck in elk-shit, his first instinct had been to send reinforcements. However, while he was considering this they had reported back once more. After just eight minutes, and on his mobile, so that none of what they had to say would be overheard by anyone listening in. It was now quarter past eight.

Remarkably, for once, regardless of their age, experience and reputation, they had got everything right. They had done all that could have been expected of them, and one of them had even done more. Got himself a little gold star in his service record, in a way that had previously been unheard of in the records of the Växjö Police Authority.

In the bedroom of the flat they had found a dead woman. Everything indicated that she had been murdered, and that this had only happened a few hours before. There were no signs of the perpetrator, apart from an open bedroom window at the back of the building, which at least gave some indication of how he had left the scene of the crime.

Unfortunately there was a complication. The young officer who spoke to the duty officer was convinced that he recognized the victim. And if she was who he thought she was, it meant that the duty officer had met her on numerous occasions over the summer, most recently on the previous day.

'Not good, not good,' the duty officer muttered, apparently largely to himself. Then he had pulled out the little reminder list of what he should do if the worst happened to him at work. A laminated sheet of A4 with ten things to remember, and the thought-provoking heading *If the stuff hits the fan at work*. He put it under the blotter on his desk at the start of each shift, and it was almost four years since the last time he had any reason to take it out.

'Okay, boys,' the duty officer said. 'This is what we're going to do . . .'

Then he too had done everything that could reasonably have been expected of him. But no more than that, because you don't want that sort of excitement at his age.

The patrol car that had arrived at the crime scene first contained two young police officers from Växjö. One was Acting Police Inspector Gustaf von Essen, thirty years old and known in the force as the Count because of his name, even though he was always careful to point out that he was actually just 'a perfectly ordinary baron'. The other officer in the car was four years younger: Police Constable Patrik Adolfsson, known as Adolf for reasons which were sadly not limited to his family name alone.

When they responded to the call, they were a couple of kilometres from the reported address, on their way back to the police station. Because there was practically no traffic at all in the area at that time of the morning, Adolf had done a 180-degree turn, put his foot down and headed back the quickest way without lights or siren, while the Count kept a sharp eye out for any suspicious movement in the opposite direction.

Together they made up almost two hundred kilos of prime Swedish police officer. Mainly muscle and bone, with all their senses and motor-functions in the best possible shape, taken as a whole they were the dream response for any terrified citizen calling to say that he or she had three unknown hooligans out in the porch, trying to break the front door in.

When they pulled up in front of the building on Pär Lagerkvists väg where the alleged crime was supposed to have been committed, an agitated middle-aged woman came running out into the road towards them. She was waving her arms and stumbling over her words and Adolf, who was first out of the car, had gently put his arm round her and ushered her into the back seat, and reassured her that 'everything's all right now'. And while the Count had taken up position at the rear of the building, weapon drawn, in case the culprit was still on the premises and intended to make his escape that way, Adolf had quickly checked out the entrance to the property and then gone into the flat. Easy enough, seeing as the front door was wide open.

This was the point where he won his gold star, before doing, for the very first time, all the other things that he had been taught to do at Police Academy up in Stockholm. With his pistol drawn he had looked through the flat, padding along the walls so as not to mess things up unnecessarily for their colleagues in forensics, nor to present the per-petrator with an easy target if he was still around and crazy enough to have a go. But the only person there was the victim. She was lying on the bed in the bedroom, motionless, beneath a bloodstained sheet that covered her head and torso and half her thighs.

Adolf called to the Count through the open bedroom window that the coast was clear for him to check the stairwell, then holstered his pistol and pulled out the little digital camera he had under his left armpit. Then he quickly took three different pictures of the covered body before he carefully folded back the sheet to check if she was alive or dead.

With his right index finger he had managed to locate her carotid artery, even though this was actually entirely unnecessary considering the noose around her neck and the look in her eyes. Then he had carefully felt her cheeks and temples. In contrast to the living women he had touched in the same way, her skin felt merely mute and stiff under his fingertips.

She looks pretty dead, even if she hasn't been dead for long, he thought.

But he had also recognized her. Not as someone he had merely seen before, but as someone he was actually acquainted with, had spoken to and fantasized about afterwards. Strangest of all, although he had no intention of ever telling anyone about this, he had never felt so *present* as he did just then. Completely present, yet at the same time as if he were standing outside what was happening and watching himself. As if this really wasn't anything to do with him, still less with the woman lying dead in her bed, even though just a few hours before she must have been every bit as alive as he was.

# 2

The witness who had found the victim and called the police was interviewed for the first time at about ten o'clock in the morning by two detective inspectors. The interview was recorded and typed up the same day. Approximately twenty pages of print: Margareta Eriksson, fifty-five years old, widow, no children, lived on the top floor of the building where the victim and her mother lived.

The final page of the transcript noted that the witness had been informed that she was being issued with a disclosure ban according to paragraph 10, chapter 23 of the Judicial Procedure Act. There was nothing, however, about her reaction to the fact that she was not, 'on pain of punishment', allowed to tell anyone about the contents of the interview. In itself this wasn't so strange. It wasn't the sort of thing that was usually recorded, and besides, she had reacted just as most people did when they received the same notification: she certainly wasn't the sort of person who'd go about gossiping about that sort of thing.

The building, consisting of a basement, four floors and an attic, was owned by a residents' association of which the witness was also the chairperson. Two flats on each of the lower three floors, and one double-size one at the top where the witness lived. In total seven properties, all owned by people in middle age or older, single people and couples with grown-up children who'd moved out. The majority of them were away on holiday at the time of the crime.

The flat in which the murder took place was owned by the victim's mother, and according to the witness the victim sometimes lived there too. Recently the witness had seen the daughter fairly often, but the mother herself was on holiday, spending most of her time at her country place on Sirkön, an island twenty kilometres south of Växjö.

The flat, four rooms and a kitchen, was on the ground floor when seen from the street entrance; but because the building was on a slope the flat was actually one floor up at the back looking on to the yard, which itself led into a small area of woodland surrounded by detached houses and a few blocks of flats.

The witness was a dog-owner and, according to what she said during her interview, dogs had been her main interest for many years. In recent times she had had two, a Labrador and a spaniel, which she walked four times a day. At seven in the morning she usually took them on a long walk lasting at least an hour.

'I'm a morning person. I've never had any trouble getting up early – I hate lying around once I'm awake.'

When they got home she usually had breakfast and read the morning paper while the dogs got their 'morning feed'. At twelve o'clock it was time for another walk with the dogs, again lasting about an hour, and when she returned she usually ate lunch while her two four-legged friends were rewarded with 'a dried pig's ear or something nice to chew on'.

At five o'clock she would go out again, but not for so long this time. About half an hour, so she would have time to eat dinner and 'give Peppe and Pigge their evening feed' in peace and quiet before it was time to switch on the television for the evening news. That left 'the evening pee' some time between ten and twelve in the evening, depending on what else the television had to offer.

In other words, she followed a fixed routine that largely seemed to be dictated by her dogs. She usually spent the free hours in between either running various errands in town, meeting friends – 'mostly women like me and other dog-people, really' – or working from home in her flat.

Her husband, who had died ten years ago, had been an accountant with his own business, and she had worked for him part time. After he died she had carried on helping some of their old customers with their accounts. But her main source of income was the pension left by her husband.

'Ragnar was always careful with things like that, so I really don't have anything to worry about.'

The interview had been conducted in her flat. The officers who interviewed her could see with their own eyes that there was no reason to disbelieve her on that last point. Everything they could see indicated that Ragnar had been careful to provide for his wife after his death.

At eleven o'clock the previous evening, while she was busy with the so-called 'evening pee', she had seen the victim emerge from the front door and set off in the direction of the town centre.

'It looked as though she was going to a party, although I tend to think that most youngsters look like that now no matter what time of day it is.'

She herself had been standing some thirty metres away up the road and they hadn't exchanged greetings, but she was quite sure it was the victim she had seen.

'I don't think she saw me. She was probably in a hurry, otherwise I'm sure she'd have said hello.'

Five minutes later she was up in her own flat and, following her usual routine, she had gone to bed and fallen asleep more or less at once, and that was pretty much all she could remember from the previous evening.

This incredible summer had begun as early as May, and did not seem to want to come to an end. Day after day without the slightest puff of wind, the sun hot as a barbecue, the sky bleached blue, merciless, with no clouds, no shadow. Day after day with the temperature setting new records, and the following morning she had gone out with the dogs very early, at half past six.

That was earlier than usual, but considering the 'absolutely incredible summer . . . I don't think I'm alone in thinking that . . . I wanted to avoid the worst of it'. And every responsible dog-owner knows that dogs don't cope well with too much exertion when it's hot.

She had followed the same route she always took. Turned left when she came out of the front door and walked up the road past the neighbouring properties, then down the path off to the right towards the larger patch of woodland that spread out just a few hundred metres behind the building she lived in. Half an hour later, by which time it was already unbearably hot even though it wasn't much after seven o'clock, she had decided to turn back and go home. Peppe and Pigge were both panting heavily and even their owner was longing for the shade at home in the flat, and something cool to drink.

More or less at the same time as she decided to turn back and go home, the sky had suddenly clouded over and turned black, a wind started whipping at the bushes and trees, and she could hear thunder not far off. When the first few heavy drops started to fall she was just a couple of hundred metres from home, and she had started to jog even though there really wasn't any point, seeing as the shower had already turned into a downpour and she was soaked through by the time she got back to the apartment block through the yard at the back.

That was when she noticed that her neighbour's bedroom window was open and blowing in the wind, and that the curtains inside the room were already soaked.

As soon as she got into the entrance hall – 'it must have been about half past seven, if I've got that right' – she had rung her neighbour's doorbell several times, but no one had come to the door.

'I thought she must have come home late and opened the window. For all the good that would have done, because it's far warmer outside than it is indoors. When we were out for the evening pee it was shut, at any rate, because I usually notice things like that.'

Because no one had come to the door she had taken the lift up to her floor. She had dried the worst of the rain off the dogs, and changed into dry clothes. She had also been in a bad mood.

'This is actually a shared property, and water damage isn't to be taken lightly. And then there's the risk of burglary. Admittedly, it's a few metres up to the windowsill, but it seems to me that hardly a day goes by without there being something in the paper about burglars stealing everything people have, and even if they're off their heads on drugs, it can't be that difficult to borrow a ladder from one of their friends, can it?'

But what should she do? Talk to the daughter next time she bumped into her? Call her mother and tell tales? A fortnight ago there had been a similar cloudburst, but that one had only lasted ten minutes before it stopped as abruptly as it had started, and the sun started shining in a blue, cloudless sky once more, and it had actually been good for the lawns and other plants. But not this time, and after quarter of an hour, while she sorted out the dogs' food bowls and made herself some coffee, it was still raining just as heavily, and she suddenly came to a decision.

'As I said, I'm chair of the residents' association, and we usually look out for each other here. Especially during the summer when so many people are on holiday. So I've got spare keys to most of the flats in the building.'

So she had fetched the key that the victim's mother had given her, taken the lift down to the ground floor, rung on the bell a few more times, 'just in case she was home after all', then unlocked the door and gone into the flat.

'I suppose it looked the way you'd expect when youngsters are left at home alone, so I didn't really think anything of it. I think I called out to see if anyone was home, but no one answered so I went in . . . into the bedroom . . . yes . . . and then I saw what had happened. I realized straight away. So I . . . I turned and ran right out into the road. I was terrified – I thought that he might still have been there. Fortunately I had my mobile with me so that's when I called . . . called the emergency number . . . you know, one one two. And they actually answered at once, even though you read in the paper that there are never any police.'

She never did get round to closing the open bedroom window, which didn't really matter because it had stopped raining by the time the first patrol car arrived on the scene, and any eventual water damage was by then completely irrelevant. Police Constable Adolfsson naturally had no intention of closing it. He had actually noticed that there were extensive traces of diluted blood on the windowsill outside, but he decided to leave that particular detail to his colleagues in the forensics division.

The hottest summer in living memory, a neighbour who took the same walk with her dogs every morning, and also happened to have spare keys to the victim's flat, a sudden downpour, an open window. Circumstances working together, the hand of fate if you like, but, whatever you called it, this was why the police were able to work out that things had happened one way and not another. And, considering the alternatives, that was far from being the worst possible outcome.

# 3

The duty officer had certainly done his bit. Within less than two hours everyone who should have been at the crime scene was actually there. Unfortunately there were also a whole load of other people that they could happily have done without, but there was nothing he could do about that, and the area around the building had been cordoned off, as had the road in front of it, in both directions.

Uniformed officers had systematically begun to search through the neighbouring properties and the immediate locality, while a dog patrol was trying to pick up the trail they assumed the perpetrator must have left when he jumped from the open window at the back of the building. Without success, however, but considering the downpour a couple of hours earlier that was hardly surprising.

Forensics had started searching the flat; the medical officer had been contacted and was on his way in from his house in the country. Officers from the county crime unit had already conducted a first interview with the witness who had found the body, and both the victim's parents had been informed of what had happened and had been taken to the police station. Soon the uniforms would start going door-to-door in the area, and all the points on the duty officer's list – with the exception of the last one – had been actioned and ticked off.

When he was sure that all the pieces were in place, or at least on their way, he got to grips with the final point on the list and called the county police commissioner. Astonishingly, even though it was a Friday during this endless summer and the man was supposed to be on holiday, he wasn't at his place in the country, on the coast outside

Oskarshamn, some hundred kilometres from Växjö, but behind his desk a few floors above in the same building as the duty officer. They spent almost fifteen minutes talking on the phone. Mostly they talked about the victim, and when the conversation was over, regardless of how experienced and hardened he might have been, the duty officer suddenly felt inexplicably depressed.

It was odd, really, because he usually felt strangely elated when he thought back to what had happened the last time he had needed to consult his handwritten list. He had been on a lengthy secondment to the neighbouring force in Kalmar, and two of the town's worst hooligans had started shooting madly, in the middle of the day, in the middle of town, in the midst of all the decent, law-abiding citizens, firing off a couple of dozen shots in every possible direction. As if by some miracle, they had only succeeded in hitting each other, and a thing like that could only happen in Småland, the duty officer had thought at the time.

The county police commissioner wasn't happy either. Admittedly, he wasn't a murder detective, and one of his maxims in life was never to meet trouble halfway, but this case really didn't look good. It had all the signs of a classic murder inquiry, and if things turned out badly – which wasn't improbable, considering who the victim was – there was a serious possibility that he would be left feeling the way people like him always felt when things at work went as unfairly as they possibly could.

During an after-dinner speech he had given the previous week he had spent a long time talking about the limited resources of the police, and had concluded by comparing his force to 'an inadequate and poorly maintained fence trying to hold growing levels of criminality at bay'.

It had been a much appreciated speech, and he himself had been particularly pleased with the metaphor of the fence, which he thought both ingenious and well phrased. Nor was he alone in this: the editor-in-chief of the largest local paper had been at the same dinner and had congratulated him over coffee and cognac. But that was then, and the county police commissioner would rather not imagine what direction the editor-in-chief's thoughts would be taking over the next few hours.

Worst of all were his personal, entirely private, feelings. He was acquainted with the victim's father, and he had met the daughter – the murder victim – on a number of occasions. He remembered her as a delightful young woman, and if he had had a daughter he would have been happy if she could have looked and behaved like her. What's going on, he thought. And why the hell was it happening in Växjö, where there hadn't been a murder case during all the years he'd worked there. In my patch. And in the middle of summer, to top it all.

That was when he made up his mind. No matter how stretched his fence was right now, and regardless of the fact that holidays and other investigations were hardly helping, it was high time for him to prepare himself for the worst that could happen. So he picked up the phone and called his old friend from their student days, HNC, to ask for help. Whom else could he possibly turn to in a situation like this?

After the conversation, which lasted less than ten minutes, the county police commissioner felt noticeably relieved, almost liberated. Help was on its way, the best possible help, from the murder squad of the legendary National Crime Unit, and their head had promised that it would arrive that very day.

He too had managed to acquit himself with honour during the early stages of the task. No gold star, admittedly, nor even a silver star, but probably a little bronze one because he had managed to think about a not inconsiderable practical detail. Straight away he had his secretary call the Town Hotel and book six single rooms for the foreseeable future, and had requested that the rooms be close together, and preferably separate from the rest of the hotel.

The people at the Town Hotel were happy, because it was the middle of the summer lull and there were plenty of vacancies, which wasn't the case just a few hours later that same day, when there wasn't a single hotel room to be had anywhere in the centre of Växjö.

# 4

## *Stockholm, Friday 4 July*

Even though it was only ten o'clock in the morning – during this remarkable summer that had begun in May and didn't seem to want to end – one of the great legends of the National Crime Unit's murder squad had already arrived at work. Unlike most of his colleagues, Detective Superintendent Evert Bäckström hadn't gone off to the country to battle with gnats, a cross wife and whining kids. Not to mention all the crazy neighbours, stinking outdoor toilets, barbecues that smelled of petrol, and warm lager.

Bäckström was short, fat and primitive, but when necessary he could be both sly and slow to forget things. He regarded himself as a wise man in the prime of life, an unfettered free spirit who preferred the quiet life of the city, and since a sufficient number of appetizing and scantily clad ladies seemed to share the same view, he had no reason at all for complaint.

Summer holidays were a source of pleasure for people who didn't know any better, a device used excessively by almost all his colleagues, and thus a very good reason to stay at work: you finally got the opportunity to govern your own time. Last in and first out, and no one around to make any comments. And that was the whole point. Plenty of time for various errands outside police headquarters, and if any remaining boss should happen to look into his office, he was well prepared.

The day before his immediate superior went on holiday Bäckström had announced that as well as looking after practical matters if the worst should happen, he intended to fill any spare time by going back through old cases which had now gone cold. His boss hadn't made any objection, largely because he just wanted to get away from police headquarters on Kungsholmen, and partly because the last thing he wanted to do was talk to Bäckström. So Bäckström's desk was now covered by a mountain of unsolved murders which his less mentally blessed colleagues had messed up for no good reason.

The first thing he did when he arrived at work was to rearrange the piles of paper, in case anyone happened to poke about in there. After planning the rest of his day from the not inconsiderable comfort of the office chair behind his overburdened desk, he clicked on his telephone to activate a suitable reason for his absence. There were several to choose from, and to avoid any suspicious pattern he threw a dice to let fate decide if he would be spending the rest of the day 'in a meeting', 'out of the office on official business', 'temporarily out of the office', 'on external business', or possibly even 'away on business'. By the time this recurring task had been dealt with, it was usually high time to continue the trials and tribulations of the day by having 'lunch'. A fundamental human requirement, a right enshrined in employment legislation, and naturally an absence worthy of its own code in the police telephone system. He didn't even need to throw the dice.

The only practical problem was that there was a distinct shortage of overtime and other small pecuniary advantages, because, as so many times before, he was suffering from a slight shortage of funds even though it was only a week since payday. Something will turn up, Bäckström thought. There's always the weather, and all the half-naked ladies in the city. Soon enough a lunatic will beat some poor bastard to death in some three-star destination worthy of a trip in its own right, and then there'll be overtime, expenses and all the other tax-deductible advantages for a simple police officer. And while he was in the middle of these encouraging thoughts his phone had suddenly rung.

The head of the National Crime Unit, Sten Nylander – or HNC as he was usually known among his eight hundred fellow officers – had also been deep in thought when the county police commissioner had called him from Växjö. Elevated thoughts about an intricate operational problem he'd set out on the vast planning desk in his own control room, or op-centre as he preferred to call it, principally about how best to deploy his rapid-response unit, in case international terrorists should hit upon the foolish notion of trying to hijack a plane out at Arlanda.

His colleague down in Växjö evidently didn't have the same ability to differentiate between large and small concerns, and in order to prevent half his day from being wasted he had promised to send down some people from the murder squad at once. The worst that could happen, in the event that they were busy, was that they would have to rearrange their priorities, he thought as he hung up and asked his secretary to 'get hold of that little fat bastard from National Crime, the one whose name I can never remember'. Then he had returned to more important matters.

'HNC seems to have a lot on, even though it's the height of the holiday season,' Bäckström said, as he smiled his most ingratiating smile at his boss's secretary and nodded towards the closed door behind her back. Op-centre, HNC, yeah, right! he thought.

'Yes, he's certainly very busy,' the secretary said in a measured tone, without looking up from her papers. 'No matter what time of year it is,' she added.

Naturally, Bäckström thought. Or else he's been on a course and learned that people like him should always make people like me sit and wait for quarter of an hour while he reads the editorial in *Svenska Dagbladet*.

'Yes, we live in troubled times,' he lamented.

'Indeed,' the secretary said, giving him a stern look.

Unless you're HNC, of course, Bäckström thought. The bastard had a nice title as well. HNC sounded military, as well as macho. Definitely better than being National Police Chief, the biggest bird in the farmyard, and being called NPC. Who the hell wants to be NPC? Sounds like something you pick up if you've been out with the wrong sort of woman.

'HNC is free now,' the secretary said, nodding towards the closed door.

'Humble thanks,' Bäckström said, bowing slightly from where he sat. Exactly quarter of an hour. Even a child could have worked that out. Even you, you nice little attack-dyke, he thought, smiling cheerily towards the secretary. She didn't respond, and just glared suspiciously at him.

Bäckström's most senior boss seemed to be lost in his own thoughts. He was still stroking his manly and well-defined chin with his right thumb and index finger, and when Bäckström came into the room he hadn't said a word, merely given him a curt nod.

Odd character, Bäckström thought. And what ridiculous clothes, when it's thirty degrees outside.

The Head of National Crime was, as usual, dressed in an impeccable uniform, and for that day this consisted of a pair of black riding boots, the blue trousers of the police horse unit, and a blindingly white uniform shirt with epaulettes bearing four gold bars and an oak leaf topped by a regal crown. On the left side of his chest was a four-barred ribbon, and on the right the two crossed golden sabres that for some reason had become the emblem of the National Crime Unit. A tie, naturally, fixed at exactly the right angle with the help of the police service's own tiepin for senior commanders. Back straight as a poker, stomach pulled in and chest puffed out, as if it were trying to compete with his most prominent physical feature.

What a fucking chin! He looks like a bloody oil tanker, Bäckström thought.

'If you're wondering about the way I'm dressed,' HNC said without gracing him with so much as a glance or taking his fingers from the part of his face that was occupying Bäckström's thoughts, 'I'm planning to go riding on Brandklipparen later on.'

No flies on him. Better be careful, Bäckström thought.

'A regal name for a noble steed,' HNC added.

'That's what Charlie the Twelfth's nag was called, isn't it?' Bäckström said obsequiously, even though he had skived off most of his history lessons.

'Both Charles XI and Charles XII,' HNC said. 'The same name, but naturally not the same horse. Do you know what this is?' he added, nodding towards the intricate model set out on the vast planning desk.

Considering all the terminals, hangars and aeroplanes, it probably isn't the battle of Poltava, Bäckström thought.

'Arlanda,' he guessed. What on earth did Arlanda look like from above?

'Exactly,' HNC said. 'But that's not why I wanted to see you.'

'I'm listening, boss,' Bäckström said, trying to look like the cleverest pupil in class.

'Växjö,' HNC said emphatically. 'A murder inquiry, a young woman, found strangled in her home this morning. Probably raped as well. I promised them our help. So put a team together and set off at once. You can sort out the details with Växjö. If anyone here has any objections, refer them to me.'

Excellent, Bäckström thought. Damn, this was even better than the age of the three musketeers, which was one book he had actually read. When he was playing truant from school.

'No problem, boss,' Bäckström said. Växjö, he thought. Wasn't that by the sea somewhere, down in Småland? It must be crawling with women at this time of year.

'And one more thing,' the Head of National Crime said. 'Before I forget. There's a slight complication. The identity of the victim.'

Let's see, said the blind man, Bäckström thought, as he sat at his desk half an hour later, busy arranging the practical details. First of all, a serious injection of liquid assets in the form of a postal order he had managed to pick up from accounts even though it was a Friday at the height of the holiday season. This he had reinforced with a few thousand-kronor notes from the gratuities box of the violent crime unit. There was always something there in case of urgent, unexpected expenses, and Bäckström always kept a close eye on it, because no matter how malnourished his own bank account might look, he had no intention of ever suffering any form of deprivation.

He had also managed to scrape together all of five colleagues, four of whom were proper police officers and only one a woman. But, on the other hand, she was a civilian employee and would mostly be busy trying to keep the paperwork in order, so he could probably live with that. And one of his colleagues would appreciate her being there, seeing as he usually jumped on her whenever he had the chance, at a sufficient distance from his miserable wife. Maybe it wasn't the absolute elite, Bäckström thought as he looked over the list of his team, but good enough considering how many people were on holiday. Besides, he was going to be there as well.

Which left transport for the trip down to Växjö, as well as while they were there. For some reason there were plenty of cars, and Bäckström laid claim to the three best. For himself he picked the largest four-wheel drive Volvo they had, with the biggest engine and so much extra equipment that the boys in the technical section must have been on a high when they fitted it out.

That's pretty much it, Bäckström thought, ticking off his little list. All that remained was his own packing, but when he started thinking of that he suddenly began to feel uneasy. Drink wasn't a problem. For once he had a hell of a lot of booze at home. One of his younger colleagues had been on a big shopping trip to Tallinn over the weekend and Bäckström had bought a considerable proportion of the booty: whisky, vodka and two crates of export-strength lager that was absolute dynamite.

But what the hell am I going to wear? In his mind's eye he could see his broken washing machine, the overflowing linen basket and the piles of dirty laundry that had been growing in the bedroom and bathroom for almost a month now. Only that morning before he set off for work he had run into problems. Freshly showered and sparkling clean he had stood there, for once not the slightest bit hungover, and he'd had a devil of a job before finally sniffing his way to a shirt and a pair of underpants that wouldn't make people think of a Danish cheeseshop if he had to talk to them. It'll sort itself out, Bäckström thought, suddenly struck by a brilliant idea. First a quick detour past the shopping centre on Sankt Eriksgatan to get something nice and new. He wasn't short of cash any more, and – on further reflection – he could simply take the dirty laundry from home with him and hand it in at the hotel down in Växjö. Brilliant, Bäckström thought. But first a bit of lunch, because it would be a serious dereliction of duty to embark upon a murder case with an empty stomach.

*

Bäckström had eaten a decent lunch at a Spanish restaurant in the vicinity, with a lot of tapas and other suitably summery delights. Because he had decided that his employers could foot the bill for this, he added a not entirely present informer to the receipt. This inform-ant had had the good sense to drink two large glasses of beer. Bäckström himself, because he was on duty, had made do with a simple mineral water, and when he emerged, replete and fortified, on to the street again he felt better than he had in ages. The sun's shining and life is looking up, he thought, setting off towards his own flat. He didn't even need to take a taxi, because for the past few years he had lived in a nice little flat on Inedalsgatan, just a couple of minutes' walk from police headquarters close to Kronoberg Park.

He had got the flat from an old colleague who had retired some years ago, someone he had got to know during his time in the violent crime division in Stockholm. His former colleague had moved out to his summer cottage, out in the archipelago, where he could drink him-self to death in peace and quiet, doing a bit of fishing while he was at it. As a result, he no longer had any need of his flat in the city, and had transferred the contract to Bäckström.

Bäckström himself had sold his own flat to a younger colleague in regional crime who had been kicked out of his place because he'd had an affair with a uniformed officer, but because she was already married to a third colleague who worked in the rapid-response unit and could be a mean bastard at times couldn't move in with her. So instead he had bought Bäckström's flat. Cash, no tax, and an affordable price, in return for helping Bäckström move his things to his new place on Kungsholmen. Two rooms, kitchen and bathroom, on the second floor in a block tucked inside a courtyard. Reasonable rent, mostly elderly neighbours who never made any noise and had no idea that he was in the police, so things couldn't be better.

The only problem was that he had to get hold of a woman who would do his cleaning and washing in return for a few good seeings-to in Bäckström's sturdy pine bed from Ikea. Because right now it looked like shit, Bäckström thought as he packed his dirty washing in a suitably large sports bag for onward transportation to the Town Hotel in Växjö.

It would have been best if he could have taken his whole flat with him and handed it in at reception, he thought. What the hell, it'll sort itself out. Bäckström fetched a cold beer from the fridge. Once he'd packed a second bag with everything else he needed, he was suddenly struck by a terrible thought. It was as if someone had grabbed him from behind by the collar and shaken him: in recent years, this had happened rather too often. What the hell am I going to do with Egon?

Egon was named after the retired colleague who had sorted the flat for him, but otherwise they weren't terribly similar, because Bäckström's Egon was a goldfish of the most common variety whereas the man whose name he bore was an almost seventy-year-old former police officer.

Bäckström had been given Egon and his aquarium by a woman he had met six months ago. He had replied to a contact advert he had seen on the internet. What had prompted him to reply was partly the advertiser's description of herself, but mainly the way she signed off: *uniform a plus*. Bäckström might have been careful to avoid wearing a uniform since he became big enough in the force to defend himself, but who cared about details like that?

To start with it had worked very well. Her description of herself as *a liberated and broad-minded woman* hadn't been entirely without foundation. Not to start with, only after a while, when she turned out to be remarkably similar to all the other whining women who had passed through his life. And things had turned out the way they usually did, with the exception of Egon, because he was still there. Things had now got so bad that Bäckström had started to feel attached to him.

The emotional breakthrough in Egon and Bäckström's relationship had happened a couple of months before, when Bäckström had been forced to go off into the country for a week on a murder case, and consequently had no opportunity to feed a goldfish each day.

First he had called the woman who had lumbered him with his little swimming dilemma, but she had just shouted at him and hung up. Oh well, if it works, it works, Bäckström thought, and in spite of the warning on the side of the container he had tipped half a pot of food into the aquarium before he set off. That's the advantage of having a goldfish, he thought as he sat in the car on the way to the murder investigation. You can't flush a dog down the lavatory if it croaks, and he could probably get a few hundred for the aquarium if he put an advert online.

When he returned ten days later it turned out that Egon was still alive. Admittedly, he had seemed considerably brighter before Bäckström had set off, and he had spent a few days swimming at an odd angle, but after that he had been his usual self again.

Bäckström was impressed and had even mentioned Egon in the staffroom at work – 'an unusually tenacious little bastard' – and that was more or less when he started to get attached to him. Sometimes he even found himself sitting there in the evenings, sipping a well-earned drink after a long, trying day at work, just looking at him. Watching how Egon swam back and forth and up and down, apparently not the slightest bit bothered that there were no little fishy ladies in the vicinity. You've got it worked out, lad, Bäckström would think. Compared to all the useless nature documentaries on television, Egon was a clear winner.

I'll just have to make sure the case doesn't take too long, Bäckström thought, feeling slightly guilty as he measured out a hefty dose of food with his thumb and tipped it into his silent little friend's aquarium. And if things looked likely to drag on, he'd simply have to call work and ask one of his colleagues to take over the daily routine.

'Take care, lad,' Bäckström said. 'Daddy's got to go away and do some work. See you soon.'

Quarter of an hour later he was sitting in the car on the way to Växjö together with two of his colleagues from the murder squad.

# 5

Two of the younger talents in the unit, Detective Inspectors Erik Knutsson and Peter Thorén weren't particularly bright sparks but at least they usually did what Bäckström told them. At work they were known as Hans and Fritz, after the old cartoon characters, and apart from the fact that Hans was fair and Fritz had dark hair they were easily mixed up. They almost always appeared together, they talked more or less incessantly over each other, and if you closed your eyes it was actually impossible to work out which of them was speaking.

Knutsson was driving while Thorén sat alongside reading out loud from a tourist guide to Växjö that he had downloaded from the internet. Bäckström himself had spread out across the back seat in order to be able to think about the case in peace and quiet, accompanied by another cold beer.

'Sorry, Bäckström,' Thorén said. 'Växjö's not on the coast. It's about a hundred kilometres from the Baltic. It's got a cathedral, a county governor and a university. You must be thinking of Västervik. Or Kalmar, maybe. Kalmar and Västervik are both on the coast. In Småland. You know, Astrid Lindgren and all that. Looks like there are about seventy-five thousand people in the town. In Växjö, I mean. How many available women does that work out at? Any idea, Erik?'

'Is it too much to hope that we might hear something about the case?' Knutsson asked crossly. 'Probably a couple of thousand, at least,' he added, sounding much happier all of a sudden.

'Our colleagues in Växjö are going to fax the details through as soon as they've put something together,' Bäckström said, nodding towards the instrument panel between the seats.

'They must know something by now,' Knutsson persisted.

Moan, moan, moan, Bäckström thought with a sigh.

'This morning they found a young woman murdered in her flat. Strangled. If you can believe what the local sheriffs say, it seems to have been about sex. Perpetrator unknown, and all that. If we're lucky, they're wrong and we can go and pick up her boyfriend straight away.'

'And that's all we know?' Knutsson said sceptically. 'So did she have a boyfriend, then?'

'Doesn't look like it,' Bäckström said hesitantly. 'There's also a minor complication. She's one of our own.'

'What?' Knutsson exclaimed. 'A police officer?'

'That's bad,' Thorén said. 'A police officer. That doesn't happen every day. Not if it's a sex crime, I mean.'

'Almost a police officer,' Bäckström clarified. 'She was training in Växjö. Was due to finish next year. Looks like she was spending the summer working in Växjö police station. Behind the reception desk.'

'What the hell's going on?' Knutsson wondered, shaking his head. 'What sort of moron kills a trainee police officer for sex?'

'If it's someone she knows, there's a fair chance it's another officer,' Bäckström said. 'Mind you, it might not be as bad as that,' he added when he saw the hostile look in Knutsson's eyes in the rear-view mirror.

'Looking on the bright side, it ought to be easier than your average prostitute murder,' Thorén said encouragingly. 'I mean, at least we won't have to deal with all the weird clients and criminal contacts and all that.'

That's hardly likely to be the big problem this time, lad, so you can forget about that, Bäckström thought. 'Let's hope so,' he said. 'Let's hope so.'

They were just passing Norrköping when their colleagues down in Växjö sent the fax, but considering what they sent they might as well not have bothered. First a map of Växjö with the scene of the murder marked by a circle, and the way to the hotel marked with arrows. Completely unnecessary, since Thorén had already found the same map on the internet and the first thing Knutsson had done was type in the address of the hotel on the car's sat-nav.

Then came a short message from the head of the local investigating team, welcoming them and informing them that the investigation had started and was being conducted according to routine, that further information would follow as soon as he had anything to send, and that the first meeting of the team was due to take place at nine o'clock the following morning in the police station in Växjö.

'DS Bengt Olsson from regional crime in Växjö is evidently going to head up the preliminary investigation,' said Thorén, who was sitting closest to the fax machine and had both hands free. 'Anyone you know, Bäckström?'

'I've met him,' Bäckström said, swallowing the last drops from the can. Slightly retarded, so things couldn't be better, he thought. At least not for him, seeing as he had already worked out how he was going to manage this.

'So what's he like?' Knutsson asked.

'He's the sympathetic type,' Bäckström said.

'Does he know anything about murder, then?' Knutsson persisted.

'I doubt it,' Bäckström said. 'But I dare say he's been on lots of courses about violence against women and children and incest and debriefing and all that sort of thing.'

'But he must have led at least one murder investigation?' Thorén suggested.

'A few years ago he made a big deal out of the ritual killing of a young immigrant girl that was supposed to have taken place in Småland some years back. He had some crazy informant who claimed she was there at the time.'

'So what happened?' Knutsson asked.

'It was all fine. They sent the case up to us and we wrapped it up the following day. Then we sent them a letter explaining that the murder in question never actually took place. We thanked them for their concern and asked them to get back in touch if they had any more old ghost stories in their files.'

'I think I remember that,' Thorén said. 'It was before my time, but isn't he the one, Bengt Olsson, I mean, who's known as the Ritual Killer detective among our older colleagues?'

'That's him,' Bäckström said. 'That's his speciality. Ghosts and creepy old blokes and incense and sharpened canine teeth, capes and so on, then a nice debriefing before the officer staggers home from work.' What do you mean, older colleagues? he thought. Fucking age-fascists.

'What on earth's happening to the force? Where are we heading?' Thorén moaned.

'I thought I just said that,' Bäckström said. 'So if you two gentlemen would be so kind as to shut up for a while, I'll try to rest my weary head.' Off he goes as well, he thought. Two idiots sitting in the front of the car.

The rest of the journey passed in relative silence. No more faxed messages. Knutsson and Thorén had carried on chatting to each other but at lower volume and without trying to draw Bäckström into the conversation. When they reached the Town Hotel in Växjö it was five o'clock in the afternoon, and because Bäckström was still feeling a little drowsy he decided to stretch out on his bed for a couple of hours before they met for dinner. Besides, their other colleagues hadn't shown up yet.

He had been smart and called the hotel before they arrived so they could sneak straight up to their rooms without having to fight their way through the vultures from the fourth estate who had already started to gather in the lobby. He had also taken the opportunity to share out some work. After all, he was in charge. He told Knutsson to get in touch with the local force and pass on a message that he was otherwise engaged at the moment but would contact them as soon as possible, and would be there for the big meeting the following morning. Thorén had promised to organize Bäckström's laundry, and would then take a trip out to the scene of the crime. He himself intended to take a well-deserved little nap.

'After all, I've been on the go since first thing this morning,' he said, already stretched out across the bed in his room. 'And don't forget to book a discreet table down in the restaurant for eight o'clock.' At last, he thought when Thorén closed the door behind them. Then he adjusted the pillow and fell asleep more or less instantly.

# 6

Half an hour before dinner they all met in Bäckström's room to catch up. Entirely natural, seeing as he was in charge, and if they met anywhere other than in the boss's room there would be mutinous talk. Bäckström knew this of old, from both sides, having been both captain and crew member during his years in violent crime. But so far everything seemed calm. All of his team had turned up. Alert and happy and almost a bit expectant, as if this were just some ordinary conference trip to Finland rather than a murder investigation.

First into Bäckström's room was his old colleague, Detective Inspector Jan Rogersson, whom Bäckström had known ever since his days on the old violent crime division in Stockholm. He had travelled down alone and taken a detour via the police station in Nyköping to hand back some case notes on an investigation that had gone reassuringly cold. The victim's widow had finally turned up her toes and stopped writing to complain to the judicial ombudsman. Rogersson had turned up at the hotel in Växjö a couple of hours after Bäckström. A good bloke, in Bäckström's opinion, and practically the only one of the people he worked with that he could bear to spend time with outside work.

Bäckström felt alert and in the best of moods, freshly woken and freshly showered as he was, and he and Rogersson had taken the chance to down a couple of lagers and a bracing chaser or two before the others trooped in and disturbed the peace. Knutsson and Thorén arrived together, naturally. Knutsson had been at the police station, where he had met their new colleagues and been given a mass of documents. Thorén had handed in Bäckström's dirty laundry and visited the crime scene, and neither of them was offered either beer or anything stronger when they turned up. On the contrary, as soon as they knocked on the door Bäckström had tucked away both bottles and glasses before opening up. They could do their drinking in their own time, he thought.

Last to arrive was Detective Superintendent Jan Lewin, who had driven down with their civilian assistant, Eva Svanström. It was a bit odd, because they had set off from Stockholm together before all the others and goodness knows how it could take seven hours to drive four hundred kilometres, but they all knew the answer so no one asked straight out.

'Hope you had a good drive,' Bäckström said with an innocent expression, looking at the only woman in the group. Alert, rosy and recently fucked, he thought. But far too skinny for his taste, so he might as well keep his mouth shut and let them get on with it.

'It was very good,' Svanström twittered. 'Janne had a couple of things to do on the way, that's why it took so long.'

'I see,' Bäckström said. 'Well, maybe we should take the opportunity to get something done while we're on our own, so that we can have a bite to eat without having to talk about the case among all the vultures down there. Erik, you brought a load of papers with you. Have you got copies for everyone?' Completely useless, he thought.

Knutsson had brought with him pretty much everything that was available and ready when he visited the police station. And six copies of everything, enough for one each. In their bundles they each had the initial alarm call, a report from the first responders, various photographs of the crime scene and the surrounding area, a sketch of the flat where the body had been found, a short description of the victim, and a log detailing what their colleagues had already had time to make a start on.

Bäckström felt slight disappointment when he glanced through the file. They didn't seem to have missed anything obvious. Not yet, at least, and considering that he was about to take charge things would doubtless be fine.

'Any questions?' he asked, to a unanimous shaking of heads.

'Well, it's not time for food yet,' he said with a crooked smile. Lazy fuckers, he thought. All they think about is food, drink and fucking.

'Do we know when we might get anything from the medical officer and forensics?' Rogersson asked.

'The post-mortem's tomorrow,' Knutsson said. 'They've evidently driven her down to the Institute of Forensic Medicine in Lund. The forensics team are hard at work but the one I spoke to thought that they'd managed to get samples of semen from the perpetrator, as well as blood from the windowsill outside the bedroom. There were also some clothes that they think belong to him. Things he left behind when he ran off. Looks like he was in a hurry, and the officer I spoke to is pretty sure he jumped out of the bedroom window. That's probably when he cut himself on the windowsill.'

'You mentioned something about clothes,' Bäckström grunted. 'Don't suppose we're lucky enough that he ran off without his trousers?'

'Looks pretty much like it,' Knutsson replied. 'Well, I don't know how he was dressed when he arrived, but it looks as though he left without his underwear.'

'That was rather careless of him,' Bäckström said. 'Still, I don't suppose that's where he kept his driving licence, because that would be a bit too much to hope for.' Hardly anyone's that stupid, he thought, although this one seemed stupid enough, and that was usually a good sign.

'Bäckström,' Rogersson said, apparently in a very good mood all of a sudden. 'Do you remember that idiot who strangled that woman in her flat on Högalidsgatan? The Ritva murder. That was her name. He spent ages cleaning up after him, wiping away fingerprints and pretty much scrubbing the walls, floor and ceiling before he left. The idiot spent hours at it. It was just a shame that little Ritva who lived there didn't get to see the benefit of having everything so clean.'

'I remember,' Bäckström said. 'We were both on the case, and it's pretty much the only one you've ever talked about in the past twenty years.' Must be all the drink, Bäckström thought.

'Now, now, there's no need to be like that,' Rogersson said, no less cheerfully. 'I wonder how he felt when he slammed the door behind him and suddenly realized what he'd forgotten.'

'I don't suppose he felt too great,' Bäckström said. He nodded towards Thorén. 'Peter, you've been to look at the crime scene. What does it look like?'

'What was the point?' Thorén asked. 'Forgive a young man's ignorance, but what was the point?'

'What do you mean, the point?' Bäckström said. What the hell's he going on about? How about answering a perfectly simple question instead?

'With the bloke on Högalidsgatan?' Thorén persisted.

'Oh, him,' Bäckström said. 'Well, he'd forgotten to pick up his wallet, with his driving licence and all the other things people usually have in their wallets. He left it on the victim's bedside table. But apart from that he'd left everything beautifully neat and tidy. Forensics didn't actually find a single strand of hair. But to get back to the matter in hand . . .'

'I don't believe it,' Knutsson exclaimed, looking almost as happy as Rogersson.

'Our case,' Bäckström reminded them. 'What about the crime scene?'

According to Thorén, it looked the way crime scenes usually looked. Just as miserable as they always were when a woman had been raped and murdered. Possibly slightly more miserable this time, as the perpetrator had been alone with the victim in her home and seemed to have had complete control over her, and had evidently had plenty of time.

Unfortunately none of the usual classic suspects had been identified. No former or current boyfriend, nor anyone else that she knew and trusted. She didn't appear to have had a boyfriend for a while, and there were no known madmen or particularly suspicious characters either in the neighbourhood or among the people she knew. Which left the typical police nightmare. A perpetrator who was unknown to the victim. Someone she had never met before, and, in the worst cases, someone no one else had ever met either.

'So it looks like it's going to be a proper murder investigation after all,' Thorén concluded.

'Okay,' Bäckström said. 'We'll sort it out. You can all read through the file in peace and quiet before going to bed. Make sure you look after them, so I don't have to see it in the paper. This whole building's crawling with reporters and other body-snatchers. Well, I for one could do with some food now. I haven't eaten a thing since this morning and I'm hungry as hell.'

'If you all write your names at the top of your file and give them to me, I'll lock them in my safe while we eat,' Svanström said.

'Excellent idea,' Bäckström said. You jumped-up little nightmare, he thought. And he was right: she was far too skinny as well.

After dinner they had all gone back to their rooms to start studying the case. At least that's what they told Bäckström they were going to do, and Knutsson and Thorén were naturally going to do it together. Even Rogersson, who was usually a perfectly normal officer, seemed to have been afflicted by the desire to do some reading. Although he had accompanied Bäckström back to his room first and borrowed a couple of export-strength lagers from him, he had declined Bäckström's invitation to join him in a post-prandial snifter.

'You're not coming down with something, are you, Rogge?' Bäckström asked. 'I'm starting to worry about you.' Feeble little bastard, he thought.

'No,' Rogersson said, shaking his head. 'No need to worry. I just need to get a few hours' sleep so I can keep up tomorrow.'

So they had gone their separate ways, which was just as well really, considering that Bäckström was thinking of taking a discreet little walk round the town. To check the lie of the land, if nothing else, and that sort of thing was best done alone.

He had snuck out of the back of the hotel, and spent a while strolling at random round the centre of town. He had never visited Växjö before, either on business or privately, and now he wandered past the governor's residence and the cathedral, past all the nice old buildings that had been restored the way buildings like that demanded, and past a number of outdoor bars full of people dressed for summer who didn't look particularly upset by the event which had brought him here. How on earth could anyone kill someone else in that way in a place like this, Bäckström wondered. It must be the first time in local criminal history.

There were several pleasant hostelries along his route, and even though it was after eleven o'clock in the evening it was almost twenty degrees, but Bäckström had been steadfast in resisting temptation until he got back to the hotel.

There he ordered a beer on the terrace, and went and sat in the gloom of the far corner so he could have some peace. Not too many people about, either, he thought. His colleagues were conspicuous by their absence, and the simplest explanation was that they had all actually done what they had promised to do. He had his doubts as far as Lewin and little Svanström were concerned, because he doubted that reading came very high up their list, but Knutsson and Thorén were probably more straightforward. They would be sitting in one of their rooms talking about murder cases, and they'd probably carry on like that half the night if no one stopped them. Who on earth would do something like that, Bäckström wondered. And they're stone-cold sober as well, the little idiots, he thought, sipping his beer.

'Is this seat taken?'

The person asking was a woman. In that indeterminate age between thirty-five and forty-five, and obviously past the best-before date for women, but at least she was verging on the well-rounded side, Bäckström thought.

'That depends who's asking,' he said. Journalist, he thought.

'Yes, maybe I should introduce myself,' she said, putting her own beer on the table and sitting down in the empty chair. 'My name's Carin Ågren.' She handed over a business card. 'I'm a reporter for local radio here in town.'

'What an astonishing coincidence,' Bäckström said with a smile. 'So what could I possibly help you with, Carin?' Other than giving you a shot up the snatch up in my room, he thought.

'Yes, isn't it?' she said, smiling and showing her white teeth. 'Funny the way things turn out sometimes. I actually recognize you. I've seen you before, when I was working for TV4 in Stockholm a couple of years ago. I was covering a trial and you were one of the witnesses.

Three Russians who'd robbed and killed an elderly couple. Might I ask what National Crime's murder unit is doing in town?'

'I haven't the faintest idea,' Bäckström said, taking a large gulp of his beer. 'I was thinking of paying a visit to Astrid Lindgren's childhood home.'

'Maybe we could meet some other time,' she said with a smile. Just as broad as before, the same white teeth.

'Maybe,' Bäckström said, and put her card in his pocket. He nodded and finished the last of his lager. Then he stood up and gave her his most effective smile. The battle-scarred cop from the big city. Tough against the tough guys but the nicest man in the world if you were gentle enough and stroked him in the right way.

'I'll take that as a promise,' she said. 'Otherwise I'll have to start stalking you.' She raised her glass and smiled at him for a third time.

Definitely up for it, Bäckström thought quarter of an hour later as he stood in front of the bathroom mirror brushing his teeth. It was just a matter of taking it slowly and in the right order, and she'd soon get a taste of the Bäckström super-salami.

# 7

In marked contrast to Bäckström's imaginings, Detective Superintendent Jan Lewin had sought the tranquillity of his own room immediately after dinner, so that he could read the file on the case in peace and quiet. He had summarized everything that was good and everything that was bad, and even though most of it was little more than preliminary information, there seemed to be quite a lot working in his and his colleagues' favour.

They had a victim whose identity was known, a crime scene, an approximate idea of how it had all happened and when the crime was committed. He and his colleagues were on the scene less than twenty-four hours after the murder, and that wasn't always the case if you worked for the murder squad. The crime had been committed indoors, which – all things considered – was better than outdoors, and their victim seemed to be a perfectly normal young person without any extravagant habits or contacts.

In spite of all this, he hadn't been able to shake off the usual sense of gnawing unease. First he had considered going to visit the crime scene on Pär Lagerkvists väg, to get an impression of what had happened with his own eyes, but because every indication suggested that their colleagues from forensics were still busy there he had decided not to disturb them unnecessarily.

In the absence of anything else and largely to give himself something to do, he had hooked up his computer and gone on to the internet to read about the author and Nobel Prize-winner Pär Lagerkvist, who had lent his name to the road where their victim had lost her life. Whatever he might have to do with anything, Lewin thought. He'd been dead for the past thirty years.

Not entirely unexpectedly, it turned out that Pär Lagerkvist came from Växjö. Born in 1891, the youngest of a clutch of seven children. Meagre financial circumstances, father a foreman of the goods yard at Växjö railway station, the highly talented youngest son who, in contrast to his older siblings, had the opportunity to study and graduated from high school in Växjö.

Then he had left his childhood behind and gone away to become a writer. At the age of twenty-five, in 1916, he made his literary break-through with a collection of poetry, *Angst*. Eventually he was elected to the Swedish Academy, and in 1951 he was awarded the Nobel Prize for Literature.

He was evidently held in high regard by his hometown, because just a few months later a road was named after him in the town where he had been born and grew up. And this more than twenty years before he died, which tended to be when such accolades were bestowed upon people like him. And at the time the buildings which would eventually be constructed along the road bearing his name only existed in the designs of the town planning office.

Now one of them had become Jan Lewin's latest crime scene, and as soon as he had time and it seemed appropriate, he planned to pay it a visit. But not tonight, he thought. Not tonight, when their colleagues in forensics needed to get on in peace.

Instead he had taken a walk through the town. Night-empty streets that led him, after just four hundred metres, to the new police station that would be his workplace for the immediate future.

The building was situated on Sandgärdsgatan, on one of the town's squares, Oxtorget. It had been put up at the start of the new millennium, and was a temple to justice typical of its time. A boxlike building of four or five floors, depending how you counted, with a pale yellow façade, where the police shared premises with the prosecutor's office, a courtroom for custody proceedings, a jail and the probation office. A justice factory, arranged in such a practical way that it covered the entire judicial chain. A clear message, of scant solace to those who ended up there, and poor support for the theory that every suspect should be treated as if he were innocent until the opposite had been proved beyond all reasonable doubt.

To the left of the entrance Lewin had found a small copper plaque which told him that back in Pär Lagerkvist's day, and even long after he had won the Nobel Prize, this had been the site of Växjö's old dairy, with pens for the local cattle market. For some reason Lewin suddenly felt depressed. He turned on his heel and headed back to the hotel, to try to get a few hours' sleep before the serious work began.

Before he fell asleep he found himself thinking about angst for some reason. Presumably not an unusual subject for a young poet, regardless of when he had been alive. And presumably a common subject for authors no matter how old they were, in the middle of a world war with the whole of Europe in flames.

Jan Lewin knew a fair amount about angst. Private and personal experience of the emotion that had been his lot ever since he was a child. Admittedly, it visited him less often the older he got, but it was still lurking out there, constantly present, always ready to attack if he wasn't strong enough to resist. Suddenly, unexpectedly, every time from a different source. Its consequences abundantly clear even if its message and origins were always shrouded in darkness.

Added to this was the angst he encountered in the course of his work, when it prompted violent attacks that he ended up investigating. Dates that had gone wrong, relationships that had gone off the rails, providing fruitful territory for fear and hatred. And sometimes ended up on his desk in the National Crime Unit in Stockholm.

And finally there was the angst that could afflict even the most hardened and ruthless criminal when he realized the enormity of what he had done. Always assuming that the police were going to catch him, of course, so it was best to hide in the darkness. Constantly aware that people like Jan Lewin were searching the same darkness, trying to find him.

If nothing else, then to ease my own angst, Jan Lewin thought, before finally falling asleep.

# 8

## *Växjö, Saturday 5 July*

Was I right, or was I right? Bäckström thought when he came down to the hotel reception for breakfast on Saturday morning. The evening papers had already arrived. Even though it was only quarter past eight in the morning, they were displayed in a stand by the reception desk. Bäckström grabbed a copy of each and headed towards the breakfast room and his colleagues. If this is just a small complication, we must sincerely hope we don't encounter anything larger, he thought.

The whole of the front page and a great deal of the rest of the papers were full of his murder, and the angle was precisely what he had expected: POLICE OFFICER KILLED IN SEX ATTACK, screamed the larger of the two, while its slightly smaller competitor tried to roar even louder: YOUNG FEMALE POLICE OFFICER MURDERED . . . *Strangled, raped, tortured.* Bäckström tucked the papers under his arm, picked up a tray and started loading it with his breakfast. No one could run a murder investigation on an empty stomach, he thought as he helped himself to liberal portions of scrambled egg, bacon and sausage.

'Have you seen the evening papers, Bäckström?' Lewin asked as he sat down at the table where the others were sitting. 'Wonder how her family will feel when they see that?'

Are you stupid, or what? Bäckström thought, leafing through the papers with his left hand while he shovelled in scrambled egg and sausages with the right.

'It's just . . . bloody vile,' Thorén, who almost never swore, agreed.

Another one, Bäckström thought. He grunted between mouthfuls and went on reading.

'Why don't the police ever do anything about them?' Knutsson said. 'There should be legislation covering this sort of thing. Abuse like this is just as bad as . . . well . . . as what the victim went through.'

Yes, imagine. Why don't the politicians do something? Stop the editors from publishing a load of crap, Bäckström thought as he continued to eat, still glancing through the papers.

They carried on like this for a good five minutes while Bäckström let his food stop him talking, and finished both his breakfast and his reading. The only one who hadn't said a word was Rogersson. But then he usually didn't say much at this time of day.

But at least there's one of them who's got the sense to keep quiet, Bäckström was thinking as the first representative of the fourth estate came over and introduced himself and wondered if he could ask a few questions. Then Rogersson finally opened his mouth.

'No,' he said, and together with the look in his eyes, this was clearly an exhaustive reply, because the man who had asked disappeared instantly.

Rogge's good, Bäckström thought. He hadn't even had to growl and bare his teeth, which was usually what he was best at.

'There's something else worrying me more,' Bäckström said. 'But we can deal with that when we're alone.'

The first opportunity for that didn't arise until they were all standing in the car park behind the closed gates of the police compound.

'I presume you've all had time to read the evening papers,' Bäckström said.

'I took a look at breakfast television, and that wasn't much better,' Lewin said.

'Not to mince words, this is just bloody vile,' Thorén repeated. He was evidently learning to overcome his reluctance to use at least the milder oaths.

'What worries me,' Bäckström said, 'is that everything we talked about yesterday evening is already in the papers. Never mind about the hypotheticals and all the fucking speculation, just concentrate on the facts in there. The only reasonable conclusion is that this ship is already leaking like a sieve.' He nodded towards the police station that was about to become their base for the foreseeable future. 'If we can't sort that out, we're going to end up far deeper in the shit than we deserve.'

None of the others contradicted him.

First Bäckström had met the county police commissioner and the officer from Växjö who was going to be the lead detective in the preliminary investigation, and thus his immediate superior. At least in theory, Bäckström thought. It always happened whenever he and his colleagues from National Crime went around the country trying to mop up the mess made by the local sheriffs.

'In spite of the tragic circumstances, I'm still pleased and relieved that you and your colleagues are able to be here to assist us. As soon as I realized what had happened, I called HNC Nylander and asked for help . . . we've known each other since we studied together . . . so if I've cried wolf for no reason, I apologize. Thank you for coming, detective superintendent. Thank you very much.'

Bäckström nodded. What a fucking moron, he thought. Take two Valiums and go home to your little wife, and nice Uncle Bäckström will skin the wolf for you.

'I can only agree unreservedly with my boss,' Olsson concurred. 'You and your colleagues are very welcome, and your arrival keenly anticipated.'

Another one, Bäckström thought. Where do they all come from?

'Thanks,' he said. Two little poofs sitting on the same branch twittering in tandem, he thought. Now how about trying to get a bit of work done?

Before they could get to work, the division of labour had to be agreed, as well as the formal set-up for the investigation.

'We'll be doing it all according to the book, as usual,' Bäckström said. Because I presume you know how to read, he thought.

'Unless you have any objections, Bäckström, I thought I might look after external communication . . . contact with the media and so on, plus personnel issues and other administrative details. There'll be quite a few of us. Six of you, and about twenty from our side. We've brought in some people from Jönköping and Kalmar, so in total there'll be something like thirty of us on the case. You don't have any objections?'

'None at all,' Bäckström said. Not as long as they do as I say, he thought.

'Then there's one practical problem as well,' Olsson went on, exchanging a glance with the commissioner. 'Do you want me to take it, boss?'

'Go ahead, Bengt,' his boss said.

'This is a terrible event, a real tragedy, and it's the height of the holiday season and a lot of the officers we've called in are younger and perhaps not so experienced . . . So the commissioner and I decided yesterday that we should have a dedicated crisis therapist attached to the investigating team, so that anyone working on the case can have the opportunity to get professional advice at all times, to help them deal with the whole business . . . debriefing, basically,' Olsson concluded, sighing deeply, as though he were already in need of this particular service.

Christ, this can't be happening, Bäckström thought. But he managed not to say so out loud.

'Do you have anyone in particular in mind?' he asked, in a brave attempt to appear as sympathetic as the others in the room.

'A very experienced female psychologist who's worked for us before, who also runs the modules on debriefing on the police training course here in Växjö. She's also worked for the council for a number of years. And she's greatly admired as a speaker.'

'What's her name?' Bäckström asked.

'Lilian . . . Lilian Olsson, known as Lo,' Olsson said. 'No relation.'

No, you're just bloody similar, Bäckström thought. And wouldn't it be practical if all morons could have the same surname?

'I'm sure it'll be fine,' he said. 'I presume that she won't be part of the investigative team itself?' Just as well to get that clear from the start.

'No, of course not,' the county police commissioner said. 'But she thought she might sit in on your preliminary meeting and introduce herself, so that everyone knows how they can get in touch with her and so on. We've organized a room for her here in the building.'

Well, that wasn't so bad, Bäckström thought once the meeting with the police commissioner was finally over. All his colleagues were in the positions that really mattered. Lewin would be directly subordinate to him, checking all the material relating to the case as it came in. Separating the wheat from the chaff, picking out the important details. Making sure anything that looked promising was followed up, and relegating all the nonsense to the files at the far end of the shelves.

Rogersson would be in charge of interviews, while Knutsson and Thorén would get to stick together looking after internal and external surveillance. He had even managed to sort something out for little Svanström. Because of her great practical experience of the documentation involved in a murder investigation, she was going to be in charge of the local civilian employees, with responsibility for registering the paperwork that was already threatening to overwhelm the investigation.

And, most important of all: Bäckström was in charge. Not bad, he thought, as he walked into the large meeting room where they were going to be based from now on, where most of his colleagues were already sitting and waiting. Not bad at all, in spite of the fact that yet another madwoman was going to be poking her nose into his and his colleagues' business even though she shouldn't have been allowed to set foot inside the building. Not in my book, anyway, Bäckström thought.

It had begun the usual way, with each of them telling everyone else what their name was and what they did. Because there were thirty-four people in the room, this had taken a fair bit of time, but even Bäckström could put up with that seeing as he was going to get rid of two of them as soon as the introductions were finished. The female press officer for Växjö Police, and the investigation's own spiritual adviser. Practically enough, these two were the last to introduce themselves, and the press officer had been surprisingly concise and clear: she, and she alone, would manage all contact with the media, after consultation with those in charge of the investigation.

'I was a police officer for almost twenty years before I took this job,' she said. 'I know most of the people in this room, and those of you who know me as well know better than to mess with me. After reading today's evening papers, it appears that I must issue a sharp reminder to everyone here about the confidentiality that is essential in this case. If it's slipped anyone's mind, you've got some revising to do. But best of all would be to keep your mouths shut and only talk about the case with people working on it, or when there's a reason to talk. Any questions?'

No one had any questions, so she simply nodded to them and walked out. She had a fair amount to do, after all. Bloody hell, Bäckström thought. I wonder what she was like when she was a police officer? Quite good-looking too. But at the top of the age range. Must be almost forty-five, poor old thing, thought Bäckström, who was himself ten years older.

Their very own crisis therapist, trained psychologist and psychotherapist Lilian Olsson, had, unsurprisingly, required rather more time. Seeing as she matched Bäckström's expectations down to a T, a small, skinny blonde who must have seen at least fifty rainy autumns, he wasn't the least bit surprised.

'Well, my name's Lilian Olsson . . . but everyone who knows me just calls me Lo, so I hope you will as well . . . Well, I'm a trained psychologist and psychotherapist . . . and a lot of you are probably asking yourselves what one of those does. As I said, I'm a psychologist . . . a therapist . . . I give lectures and run courses . . . I work as a consultant . . . and in my free time . . . voluntary work for a lot of different charities . . . the women's helpline . . . the men's helpline . . . the crime victims' helpline . . . and I'm writing a book as well . . . and most of the people sitting here . . . it's okay to feel upset . . . a lot of us seem sensitive, confused, badly affected by crises . . . whereas others take refuge in macho attitudes and denial, not saying anything and . . . some people abuse alcohol and sex . . . themselves and those around them . . . a lot of us have eating disorders . . . we're all human . . . we have to affirm . . . we have to raise our consciousness . . . we have to take the step . . . free ourselves from all the heavy baggage that holds us back . . . we have to dare to show our weaknesses . . . dare to cry for help . . . dare to step outside all this . . . this is what it's all about, really . . . the liberation process, to put it simply . . . it's really no more than that . . . so really it's all fairly simple and straightforward. And my door is always open to you,' Lo concluded, letting her gentle smile embrace each and every person in the room.

Blah, blah, blah . . . blablah. Bäckström adjusted his position and snuck a glance at his watch. More than ten minutes of the investigation's limited and valuable time had already gone up in smoke because yet another in the endless parade of morons needed almost quarter of an hour to let everyone know that she had a door and that it was wide open, he thought.

'Well, then,' he said as soon as she'd shut the door behind her. 'Maybe the rest of us should think about getting something done. We've got a madman on the loose, and we need to get him locked up. The sooner the better.' And ideally we'd boil him down to make glue, he thought but didn't say. Every proper police officer knew that anyway. They didn't need to have it spelled out under their noses, and during Ms Crisis Therapist's performance he had already checked out a couple of the younger officers who, to judge by the looks on their faces, seemed very promising. Maybe there was even a future Bäckström in the room, Bäckström thought. However incredible that might seem.

# 9

'Okay, let's get going,' Bäckström said. He leaned forward over the head of the long table where he was sitting, resting on his elbows and jutting out his chin almost as far as if he were head of the entire National Crime Unit.

'I thought we could start by outlining the current position,' he went on. 'What we know about the victim, and what she got up to. Everything we know so far.'

Their murder victim was called Linda Wallin. She was twenty years old and would have been celebrating her twenty-first birthday exactly one week after she was murdered. That autumn she had been due to start the third term of the police course in Växjö. She was 172 centimetres tall and weighed 52 kilos. Natural blonde, short hair, blue eyes. An attractive girl, if you happened to like the skinny type that does a lot of exercise, Bäckström thought as he looked at a photograph of her. It was an enlarged version of the picture on her ID card from police college, and showed an openly smiling Linda looking straight into the camera, absorbed in the moment and full of expectation about the life ahead of her. Like this summer, for instance, when she had been working as a civilian employee for the police in Växjö, where she seemed to spend most of her time behind the reception desk, a job she had handled with great efficiency. Not just good to look at, but good at her job, competent and appreciated by visitors and colleagues alike.

She was described by people who knew her as talented, charming, sociable, clever and keen on sport. Possibly not too surprising considering the circumstances, but for once there was documentary evidence to back it up. Top grades from school and police college in both practical and academic subjects. She was also the fastest female student in her year round the assault course, and the second-best shot in her school's female football team. And she still appeared to have been socially and politically active, in the approved way. At school she had written a project on *Crime, racism and xenophobia.* Not your typical female murder victim, but probably the sort of girl who could take home anyone she liked, and it was probably no more complicated than that, Bäckström thought.

Like all children, Linda had two parents, and, like many children in her generation, those parents were divorced. In her case, for the past ten years. Linda was the only child of the marriage, and the parents had shared custody after the divorce. Just before they split up, the family had spent a couple of years living in the USA, because her father had started his own business in New York. When her parents' relationship broke down, her mother had brought Linda back to Sweden with her.

The mother was forty-five years old and had spent the past fifteen years working as a teacher in a secondary school in Växjö. The father was twenty years older, a successful businessman who had started to take things a bit easier now. He had returned to his roots in Småland a few years after Linda and her mother, and now lived in a large manor house by Lake Rottnen, a short distance south-east of Växjö.

He had two sons from a previous marriage, approximately twice the age of the daughter he had just lost. According to their inform-ation, Linda had very little contact with her two older half-brothers. But she got on well with both parents even though the parents them-selves didn't appear to have met each other since the divorce. Sounds like the usual marital mess, Bäckström thought. It was high time for a question.

'So she lived with her mother in the flat where she was murdered?' he asked.

'She seems to have lived with both parents. But recently mostly with her mother,' replied the female officer from Växjö Police who was putting together the profile of the victim.

'So what was she doing before she met her tragic fate?' Bäckström said, sounding both friendly and interested. That's what they should look like if they have to be in the police, he thought. Dyed blonde hair, a nicely pulled out top drawer, happy and friendly and in good shape for thirty. The only problem was that she was doubtless seeing some idiot country sheriff who might even be in that very room. Approach with extreme caution.

'You've asked the right person,' the policewoman said with a smile. 'We were actually in the same place, the victim and I. We were at Grace, the nightclub at the Town Hotel, because there was a big club night there on Thursday evening. But Linda left before I did. I was there until they closed. You have to make the most of it when your husband and kids are safely out of the way in the country,' she clarified, apparently not feeling the slightest bit embarrassed. Nor did anyone else either, judging by the suppressed smiles that suddenly spread through the team.

'Really?' Bäckström said, still sounding just as friendly and interested. Maybe this town is a bit desperate after all, he thought. Especially if he was going to make a move on someone in his own team. Like, for instance, officer Anna Sandberg, 33, of the Växjö Police. That was evidently her name, according to the list of team members he had on the table in front of him.

'We're making progress,' Sandberg declared. 'Gyllene Tider were playing on Öland yesterday, so there were considerably more people in town than usual, and I certainly wasn't the only member of the force, or future member, at Grace . . . well . . . I think we're starting to get a grip on who was there. If you'd like me to run through it briefly?' She glanced questioningly at Bäckström, and was rewarded with a friendly and interested nod.

Go ahead, my dear, he thought. We can deal with the details when we're on our own.

On Thursday, the day before she was murdered, Linda had spent the day working in reception in the police station. She had left the building with a friend who was also employed in a civilian capacity by the police just after five o'clock in the afternoon. They had spent some time looking in a couple of shops, then at half past six they went into a pizza restaurant in the centre of town, where they each had pizza, salad and mineral water. That was also where they decided to meet later that evening at the Town Hotel.

When they had finished their meal they split up and Linda walked home. On the way she made three phone calls on her mobile. The first of these, just after half past seven, was to her mother, who was at her summer cottage south of Växjö. A short, chatty conversation during which she told her mother about her plans for the evening.

The second and third calls were to a female friend and classmate from police college, to see if she 'wanted to come along to the club'. The classmate asked for time to think about it, but when Linda called back ten minutes later and said that she had just got home and was about to have a shower – in case her friend called and wondered why she wasn't answering – the friend had decided to go along. At quarter past eleven they had met outside the Town Hotel on the central square and gone into the nightclub together.

What she was doing between quarter to eight and just before eleven o'clock that evening was as yet unclear, but it seemed likely that she had remained in the flat the whole time. She hadn't made or received any calls on her mobile in that time. But she did call her father just before nine o'clock on the landline in the flat, and that conversation lasted about quarter of an hour. According to her father they had talked about everyday matters, things that had happened at work, and his daughter's plans for the rest of the evening. And from what Linda told her friends in the bar later that night, she had watched a music programme on MTV that had started at half past nine, and had then changed channel to watch the ten o'clock news on TV4.

Approximately an hour later the neighbour saw her as she left the house on foot and went off down Pär Lagerkvists väg, heading south towards the town centre. This information was reinforced by the fact that she withdrew five hundred kronor at fourteen minutes past eleven from the cashpoint outside the SE-Bank on the corner of the main square and Storgatan, just fifty metres from the entrance to the Town Hotel nightclub.

'I think it all fits together fairly well,' Sandberg finished. 'Any girl knows it takes a while to get ready if you're going out partying. That's probably all she was doing when she wasn't talking to her dad or watching television or just taking it easy. She was simply getting ready for a night out,' she concluded, and suddenly looked rather down in the mouth.

'What happened inside the club?' Bäckström asked. Women are all the bloody same. If things carry on like this, that psychologist bitch is going to have her hands full.

What had happened there wasn't yet entirely clear either, for quite natural reasons. It was crowded, as usual in a nightclub, and there were a lot of people that they hadn't yet had time to question. The evening was also more chaotic than usual because they had hired the services of some local celebrities who had appeared in various reality shows on television and now made a living from public appearances in nightclubs.

Nothing dramatic or even particularly interesting seemed to have occurred, in light of what happened to Linda a few hours later. She had drifted about like most of the others, the way people do in clubs. She sat down with two different groups of people. She chatted and danced and seemed to be in good spirits. She hadn't argued or even disagreed with anyone, and no one had tried it on with her. She hadn't been particularly drunk either. She drank one beer, possibly a raspberry shot, and after that a couple of glasses of wine at most, which a female colleague from the police station had bought for her.

Some time between half past two and three in the morning she had found her classmate from police college and told her that she was thinking of going home and getting some sleep. The bouncer on the door had seen her when she left – 'just before three if you ask me' – and according to him she was both sober and alone, and neither happy nor sad, when he saw her head off diagonally across the square, past the district governor's residence, towards her home on Pär Lagerkvists väg.

In the worst-case scenario, that would be where she disappeared into the mist for the police. No witnesses had seen her walk the kilometre or so between the club and her home. Or at least none that had contacted them. No calls to or from her mobile. And a quiet night in the town, and especially on the streets that Linda had probably walked down.

'Okay,' Bäckström said, looking round his investigating team. 'This bit's pretty damn important, as I'm sure you realize. I want to know in detail what happened inside that club. Every bastard who set foot in there needs to be questioned, all the staff, and not least those reality TV people. Especially them. The same thing with her walk home. No witnesses have contacted us, then?' He looked enquiringly at Police Constable Sandberg, who looked almost guilty as she shook her head.

'Surveillance cameras,' he said emphatically. 'You mentioned a cash-point. There must be some sort of camera there?' Fucking amateurs, he thought.

'We've pulled in the recording. I'm afraid we haven't had time to look at it yet. We simply haven't had a chance.'

'What other cameras are there on her route home?' Bäckström rocked on his elbows and looked fierce.

'We're looking into that,' Sandberg said. 'I've thought about it, but we haven't had a moment to check it out yet.'

'Well, we'll just have to make that a priority,' Bäckström countered. 'Before the bloke in the corner shop and anyone else thinking along the same lines realizes that he forgot to get permission to set up his little camera and decides to hide it away and delete the recordings from Friday night.'

'I see what you mean,' Sandberg said.

'Excellent,' Bäckström said. 'Then it's high time we started knocking on doors along the route between the club and her home. Get the officers who've been going door-to-door around where she lives to move on to that.'

She contented herself with a mere nod this time and made a note in her little book.

Shiiit, Bäckström thought, glancing at his watch. Into the third hour already. His stomach had started to rumble from lack of food and they hadn't even got to the crime scene yet. And if he wasn't going to end up having to spend all day listening to this, he'd just have to take over, speed up the whole process and make sure his investigative team did a decent job.

'Okay,' he said, nodding to the forensics expert, Enoksson, known as Enok, a superintendent and head of the unit. 'Correct me if I'm wrong, Enoksson. The crime scene is the flat where she lived with her mother, and it happened some time in the early hours of Friday morning, between approximately three o'clock and five o'clock. And in your opinion and that of your colleagues, she was strangled and raped, and we're probably talking about a single perpetrator.'

'I'm not about to correct you,' Enoksson said, looking like he could do with both a bit of food and some sleep. 'That's exactly what we think. And we're also pretty sure that he escaped through the window. We've found traces of blood and skin on the windowsill.'

'So why didn't he just leave through the door?' Bäckström wondered.

'If what the neighbour who found her says is true, it was locked from the inside. It's the sort of lock that doesn't click into place if you just close the door from the outside. My colleagues and I are wondering if he didn't make his escape when the newspaper was pushed through the letterbox. We think he got the impression that someone was on their way into the flat, and because the bedroom was furthest away from the door he jumped out of that window.'

'So when was the paper delivered?' Long-winded bastard, Bäckström thought.

'Just after five in the morning, and that seems fairly definite.' Enoksson nodded to underline what he'd just said.

'Do we know anything more?'

'The coded lock on the main door to the building was deactivated. It had been playing up, and the bloke delivering the papers had complained. So the building's been unlocked since Wednesday. The locksmiths promised to fix it on Thursday but evidently didn't get round to it.' Enoksson sighed and shrugged his shoulders.

'What about the door to the flat, Enoksson? Anything about that?'

'No marks to indicate a break-in,' the forensics expert said. 'And no other signs of a struggle out in the hall. So either she let him in of her own volition or she forgot to lock the door behind her when she came home.'

'Or he put a knife to her throat when she walked in the front door and forced her to open the door to the flat. Or he took her keys,' Bäckström countered. 'Remember the door was locked when he left.'

'Can't be ruled out,' Enoksson said. 'Definitely not. We'll need a couple more days inside the flat to get a clearer picture. The analysis from the National Forensics Lab will take a while, as usual, but the medical officer promised to let us know his preliminary findings by tomorrow at the latest, so presumably he's already got going on the post-mortem.'

'So there's a bit of good news after all,' Bäckström said, suddenly quite jovial. You have to mix things up, he thought. A lot of stick, with the occasional bit of carrot.

'We've got blood, semen and probably his fingerprints as well, so it's far from desperate,' Enoksson said.

'But you'd rather wait with the details?' Bäckström was still smiling.

'Yes, we'd rather do that, me and my colleagues in forensics.' He nodded as if to confirm that there was a right time for everything, and Bäckström joined in. 'I might be able to give you a couple of pointers on the way, though.'

'I'm listening,' Bäckström said. But ideally not all day, he thought. Because by now there was a full-scale rebellion going on beneath his belt.

'To start with, I think she let him in of her own accord. Or else she met him en route and took him home with her. Or had arranged to meet him earlier. The way things look inside the flat, things seem to have started off fairly amicably, at least.'

'Really?' Bäckström said slowly. The sort of person who could imagine letting just anyone in, he thought.

'And secondly, and with all due respect for what our colleague Anna said a while back, I don't think she's been living there to any great extent. I've read the interview with her mother and I appreciate that that's what she's saying.'

'Why don't you believe it, then?' Bäckström asked.

'She was sleeping in her mother's bed,' Enoksson replied. 'And that's almost certainly where he killed her. The only bed in the flat. Of course, she might have been sleeping on the sofa out in the living room, it's big enough, but there's nothing to suggest that she'd been doing so for any length of time, if I can put it like that.'

'But the mother's a teacher,' officer Sandberg said, evidently feeling picked upon. 'She's had almost a month off now, and has probably spent most of that time in the country. I mean . . . what with this weather we've been having.'

Why don't they ever give up? Bäckström thought. They've always got to argue. Always.

'I hear what you're saying, Anna,' Enoksson said. 'It just doesn't look like she was planning on moving in for good, at any rate. The only thing we've found in the flat that seems to belong to Linda is a sponge-bag in the bathroom, containing the usual things, and one of those fabric sports bags on the top shelf in a wardrobe in what looks like her mum's workroom. It contains a clean change of underwear and a blouse. So I get the impression that she was staying there while her mum was away, or when she wanted to stay in town so she could go out, for instance. Like on Thursday, when she went to the nightclub.'

'We'll have to dig deeper,' Bäckström concluded, smiling amiably. 'Well, I don't know about the rest of you, but I at least need a bite to eat.'

# 10

To begin with Bäckström and Rogersson had planned to escape into town and eat lunch at some discreet place where they could have the beer that they so richly deserved. But when they caught sight of the crowd of journalists outside the entrance to the police station they rapidly changed their minds and turned on their heels, and went and sat down in the staff canteen. They found an empty table at the back, and each ordered special of the day and a low-alcohol beer.

'What the hell's going on inside these people's heads, serving fried sausages, macaroni bake and Småland cheesecake with jam as dessert when it's almost thirty degrees outside? It looks like worms,' Rogersson said, poking his fork suspiciously at the macaroni.

'Don't ask me. I've never eaten worms,' Bäckström said. 'I think it's okay.'

'Sure, Bäckström,' Rogersson said tiredly. 'But if you're a normal person like me . . .'

'If you're worried about worms, maybe you should have a word with Egon.' And good luck with that, Bäckström thought, because Egon was even less talkative than his colleague Rogersson.

'What fucking Egon?' Rogersson asked.

'My Egon,' Bäckström said.

'You give him worms?' Rogersson was looking at him suspiciously.

'Maggots, fly larvae, same thing. But only on special occasions. Have you got any idea how much a tub of fly larvae costs?' There have to be some limits, even for Egon, Bäckström thought. After all, we both have to survive on an ordinary police salary.

'Do you want coffee?' Rogersson sighed, standing up.

'Large, milk and sugar,' Bäckström said. Best cheesecake I've eaten for ages, he thought.

After lunch Bäckström set about organizing things with renewed energy, making sure that his investigative team did a decent job. Their senior colleague Olsson showed up, took a turn about the room and tried to ingratiate himself with as many people as possible as he did so, but as he was approaching Bäckström to waste his valuable time Bäckström pulled the telephone trick, picking up the receiver and humming in concentration as he listened to the dialling tone on the line and waved his right hand in a holding gesture. For safety's sake he had a pad and pen clearly visible on the table in front of him. So Olsson returned to his room and shut the door while Bäckström called officer Sandberg over and took the opportunity to rest his weary eyes on the person who would be doing the actual work.

'The victim's sex life, Anna. Are we starting to get any idea of that?' he began, nodding towards her. The ponderous, professorial nod that he usually employed when he had to talk about difficult subjects. Decent tits on this little lady, he thought.

'We've found out a few things,' Anna said neutrally.

'Anything interesting?' Bäckström said. 'In terms of the investigation, I mean.' Walking on very thin ice. Got to watch my words carefully if I don't want to fall through.

Up until spring that year Linda had had a boyfriend, whom she had met a year earlier when he was studying economics at Lund University. As soon as he finished his exams, just before Christmas last year, he got a job in a company based up in Stockholm. He had moved there and before too long his relationship with Linda had run into the sand.

They hadn't managed to find out anything negative about either him or his relationship with Linda, and for once it turned out that he seemed to have a cast-iron alibi for the time of the murder. He had been at a party together with his new girlfriend and a few other friends. He had contacted the Växjö Police himself as soon as he heard what had happened to Linda, and then, on his own initiative, he had contacted the Stockholm Police, who had already interviewed him. He was shocked, naturally, but simultaneously more willing to cooperate than anyone had any right to expect. For instance, he had volunteered to give them a DNA sample to stop the police wasting any unnecessary time on him.

'What an accommodating young man,' Bäckström said. 'So how did he find out about it so quickly? That Linda had been murdered, I mean.'

'His mum lives here and knows Linda's family, and she called him yesterday afternoon, as soon as she found out. Her son was somewhere in Sandhamn. Way out in the Stockholm archipelago, apparently. Well, you know that, of course. Where it is, I mean. Evidently she knows the family in Sandhamn as well, so that's where she called, in case you were wondering. I've just spoken to the officer who interviewed him. He's convinced the boy didn't have anything to do with the murder. But he still took the DNA sample, and he's sending it to the National Forensics Lab,' Anna concluded.

'Well, then,' Bäckström said. 'I suppose we'll just have to wait and see. Have you found any other boyfriends since she broke up with the economist?'

'Nothing,' Anna said, shaking her head. 'And we've spoken to her three best friends and a number of her classmates at police college. We're thinking of talking to her parents as soon as they're in a fit state.'

'No short flings, nothing peculiar about her sexual preferences and so on?' Bäckström persisted.

'No.' Anna shook her head firmly. 'At least nothing that anyone we've spoken to knew about. According to what they've said, Linda seems to have been a completely ordinary girl. Ordinary boys, ordinary sex. Nothing odd.'

'Six months without a boyfriend, or even a fling.' Bäckström shook his head doubtfully. How likely is that, he thought. A pretty young girl of twenty. Even if she was too skinny for his taste.

'It's probably much more common than people think,' Anna replied, giving the impression that she knew what she was talking about. 'I think she was attacked by a madman. If you ask me, I don't think it's any more complicated than that.'

'Really?' Bäckström said slowly. 'It'll sort itself out,' he added, and smiled at her. And they all have something hidden away somewhere, he thought.

Officer Sandberg didn't say anything. Merely nodded and looked rather surprised.

That gave you something to think about, didn't it, dear? Bäckström thought, watching her as she went back to her desk. He sighed. All work and no play. He went and got a cup of coffee, then pulled Knutsson and Thorén into an empty office so that he could see how they were getting on with the surveillance in peace and quiet.

'So, tell an old man.' He had decided to adopt a relaxed and lofty posture. 'Have we found anything interesting?'

'You mean at the crime scene?' Thorén asked. 'They seem to be finding things there all the time.'

'I don't mean the crime scene,' Bäckström said, just as calmly and pedagogically. 'I mean everywhere apart from the crime scene. Along the route the victim walked home that night. In the vicinity of the crime scene. Along the presumed escape route of the perpetrator. Or anywhere else in Växjö. Or Sweden . . . or the rest of the world.'

'I see what you're thinking,' Knutsson said. 'You mean . . .'

'I can't imagine that you do,' Bäckström interrupted, having already built up a head of steam. 'I'm thinking about the tiniest scrap of paper on the road outside the crime scene, rubbish bins, skips, gutters and drains, nooks and crannies, stairwells, hiding places, other flats, attics and cellars, scrubland, and all the perfectly ordinary spaces in between. I'm thinking about peculiar neighbours, troublemakers in general, peeping toms, flashers, sex maniacs and psychiatric cases. And I'm thinking about all the ordinary citizens who might just have suffered a short-circuit in their little brains because it's so fucking hot and it doesn't seem to want to end.'

'In that case, we haven't found anything,' Thorén said.

'But we're still looking,' Knutsson said. 'I mean, what you said in the meeting was clear enough. So I think everyone's doing their best.'

'But we haven't found anything yet?' Bäckström gave them a questioning look.

'No,' Thorén said.

'No,' Knutsson agreed, shaking his round head in confirmation.

'Doesn't it seem a bit odd that a nutter can run away from the crime scene without his underwear, jumping out of a window just because the paper comes through the letterbox, not to mention all the semen and blood traces and fingerprints he seems to have left behind him, only to disappear into thin air the moment he gets outside?'

'It's certainly a bit strange,' Thorén said.

'That struck me as well,' Knutsson concurred. 'But I don't suppose his underwear was all he was wearing when he attacked the victim. Only joking,' he added quickly when he saw the look on Bäckström's face.

'You never know,' Bäckström said. 'You never know. Considering what he evidently spent a couple of hours doing to her, and what he did after he'd killed her. Because he seems to have taken a shower and done a bit of thinking.'

'He seems more than crazy enough, I agree with you there,' Thorén said.

'But apparently not crazy enough to leave any evidence outside the crime scene?' Bäckström said.

'Maybe he felt better once he'd relieved the pressure,' Knutsson said with a chuckle.

'I find that hard to imagine,' Bäckström said. 'If I see something that looks like a glow-worm, and moves like a glow-worm, and gives off a mysterious glow, what am I looking at?'

'A glow-worm?' Thorén said, looking at his boss quizzically.

'Excellent, lad,' Bäckström said. 'Have you ever thought about joining the police?'

Before they went back to the hotel that evening, Bäckström and Rogersson took a detour via the crime scene to have a look at the flat. A number of representatives from the media were naturally in position behind the extensive cordons, and to judge from the number of telephoto lenses in evidence they were clearly prepared for all eventualities. Bäckström had sat behind the wheel without changing his expression at all even though one of the photographers was practically up on the bonnet before he backed off. At last they moved through the cordon and Bäckström parked the car immediately in front of the building to avoid having to walk too far and have his picture taken unnecessarily.

'Fucking vultures,' Rogersson said as soon as they entered the building. 'I'm surprised they haven't set up a fast-food kiosk as well.'

'It's probably too hot,' Bäckström chuckled. Mind you, an ice-cream would have been nice, he thought.

The two forensics technicians there were taking a break when they arrived, but when both Bäckström and Rogersson declined a cup of coffee they quickly put theirs down and offered to show them round.

'Do you want the large or the small tour?' the younger one asked.

'The small one will do,' Bäckström said, pulling on plastic gloves and, with some difficulty, protective plastic covers over his shoes, using the wall to stop himself from losing his balance.

'Four rooms, kitchen, bathroom, a separate lavatory, plus the hall we're standing in. In total eighty-two square metres.' The older of the two technicians gestured as he spoke. 'The living room's straight ahead. Approximately twenty-five square metres, in the centre of the flat. Facing the road we've got the kitchen and an adjoining room that the victim's mother evidently uses as a workroom. By the way, you've had the plan of the flat, haven't you?'

'Yes,' Bäckström said. 'We've seen it, but it isn't the same as putting your ear to the rails yourself.'

'Quite. I couldn't agree more,' the older one said with a smile. 'At the back of the building we've got the bedroom where she was found, leading off the living room. Alongside the bedroom is a fairly large bathroom with a bath, shower cubicle, toilet and bidet, reached through a door in the bedroom. On the other side of the bathroom is a smaller room that the mother seems to have used as a sort of junk room or storage space. There's an ironing-board and a couple of big laundry baskets in there as well, among all the other clutter, and you reach that through this corridor,' he said, pointing with his arm. 'The passage also contains a number of built-in cupboards.'

Neither too flash nor too poor, Bäckström thought as he walked round the flat with the others. Neither tidy nor particularly messy when you considered what the forensics team had already been up to.

It looked just as he imagined the home of a middle-aged, middle-class female teacher would look like. A single woman with a twenty-year-old daughter who seemed to have stayed there sometimes.

A living room with a large sofa, with three removable cushions, the middle one of which was missing. In front of it was a coffee table and two armchairs. A small dresser stood against the wall beside the sofa, and because the flat was occupied by a woman Bäckström felt no great desire to inspect what was hidden behind the cupboard doors. Probably just glasses and napkins and other crap, he thought.

Bookshelves along the walls with a fair number of books, which was perfectly natural considering the woman's profession, and of course a television, fairly large, strategically positioned in relation to the sofa. A small chandelier hanging from the ceiling, a couple of floor lamps, and a total of three rugs on the floor, some Oriental design that Bäckström didn't recognize. A stereo with two separate loudspeakers positioned at chest height on the middle bookshelf. Pictures on the walls, all of them landscapes or portraits.

'We've taken the middle cushion from the sofa away,' the younger technician said. 'And the now renowned pair of underpants, which I dare say we will shortly be able to read all about in our beloved evening papers, not merely referred to as a typical item of male clothing, were found crumpled up on the floor under the sofa.'

You've got a fine way with words, Bäckström thought. I wonder if you've been on a course? But there would be better opportunities for that sort of remark, so he contented himself with a nod of agreement, while his friend and colleague was as taciturn as usual.

In the bedroom their colleagues from forensics had evidently been busy. The mattress and bedclothes were missing from the wide pine bed, and there were traces of both fingerprint powder and various chemical substances on everything in the room. They had also removed a large section of the carpet covering the floor.

'Well, this is where most of it seems to have happened,' the older technician said. 'The centre of events, if you like. Anything that hasn't already been sent to the National Forensics Lab in Linköping is back at base, if you want to take a look at it.'

'Well, thanks very much,' Bäckström said, smiling collegially. High time for a lager or two, he thought.

Bäckström and Rogersson had ordered their dinner up to Bäckström's room. A quick glance at the dining room had been enough to confirm that it would be the very worst place to be in the whole of Växjö if you were a police officer from National Crime who simply wanted to get a bite to eat in peace and have a beer or two, with maybe the odd chaser.

'Well, cheers, then,' Rogersson said, raising the little glass even before Bäckström had had time to pour out their beers.

He seems considerably happier now, poor old soak, Bäckström thought. He wasn't the sort to argue about the fact that they were still drinking his vodka.

'Cheers,' Bäckström said. Saturday at last, he thought, draining the first short and feeling the warmth and peace spread through his stomach and head. I'm a fortunate man.

# 11

## *Växjö, Sunday 6 July*

Detective Superintendent Jan Lewin had never been to Växjö before
on duty. Considering that in the almost twenty years that he'd been a
murder detective at National Crime he'd visited almost all the towns
in Sweden that were as large or larger, and some that were considerably smaller, this wasn't an entirely irrelevant fact. Whatever. Now he
was here. Finally Växjö, Lewin thought with a wry smile. Of all the
places on the planet, he thought, shaking his head.

As soon as the initial meeting was over he had eaten a quick lunch
and then sat down behind his desk to try to get some order in his
growing piles of papers. He had sat there for almost twelve hours, all
of Saturday, and when he was finally able to leave the police station on
Sandgärdsgatan to take the short walk home to the hotel, it was
already past midnight. And the piles on his desk were, if anything,
even larger than when he started on them just after lunchtime.

In the hotel corridor where he and his colleagues were staying
everything was quiet and shut up. Lewin had opened the locked door
to the landing carefully so as not to disturb his sleeping colleagues. He
had stopped for a moment outside Eva Svanström's door, wondering
if he should knock on it – a very light knock – to see if she was still
awake and maybe wanted company. Not tonight, he thought. Some
other night, one that was better than this.

Then he had crept into his room and washed in the basin with the
help of a wet flannel. Face, armpits, crotch. Just the necessary, in that
order, and even though he wanted nothing more right then than to

stand under the shower and just let the water run. Early tomorrow morning, he thought. Not half past midnight when the others were already asleep.

Then he had got into bed. As usual at the start of a new case, he had trouble getting to sleep, and when he finally managed it he had been tormented by dreams, as he often was when beginning an investigation, or when he just felt anxious or miserable for reasons that he never quite understood. Dreams that were based on real events, but always assumed new meaning, new expression. And this time the dreams were about the summer just after his seventh birthday, when he got his first proper bicycle. A red Crescent Valiant.

He woke up for the third time at half past five in the morning, and that was when he made up his mind. He put on his shorts and a short-sleeved blue top with the National Crime emblem on the front, pulled on his jogging shoes, put the pass card for his hotel room in his pocket, grabbed the tourist map of Växjö, and quickly and silently went out of the door. Just as well to get it over and done with, he thought as he waited for the lift. Considering the state of his desk, it was bound to be some time until he was able to visit the crime scene while he was on duty, and in the world he lived in he should really have been out there before now.

Outside the sun was shining in a pale blue sky and it was almost twenty degrees, even though it was only quarter to six. The main square lay empty and deserted. No one in sight. Not even a solitary abandoned beer can to indicate any traces of earlier human life. He stopped in front of the entrance to the nightclub, and with the help of the map plotted the most direct route to Linda's home. First he checked the time, so that he would be able to see how long it took, and then he started off at the pace he imagined she would have walked at, hopefully following the same route, even though that was still highly unclear.

Heading north-east. Diagonally across the main square, past the east wing of the district governor's residence, on to Kronobergsgatan, heading due north. So far, this matched the bouncer's statement.

But what next, Lewin wondered. He stopped and checked the time again. The quickest way home, he thought. Wasn't that what she had said to her friend before she left the club, that she was going to go home and sleep? In the absence of any better ideas, he took the first turning on the right and emerged on to Linnégatan just a hundred metres further on. He turned north and after another four minutes he turned right once again and found himself on Pär Lagerkvists väg. He stopped to get his bearings and sum up his impressions.

Approximately six hundred metres from the nightclub, a six-minute walk for a young, fit and sober woman walking quickly in an area that she'd known since she was a child. Broad, quiet streets in the centre, still very light: only a madman would attempt to attack anyone on that stretch. Not to mention the fact that this was Växjö.

And on Pär Lagerkvists väg itself the chances of an undisturbed night-time walk were, if anything, even better. It was approximately seven hundred metres to the door of Linda's building, and the whole length was a broad, straight road lined with small blocks of flats of three or four floors. Plastered façades, shiny HSB housing association signs that suggested careful, middle-aged, middle-class occupants, well-ordered lives and good neighbours. No undergrowth, no narrow alleyways, not even a little side road where anyone with evil intentions could potentially lie in wait for an unsuspecting victim.

His own victim lived at the end of the road, in a building that was as neat as all the others, although it lacked the HSB sign, as it was owned by a private association whose members all lived in the building. So this was where it happened, Jan Lewin thought, stopping at the blue and white cordon tape which still surrounded the scene of the murder. As the venue for a standard sexually motivated murder of a young woman, it seemed highly unlikely.

There's only one explanation, he thought as he got back to his hotel room half an hour later. That was where Linda lived. That's why the killer went there. Specifically to see her. Someone she knew, someone she trusted, someone she liked. Someone like her. Then Lewin took off his clothes, got straight in the shower and let the water stream over him for five minutes. And for the first time in a day and a half he felt completely calm and completely happy with the work that remained to be done.

# 12

At half past six on Sunday morning – while Jan Lewin was standing under the shower in his hotel room just letting the water run – the county police commissioner's mobile rang. The commissioner was asleep and had some difficulty putting on his glasses and locating his mobile before he could answer. Something must have happened, he thought after a quick glance at the alarm clock on his bedside table.

'Nylander here,' the voice at the other end said. 'I presume I didn't wake you.'

'No problem,' the commissioner said weakly. 'No problem at all.' Something terrible must have happened, he thought.

'I'm calling to see how things are going,' Nylander said abruptly. 'What's the current position?'

'Everything's going according to plan,' the commissioner said. How am I supposed to know? I've been asleep all night. 'Was there anything in particular you were wondering about, Nylander?'

There wasn't anything Nylander was wondering about – 'I'm not that sort of person'. But, in his capacity as head of the National Crime Unit, he had devoted himself to some 'strategic considerations' motivated by the current case. As a result of these, he had a proposal about 'operational contributions'.

'What were you thinking of ?' the commissioner replied. Strategic considerations, operational contributions? What on earth's he talking about?

'As I see it, there's a severe risk that there's a genuine madman on the loose,' Nylander said, 'and in all likelihood he's going to end up doing something even worse fairly soon.'

'Is there anything in particular you're thinking of?' the commissioner repeated weakly, whereupon Nylander embarked on a number of possible scenarios taken from his wealth of experience as the officer in charge of the national police force.

'Well, I'm thinking of the Samurai killer in Malmö who murdered and mutilated a number of his neighbours. The lieutenant in Falun who shot and killed ten people, most of them young women. And . . . who else?' NHC sounded just as if he was stroking his chin. 'There's that one who ran amok with an iron bar on an underground platform here not too long ago. Three dead and half a dozen injured, if I remember rightly. And that madman in Gamla Stan who mowed down hundreds of pedestrians in his car early one morning. That's just a few examples.'

'I see,' the commissioner said. Good grief, he thought. On my patch. In Växjö.

'I've already spoken to our analysts,' Nylander said, 'and they're in complete agreement with me. We're talking about a serial killer who in all likelihood is capable of mass murder, or going on a so-called killing spree.'

'You had a suggestion?' the commissioner said. Bloody hell, he thought.

The Head of National Crime had all of three operational proposals. And he had already launched two of them and completed the preparations for the third to set sail.

'I think we should let my CP group take a serious look at this madman before things get any worse. And send the case to the VICLAS unit. Forewarned is forearmed,' he said.

'CP group? VICLAS?' the commissioner said. All these acronyms, he thought.

'The criminal profiling group, to get a more exact picture of who he is. And VICLAS, the violent crime linkage analysis system, to connect him to all the previous attacks of a similar nature that he's already carried out,' Nylander explained curtly. Typical civilian, he thought.

'And you mentioned a third option?' the commissioner said defensively.

'Precisely,' Nylander said. 'When the arrest is imminent, I think it would be best if you hand the task over to our National Rapid-Response Unit here. To avoid any unnecessary bloodshed. I've already alerted them. We can usually be in place within three hours of the order's being given. We're trying to reduce that time, and assuming that we get the same good flying conditions that we've had all summer, the head of the unit thinks we can do it in two. We've already raised the state of alert from blue to orange for three of the rapid-response teams.'

'Bloody hell,' the commissioner said. Bloody hell, he thought. And exactly what sort of numbers are we talking about, as far as necessary bloodshed goes?

Quarter of an hour later the county police commissioner – in spite of the fact that it was still very early – called Olsson, the head of the preliminary investigation, and informed him that he and the Head of National Crime had unanimously and in complete agreement decided to reinforce the investigation with the experts from the CP group and the VICLAS unit, and that any potential arrest would be handled by the NRRU. Olsson himself, oddly enough, had been thinking along the same lines, and thought that this was an excellent proposal.

'I was actually thinking of calling you later today to suggest that, boss. The only reason I decided to wait was because I know you're enjoying a well-deserved holiday.'

Bäckström was stressed, tired and hungover. The previous evening he and Rogersson had done their best to compensate for the lengthy period of abstinence that their duties had imposed upon them. Bäckström had collapsed on his bed just before midnight, had over-slept, and had had to wolf down breakfast without so much as a glance at the morning papers. They were also forced to stop at a petrol station shop on the way to buy some mints and high-energy drinks to get their breath and hydration levels into some sort of order.

Things hadn't got any better when he was hurrying down the corridor to the morning meeting of the investigative team, because that idiot Olsson had jumped out on him and started going on about different worst-case scenarios that he and the county police commissioner had considered themselves obliged to deal with without Bäckström's knowledge.

'What do you think about that, Bäckström?' Olsson asked. 'Asking for the involvement of your colleagues at the CP group and VICLAS?'

'Sounds like an absolutely excellent idea,' Bäckström said. He had no intention of wasting any of his valuable time being lectured over the phone by his ultimate superior, Sten 'the Chin' Nylander.

At last, he had found his way to his place at the end of the table. Admittedly, he didn't have a Höganäs pot hanging round his neck to stop him from dying of thirst, but he did have a large mug of coffee with plenty of milk and sugar, and the whole of his team was in place.

'Okay,' he said. 'Let's get going.'

First Police Constable Sandberg told them about the surveillance cameras along the victim's route home. The one by the cashpoint where she withdrew money hadn't given them anything, presumably because the victim had been outside the range of the camera when she left the Town Hotel.

'The camera only covers the pavement and a bit of the street in front of the cashpoint,' she explained. 'But we did find something much better, and I think the credit for that should go entirely to you, boss,' she went on, nodding and smiling at Bäckström.

'I'm listening,' Bäckström said, smiling back. You're already halfway in there, lad, he thought.

Sandberg and her colleagues had found another, much better camera, albeit one lacking the requisite permits. It was above the counter of a corner shop at the start of Pär Lagerkvists väg, just five hundred metres from the victim's home, and at night it also covered the road in front of the shop. At four minutes to three on Friday night Linda Wallin had been picked up on camera when she was on her way home. But there had been no one else in the next thirty minutes, so it didn't look like she was being followed.

'The shop's open until eleven o'clock in the evening. The camera normally covers the interior and the tills, but before the shopkeeper goes home, just before midnight, he changes the angle so that it picks up people going past outside. He comes from Iran, and he's had trouble with vandalism, people spraying racist slogans on the windows and so on,' Sandberg explained.

'And we're absolutely certain it's Linda?' Bäckström asked, not about to let go of this encouraging little detail in the work of the investigation.

'Entirely sure,' Sandberg said. 'I've been through the recording with forensics. After all, a number of us know . . . knew . . . her.'

After that things rolled on in the usual efficient way they did whenever he was the one holding the tiller. And thank God for that, Bäckström thought, now that half the police force didn't have to waste time introducing themselves to the other half.

'What about the door-to-door and search of the area?' he asked. 'Have we found anything interesting since yesterday?'

Unfortunately not, according to the officer who was responsible for that part of the investigation. The last known traces of the perpetrator were the blood and skin found on the windowsill of the bedroom in the flat where the murder took place.

'Then we expand the area of the search,' Bäckström said gruffly. 'Anything odd that happened anywhere in town during the day in question. The whole lot, from the usual troublemakers, burglaries, criminal damage, stolen cars and parking fines to any mysterious vehicles, events and people. I want to see lists before lunch.' Lazy fuckers. If you want something doing you have to do it yourself.

'So has anyone been in touch to tell us anything interesting, then?' he went on, looking at Lewin. If you've managed to tear yourself away from Svanström, you randy bastard, he thought.

'We've received hundreds of tip-offs,' Lewin said. 'By phone, by email, even by text to some members of the team whose numbers are evidently known to various informants. But perhaps that isn't so odd, seeing as the officers who've received tip-offs that way usually work in surveillance or drugs, where you do sometimes have to give out mobile numbers. If anyone's sent us anything in the mail, it probably won't turn up until tomorrow at the earliest. Seems to be par for the course with the post these days.'

'So?' Bäckström asked. 'Is there anything juicy for us to get our teeth into?'

Unfortunately not, according to Lewin. Just the usual. Agitated citizens lamenting the general decline of society, and crime in particular. The usual know-alls wanting to tell the police what to do, their expertise usually acquired from watching crime series on television. And obviously a fair number of clairvoyants, visionaries and mystics wanting to share their visions, premonitions, general predictions, intuitions and vibrations.

'Nothing specific, nothing at all for us to get our teeth into?' Bäckström persisted.

'Some of them were extremely specific,' Lewin said. 'The only problem is that they seem to have got everything mixed up.'

'Give us some examples,' Bäckström said.

'Certainly,' Lewin said, looking down at his papers. 'We've got someone who was friends with Linda in high school. She's one hundred per cent sure, in her words, that she talked to Linda at a concert in Borgholm on Öland that evening. Some group called Gyllene Tider were apparently playing there on their summer tour.'

Borgholm, Bäckström thought. That must be a good hundred and fifty kilometres from Växjö.

'The only problem is that the concert was on Friday night, and by then the victim was already at the Institute for Forensic Medicine in Lund,' Lewin sighed. 'So that witness hadn't even read the evening papers. And then there's this one.' He was leafing through the bundle of tip-offs in front of him. 'One of Växjö's young talents has been in touch with one of the uniformed officers here to say that he saw Linda five hundred metres west of the Town Hotel early on Friday morning. On Norra Esplanaden, close to the council offices, if I've understood it correctly.'

'So what's wrong with that, then?' Bäckström wondered.

'The problem with him,' Lewin replied, 'apart from his general credibility, is that this is supposed to have been at around four o'clock in the morning, on a road in completely the wrong direction from where she was going, and in the company of – and these words are the witness's and not my own – a fucking big nigger.'

'In that case I think I know who the witness is,' one of the local officers towards the end of the table said. 'There are a lot of evil dark-skinned people in that young man's world.'

'I realized as much when I read his criminal record,' Lewin said with a half-smile.

'Okay,' Bäckström said. 'Questions? Opinions? Suggestions?' Not a single one with anything sensible to say, he thought as he saw the headshakes round the table. 'Let's get going, then,' he said, standing up with a jolt. 'What are you waiting for? Don't just sit there. Go and do some work. I want the name of the man who did this by lunchtime at the latest. If you give me something good I'll get cake to go with the afternoon coffee.' Happy faces round the table. They're like children, Bäckström thought. There was no way he was going to waste his hard-earned money on any damn cake.

Equipped with paper and pen, he sought out the seclusion of an empty interview room to think in peace and quiet. He switched on the red sign, closed the door and dropped the massive fart he had been nursing throughout the meeting. Finally alone, he thought, waving the worst of the previous evening's fug away from him.

Okay, so she gets home to her flat just after three o'clock. Doesn't look like anyone followed her, or had arranged to meet her at the flat. But the perpetrator shows up in the story shortly thereafter. Things go rapidly downhill and, considering the way the crime scene looked, the little psychopath must have had his hands full for at least an hour and a half. So in all likelihood she died some time between half past four and just before five, he thought.

He goes out into the bathroom to shower the worst of it off. Then the newspaper gets delivered at about five o'clock and he imagines someone's on their way into the flat. So he throws on the essentials and jumps out of the bedroom window, and by then it's just after five o'clock. So where does that get us? he thought. Bäckström looked at his watch and started to count forward from early Friday morning to Sunday morning. It would soon be two and a half days since she died. The bastard could be on the moon by now, he thought crossly. He gathered his papers and decided to go back out and give the members of the team a bit of a kick.

On the other hand, he thought when he emerged into the corridor, it would be pretty stupid to do that on an empty stomach, and seeing as the staff canteen was open even though it was Sunday, because of what had happened, it probably made sense to get a bite to eat.

Småland stuffed potato dumplings, he thought greedily as he inspected the menu. That would do nicely. He rounded the meal off with a large cup of coffee and an almond bun, quietly reading the evening papers he had pinched from the hotel but hadn't yet had a chance to look at. No new facts, Bäckström thought as he sipped the hot coffee. Mostly speculation, making a lot of waves.

One of the papers had launched a new variation on the classic police angle. The perpetrator was probably a violent criminal who hated the police and 'harboured an irrational hatred of the victim because she worked for the police', as one of the members of the paper's own panel of experts put it. As soon as the opportunity presented itself, they were always quick to put together a fine selection of the most confused minds in the country.

Yeah, yeah, Bäckström thought, chewing on the almond bun. Must be some lecturer she had at police college in Växjö. Maybe that crazy woman in charge of debriefing. The semen didn't necessarily rule her out: it could be a cunningly laid plan to mislead them.

According to the other main evening paper and their experts, the case was entirely different. It was actually about a serial killer with an obsessive hatred of women and an almost ritualistic method of carrying out his crimes. This sounded pretty much like his dear colleague Olsson, Bäckström thought. Where the hell do they get it all from?

There were also some elements common to both of the papers' accounts. It was a thin connection, but it was there. Another expert, one who espoused the police angle in the first paper, didn't think it impossible that they were dealing with a specific type of serial killer who was targeting police officers in particular, because uniforms were what turned him on sexually. His special 'trigger', according to the paper.

They must all have access to the same insane website where they could recharge their stock of cretinous ideas, Bäckström thought. He was about to put the papers down when he caught sight of an article that made him pause: an interview with yet another expert, professor of something called forensic psychiatry at Sankt Sigfrid's psychiatric hospital in Växjö, with a big picture of him. He gave a long description of the torture wounds that the police had discovered on the body. Either he had seen the same pictures that the core members of the investigative team had received the previous evening, Bäckström thought, or one of the people who had seen them had described them to him in exhaustive detail.

Even the professor with the remarkable insight into the workings of the investigation appeared to subscribe to what could probably be called the main thread in the case. They were dealing with a serial killer. Considering the brutality of this case, he must have committed similarly brutal crimes in the past, and there was a high probability of his doing so again within the near future. In fact it was almost certain.

At the same time, he was 'no ordinary sexual sadist with highly developed sexual fantasies', as the professor's incompetent colleagues appeared to believe. Still less was he someone who got turned on by trainee female police officers, either in or out of uniform. No, this was a case of a 'severely mentally disturbed', possibly even a 'chaotic', perpetrator. He was also 'a young man from an immigrant back-ground who had been exposed to violent and traumatic experiences in his childhood or youth'. For instance, he might himself have been tortured or subjected to serious sexual abuse. When he reached this point in his reading, Bäckström quickly drank the last of his coffee, put the paper in his pocket and went to find the investigation's press spokeswoman.

Five minutes later he was sitting in her office. He passed her the paper, open at the article. 'Have you seen this?'

'I understand what you mean,' she said. 'I read it this morning, and my reaction was the same as yours. This little boat's got a serious leak. Mind you, trying to look on the positive side, perhaps it isn't so odd that this particular expert is involved. I take it you're aware of Sankt Sigfrid's? It's the big psychiatric hospital here in town and it houses some of the very worst offenders, who've been sentenced to secure treatment. Our friend the professor is a regular lecturer both at the police college and here at the station. I don't know how many times I've heard him speak.'

'Really,' Bäckström said. 'Is he worth listening to, then?'

'I'd say so,' she said. 'He gets things right pretty often, in my opinion.'

Maybe it would be worth having a word with the bastard, Bäckström thought. That business about a young, foreign perpetrator didn't sound so crazy. Besides, the victim probably had a bit of a weakness for that sort of bloke. Maybe to the extent that she let him in when he knocked on her door.

When Bäckström returned to the large room where the investigation was based, he adopted his field-marshal expression and surveyed his troops.

'Well,' he said, 'what are you waiting for? I've had my lunch, and now I want a good solid name.' To underline his point, he patted his bulging stomach without even thinking about it.

'You can have some names from me. We've just finished putting together the first list of door-to-door enquiries,' Knutsson said, waving a bundle of printouts.

'Anything good, then?' Bäckström took the papers and went to sit in his usual chair.

'Well, there are a lot of names, at any rate,' Knutsson said, sitting down beside him. 'Seventy-nine, to be precise, and that's just the neighbours in the immediate vicinity, people who knew the victim and the likely suspects here in Växjö.'

'Tell me,' Bäckström said. 'Give me something to work on.'

'Take it easy,' Knutsson said. 'I was getting to that.'

# 13

Knutsson and his team had begun by going through the victim's family, friends and acquaintances to see if any of the many registers that the police had at their disposal had anything interesting to say about any of them. The fact that they didn't hardly came as a surprise. About a third of the twenty or so names were Linda's colleagues from police college, and you didn't get accepted there if you had a criminal record.

'As unimpeachable as our victim,' Bäckström declared happily, leaning back in his chair with his hands clasped over his stomach.

'In terms of the registers, at least,' Knutsson said judiciously.

'Seeing as we're going to be getting the perpetrator's DNA profile, I want samples from the lot of them. Preferably voluntarily, and mainly to get them out of our investigation as quickly as possible.'

'That shouldn't be a problem,' Knutsson said.

'No, it certainly shouldn't,' Bäckström agreed. Honest people had nothing to fear from their DNA, he thought.

The second category was the opposite of the first, in that its members all had comprehensive files in the police registers. With the help of their computers, Knutsson and his team had managed to dredge up about a hundred misogynists, street-fighters, rapists and other madmen with connections to Växjö and the surrounding area. Then they had written off the ones who were already in prison or had other reasonable alibis. That left eighty people lined up for a more thorough and time-consuming examination. Ten of these were of particular interest, because they were receiving treatment or had been treated in the past at Sankt Sigfrid's hospital for serious sexual offences.

'Get DNA samples. The whole lot of them get to stick a cotton-bud in their mouths to help the nice police.' Bäckström nodded happily. Finally, this is starting to look like something, he thought.

'Sure,' Knutsson sighed, suddenly seeming considerably less happy. With a bit of luck we'll already have some of them on file, he thought.

Which left the neighbours. In total almost a thousand people, approximately half of whom had contacted the police or happened to be at home when they went door-to-door. Considering that it was summer, and the holiday season, and that the area was primarily inhabited by the elderly or middle-aged middle class, the high level of absenteeism was hardly surprising.

'I don't care if they've spent the whole summer out in the country and haven't got anything useful to contribute, I still want them questioned and ticked off the list,' Bäckström said.

'I can't disagree with that,' Knutsson said, 'but I'm assuming that you don't want us to get DNA samples from the lot of them.'

'Doesn't do any harm to ask,' Bäckström said, shaking himself. 'How many of them did you pick up on the criminal record check, by the way?'

'I thought I told you,' Knutsson said, glancing at his list. 'Seventy-nine, minus seventy public order offences, leaving a total of nine.'

'And what did they do?'

'Three drunk-drivers. One of them with four convictions in twelve years – one of our colleagues from Växjö described him as a gay old dog. Bearing in mind that one of them is fifty, another fifty-seven and the gay old dog himself seventy, then . . .' Knutsson sighed once more and shrugged expressively. 'Then there's one who had his hand in the cookie jar at work. He got probation for embezzlement. Another one hit his wife nine years ago, but we didn't catch him on the door-to-door; he's evidently at his place in the country. There's one who was caught dodging tax, plus a couple of youngsters, sixteen and eighteen respectively, who've done most of the usual stuff, shoplifting, graffiti, throwing a brick through a shop window, fighting with other kids.' Knutsson sighed again.

'The one who beat his wife?' Bäckström asked curiously.

'Supposed to be in the country with his wife. Happily married according to the neighbours our officers spoke to in the door-to-door,' Knutsson said.

'Then he won't have anything against volunteering a DNA sample,' Bäckström said. Happy people usually don't, he thought.

'There might just be one that I think could be interesting,' Knutsson said. 'His name's Marian Gross, originally from Poland. He's forty-six, arrived with his parents as a child, they were political refugees, he's had Swedish citizenship since 1975. He was reported last winter for threatening behaviour, sexual harassment, and a number of other offences. Single, no children, works as a librarian at the university here.'

'Hang on a minute, Knutsson,' Bäckström said, raising his hands to slow him down. 'He's a poof. You can tell just from the description, can't you? Marian. Who the fuck's called Marian? Librarian, single, no kids.' He stuck his little finger out. 'We'll have to have a word with the arse-bandit who reported him.'

'I don't think so,' Knutsson said. 'The person who made the complaint is a female work colleague, fifteen years younger than him.'

'Sigh,' Bäckström said. 'Another librarian. So what's he done to her, then? Shown her his Polish bratwurst at the Christmas party, or what?'

'He sent a load of anonymous emails and other messages that strike me as quite offensive. Just the usual dirty stuff, admittedly, but there's something threatening about them.' Knutsson shook his head with a look of disgust.

'The usual dirty stuff?' Bäckström looked questioningly at Knutsson. 'You couldn't be a bit more . . .' Bäckström waved his right hand expressively.

'Of course,' Knutsson said, with a heavy sigh, as if he were taking a deep breath. 'I'll give you a few examples. We've got the old classic of the dildo sent to her workplace. The biggest size, in black, with an anonymous note in which the sender says it was modelled on him.'

'I thought you said he was Polish?' Bäckström grunted. 'Maybe the bastard's colour-blind. Or else it's about to drop off.' He was laughing so much that his bulging stomach was bouncing up and down.

'The usual emails and notes, saying he's seen her in town and at the library, expressing an opinion on her choice of underwear. Will that do?'

'Sounds like a perfectly normal dirty old man,' Bäckström said. So what's made little Hans reveal the softer side of his character? Maybe he's been to see the crisis therapist?

'Well, that's not really what interests me,' Knutsson said sullenly.

'So what is it, then?' Bäckström asked. 'The fact that he's Polish?'

'He lives in the same building as the victim,' Knutsson said. 'In the flat immediately above.'

'Get a DNA sample,' Bäckström barked, then straightened up and pointed a stubby index finger at Knutsson. 'You could have said that straight away. Send someone out to get a sample from him, and if he doesn't want to give one we'll just have to bring him in.' Finally, this is starting to look like something.

It was late in the afternoon when they finally received the promised preliminary report from the medical officer. It arrived on the forensic team's fax and was addressed to the chief technical expert on the case, Enoksson from regional crime in Växjö, and as soon as he'd read it he went to find Bäckström to discuss what it said.

'According to the medical officer, she died between three and seven in the morning. Suffocation as a result of strangulation,' the forensics officer said.

'You don't need a white coat to work that out,' Bäckström said. 'If you ask me, she died between half past four and five o'clock at the latest.' Typical medical officer, he thought. Bloody cowards.

'I agree with you about the timing,' Enoksson concurred. 'As far as the rest of it goes, it looks like she was raped at least twice. Once vaginally and once anally, and probably in that order. Possibly more than twice. And the perpetrator ejaculated both times.'

'Does he have anything to say that we haven't worked out for ourselves?' Bäckström asked. 'Those stab wounds on her . . . lower back, then?' You can't even say backside any more, he thought. Where the hell have I ended up?

'Stab wounds is putting it a bit strongly,' Enoksson said. 'More like cuts, even though she did bleed a fair bit. Yes, he's measured those for us. That's not part of our job, of course. But even we managed to count them, and we agree with him. Thirteen cuts, curving up towards her midriff and the middle of her body, probably made from the left-hand side to the right.'

'I'm listening,' Bäckström said.

'A non-serrated knife, probably the one we found at the crime scene. The cuts are between two and five millimetres deep, with the deepest about a centimetre. They seem to have been made with some degree of control, considering that she must have resisted and been thrashing about. They're deeper on the right than they are on the left. We can probably deal with the restraints and gag, and the marks they made on the body, when we get the final report from the National Forensics Lab.'

'I don't have any objection to that,' Bäckström said. 'After all, everything our esteemed medical colleague has had to tell us so far is what we already knew.' Well, me at least, he thought.

'Yes, to a great extent. But he's happy to come and talk to us if you like,' the forensics officer said. 'I thought it might be best if he did that once I and my colleagues have finished our bit and had the results back on all our tests. It's possible that there's something he'd like to talk to us about in person when we meet him. So we can take everything at once. Unless you'd rather not?'

'Sounds good,' Bäckström said. But preferably before the end of the summer, he thought.

After that, Bäckström took his colleague Sandberg to one side to orientate himself a little further regarding the victim's character, but mainly to rest his weary eyes.

'I hope you don't think I'm being a nuisance, Anna,' he said, smiling amiably, 'but I'm sure you realize that this business about who the victim was is possibly the most important aspect of the whole investigation.' Softly, softly, he thought. Goodness, the lengths he went to for their sake.

'I don't think you're being a nuisance at all,' Anna replied. 'On the contrary, I like hearing what you've got to say. Far too many people here don't take the victim seriously.' She looked at him solemnly.

Nice to hear that there are a few sensible officers even in Växjö, Bäckström thought, but he had no intention of saying so.

'Exactly,' he said. 'I understand that you've spoken to the father? To Linda's father?'

'That's putting it a bit strongly,' she said. 'I was there when we visited him and told him what had happened. An older colleague did most of the talking. He was a vicar before he joined the police, and he's been a neighbourhood officer here in town for years. He's very good at that sort of thing. It's terrible, when you think about it. It was an awful shock to her father. As soon as we got back to the station we had to get a doctor.'

'Terrible,' Bäckström said. Now she's got that look on her face again. I'd better speed up before she starts crying. Women are all the same — women, vicars, and neighbourhood officers. Bloody babies. 'I thought she was registered as living with her father? I presume she has her own room there?'

'Oh yes,' Anna said. 'It's a huge place, a manor house. Lovely, actually.'

'So did you find anything interesting when you searched her room out at her father's place? Diaries, personal notes, calendars and so on, old letters, photos, videos from family occasions. Well, all that sort of thing. You know what I mean.'

'We didn't actually have time for that,' Anna said. 'We didn't get much further than the hall before we drove away. Her dad was in pieces. But we have got her pocket diary. It was in the bag she had with her when she went out on Thursday evening.'

'Is there anything interesting in it, then?' Bäckström asked.

'No,' Anna said, shaking her head. 'Just the usual. Meetings, lectures at college, friends she was seeing, and so on. You're welcome to take a look at it, if you like.'

'Later,' Bäckström said. 'What about after that? Have you been back?'

'No,' Anna said. 'I raised it on Friday with Bengt — I mean, Superintendent Olsson — after her father had left here with a doctor and a couple of family friends, but Bengt thought we should wait. Leave him in peace, in light of what had happened, I mean.'

'So we still haven't searched her room in her father's house?' *Where the hell have I ended up?*

'No, not as far as I know,' Anna said, shaking her head. 'Forensics have had their hands full with the crime scene. But I see what you mean.'

'I'll raise it with Olsson tomorrow,' Bäckström said. *That'll give him another half-day to fuck things up in,* he thought.

Rogersson was sitting with his office door shut, a pair of headphones over his ears and a tape machine on the desk in front of him, when Bäckström walked into his room.

'And how can I help you, detective superintendent?' Rogersson said, taking off the headphones and nodding gloomily as he switched off the tape machine.

'You can come back to my hotel room with me, have a bite to eat, and then help me drink a couple of lagers,' Bäckström said.

'I think I'm getting eczema in my ears after spending all afternoon and half the evening listening to a load of utterly meaningless interviews,' Rogersson said. 'Right up until my dear colleague Bäckström comes in, when all I hear is the sweetest music.'

'Bollocks to that. Let's go,' Bäckström said. *The bastard's starting to get all sentimental. Must be the alcohol.*

'Aaah,' Rogersson said. He gave a deep sigh of contentment and wiped away the head of the beer from the corner of his mouth with his left hand. 'Whoever invented lager ought to get all the Nobel Prizes there are. Everything from the Peace Prize to that one in Literature. He should get the whole lot.'

'I dare say you're not alone in thinking that,' Bäckström said. 'And the only thing better than a cold beer would probably have to be a free cold beer. So he should probably get the Prize for Economics as well, considering the amount you've managed to get through, you tight bastard.'

Rogersson ignored the insult. But he did change the subject suddenly.

'That Polack, the one Knutsson's trying to get us to go for,' he said, shaking his head.

'We're thinking of talking to him again first thing in the morning, and doing a DNA test,' Bäckström said. Let's talk about all the free beer you're putting away instead, he thought.

'I'm not getting it,' Rogersson said. 'He just doesn't feel right.'

'Really?' Bäckström said. 'Why doesn't he feel right?'

'I've read the interviews with both the newspaper bloke and the Polack. And I've spoken to our colleague Salomonson down here, the one who was in charge of the sexual harassment case. He actually seems pretty normal, by the way. The Polack just doesn't feel right. That's all.' He emphasized his point by taking a deep gulp of free lager.

According to Rogersson, there were three good reasons why Linda's Polish neighbour, Marian Gross, wasn't the murderer. The first was the interview with the man who delivered the morning papers at the same time every day to the people who paid to receive it.

'He should have realized,' Rogersson said. 'I mean, that it was just the paper being delivered, not someone coming home. He even gets the same morning papers as the victim's mother. The *Småland Post* and *Svenska Dagbladet*.'

'Maybe he's normally asleep when the papers arrive,' Bäckström countered.

The second reason was the interview conducted with Gross by the police when they were going door-to-door on Friday afternoon, when Gross volunteered that earlier that week he had spoken to Linda's mother, and that she had said she was going away, but her daughter would be living in the flat.

'Surely that implicates him, if anything,' Bäckström said. 'He knew there weren't any obstacles.'

'So why would he have gone out through the window?' Rogersson repeated. 'Surely the simplest solution would have been to go the normal way, out through Linda's door and up to his own flat?'

'But there was someone outside the door,' Bäckström objected.

'Yes, delivering the papers,' Rogersson said emphatically. 'All he had to do was wait until he'd gone.'

Sigh, Bäckström thought, and contented himself with a nod.

The third reason concerned Gross's physical condition, combined with the perpetrator's choice of escape route. According to the forensic report, the windowsill was almost four metres above the lawn below. Gross was one metre, seventy centimetres tall, and weighed approximately ninety kilos. Not particularly agile, and out of shape.

'According to Salomonson, he's a fat little bastard, and bloody unpleasant with it. Salomonson says he's completely out of shape as well. Pants like a steam engine after just half a flight of stairs,' Rogersson said. 'So he'd probably have killed himself if he went out that way. If he managed to get himself out of the window in the first place.'

A fat little bastard, Bäckström thought. He was scarcely any taller and not much thinner himself, and had a considerably more athletic perpetrator in mind. Hm. 'There's something in what you say,' he agreed. 'But there's no harm in taking a sample, is there?'

'Good luck with that,' Rogersson said. 'From what I've heard, Gross is a uniquely difficult character.'

# 14

*Växjö, Monday 7 July*

Day four, and still no perpetrator, Bäckström thought as he sat down at the large meeting table. And Detective Superintendent Olsson had evidently decided to play at being in charge of the preliminary investigation, and was waving his flag. What was more, they were still reporting on the basic state of an investigation that hadn't given them much to go on so far, Bäckström thought. Olsson was in charge, the usual arse-lickers were agreeing with him, and time was passing. He tried to shut his ears as he pretended to read some documents.

To start with, they had decided to end the search for evidence in the vicinity of the crime scene and along the perpetrator's presumed escape route. They'd been at it for three days already, and if they hadn't found anything by now the chances were that they weren't going to.

'I think it makes more sense to focus our resources elsewhere,' Olsson said, and was rewarded with nods of agreement.

Like for instance a little search of her room in her father's house, Bäckström thought, but he didn't say so out loud because he was planning to take that up with Olsson in private.

'Well, I'd just like to thank everyone involved in this case,' Olsson went on. 'You've all done a fantastic job.'

Don't mention it, Bäckström thought. All I did was find a surveillance camera that the other idiots managed to miss.

The door-to-door enquiries were also being scaled back. The neighbours who still hadn't been interviewed had received notes through the letterbox, and the most interesting ones – whoever those might be – would have to be tracked down to their places in the country.

'That will mean that we can free up a number of colleagues who are needed elsewhere,' a cheerful Superintendent Olsson declared.

Like for instance a little search of her room in her father's house . . .

Then it was time to go through the investigative capital that they had somehow managed to scrape together from the crime scene and in the forensics lab down in Lund.

'As far as we're concerned,' Enoksson said, 'things are looking pretty good. But you'll just have to be patient for a couple more days. Partly because we're waiting for a load of test results, but after that I promise we'll get back to you. Until then you'll have to make do with what they say in the evening papers, although I think I'd exercise a bit of caution there.'

Aha, Bäckström thought. Bloody hell. Enoksson's not a happy bunny.

Olsson didn't appear to note the comment, and evidently had no intention of letting go of the crime scene yet. 'If I've got this right,' he said, 'she was strangled and raped at least a couple of times, and she died just before five o'clock.'

'Yes,' Enoksson said. 'She died between half past four and five.'

Good lad, Bäckström thought, stick to your guns. If you give someone like that so much as your little finger, he'll take your whole arm.

'The more ritualized elements in the case . . . almost torture . . . to put it bluntly, he tied her up, gagged her, and then stabbed her a number of times. How far have we got with that?'

'Stabbed is putting it a bit strong,' Enoksson objected. 'It's more like he cut her.'

'If I've got this right,' Olsson repeated, 'he stabbed her thirteen times. Or cut her, if you prefer.'

'Yes. Thirteen, and I don't think we've missed any. She bled a fair amount when he cut her, even though the wounds aren't particularly deep, which means that she was alive and struggling, and that was probably the whole point.' Enoksson suddenly looked exhausted.

'Stabbed thirteen times,' Olsson said, sounding like someone who'd seen the truth and the light. 'That can't be coincidence, can it?'

'I don't think I understand what you mean.' Enoksson looked like he meant it.

'Why thirteen in particular?' Olsson persisted. 'It's everyone's unlucky number. If you ask me, it's no accident that it was thirteen. I'm fairly sure that our perpetrator wanted to send us a message.'

'But on the other hand, I happen to think it was pure coincidence that it was thirteen, and not ten or twelve or twenty,' Enoksson said curtly.

'Let's think about it.'

Bäckström had had enough. He grunted loudly enough to get everyone's attention.

'I'm inclined to agree with you, Bengt,' he said, smiling amiably at Olsson. 'And the date she was killed on can hardly be a coincidence either, although I didn't realize that until I recalled Anna's excellent profiling work. She pointed out that the victim had actually spent a couple of years living in the USA when she was younger. I mean, the fourth of July. Surely that can't be a coincidence?'

'I don't quite follow,' Olsson said hesitantly.

But everyone else seemed to, to judge by their cupped ears and craned necks, Bäckström thought. A Mexican wave.

'The American national day,' Bäckström said, nodding for emphasis. 'You don't think we could be dealing with someone from al-Qaida?'

The number of people who shuffled on their chairs was slightly larger than those grinning or smirking, but the message had got through.

'I understand your point, even if it was subtle,' Olsson said with a stiff smile. 'Well, to move on, I understand that we've got wind of an extremely interesting individual.' He turned towards Knutsson.

The rats are thinking of jumping ship, Bäckström thought, looking at Knutsson, who suddenly seemed absorbed in his papers.

'Yes,' Knutsson said. 'The victim's Polish neighbour. Marian Gross, a man many of you here evidently already know.'

Exactly, so why didn't you deal with him on Friday so that I didn't have to? Bäckström thought. But of course the uniformed officers who were conducting the door-to-door enquiries hadn't known who he was, because the prosecutor who had been considering his case since last winter hadn't realized that he lived in Linda's building until little Hans from National Crime in Stockholm starting waving it in front of his nose.

They discussed the Polish neighbour within the frame of 'already known sex maniac', and as not merely a potential but also the probable perpetrator. The discussion rolled back and forth for almost quarter of an hour, while Bäckström tried to focus on other matters, and when Olsson suddenly asked him a direct question he had no idea what it was about. Other than the fact that it must concern the Polack, of course.

'What do you think, Bäckström?' Olsson said.

'I suggest that we do the following,' Bäckström said. 'Pay the bastard a visit and question him. And make sure we get a DNA sample.'

'I'm afraid there might be a few problems with that,' Salomonson interrupted from his place further down the table. 'I'm the one who was in charge of the allegations of sexual harassment, in case anyone's wondering. Gross is a difficult individual.'

Well then, if he's that bad we'll just have to drag him back here, Bäckström thought. Put a pair of cuffs on him and lead him in through the main entrance on Oxtorget so the reporters get plenty of good pictures of the bastard.

'As the officer responsible for this, I'm happy for him to be brought in for questioning,' Olsson said, straightening his back. 'Brought in for questioning under paragraph twenty-three, section seven of the Criminal Justice Act,' he clarified, looking very pleased with himself as he did so.

You do that, lad, Bäckström thought, nodding in agreement like everyone else sitting round the table, with the exception of Rogersson, whose expression didn't change.

After the meeting Bäckström caught Olsson before he had time to disappear into his office and shut himself in.

'Have you got a minute?' he said with a friendly smile.

'My door's always open for you, Bäckström.' Olsson sounded just as friendly.

'She seems to have spent most of her time at her father's house,' Bäckström said. 'Her room there ought to be searched as soon as possible.'

Olsson looked troubled, nowhere near as energetic as he had towards the end of the meeting. Her dad was in a bad way. A few years earlier he had had a heart attack and had almost died. His only daughter had been taken from him in the most brutal way, and whenever he switched on the television or the radio or tried to read a paper he was constantly reminded, in the most inconsiderate way, of the tragedy that had befallen him. Besides, it was practically unimaginable that he had anything to do with his daughter's death. For instance, he had volunteered his fingerprints for the usual comparisons when he was in the police station.

'I don't think he had anything to do with his daughter's death either,' Bäckström agreed, already focusing elsewhere. Just as little as that fucking Polack, he thought, but that wasn't the issue just then.

'It's reassuring to know that we agree on that,' Olsson said. 'I suggest that we wait a few more days, to give Linda's dad a chance to get back on his feet. I mean, if we're in luck with this Pole, Gross, the whole thing might be over as soon as we get the DNA results back.'

'Your decision,' Bäckström said, and walked away.

After lunch Bäckström received a new list from Knutsson, who for some reason seemed almost guilty.

'I understand from Rogersson that you don't believe in the Pole,' the detective inspector said apologetically.

'What did Rogersson say, then?'

'Well, you know what he's like when he's in that mood.'

'So what did he say?' Bäckström said, looking expectantly at Knutsson. 'Give me a direct quote.'

'He said I could shove Gross up my . . . well . . . my backside, you know,' Knutsson said stiffly.

'That wasn't a very nice thing to say,' Bäckström said. Mind you, it was pretty nice for Rogersson, he thought, considering the things he was capable of saying when he was in that mood.

'If you're interested, here's the latest list,' Knutsson said, evidently keen to change the subject.

'My door is always open,' Bäckström said, leaning back in his chair.

In Knutsson's opinion, work had been going well since their previous conversation on the subject the day before. He and his colleagues had, amongst other things, been able to get through twenty or so of the seventy most interesting and violence-prone hooligans in Växjö and the surrounding area. DNA samples had already been taken from another ten, in conjunction with earlier offences, and as soon as the National Forensics Lab sent their findings through they'd be able to check for a match.

'Sounds pretty good,' Bäckström said. 'Make sure they all give samples as soon as possible.'

'There's just one small problem,' Knutsson said.

'I'm listening,' Bäckström said.

After going through the list with the others working on the same thing, Knutsson and Thorén had decided to expand the list of potential perpetrators.

'There are a lot of burglaries at this time of year, when people are away on holiday,' Knutsson explained. 'So we added the most serious repeat offenders, regardless of whether or not they'd ever shown any signs of violence in the past.'

'So how many have we got now? A thousand?'

'It's not quite that bad,' Knutsson said. 'The list now contains eighty-two men with links to the area who have previous convictions.'

Later, the VICLAS unit from National Crime rang Bäckström to share their findings.

'I've got a lot to do, so the short version will do fine,' Bäckström warned. He knew the officer up in Stockholm and thought he was unbelievably long-winded. The Chin must have put the fear of God into the useless bastards, he thought.

The VICLAS unit looked for serial offenders by trying to find connections between new crimes and old cases, preferably solved ones. To start with they had fed in all the known details about Linda's murder, and then compared it with previous cases and known perpetrators who were already in the unit's computer.

'We got a match with a known criminal,' Bäckström's colleague said, sounding proud as a peacock. 'Your case is very similar to the one he's serving time for. Not bad. But you should know, Bäckström, they don't come much worse than this one.'

'So who is he, then?' Bäckström said. Almost sounds like you're talking about your own son, he thought.

'It's that crazy Pole who killed that beautician out in Högdalen. The Tanja murder. That was her name. The victim. You remember it? Leszek, Leszek Baranski. Calls himself Leo. He'd raped a whole load of women before that. A really nasty character. Used to run the whole repertoire, tying them up and gagging them, then torture and rape and strangulation. More than one strangulation on the same victim, actually. He used to strangle them a little bit until they lost consciousness, wake them up again by hacking at them with an ice-pick until they came round, then start all over again. A really nice guy.' The officer was almost bursting with enthusiasm.

'Hang on a minute,' Bäckström said. He had suddenly remembered who they were talking about. 'Didn't he get life?' Is that fucker already on the loose?

'First he got life imprisonment in the district court. But the appeal court sentenced him to a secure psychiatric ward with specific probationary requirements, and according to our records he's still inside, even though it's now six years since he was sentenced. Must be a new record for a secure psychiatric unit.'

'So what are you calling me for?' Bäckström said. We've already filled our quota of Polacks, he thought.

'Ah, I forgot to say,' his colleague said. 'He's in Sankt Sigfrid's, in Växjö, or at least he should be. Come on, Bäckström, you've been doing this for a while now. You know how things are with psychiatric units. Maybe the shrinks thought some fresh air would do him some good, let him get a bit of a tan and so on, and just forgot to tell us.'

'You mean he could have got day-release or something?' Bäckström said. Not him. Even shrinks aren't that fucking crazy, are they?

'No idea,' his colleague said. 'Why don't you call them and ask? I'll fax you everything we've got on him.'

'Thanks,' Bäckström said, and hung up. Right man in the right job: that fool he'd just spoken to would work for nothing if he had to. Who the hell are they letting into the force these days?

Bäckström stood up and lumbered over to the fax machine. Maybe he'd be lucky enough to both catch his perpetrator and fuck over the whole psychiatric industry at the same time.

The investigation's first Pole, librarian and holder of a doctorate, Marian Gross, had been contacted by the police that morning. Through the letterbox of the closed door of his flat he indicated to Inspector von Essen and his colleague Constable Adolfsson from Växjö Police that he was extremely busy all day, but that he could be reached by telephone the following day. Seeing as neither von Essen nor Adolfsson was in the mood, not where this case and, in particular, that building were concerned, Adolfsson had roared at him to step aside so he didn't get hit by his own door, and then landed an exploratory kick to check if he needed to get the ram from the boot of the patrol car. For reasons that were never entirely explained – the accounts of those involved differed quite dramatically in the report that was sent shortly afterwards to the police complaints authority – Gross had immediately opened the door.

'Ah, there you are, Gross,' Adolfsson said, smiling broadly at the flat's owner. 'Would you like to come with us, or do you want us to drag you?'

Quarter of an hour later von Essen and Adolfsson, with Gross between them, walked into the premises occupied by the investigating team. Gross had decided to walk under his own steam. He wasn't cuffed, and they had arrived discreetly via the garage of the police station.

'One Polack, as requested,' Adolfsson declared, as he handed him over to Salomonson and Rogersson, who were going to conduct the interview.

'I heard that,' roared Gross, whose face had been bright red the whole time although up to now he hadn't made a sound throughout the entire journey. 'I'll file a complaint for unlawful discrimination. You fucking fascists.'

'If Dr Gross would be so kind as to follow me and my colleague here, we'll sort out the practical details at once,' Salomonson said with a polite gesture towards the interview room.

The interview with the murder victim's neighbour, Marian Gross, started just after eleven o'clock in the morning. Lead interviewer was Detective Inspector Nils Salomonson of regional crime in Växjö, and the witness was Detective Inspector Jan Rogersson from National Crime in Stockholm. It would last almost twelve hours, with a break for lunch, two coffee breaks, and a couple of pauses so everyone could stretch their legs. At the end of the interview Martin Gross refused the offer of a lift home, and asked them instead to order him a taxi. At quarter past ten he left the police station. Considering what they had managed to get out of him, they might as well not have bothered.

Gross was mainly interested in talking about himself and the harassment the police had subjected him to for almost six months now, based on a ridiculous complaint filed by 'a mad woman at work whose sexual advances I have turned down'. Her accusations had started the ball rolling, and now that his neighbour's daughter had been murdered the police obviously thought he was fair game.

'You don't seriously believe that someone like me would be capable of doing something like that?' Gross had asked, looking in turn at Salomonson and Rogersson.

Naturally he hadn't received an answer. Instead Salomonson had changed track to a related issue where the fingerprints that they already had on file for Gross, as a result of the earlier investigation into the sexual harassment allegation, might come in handy. Unfortunately they had neglected to take a DNA sample on that occasion.

'You and Linda's mother, Liselotte Ericson, you've been neighbours for several years now,' Salomonson had said. 'How well do you know her?'

Normal neighbourly encounters, nothing more, nothing less, even if Linda's mother might not be averse to a closer relationship, according to Gross. And he'd also taken the opportunity to put them right.

'People call her Lotta. That's the name she uses herself,' he had said, and for some reason he seemed rather pleased. 'A not unattractive woman, unlike her anorexic daughter. They're not very similar at all. Lotta looks the way a woman's supposed to look.'

Salomonson had ignored his description of the murder victim. 'But Lotta Ericson isn't your type either?'

A bit too simple, possibly even a bit vulgar generally, and she was bound to be the clingy sort that he couldn't stand. And far too old, according to Gross.

'I see from our records,' Rogersson interjected, 'that she's a year younger than you. She's forty-five, you're forty-six.'

'I prefer younger women,' Gross said. 'Not that that's any of your business.'

'Have you ever visited Lotta in her flat?' Rogersson wondered.

Gross had been inside her flat on several occasions. A couple of times along with their other neighbours, when they'd discussed matters concerning the residents' association, and a couple of times on his own. Most recently just a month or so ago.

'She insisted on asking me in even though I was trying not to give her any signals in that direction,' Gross said. 'Like I said, she was fairly clingy.'

Whereabouts in the flat had he been? The hall, the living room, the kitchen, the usual places you went when you visit someone who's invited you for coffee. Possibly also the lavatory.

'The one beyond the bedroom?' Salomonson asked.

'I know what you're getting at,' Gross said. 'To avoid any mis-understanding: I've never set foot inside her bedroom. I might have been to the toilet out in the hall, and because our flats are identical I had no trouble finding it. So if you do happen to find my fingerprints anywhere – the same fingerprints you got hold of without any legal justification –- there's an entirely natural explanation.'

He's not your average idiot, Rogersson thought. No fingerprints from Gross had yet been found at the crime scene, and if any were in future their value was now extremely limited as a result of what he'd just said. So they had changed the subject and asked about his neighbour's daughter, the murder victim, instead.

'I hardly ever spoke to her,' Gross said. 'How could I have any opinion of her? She seemed a bit self-absorbed, spoiled and badly brought up, like every other young lady of her age.'

'Self-absorbed, spoiled, badly brought up. What do you mean by that?' Salomonson asked.

She'd hardly said hello to him on the few occasions when they had bumped into each other. She had avoided meeting his eyes and seemed to made a big deal of being completely uninterested the only time he could recall actually talking to her. And on that occasion her mother had also been present.

They hadn't taken a break for lunch until two o'clock. Gross himself had determined the late timing, presumably mainly to make things difficult for them. While Salomonson organized the food, Rogersson had gone to the bathroom. When he emerged, Bäckström was the first person he encountered.

'So how's it going with our Polish sex pest?' Bäckström asked.

'Had to ease the pressure,' Rogersson said. 'I seem to spend half my time in there these days. I'm finished as a lead interviewer. The only time I don't have to run to the toilet is when I'm drinking a load of beer. Then I don't even think about going. It's all very strange.'

'Yes,' Bäckström said with a grin. 'I only go when I wake up and before I go to bed. Twice a day, in fact, regardless of whether or not I need to.'

'In answer to your question, it's going pretty much as expected,' Rogersson said, ignoring Bäckström's last remark.

'Has he given a DNA sample?'

'We haven't got to that yet,' Rogersson said with a sigh. 'We've had our hands full listening to how badly we've been treating him. If you're interested, I can tell you how this is going to end.'

'So how's it going to end, then?' Bäckström said.

'We'll spend the next three hours listening to him droning on. Then Olsson will show up and decide that we need to listen to the same thing for another six hours. Then he'll refuse to give us a DNA sample, and then Olsson will back down because he hasn't got the balls to declare him an official suspect and ask the prosecutor to remand him in custody so that we can take the sample without his permission. Then Gross, Salomonson and I will all go home in our separate directions.'

'Well, at least you can have a couple of beers then,' Bäckström said sympathetically. 'To stop you having to run to the toilet, I mean.'

'Sure,' Rogersson. 'Gross didn't kill Linda, he didn't see anything, he hasn't heard anything, and he hasn't worked anything out for himself, so what's he doing here? In summary, it's just another perfectly routine day lost from a detective's life. So what are you up to?'

'I'm going to the madhouse,' Bäckström said.

# 15

Because Bäckström didn't like driving, he'd organized a driver. The person accorded this honour was young Adolfsson, and they had got the introductions out of the way on the way down to the garage.

'I understand that you and your partner were the ones who found her?' Bäckström said.

'Yes, boss,' Adolfsson said.

'So how come you're in the investigating team?' Bäckström asked, although he already knew.

'They're short of people, what with the holidays and everything,' Adolfsson said.

'I spoke to Enoksson,' Bäckström said. 'Sounds like he'd like to adopt you.'

'Yeah, that's probably not far from the truth. Enok's a good bloke. He and dad go hunting together.'

'Holidays and a shortage of people and Enoksson. So things went the way they did no matter what our esteemed Superintendent Olsson thought about the matter,' Bäckström summarized.

'Yes,' Adolfsson said. 'That just about covers it, boss.'

'That's not the first time either,' Bäckström said, squeezing into the passenger seat with some difficulty. Nice lad. Reminds me of myself at that age, Bäckström thought.

'Can I ask you a question, boss?' Adolfsson wondered politely as they were heading up out of the garage.

'Go ahead,' Bäckström said. Nice and polite as well, he thought.

'To what does our madhouse owe the honour of a visit from you, boss?' Adolfsson asked.

'We're going to take a look at a proper nutter,' Bäckström said. 'And we'll take the opportunity to have a look at the person taking care of him. If we're lucky, we'll get two nutters in one afternoon.'

'The Tanja man and Professor Brundin,' Adolfsson said. 'If I'm allowed to guess.'

A talented young man, Bäckström thought. But what else could you expect?

'That's pretty much it,' Bäckström said. 'Have you met either of them?'

'Both,' Adolfsson said. 'I've heard Brundin when he gave us a lecture. And the other one was wounded by another inmate on the ward a year or so ago, and had to be taken to hospital to be stitched up. My partner Essen and I oversaw the transfer.'

'So what are they like?' Bäckström asked. 'Brundin and the Tanja man, I mean.'

'They're both more than crazy enough.' Adolfsson nodded emphatically.

'Which one's craziest?' Bäckström said, looking at his new-found young friend curiously.

'Horses for courses,' Adolfsson said, shrugging his big shoulders. 'They're crazy in different ways, if I can put it like that. Mind you . . .'

'Shoot,' Bäckström said encouragingly.

'If I had to share a room with either of them, I'd probably prefer the Tanja man. No question.'

Sankt Sigfrid's Hospital was just a couple of kilometres from the police station, a mix of old and more modern buildings surrounded by a fairly large park which sloped towards a lake. It was airy and green, with shady trees, and well-kept lawns in spite of the summer drought. More than anything, it reminded Bäckström of the Grand Hotel in Saltsjöbaden outside Stockholm, where National Crime usually held their conferences and staff get-togethers. Professor Brundin's office was in an old, respectfully restored nineteenth-century building of white-plastered stone. Doesn't look like our criminal lunatics suffer too much, Bäckström thought as he and Adolfsson got out of the car.

'Wonder what all this cost?' he said as they rang the entry-phone at the entrance. 'The lunatics have got their own tennis courts, mini-golf and a fuck-off great swimming pool. What the hell's wrong with a bit of basic barbed wire?'

'Yes, our criminal lunatics don't exactly go short of anything in this country,' young Adolfsson agreed.

This boy's going to go far, Bäckström thought.

Professor Robert Brundin was rather reminiscent of a young Oscar Wilde, although unlike the original he had perfect teeth that he was happy to show off when he smiled. He was sitting comfortably, leaning back in the big chair behind his big desk in his big office, and appeared to be in complete harmony with both himself and his surroundings.

Bloody hell, he really is like that English poof who wrote stuff, the one who ended up in prison, Bäckström thought, temporarily unable to think of the name of the film and its lead character. Hardly surprising, he thought. It was a shit film and there weren't even any decent arse-bandit scenes, even though the TV supplement had said it was about poofs.

'So the police are anxious that I might have let my little Leo out into the town's streets and squares?' the professor said, showing all his white teeth.

'Well, unfortunately it's happened before,' Bäckström said.

'Not here, and not with me,' Brundin declared. 'If you like, I'd be happy to explain why.'

'We're listening,' Bäckström said. Young Adolfsson had already taken out his little black notebook and a pen.

Leo, Leszek Baranski, thirty-nine years old, was an extremely dangerous individual, and the crown jewel in Professor Brundin's remarkable collection of dangerous individuals. Leo alone had inspired him to write a number of articles in academic psychiatric journals, and he had been the central character in countless lectures.

'A unique example of a sexual sadist with highly developed fantasies,' Brundin declared happily. 'Each week we have several conversations on the subject, he and I, and I've never encountered anything like it before. Generally speaking he's very intelligent – his IQ is over 140, enough to get him into NASA's training programme for astronauts, for instance – but in terms of tormenting young women for his own sexual gratification he's an absolute genius. When it comes to thinking up new ways of expressing his sexual sadism, his creativity knows no bounds.'

'So you're not planning on letting him out,' Bäckström said. Sounds like a charming bloke, he thought, not quite sure if it was Leo or his doctor that he had in mind.

Brundin wasn't planning on letting Leo out. The idea had never even occurred to him. But his boss, in contrast, an older colleague who was – admittedly – 'a decent person but I'm sorry to say badly afflicted by the liberalism of his generation, generally lethargic in his attitudes and with occasionally clear signs of a refractory personality', had suggested various measures which could eventually, in his opinion, facilitate Leo's rehabilitation for a life outside the goldfish bowl in which he was currently being kept.

'Such as?' Bäckström said. Why not just boil him down and make glue out of the bastard?

'Voluntary castration,' Brundin said, with a broad smile. 'My boss suggested that if Baranski agreed to let himself be castrated, then over a long period of time he could gradually be let out on supervised excursions.'

'Castration?' Bäckström asked. 'Do you still do that?' Fucking hell, he thought, unconsciously crossing his legs.

'Voluntarily, of course. Voluntarily,' Brundin said, leaning back comfortably and letting his fingers form a tall steeple.

'So what did he think about that, then?' Bäckström asked. There had to be some limits, surely? Boiling him down into glue seemed lenient by comparison.

'He wasn't exactly keen,' Brundin said. 'After all, it would completely extinguish his considerable sexual drive – he usually masturbates between five and ten times a day. And patients like that normally suffer dramatic weight gain, particularly when they're in an environment like this. Obviously, he's worried about losing both his urges and his looks, because he's a very vain man. I myself was strongly – I might almost say categorically – opposed to the idea of castration.'

'Why?' Bäckström said. Because the bastard probably looks like you, he thought.

'Extinguishing his sexual desires would obviously also affect his sexual fantasies. In the worst case, he'd be lost to psychiatric research,' Brundin said, without a trace of a smile.

'I see,' Bäckström said, who for once wasn't sure what he thought.

'I presume that you gentlemen would like to see him,' the professor said.

'Why not?' Bäckström said. If nothing else, it would give him something to talk about in the staffroom at work, he thought. Adolfsson contented himself with a nod, a youthful and expectant glint in his deep-set blue eyes.

'He's been in isolation since yesterday evening,' Brundin said. 'We had to sedate him and put him in a straitjacket, so I'm afraid you won't be able to talk to him. It's entirely likely that he just heard one of the staff say something about the Linda murder and it got him extremely excited.'

Leszek 'Leo' Baranski seemed anything but excited, even though he looked like an illustration from one of the fantasies that usually occupied his mind, possibly even now when he appeared to be fast asleep. He was lying in a ten-metre-square room in the secure unit's corridor of isolation cells. The only furnishing was a metal bunk that was bolted to the floor. Leo lay immobile on top of it, flat on his back, his head to one side so that he was lying on his right cheek. Small and thin, dark curly hair and sensitive, almost feminine facial features. The only thing he was wearing was a pair of hospital boxer shorts, stamped with the logo of Sankt Sigfrid. His arms were fastened to his sides by thick leather straps. His legs were stretched out, apart, and held down at the ankles by leather straps fixed to the end of the bunk.

'It normally takes about six hours before he comes round,' Brundin told them. 'We usually start by untying his right arm so he can relieve the worst of the angst.' He smiled.

'That sounds practical,' Bäckström said. While you and your colleagues stand here watching him through this pane of glass, he thought.

When they left, Professor Brundin wished them luck with their work, and hoped that he would soon have an opportunity to meet them again. He had already started to sketch out a future research project about a new and very interesting group of young men with foreign backgrounds who committed serious sexual offences because they themselves had suffered similar abuse in their childhood or youth. Chaotic and severely disturbed, of course, yet still capable of holding things together, and not to be confused with men like Leo.

'I'm looking forward to meeting the Linda man. Especially as he represents an entirely different category of offender from the one Leo belongs to,' Brundin said, smiling warmly at them.

'Who isn't looking forward to meeting him?' Bäckström said, with feeling.

'Do you mind if I make a personal remark, boss?' Adolfsson said as they were driving out through the hospital gates.

'Shoot,' Bäckström grunted.

'That Brundin seems an odd character. Right man in the right job, I'd say.'

You're going to go far, lad, Bäckström thought, contenting himself with a grunt of agreement.

# 16

When they got back to the police station, Bäckström asked young Adolfsson to write a report of their visit to Sankt Sigfrid, while he got to grips with the various piles that had built up on his desk. Nothing exciting, and none of the others in the room appeared to be in need of a kick up the backside to get something done. High time for the hotel and a little glass of beer, Bäckström decided after a quick glance at his watch. But of course that was when his mobile phone rang. It was the long-winded colleague from the VICLAS unit, wanting to hear how things had gone with Leo.

'We met both him and Brundin,' Bäckström said.

'Is Brundin in charge of looking after him?'

'Yes,' Bäckström said, glancing at the time again. 'He says hello, by the way.'

'In that case there's no need to worry,' his colleague assured him. 'Brundin's the only person in that entire profession who's completely normal. So how was Leo?'

'Fine. Having a great time. He says hello too,' Bäckström said, and ended the call.

On the way out he went past Rogersson's room to see if he was done for the day, but the red light outside the interview room was still on. Six hours, plus six more, Bäckström thought. Oh well, he could always order a taxi. Who has the energy to walk in this sort of heat? He fished up his mobile from his pocket again, but before he had time to make the call the investigation's very own crisis therapist popped up and almost threw herself at him even though she was skinny as a golf club and not much taller.

'I'm so pleased I've found you, Superintendent,' she said, smiling warmly and tilting her head to one side. 'Can you spare me a few minutes?'

'What can I do to help you, Lo?' Bäckström said, smiling just as warmly back. Probably makes sense to deal with the old cow while I've built up a head of steam, he thought.

Once they reached her room it took several minutes before Lo got to the point. But because Bäckström already knew exactly how he was going to handle this, it was a pleasure watching her put her scrawny neck in the noose he had set up for her. He leaned back comfortably in the armchair she kept for visitors, folded his hands over his protruding stomach and nodded encouragingly at her.

'You're practically the only person I haven't spoken to, superintendent,' she began.

'Well, Lo, as I'm sure you appreciate, I've had quite a bit to do,' Bäckström said, with a thoughtful nod. So much so that I haven't had time to sit here babbling with a nagging old cow like you, he thought.

'I certainly do appreciate that,' Lo agreed, tilting her head a few more centimetres and flashing him an almost vertical smile.

'That's good to hear,' Bäckström said tranquilly, simultaneously trying out the contemplative nod that he usually saved for just this sort of situation.

According to Lilian Olsson, Bäckström, because of his long experience as a murder detective with National Crime, must have been confronted with more misery than almost any other officer in the force.

'How have you managed to handle all that?' she asked. 'You must be carrying around some terrible experiences.'

'How do you mean?' Never give them a millimetre, because then you're fucked, Bäckström thought.

All the awful things he'd seen in the course of his duty? A lot of police officers, not to say most, or even all, ended up getting burned out because of the job. Marching in file towards the wall until they hit it, while they tried to struggle through to their next shift by abusing alcohol and sex.

'And that's probably the very worst way to try to deal with psychological problems,' Lo said.

Fucking good fun though, Bäckström thought as he nodded in agreement. 'It's tragic,' he said, shuddering with distaste. 'Tragic,' he repeated. Maybe I ought to tip her the wink about Lewin and little Svanström, he thought.

'I've even come across young officers who developed eating disorders while they were still at police college,' Lo went on.

'Tragic,' Bäckström repeated. 'Young people too. Terrible.' He sighed deeply. Considering the food they served there, the big mystery was how any of them managed to eat anything at all.

In Lo's firm opinion, based on the many years she had spent working as a psychologist with the police, the problem was hidden within the culture of the police itself, in the spirit of 'machismo, denial, silence and destructive behaviour patterns, all acting together', which had for so long governed the working environment within the force, and handicapped the people who were forced to work within it. Even she could feel it flowing towards her, from the floor, walls and ceiling, each time she set foot inside a police station.

'How do you deal with all these traumatic experiences, Bäckström?' she repeated, bobbing her head encouragingly.

'With the help of our Lord,' Bäckström said, and raised his pious face towards the ceiling. Suck on that, bitch, he thought.

Lo smiled hesitantly. 'Sorry, I don't think I quite follow you, I'm afraid,' she said.

'Our Lord,' Bäckström repeated in an inviting voice. 'Our Almighty Lord, ruler of heaven and earth, and also my guide and salvation during my time on earth.' Is that what someone looks like just before their ears and jaw drop off, he wondered.

'I had no idea that you were born again, Bäckström,' Lo said, looking at him weakly.

'It's not the sort of thing you go round talking about,' Bäckström said, giving her a look of admonition and shaking his head. 'It's between me and my Lord.'

'I understand that so well,' Lo said. 'But these things aren't mutually exclusive, of course. You've never considered altern— well, trying other ways of achieving mental peace, I mean?'

'Such as what?' Bäckström said grimly, giving her his police stare. Time to turn the screw, he thought.

'Well, like different forms of therapy, such as debriefing, which is itself actually a form of therapy,' Lo said, smiling stiffly at him. 'My door is always open, and I have a lot of ordinary believers . . .'

'Thou shalt have no other gods before me!' Bäckström thundered, pointing at her with his outstretched hand as he stood up from the armchair. 'This arrogance that you and your colleagues exhibit by trying to put yourselves in the place of our Lord. Are you aware that you're breaking the first commandment?' Unless it was the second? Well, what the fuck.

'I really didn't mean to upset you—'

'The deeds of men are mere fragments,' Bäckström interrupted. 'Ecclesiastes twelve, fourteen,' he went on, staring hard at her. A shot in the dark, and a bit of a gamble in Småland, of all places, but she didn't seem the churchy type.

'Well, I really do apologize if I've upset you at all,' Lo said with a weak smile.

'My door is always open,' Bäckström said, as he opened hers as if to underline what he was saying. 'Just think about one thing, Lilian,' he said cajolingly. 'We human beings . . . we are but fools . . . for our dear Lord rules.'

Gently, he closed the door behind him. And now to lock myself in the toilet and laugh until I give myself a hernia.

As soon as he reached his room he poured himself a cold lager. There must be something wrong with people who drink direct from the can. No damn better than monkeys, Bäckström thought, taking a few deep gulps and greedily licking the froth from his upper lip. Then he threw himself on to the bed, turned on the television and began looking through all the phone messages that had been left for him down in reception. There were quite a lot, mostly from little Carin from local radio. In one message, left just a couple of hours ago, she had even sworn that 'we don't have to talk about work', and to show she meant it she had left her home number. 'Can I offer to get you a bite to eat at a discreet little place?' A woman in dire straits, Bäckström thought as he reached for the phone on the bedside table. She seems completely desperate.

*

The 'discreet little place' was a small inn with an outside terrace over-looking yet another Småland lake. It was a fair way out of town, but since his employer would be paying for the taxi he didn't much care. Not a single damn journalist as far as my detective's eye can see, he thought as he pulled out the chair for his companion.

'Finally alone, superintendent. Hint, hint,' Carin said, smiling with her mouth and eyes. 'What would you like? My treat.'

'Absolutely not.' Bäckström had already decided in the taxi to award himself overtime for meeting another secret informant, and obviously he would need the receipt to prove that the meeting had taken place. 'I want something nice,' he went on, glancing at Carin's tanned arms and legs. She was wearing a thin summer dress, and she must have forgotten to do up the top three buttons. Maybe a bit too easy, he told himself.

Very pleasant, he thought as he dropped her off three hours later. He had put a stop to all attempts to get him to talk about the Linda case. To keep the conversation going, and to tell her a bit about himself in an unforced way, he had offered her the usual police classics, and had concluded with a fat promise about the future.

'Still, you have to appreciate how I feel,' Carin had sighed, fingering her wine glass. 'We're sitting down here, and all the news keeps coming out in the Stockholm papers. That's where you find out what's going on. Even though it's our murder. I mean, the girl who was killed did actually live here. One of our own, if you like.'

'Most of what they print is rubbish, if that's any consolation to you,' Bäckström had said. Ah, the things I do for the poor wee souls, he thought.

'Really?' she said, with a glint of hope in her eyes.

'Okay, this is what we do,' Bäckström said, leaning forward and just happening to touch her arm. 'When I've got the bastard and am con-vinced it's him, I promise I'll let you know ahead of all the others. Just you. No one else.'

'You promise? You really mean it?' she said, staring at him.

'I really mean it,' he lied, and left his hand touching her arm. 'You, and only you.' This is way too easy.

As soon as he got back to the hotel he headed straight for the bar. Only three beers throughout a whole meal, and he was as thirsty as a camel that had gone on a pilgrimage from Jerusalem to Mecca. And Rogersson was sitting towards the back of the bar with a huge glass in front of him, looking more than usually miserable even though there were plenty of empty tables around him. The two dozen reporters and other civilians in the room had for some reason chosen to sit as far away from him as possible.

'I said I'd break the arm of the first vulture who tried to sit down, so everything's okay,' he explained. 'What do you want? It's my round.'

'Beer, a large one,' Bäckström said, waving over a waiter who for some reason looked reluctant. You're always so diplomatic, Rogge, he thought.

'So what have you been up to?' Rogersson asked when Bäckström had got his beer and had had a chance to dull the worst of his thirst.

'I had a long talk with our very own crisis therapist,' Bäckström said with a grin. 'Then I had to go to the toilet. So that'll make three times today.'

'And I thought you were a normal person. What the fuck are you talking to someone like that for?' Rogersson sighed, shaking his head.

'Just listen,' Bäckström said, and leaned over the table to tell Rogersson the whole story. Rogersson livened up considerably, and they sat there and drank their way through several more rounds of beer and chasers, which Bäckström told the staff to put on the bill for their rooms which, along with everything else, would be paid by their employer.

When it was time to go upstairs and get some sleep, the bar was practically empty. Rogersson was considerably happier, and had even said goodnight to the few reporters who were still sitting there, evidently determined to drink their heads off.

'Go home, you stupid fuckers,' he said.

# 17

## *Växjö, Tuesday 8 July*

Evidently not all the reporters had followed Rogersson's advice the previous evening, because over breakfast Bäckström and his colleagues were able to enjoy the latest scoop in the largest evening paper. HE TRIED TO KILL LINDA'S NEIGHBOUR, screamed the headline, referring to the three-page article inside, on pages six, seven and eight: *'Police murderer tried to kill me too.' Linda's neighbour Margareta tells her story.*

'What the fuck's all this?' Bäckström said to a silent Rogersson, who was driving them the four hundred metres from the hotel to the police station. *'At three o'clock in the morning I was woken by someone trying to break into my flat,'* he read out loud. *'But my two dogs started barking furiously and he ran off. I heard him running down the stairs.* What the fuck is this?' he repeated. 'Why hasn't she mentioned this before? We've questioned her a couple of times at least, haven't we?'

'She's been questioned three times,' Rogersson confided. 'I've read them all. To begin with she spoke to the first patrol on the scene. Then our colleagues in regional crime had a long interview with her, when she was also issued with a disclosure ban. Then she was questioned a third time during the door-to-door enquiries.'

'And not a single word about him trying to break into her flat?'

'Not a peep.'

'Go and see her, and question her again,' Bäckström said. 'Straight away. Take young Salomonson with you.'

'Sure,' Rogersson said.

Could it simply be the case that this is the truth, Bäckström thought. That the same crazy bastard knocked on Linda's door and she was stupid enough to let him in?

The morning meeting was a dull affair, even though it was led by Bäckström. Most of them seemed to be waiting for the forensics report of what had happened at the crime scene, particularly the long anticipated results from the National Forensics Lab about the perpetrator's DNA profile. Most of the meeting had been devoted to a discussion of what they had read in that morning's paper, which upset Bäckström so deeply that he had no intention of saying why: that the media had taken the initiative in his murder investigation.

As so many times before, opinion had been divided.

'I think it could simply be that she didn't dare tell us when we questioned her. She was just scared,' said the first person who spoke.

'Another possibility is that she's made it all up to make herself more interesting, or that the reporters put words in her mouth,' the next said.

'Maybe the truth is somewhere in between,' the third said. 'That her dogs started barking in the middle of the night, but not necessarily because someone was trying to get into her flat. Could have been a car, or a drunk out in the road?'

Things had carried on in that vein until Bäckström straightened up and raised his hand to interrupt the discussion.

'It'll sort itself out,' Bäckström said, then turned to Enoksson, who hadn't said anything either. 'Is there any point sending you and you chums to dust down her door?'

'They're already on their way,' Enoksson said.

Finally, Bäckström thought. A proper police officer.

After the meeting Bäckström had taken officer Sandberg to one side to rest his weary eyes once more, and to see how far they had got with the profiling of people connected to the victim.

'How's it going, Anna? Are we starting to get an idea of who was at the nightclub on Thursday?'

According to Sandberg, they were looking at a total of approximately two hundred people who were either inside the club when

Linda showed up just after eleven o'clock, or arrived later that night while she was still there. Of these, almost a hundred had already been questioned. Most of those had contacted the police themselves after members of the investigating team appeared in the local media and appealed for them to get in touch. This group included six of Linda's colleagues from police college, the friend who was also a civilian employee at the police station, and four other police officers, including Anna Sandberg herself.

'And you haven't got any suspicions about any of our colleagues, or any of the students?' Bäckström said cheerfully.

'No,' Anna said, apparently less amused by the subject. 'At least, not from what I've been able to find out. So: no.'

'What about the rest, then? Were there many troublemakers there? And all the weirdos who haven't contacted us? What do we know about them?' Bloody hell, don't any women have a sense of humour? he thought.

Nothing unusual, according to Anna. A few local troublemakers, but anything else would have been odd considering the time and place. They'd managed to speak to a number of them, and they were as upset as everyone else that Linda had been murdered.

'So there are at least fifty people we haven't got a clue about?' Master Detective Anna Blomkvist, like Astrid Lindgren's young detective, Bäckström thought.

'Yes,' Anna said. 'At most, if we're only talking about men. But I don't think it's as many as that.'

'So how do we get hold of them, then?'

According to Anna, it was bound to take a bit of time. Partly because it was the middle of the holiday season, and partly because a lot of them simply didn't want to admit that they were in the club, even if they hadn't seen or spoken to the murder victim. Besides, officer Sandberg also had an idea of her own that she wondered if she could mention.

'I've spent a lot of time thinking about this, and to be honest I'm wondering if it's worth the trouble.'

'Why wouldn't it be?' Bäckström said. So she's lazy as well, he thought.

There were several reasons, in Anna's opinion. It involved a great deal of work, yet no matter how hard they tried they weren't going to get hold of everyone who was there.

'Any other reason?' Bäckström said. Sigh, he thought.

'Is it really that interesting?' Anna said. 'Nothing suggests that anyone went home with her from the club, or followed her home. Or even that she agreed to meet up with someone she met there. If what the neighbour said in the paper is true, it looks like she just got caught by a maniac, doesn't it? I think that looks most likely.'

'We don't actually know that,' Bäckström said curtly. 'You don't, and I don't,' he added. Least of all you, he thought.

'So we carry on?' Anna said.

'Exactly,' Bäckström said. 'I want everyone in that club identified and questioned, and if we happen to find the perpetrator somewhere else in the meantime, then we'll stop. I'm not that stupid.'

'Understood,' Anna said curtly.

'One more thing,' Bäckström said. 'You said I could take a look at her diary?'

'Of course,' Anna said. 'Although I'm afraid that doesn't contain anything interesting either. At least not that I've been able to find.'

'Are forensics finished with it?' Bäckström asked. What do you mean, either? he thought.

'Yes,' Anna said. 'Just Linda's prints. No one else's.'

'Thank goodness,' Bäckström said with a grin.

'What do you mean?' Anna looked at him warily.

'I won't have to wear those damn plastic gloves,' Bäckström said.

'No, you won't,' Anna said curtly. 'Are we finished?'

'Sure,' Bäckström said with a shrug. How can a woman with such decent tits be so fucking miserable? he thought.

# 18

A remarkable summer. The most remarkable both in living memory and in perfectly ordinary memory as well, assuming people were old enough, of course. It had started as early as May, day after day of scorching hot sun with new record temperatures being set all over the country, fairly evenly distributed.

And on Tuesday 8 July it was time for a new national record. The previous Swedish record had actually been set in Småland almost sixty years before. On 29 June 1947, a temperature of 38 degrees was reached in Målilla, and if our Lord was actually in charge of the weather, then he was certainly taking care of his own. What other explanation could there be for the fact that at three o'clock in the afternoon of Tuesday 8 July, the pious village of Väckelsång, a short distance south of Växjö, recorded a temperature of 38.3 degrees Celsius? In the shade, naturally.

In Växjö it was relatively cool. When Jan Lewin and Eva Svanström left the police station just after one o'clock for a late lunch out in town, Oxtorget was quivering with heat haze, even though it was only a modest 32 degrees outside. Lewin had spent most of his waking hours in his air-conditioned office inside the police station, so he wasn't exactly prepared.

'Maybe we should stay inside?' he suggested, smiling hesitantly at Eva Svanström. What's going on, he wondered. In Sweden, in the middle of the summer?

'I think it's lovely,' Eva replied with a happy smile, throwing out her arms in an extremely un-Swedish gesture. 'Come on, Janne, let's go. I promise you can sit in the shade.'

The news the previous evening and that morning had focused largely on the weather, and in the local media there had been a fair degree of local pride. The warmest part of Sweden was still in the Småland of our Lord. The *Barometer* in Kalmar had even seen fit to declare Småland the Riviera of northern Europe, although the *Småland Post* was, as so often, more restrained: after all, every right-thinking Småland resident knew the penalty for false pride.

Just as in the bigger papers, various experts had been asked for an opinion, both those who warned of the greenhouse effect and those who dismissed it, referring to historical and long-term variations in temperature, such as the fact that grapevines had been grown way up in Norrland during the Bronze Age. And of course there was plenty of medical advice. People should stay in the shade, avoid unnecessary physical exertion, drink a lot and cover their heads with a cap or a hat. This was particularly important for the elderly and the very young, and for people with high blood pressure or heart problems. And obviously under no circumstances should dogs or small children be left inside locked cars, even for a short while.

The evening papers had followed their usual tradition. After doing their duty and getting the meteorological details out of the way, they had focused on the really important aspects, such as the link between the unbearable heat and the increase in violent crime – not forgetting the Linda murder, of course.

One of the experts consulted by the largest of the evening papers had detailed the clear connection between the emergence of serial killers and the temperature at the time of the crimes. According to his own research, the likelihood of multiple murders increased along with the temperature. The summer months were far more critical than winter, whether you were an Eskimo or an African. And it was no coincidence that the majority of known serial killers, in the US for instance, preferred to work in the southern states of California or Florida than in the mid-western or northern states. His conclusion: heat triggers violence, particularly in mentally ill, unstable or fragile criminals.

# 19

Life goes on. First I have to argue with a miserable bitch before lunch, then I have to eat with two complete idiots because Rogersson is evidently still listening to another bitch, Bäckström thought. And as if that wasn't more than enough, they're serving soggy pasta and some bastard fish sauce for lunch. What's wrong with a bit of beef stew with beetroot? For God's sake, this rural hell-hole was right next to Skåne, and they had decent food there.

Knutsson and Thorén were considerably more cheerful, and Knutsson was most cheerful of all, because he had decided to check the list of burglaries even before the neighbour had stepped forward and told her story to the paper.

'Very far-sighted of you, Erik,' Thorén said in admiration. 'When I read what she said, I was convinced it was true. I think you're on the right lines.'

'Tell me,' Bäckström said. Fucking idiots, he thought.

According to Thorén, it was very simple. 'Typical behaviour for burglars. First they go to the top of a building, where there's least chance of someone living lower down going past.'

Because at three o'clock in the morning in the middle of the holiday season that risk was pretty damn significant, Bäckström thought, nodding encouragingly at him.

'Well, then he probably tried ringing on the door to see if anyone was home, and then the dogs started barking,' Thorén went on.

'Or he looked through the letterbox,' Knutsson added helpfully.

'So he left. Burglars hate dogs,' Thorén explained.

And I can tell you've never worked in the drug squad, Bäckström thought, nodding. 'So what was wrong with the floor below? There wasn't anyone there at all,' he said.

'Far too close, considering he'd just woken up the upstairs neighbour,' Knutsson said confidently.

'The next floor, then?' Bäckström asked.

'The Pole was home,' Thorén said. 'But that's not to say the burglar didn't check his door too.'

'I still think he went all the way to the ground floor,' Knutsson said. 'To be on the safe side, I mean.'

'So that's when he rings on Linda's door?' Bäckström asked. This is getting better and better.

'Yes,' Knutsson said. 'And looks through the letterbox and everything they usually do. That's the usual modus for people like that. Well. Their modus operandi, I mean.'

'And Linda gets up and opens the door for him?' Bäckström said.

'Yes,' Knutsson said. 'Even if it sounds a bit strange. Of course she could have just forgotten to lock the door.'

'She must have done, seeing as there were no signs of a break-in on the door,' Thorén said. 'Either opened the door, or forgotten to lock it, I mean.'

'Hang on a moment,' Bäckström said, raising his hands to stop them. 'Just so I'm following your reasoning, gentlemen. At three o'clock in the morning a typical burglar comes along, your standard addict with needle-tracks, saliva hanging from the corner of his mouth and so on, and he rings on Linda's door to see if the Ericson whose name is on the door is at home, or, preferably, isn't. Meanwhile, the neighbour's dogs up on the fourth floor are barking like mad. So our thief rings on the door, ring, ring, ring. Then he takes a quick look through the letterbox as well. And Linda, who's left the club to go home and get some sleep, and who I believe was training to join the police, goes up to the door, looks through the peephole, and what does she see? A typical thief. Wired. Wow, I must let him in! Straight away. There's lots here he can pinch. As long as he promises to take off his shoes and leave them in the shoe-rack in the hall, so he doesn't make a mess. Is that it?'

Neither Thorén nor Knutsson said anything. Bäckström got up, put his tray on the trolley, then went and got a cup of coffee with plenty of milk and sugar, and took it with him back to his office, cursing silently the whole way.

When Rogersson and his fellow officer Salomonson rang on the door of the neighbour, Margareta Eriksson, she was already busy. She had invited in a reporter and photographer from the second largest evening paper, who had missed the scoop but hadn't given up hope of getting a fresh angle. They were sitting in the kitchen drinking coffee.

'So it would suit me much better if you could come back later today,' she explained.

'Perhaps you'd rather do this down at the station, Mrs Eriksson,' Rogersson said with an expressionless voice and a blank look in his eyes. 'We can send a patrol car to pick you up. Just let us know when.'

Upon further consideration, right now turned out to be a very good time after all, and just a few minutes later Mrs Eriksson was sitting with Rogersson and Salomonson around the same kitchen table that the reporters had just vacated.

'Perhaps you'd like a cup of coffee?' their hostess asked. She had evidently decided to draw a line and move on.

'Yes, that would be great,' Salomonson said before Rogersson had time to decline the offer.

'Well, of course I understand that you're wondering about that article in the paper,' Mrs Eriksson said, and from the look on her face she wasn't feeling entirely comfortable. 'Why I didn't say anything when I spoke to your colleagues, I mean.'

Rogersson made do with simply nodding at her, while Salomonson focused on stirring his coffee.

'Of course you can't believe everything they say in the papers,' Mrs Eriksson said with a nervous smile. 'Absolutely not, because I didn't actually say everything that they printed. What I said was that I'd woken up in the middle of the night because my dogs were barking. But all the rest, about someone trying to break in, and that I heard someone running downstairs . . . I didn't say any of that. If anything like that had happened, I'd certainly have called the police.'

'Do your dogs often start barking when someone comes, Mrs Eriksson?' Salomonson wondered.

Their owner said that it certainly happened sometimes. Occasionally they would bark when the neighbours came home, especially if it was late, or sometimes just when there was someone making a noise out in the road. 'That awful Pole' that she unfortunately had as a neighbour had even complained to the residents' committee because of it. Without success, according to the dogs' owner and chair of the committee. But certainly Peppe could be very sensitive.

'He has a very gruff bark,' Mrs Eriksson said proudly, patting the large Labrador that was resting its head in her lap. 'And then little Pigge joins in to help his big brother.'

'What did you do when the dogs started barking, Mrs Eriksson?' Rogersson asked.

Because she was in bed asleep, and was woken by their barking, she had lain there listening. Then she had told them to stop, and when they did she had assumed that there was nothing wrong.

'If someone had been standing out on the landing, obviously they would have carried on barking, even if he was quiet as a mouse,' Mrs Eriksson explained.

'So the dogs stopped barking,' Rogersson said. 'Then what did you do?'

First she had crept out into the hall and looked through the peephole, but she hadn't heard or seen anything. Then she had gone back to bed again, and eventually went back to sleep. That was all, and she apologized once more for not thinking of it sooner when she was talking to the police. As to why the journalists had written what they did, she 'honestly had no idea'.

Because you tried to make yourself sound interesting, Rogersson thought, but he didn't say it. Instead they concluded the interview, thanked her for the coffee, and left. Rogersson hadn't even bothered saying anything about the disclosure ban. Every proper police officer knew that they were just a bad joke.

On the way down the stairs they met two forensics officers who were on their way up to dust Mrs Eriksson's door, and any other potentially interesting surfaces.

'If you're quick, you'll get a cup of coffee,' Salomonson said, whereas Rogersson made do with a nod and grunt.

Because they were passing, they rang Gross's bell to see if he had noticed anyone outside his door early on Friday morning. Gross had refused to open the door. Through the letterbox he told them to stop harassing him.

'I've got some reporters here. I've got witnesses in the flat. I'm warning you,' Gross said. 'Get lost, right now.'

'Well, that was pretty much it,' Rogersson said. He looked up at Bäckström and sighed.

'So what do you think?' Bäckström asked.

'That the old bag woke up in the middle of the night because her dogs were barking,' Rogersson said. 'She doesn't know when exactly. I'm guessing they bark all the time. They were barking like mad when we rang on the door.'

'So why did she go and look through the peephole, then?' Bäckström asked. 'Does she do that every time the dogs bark?'

'Not according to her, anyway,' Rogersson said. 'But if you want to know what I think?' Bäckström nodded. 'It was the middle of the night, it's summer, she's read in all the papers about break-ins and thieves running wild, pretty much all her neighbours are away on holiday. That's enough to explain why she decided to take a look this time.'

'But why were the dogs barking, then?' Bäckström persisted.

'Don't ask me about dogs. Talk to someone in the dog unit. It would probably cheer them up. Their dogs are the only thing those poor bastards have in their tiny minds.'

'Why did the dogs bark?' Bäckström repeated.

'The simple explanation is that they started to bark because they heard Linda come home. If we're to believe their owner, they've got fucking brilliant hearing. See you at the hotel,' Rogersson said.

'Don't forget to pick up supplies,' Bäckström reminded him. 'No need to get me anything; it'll be fine if you just replace all the cans you've had off me.'

Before Bäckström left the police station he called Enoksson in forensics to ask how things were going with the examination of Mrs Eriksson's door.

'We examined everything under ultra-violet, and dusted it,' Enoksson said. 'The door, the handle, the letterbox, the frame, the walls on either side, the banister on the stairs up to her floor. We've already checked the lift, as you might remember.'

'And?' Bäckström said.

'Nothing,' Enoksson said. 'Just her prints. She's probably just lonely and wanted some company. And maybe exaggerated to make herself more interesting.'

When Bäckström returned to his room in the hotel, he found that his laundry had been returned. The neatly folded piles covered pretty much every available surface of the room. And they had written it up on the bill as 'care of equipment', as he had requested. Then Rogersson turned up with the crate of export-strength lager that he owed Bäckström. Christmas, Bäckström thought, instantly forgetting any thought of calling little Carin and telling her anything.

'I've got some cold ones in the minibar,' he said. 'I suggest we deal with those before going to get something to eat.'

# 20

## *Växjö, Wednesday 9 July*

The day had begun with unusual promise. The second largest evening paper was refusing to give up the fight. They were out for revenge, and had managed to make more of Marian Gross's story than even their editor could have hoped for. A double-page spread, with a big picture of the hero of the piece, librarian Marian Gross, 39, which perfectly matched the headline: HE SCARED OFF THE SERIAL KILLER. How the hell had the photographer managed that, Bäckström wondered. *The little fucker does look almost scary. They must have shot him from below.*

'Listen to this,' he said, and began to read from the article.

'Hang on,' Thorén said pedantically. 'Isn't he forty-six, not thirty-nine?'

'Who cares,' Bäckström said. 'Just listen to this. *Marian woke up in the middle of the night because someone was trying to break into his flat, and he ran out into the hall. Through the peephole in the door he saw a young man in his early twenties trying to pick the lock of his flat.*'

'Which one?' Rogersson said sullenly. 'He had three different locks on his door when I was there yesterday.'

'Don't get hung up on details,' Bäckström said, and carried on reading. '*I asked him what he was doing, Marian says, but before I had time to open the door and grab him he ran off down the stairs and disappeared.*'

'So does he give a description?' Knutsson asked.

'A very good one, actually,' Bäckström said. 'Although the perpetrator's face was covered by the peak of a so-called baseball cap, our Polish friend saw that he had short hair, almost shaved, and looked typically Swedish. Like a football hooligan or a right-wing extremist, at any rate. Big and strong. About one metre eighty, about twenty years old. Wearing a green and brown camouflage jacket, and black trousers made of some sort of shiny material, stuffed into a pair of high boots.'

'Interesting,' Lewin said, sipping his coffee and at the same time running the big toe of his right foot along Eva Svanström's left ankle and suntanned shin under the table. 'The way he was dressed, considering it was about twenty degrees outside, I mean.'

'There's something here that doesn't make sense,' Knutsson said hesitantly, shaking his head.

'Tell us,' Bäckström said eagerly, putting the paper down and leaning forward so as not to miss a word.

'Would the perpetrator really have run down to the ground floor and rung on Linda's door?' Thorén clarified, shaking his head again.

'Perhaps he was finished with Linda,' Bäckström suggested helpfully. 'And he thought he'd work his way back up the building?'

'So why didn't he call the police?' Knutsson said obligingly. 'Gross, I mean.'

'He's already been asked that, actually,' Bäckström said with a grin. 'Along with most of the other citizens of this country, Gross doesn't have a lot of faith in the police.'

'Thank heavens for that,' Thorén said. 'Considering what he's been up to himself.'

'I don't believe any of this,' Knutsson said, shaking his head firmly. 'I think he's made it all up. Although someone could have rung on his door, of course. Like the woman upstairs, I mean.'

'I don't think we're going to get much further,' Rogersson sighed, getting up from the table. 'Do you want me to question him again?' He was looking at Bäckström.

'Does the Pope wear a turban? Does Superintendent Bäckström wear a uniform? Does Dolly Parton sleep on her stomach?' Bäckström said, getting up as well.

# 21

That same morning the investigating team finally received the much anticipated forensic report, and everyone was present for the morning meeting. The atmosphere was charged as they heard that the results were conclusive. If they could only get hold of whoever left the DNA at the crime scene, Linda's murder would be solved beyond any doubt. From the point of view of evidence, it was so overwhelming that anything the perpetrator might say after his arrest was completely irrelevant.

His DNA had been secured from seven different places. In the form of semen from the sofa in the living room. In the form of various bodily fluids on the dark blue Jockey shorts, size S, found under the same sofa. In the form of semen in the victim's vagina and rectum. In the form of semen on the wall of the shower in the bathroom. In the form of blood on the windowsill. And finally from one other place that forensics hadn't mentioned before. In the hall they had found a pair of trainers, size 42, Reeboks. The DNA that forensics managed to secure from these identified them as the perpetrator's shoes.

'We weren't sure to start with,' Enoksson explained. 'That's why we haven't said anything before. But according to Linda's mother, she'd never seen them before, so we sent them off to the National Lab, and it worked out.'

A pair of Jockey shorts and a pair of Reebok trainers. Worn by hundreds of thousands of men, and sold in their millions. Trying to track down whoever had bought them was out of the question. So they would have to rely on other leads, and according to Enoksson and his colleagues the nature of the traces that had been secured gave a good idea of the sequence of events.

The perpetrator comes in through the front door of the flat. Most of the evidence suggests that Linda lets him in. He takes off his shoes and puts them on the shoe-rack in the hall.

Then he and his victim end up on the sofa in the living room, where the perpetrator takes off his trousers and underwear and ejaculates on the sofa.

Then the action moves to the bedroom. The perpetrator ties Linda's hands behind her back, gags her, and ties her ankles to the foot of the bed, probably in that order. Then he rapes her twice, first in the vagina, and then in the anus, and ejaculates both times. It seems probable that in conjunction with the second rape he makes the cuts on her lower back. Then, during or after this final assault, he strangles her.

Then he goes into the shower, washes, masturbates, and ejaculates once more.

'And finally he escapes through the bedroom window,' Enoksson said. 'He goes out backwards, with his chest and stomach against the windowsill, to make the drop smaller. As he crawls out and lets go of the window-frame, he scratches himself on the edge of the windowsill, which is rusty and quite sharp.'

The clothes Linda was wearing on the night she was murdered had also helped the forensics experts to map the course of events.

'According to witnesses who met her in the club, she was wearing the following,' Enoksson said. 'A pair of leather sandals with a slight heel and leather straps fastened above the ankle. A pair of low-cut and fairly loose dark blue linen trousers. An untucked linen blouse of the same colour, collarless and with five buttons. Over the blouse a black velvet waistcoat with black embroidery and blue pearls and sequins. She was also carrying a small rucksack made of blue velvet, with straps and detailing in blue suede, which could also be used as an ordinary handbag by adjusting the straps. Okay, so where have I got to? Ah, yes.' He scratched his head. 'Underneath she was wearing a pair of black pants and a black bra. So, a pair of shoes, a rucksack, and a total of five items of clothing. And now I'm getting to the real point.'

Linda seemed to have taken off her shoes and bag as soon as she got through the door. The shoes were kicked off and left on the floor beside the doormat, and her bag was leaning against the wall half a metre away. The velvet waistcoat, linen trousers and blouse were found in the living room, neatly folded in a pile on the arm of one of the armchairs. The waistcoat at the bottom, then the trousers, with the blouse on top.

Her pants and bra were on the floor of the bedroom. The pants were intact, albeit turned partly inside out, and were found on the floor on the side of the bed closest to the living room. Her bra was on the other side of the bed. The catch at the back had been undone, but the shoulder-straps were both broken.

'The probable explanation is that the perpetrator took it off after tying her hands behind her back,' Enoksson said.

The next item on Enoksson's agenda was Linda's jewellery. According to various witnesses questioned by the police, she was wearing a wristwatch on her left arm, a thin gold bracelet on the same arm, three different rings on her left hand,  and one on the little finger of her right hand.

'The watch plus five items of jewellery makes six in total,' Enoksson said. 'All six items were found in the big ceramic bowl on the coffee table in the living room.' He clicked to bring up an image on the overhead projector showing the coffee table and the ceramic bowl. 'Our interpretation is that she probably took her watch and jewellery off herself. Exactly as we think she did with the waistcoat, trousers and blouse.

'If you look a bit closer at the ceramic bowl on the table,' Enoksson went on, clicking to bring a close-up on to the screen, 'you'll see her mobile phone as well. Which leads us to my next point: the contents of her bag.'

Inside Linda's bag they had found everything that might be expected to be in a bag like that. A total of one hundred and seven different objects. Her pocket diary, a leather wallet containing her ID card from police college, her driving licence, four small photographs of her father, mother and two of her female friends, her own visiting cards and four from other people, a bank card and various other plastic cards: membership cards, a VIP card for Grace, and another one for Café Opera in Stockholm.

The wallet also contained money: six hundred kronor in Swedish notes, thirty-two kronor and fifty öre in coins, and sixty-five Euros, making a total equivalent to approximately one thousand, two hundred kronor. There was also a small bag containing lipstick, eyeshadow and other items of makeup, a bag of mint throat sweets, a lip salve, a small plastic container of dental floss, a toothpick in a plastic sleeve, a small matchbox containing twelve matches, and various till and credit card receipts from different bars and shops. As well as the usual bits of fluff and other fragments that a careful forensics officer always finds at the bottom of any bag, no matter how fastidious its owner might have been.

'Talking of makeup, she didn't take hers off, which could be of some interest in terms of the sequence of events. She was still wearing it when she was found later that morning. Lipstick, eyeshadow and something I've forgotten the name of. Seems to have been her own. The thing I've forgotten is in the report. Nothing unusual.'

Finally, the bag also contained a key ring with a number of keys that matched the front door and various other locks at her father's house. A car key, to a two-year-old Volvo S40 that Linda had been given as a graduation present from her father. Neatly parked in one of the private spaces right in front of the building. It was currently in the compound of the police station, but a forensic examination hadn't come up with anything.

'Well,' Enoksson said. 'Some of you are probably wondering about the key to her mother's flat? That's in the bowl on the coffee table as well.'

He showed another close-up of the ceramic bowl, and he had added a little red arrow pointing to an ordinary door key on a white metal key ring. The simple explanation for this – according to Enoksson – was that she usually kept the key to her mother's flat in her pocket, whereas the bulkier key ring with the keys to her father's house was kept in the bag.

'To round off the story of the bag,' Enoksson said, 'there doesn't seem to be anything missing from it. And it doesn't look like anyone went through her things. So theft doesn't seem to have been a motive. Money in her wallet, jewellery in the ceramic bowl, and her watch –

one of those gold and steel Rolexes that her father apparently gave her on her birthday when she came of age, supposed to be worth about sixty thousand.'

After finishing with the contents of Linda's bag, Enoksson went on to account for the various items the perpetrator used while he was raping, torturing and murdering his victim. This meant a Stanley knife and five different men's neckties. There were pictures of each of these, and it looked like the perpetrator had been fortunate enough to find all of them in the flat after he got there.

The forensics team had found the knife on the floor of the bedroom, but before it got there it had been in a red plastic bucket on the draining board in the kitchen, along with other decorating tools. An ordinary Stanley knife, used for cutting wallpaper, fabric or floor tiles. A single-sided knife with a slanted and adjustable blade, capable of cutting to a depth of approximately one centimetre, and with a sharp point at the end of the blade.

'This is what he used to cut her,' Enoksson said. 'Her blood is on the blade and handle, but the perpetrator's prints aren't. It looks like he wiped it on the sheet he used to cover her.'

The five neckties had been at the top of a box out in the hall. Linda's mother was clearing out some old bedclothes, towels and clothes that were going to be thrown away.

The five men's neckties were of the older, slimmer design, originally bought by the victim's father. For some unexplained reason they had ended up with her mother after the divorce and were about to be disposed off, until the perpetrator decided to use them to bind and strangle their daughter.

Three of them were still on Linda's body when she was found. The first was wound tightly round her neck, with the knot at the back to make things easier for the perpetrator, who seemed to have sat astride her thighs when he strangled her. The second had been used to tie her hands behind her back. The third was tied round her right ankle. A fourth was crumpled up on the floor. It held traces of Linda's saliva and marks from her teeth. That was the one he had used to gag her, and presumably removed after he had strangled her. The fifth tie was fastened round the bottom end of the bed frame, and to judge from the evidence it had been used to secure Linda's left ankle.

'A very sad story,' Enoksson concluded, shutting off the projector.

'How are we doing with other evidence?' Bäckström asked. 'Hair, fingerprints, other remnants and fibres, all the stuff you lot usually find in places like this?'

There was a fair amount, according to Enoksson. They had found ten different strands of hair that had been sent to the National Forensics Lab. Various sorts: ordinary head hair, body hair and pubic hair.

'Some of that's bound to come from our perpetrator,' Enoksson said. 'But they haven't finished the analysis yet. We took the easiest bits first.'

Same thing with fingerprints, other traces and fibres. Assuming that they found the right person, a considerable quantity of the evidence could be tied specifically to him.

'Considering what we've already got, that's almost overkill,' Enoksson said. 'But better too much than too little. Mind you, sometimes I think we suffer from a sort of evidential hysteria in this country. Probably thanks to all those programmes people see on television.'

You're a proper little philosopher you are, Enok, Bäckström thought. 'Have you got anything else for us?'

Enoksson looked hesitant. Shook his head.

'Don't sit there holding anything back,' Bäckström said. 'Out with it, Enok. Unburden your heart. Help your hardworking colleagues slaving away on the factory floor.'

'Well,' Enoksson said, 'as far as that goes, I think I and my colleagues in forensics have done our bit. When I spoke to the National Lab about our DNA ... but this is a long way from being certain, because research in this area is still in its ... well, in its infancy, really, so there's a serious risk that this could be wrong, but ...'

'Enoksson,' Bäckström said sternly. 'What did the bloke at the lab say?'

'It was a she, actually,' Enoksson said. 'Well, in her opinion there are certain things that suggest that our DNA isn't typical Nordic DNA. There's some evidence to suggest that it comes from a perpetrator with a different background, if I can put it like that.'

Surprise, surprise, Bäckström thought, but he contented himself with a nod.

After a break for coffee and a bit of leg-stretching – Enoksson's presentation had taken almost two hours – the medical officer took over. Nothing he had to say in any way contradicted what the police had managed to work out on their own, although he stressed that these were just his preliminary findings. His final report wouldn't be with them for another couple of weeks, when all the analysis would be complete and he had had time to reflect on the results.

'But what I can tell you at this stage,' the medical officer said punctiliously as he leafed through his papers, 'is that the victim died of asphyxiation through strangulation. Evidence from the post-mortem indicates that she was strangled with the tie round her neck, and that death occurred some time between three o'clock and seven o'clock, in the early hours of Friday morning.'

Sigh, Bäckström thought.

'And the knife-wounds found on her left and right buttocks, according to the post-mortem results, are a good match for the knife in question.'

Sigh and groan, Bäckström thought.

'Similar wounds have become more common in recent years in connection to this sort of crime. The popular description of them as torture wounds isn't entirely misleading, even if people in my profession ought to refrain from speculating about a perpetrator's possible motivations. There are a number of previous cases in which the perpetrators have used knives or other similar weapons, or lit cigarettes. We've also had a couple of cases where a taser has been used . . .'

And nobody cares about that right now, Bäckström thought.

'The fact that there was considerable bleeding from the wounds, considering their nature, I mean, suggests that the victim was alive when the injuries were inflicted, and she probably put up considerable resistance. The body pumps adrenalin, and the blood pressure goes up significantly.'

Well, that's always something, Bäckström thought. Our perpetrator isn't crazy enough to torture a corpse.

'The marks on her wrists and ankles are a good match with the ties secured in the forensic examination . . .'

Who'd have thought it? Bäckström thought, glancing at his watch.

'Well,' he said quarter of an hour later as he gazed imperiously round his troops. 'What are you sitting here for? Get out there and find the bastard.'

# 22

That evening, after dinner in the hotel, Bäckström gathered his core team in his room to discuss the case in peace and quiet without a load of rural sheriffs trying to impose their cretinous opinions.

'If we take this point by point, maybe you could take notes, Eva?' Bäckström said, turning to the only woman in the group. What the hell's the point of scrawny women? he thought.

'Ready, boss,' Svanström twittered, holding up her notepad and pen.

'Okay, point by point,' Bäckström said. 'How did he get in?' And she's ingratiating, he thought.

'She let him in,' Rogersson sighed. His mind seemed to be elsewhere. 'Just after she got home he rang on the door, and she let him in. It's not just someone she knows, it's someone she likes.'

'Or trusts, at any rate,' Thorén said. 'Or at least isn't scared about letting in.'

'Mind you, he might well have tricked her,' Knutsson said.

'Are you completely stupid, Erik?' Rogersson said, glaring at Knutsson. 'You too, Thorén,' he said, glowering at him as well. 'She's planning to go to bed. It's three o'clock in the morning. The first thing he does is take off his shoes and put them in the rack. I don't think we're talking about dear little Gross wanting to borrow a bit of Nescafé.'

'On an entirely different subject,' said Bäckström, who had been struck by the same thought that was probably troubling Rogersson, 'how about a little evening beer?' If it comes to the crunch, I can always put it on expenses, he thought.

For once they all seemed to be in agreement. The age of miracles didn't seem to be quite at an end either, because Thorén and Knutsson offered to get some of the supplies they had in their rooms.

'We bought a whole case on Friday, but haven't had time to drink any,' Thorén explained.

They're both completely mad, Bäckström thought.

'Okay,' he said five minutes later, licking the froth from his top lip. 'So what do you think, Jan?' He nodded at Lewin, who also seemed to have his mind elsewhere. Pull yourself together, you randy bastard, Bäckström thought.

'I agree with Rogersson,' Lewin said. 'It was someone she knew and liked. I don't think they planned to meet, either. He just turned up unannounced.'

'I agree with Janne,' Svanström said. 'Someone she really likes just turns up out of the blue.'

And who the fuck asked you? Bäckström thought.

'So how did he know she was at home?' Thorén said.

'Her car was parked outside, maybe he saw lights on inside the flat, maybe he was just trying his luck.' Lewin shrugged.

'Okay,' Thorén said, apparently prepared to negotiate. 'But I still think he tricked her.'

'Considering the way it ended, you mean?' Rogersson said, now sounding more ironic than annoyed. 'In that case, I agree with you entirely. I don't think Linda reckoned it was going to end the way it did when she let him in.'

'So what happens in the living room?' Bäckström said. They're like children, he thought. Squabble, squabble, squabble.

'She takes her clothes off, he takes his off. Then they get started,' Rogersson said. 'Entirely voluntarily, if you ask me. She starts with a basic handjob. He comes all over the sofa, after all, and it doesn't look like they found any of her saliva.'

'Hang on,' Thorén said, stopping the flow by holding up his hands.

'We don't know that. Maybe she just wanted to sit down and talk for a while.'

'Exactly,' Knutsson said. 'He says he wants a glass of water, goes out to the kitchen, and sees the knife. He goes back and says he's had enough of talking.'

'Fuck, that's complicated,' Rogersson sighed. 'What's wrong with a bit of voluntary sex?'

'I'm inclined to agree with Rogersson again,' Lewin said. 'Neatly folded clothes, the fact that she probably took the key to the flat out of her trouser or waistcoat pocket before folding them over the edge of the armchair. That's not the sort of thing our perpetrator would have done, or something she'd have thought of doing if she had a knife at her throat.'

'I agree with you, Janne,' Svanström said.

'But he does seem to have been in more of a hurry than her,' Knutsson said. 'We can agree on that, can't we? He pulls off his trousers, drops his pants on the floor. But the girl, Linda, takes it much more slowly.'

'Maybe she was trying to get him excited,' Rogersson said with a shrug. 'Considering what happened when they ended up in her mum's bed, I'd say she succeeded beyond all expectation.'

None of the others said anything. Knutsson and Thorén contented themselves with just looking sceptical. Lewin seemed mainly interested in the ceiling of Bäckström's room, while Svanström was busy making notes.

'Do you mean she went along with that as well?' Bäckström asked. 'That it was some sort of sex game that got out of hand?' Even though she seems so straitlaced, he thought.

'The first thing that happens in the bedroom could easily be normal intercourse,' Rogersson said. 'According to our esteemed medical colleague, she didn't have any significant injuries in or around her vagina. I don't think it's out of the question that he tricked her into putting on a couple of the ties without her objecting. Either then or later.'

'Then what happens?' Bäckström asked. Rogge's good, he thought. Even though he drinks like he worked for our colleagues in Tallinn.

'Then I think things get way out of hand,' Rogersson said. 'When he decides to take her up the arse. But by then it's too late. Properly tied up, gagged so she can't scream, then out with the knife to get her to do what he says. And that's when she gets the injuries that our esteemed medical colleague described in such detail. Small tears to the anus, scratches round her neck, on her upper arms, wrists and ankles. When he's pulling her about and she's struggling to get free.'

'The inhibitor in our perpetrator's brain has gone,' Bäckström said.

'Every single fucking fuse in that bastard has blown,' Rogersson said with feeling. 'By the way, is there any more beer?'

'So who is he, then?' Bäckström asked his team. 'Who are we looking for?'

'The perpetrator is probably a man,' Thorén said solemnly. 'I'm joking, of course,' he added. 'I was thinking of our colleagues in the CP group. Isn't that what they usually put in their profiles? "The perpetrator is probably a man. In all likelihood he already knew the victim, but we can't rule out that he had no previous connection to the victim and met her in conjunction with the offence in question,"' he went on in a sombre voice.

'Are you thinking of changing jobs?' Bäckström said. 'A young man who already knew Linda,' he went on, looking at the others encouragingly.

'Young? Peter didn't actually say young,' Knutsson said.

'So how old is he, then?' Christ, they're just like stroppy teenagers, Bäckström thought.

'Well,' Knutsson said, 'between twenty and twenty-five, something like that, a few years older than Linda.'

'Fine,' Bäckström said. 'I thought that's what I said?' Idiots. 'So how well does he know her?'

'This is what I think,' Lewin said, sounding as though he'd given the matter some thought. 'Eva and I were actually discussing this before dinner.'

'I'm listening,' Bäckström said. So you talk to each other as well?

'A young man, twenty-five, thirty or so. He knows Linda well, although they don't meet very often. But she's still very fond of him even though it's been a while since they met. Someone she's had sex with at least once before. Probably perfectly ordinary sex, because I get the impression that's what she likes. I don't think she's particularly sexually experienced either. I actually asked the medical officer after the meeting, and according to him there's nothing to suggest that she had ever engaged in anal sex or any of the more violent sadomasochistic practices before. No healed wounds or old scar tissue, nothing like that. And I think she trusts him. And they haven't seen each other for a while. Then he suddenly shows up again. In the middle of the night.'

'She's still fond enough of him to let him in,' Svanström said. 'I don't think he's necessarily that young, either. He could easily be a bit older.'

I didn't expect that of Lewin, Bäckström thought. That he's still got that much going on. 'He still manages to come four times in not much more than an hour,' he said.

'Yes, that was a while ago,' Rogersson said. It sounded as if he were thinking out loud.

'I get the impression that he was high on something,' Lewin said. 'That he'd taken amphetamines or something like that.'

'Yes, or maybe a slightly older man who's been at the Viagra,' Thorén added.

'Someone who uses drugs?' Rogersson said hesitantly. 'I can't quite get that to fit with our victim. Especially not if I buy the bit about her trusting him. I think she trusts him more or less unconditionally. Would she really have that sort of trust for someone with a drug problem?'

'Not a drug problem.' Lewin shook his head. 'It doesn't work if that's the case. Someone who's tried it a few times. Maybe just uses it for sex.'

'Someone that Linda knows and trusts,' Bäckström said slowly. 'So where does he live, then?' Makes sense to change track, he thought.

'Here in town,' Knutsson said. 'In Växjö.'

'Or close to the town, Växjö and the surrounding area,' Thorén elaborated.

'A man of twenty-five or slightly older, someone she knows already, likes, and trusts completely. Who lives in town or at least nearby. Who isn't an addict but occasionally takes amphetamines because he knows the way they work, which is to help him lose his inhibitions and make his cock go like an electric toothbrush,' Bäckström summarized. 'You don't think things could be so bad that we're looking for a fellow officer? Some crazy bastard who manages to hold it together apart from one fateful day?'

'That thought has been at the back of my mind ever since I got here,' Rogersson said. 'All the crazy fuckers you meet in the force. All the stories you hear. They can't all be made up, sadly.'

Lewin was shaking his head dubiously. 'Admittedly, worse things have happened in the force,' he said slowly. 'The thought's occurred to me as well. But I still don't quite believe it.'

'Why not?' Bäckström said. Because he isn't like you, he thought.

'He seems a bit too uninhibited for my taste,' Lewin said. 'All the evidence he left behind. Wouldn't a police officer have tidied up after him?'

'Looks like he wiped the knife,' Bäckström said. 'Maybe he didn't have time to clean up if he thought someone was coming.'

'There's something about this that just doesn't feel right.' Lewin shrugged. 'But of course I've been wrong before.'

'Anything else?' Bäckström said, looking round the room. Or am I going to have the good fortune finally to be able to collapse in bed with a bit of liquid assistance before I fall asleep?

'I think he's good-looking,' Svanström said suddenly. 'Our perpetrator, I mean. Linda was very attractive,' she went on. 'And she seems to have taken a lot of trouble over her appearance, not least her clothes. Have you any idea how much clothes like that cost? The things she was wearing. I think he's the same. Birds of a feather. Isn't that what people say?'

Yep, and you and Lewin are both fucking scrawny, Bäckström thought.

Before Bäckström fell asleep he called his little reporter from local radio. To help keep her on the boil, if nothing else.

'I understand you've had the results of your DNA samples,' Carin said. 'I don't suppose that's something you'd like to tell me about?'

'I don't know what you're talking about,' Bäckström said sternly. 'You got home okay the other night?'

Evidently she had, without going into detail. Then she suggested that they ought to meet again soon. And they still didn't have to talk about work.

'Sure,' Bäckström said. 'That sounds good. But things are pretty busy, so it might not be for a day or two,' he added. Way too easy, he thought.

'Should I interpret that to mean that things are coming together?' Carin said, her voice suddenly sounding eager.

'*You will be the first to know*,' Bäckström said, in his best television American.

# 23

## *Växjö, Thursday 10 July*

On Thursday Lewin decided to stop reading the evening papers. His decision was final and irrevocable, and encompassed *Aftonbladet*, *Expressen* and the latter's two smaller and, if possible, even nastier siblings, *Göteborgs-Tidningen* and *Kvällsposten*.

The double-spread article that had particularly attracted his disgust was in that day's copy of *Kvällsposten* and taken alongside everything else the Swedish evening papers had already printed about the Linda murder it looked almost innocuous. Shipwrecked-Micke had come forward and revealed that 'I met Linda the night she was murdered'.

Shipwrecked-Micke, in his capacity as a reality television celebrity with local connections, had accepted a small job at the Town Hotel on the evening of Thursday 3 July. The same evening that Linda went to the hotel's club, just a few hours before she was murdered. He had been accompanied by two fellow celebs – Farm-Frasse and Big Brother-Nina – and their shared duties involved helping out in the bar, mingling with the guests and generally contributing to raising the atmosphere in the venue.

Around ten o'clock in the evening, about an hour before Linda arrived at the nightclub, Micke, severely intoxicated, bare-chested and with nothing on his feet, had been dancing up on the bar, but tumbled off and broke a load of glasses, and ended up flailing about in the shattered fragments. At quarter past ten he was taken by ambulance to hospital in Växjö to be sewn up. His colleague, Frasse, had gone with him, and had called a journalist he knew while they were in the ambulance. The interview with Micke and Frasse had been conducted while they were waiting in A&E, and the next morning, the same morning that Linda was found murdered and before news of the killing reached the papers, *Kvällsposten* had led with a big report about the fact that Shipwrecked-Micke – famous from *The Bar* and ordinary *Shipwrecked*, and because of the double accolade of having also appeared in *Celebrity Shipwrecked* – had been attacked and beaten up in the Town Hotel in Växjö the previous evening, even though he was born and raised there, and was now one of the town's most famous inhabitants.

After the conclusion of the interview and a further hour of waiting for the doctors to take care of his colleague, Farm-Frasse had got fed up and gone back to the Town Hotel. There the bouncer had refused to let him back in and a fight had broken out, the police had been called, and shortly after midnight Farm-Frasse had found himself in the holding cells of Växjö police station on Sandgärdsgatan, where he was left to sober up.

A couple of hours later he was joined by Shipwrecked-Micke, who had kicked up a fuss in A&E, been picked up by the police and thrown into another cell in the same police station. At six o'clock the following morning they had both been allowed to leave the station, and, leaning on his friend Frasse, a limping Micke had crossed Oxtorget and disappeared from any sort of police interest, destination unknown.

What Shipwrecked-Micke was now telling the paper a week after the murder was a pack of lies from beginning to end. He couldn't have spoken to Linda during the evening before the murder, and she hadn't 'told him in confidence that she had often felt threatened recently, because of her job with the police in Växjö'.

Being in the same predicament as Shipwrecked-Micke, in the same corridor of cells mainly used for drunks, Farm-Frasse couldn't have met Linda the night she was murdered either. Which left the third member of their company, Big Brother-Nina, who at least had been in the nightclub until it closed at four o'clock the next morning.

Nina had been questioned by the police as early as Friday afternoon, and it had taken some time before she realized that the police didn't want to talk to her about the alleged attack on her friend Micke. She didn't have a clue about the fact that Linda had been murdered. She didn't know her. Had never met her, still less spoken to her, not on any previous occasion, and not on the night of the murder.

The reporter who had written both articles could hardly have been quite as ignorant, but what irritated the usually sanguine Lewin was the fact that the reporter had the bad taste to drag him into the lies he had woven together. The day before the second article appeared he had called Lewin to give him the opportunity to respond to the serious allegations that Shipwrecked-Micke was now directing at the police. What had they done to investigate the threats that Linda had told Shipwrecked-Micke about, which Micke claimed he had informed the police in Växjö about at the earliest opportunity?

Lewin had declined to comment, and referred the reporter to the press officer. Whether he followed that advice was unclear. The only thing revealed in the article was that the paper had contacted the detective in charge of the case, Superintendent Jan Lewin from the National Crime Unit, but he had 'refused to address the serious allegations directed at his and his colleagues' work'.

And that was when Lewin had made up his mind. He was never going to read another Swedish evening paper as long as he lived.

# 24

At the morning meeting that day, Enoksson was able to report the first concrete surveillance results.

With the help of the perpetrator's DNA, they had already been able to discount ten people from the inquiry. First in and first out was Linda's former boyfriend, along with a couple of Linda's fellow students who had met her at the club on the night of the murder, as well as half a dozen serious sexual offenders whose DNA profiles were already in the police database. Including Leo Baranski.

'It's like going out into the fields with a good sharp scythe,' Enoksson said happily. 'You take a couple of good swings and get rid of anything that's got no business being there.'

'Okay,' Bäckström said. 'You hear what Enok's saying. Let's swing that scythe. We need samples, samples, and more samples. Anyone with a clear conscience has nothing to fear, and every decent citizen wants to help the police, so there shouldn't be any problems getting people to volunteer.'

'What about if anyone doesn't want to?' one of the younger local officers said from the far end of the table.

'Then things get really interesting,' Bäckström said, smiling as warmly as the big bad wolf in the tale of the three little pigs. What the hell are they letting into the force these days?

Later that morning the head of the National Crime Unit, Sten Nylander, arrived in Växjö. Nylander came by helicopter together with his chief of staff and staff officer. The simpler members of the rapid-response unit, who would be responsible for the practical details, had travelled down in advance in two of the large American Hummer jeeps that the force had at its disposal.

When Nylander landed at Småland Airport, some ten kilometres outside Växjö, the welcoming committee was already in place, and the NRRU was making sure that the area was kept clear of anyone who shouldn't be there. The county police commissioner had driven in from his place in the country, and had even changed out of his shorts and Hawaiian shirt into a grey suit and tie, even though it was almost thirty degrees outside. By his side stood Superintendent Bengt Olsson, in full uniform, and they were both sweating profusely already.

Nylander himself, in contrast, was both immaculately dressed and not showing the slightest sign of bodily fluids. In spite of the weather, he was wearing the same outfit as when he met Bäckström the previous week, plus a neatly peaked uniform cap that he put on the moment he stepped out of the helicopter. The ensemble was completed by a pair of dark frameless sunglasses, with reflecting glass, and a riding crop. This latter detail aroused a certain amount of local surprise, since no one had seen any trace of Brandklipparen.

First they 'reconnoitred the operational terrain' – Växjö and the surrounding area – in advance of the impending operation, partly to 'get a feel' for the district, partly to identify suitable locations where they could 'disembark' their forces, and partly to determine the 'optimal point' for the actual seizure of the perpetrator.

'But can you really work all that out in advance?' the county police commissioner said, as he sat squashed into the rear seat of the jeep surrounded by half a dozen silent figures in camouflage uniforms. 'I mean . . . we don't actually know who he is. Not yet, I mean,' he added quickly.

'Affirmative,' Nylander said from his seat at the front, without even turning his head. 'It's all a question of planning.'

A couple of hours later they were finished. Nylander had declined a meeting in the county police commissioner's office, the planned lunch, and other formalities. He had to fly on to Gothenburg on a similar mission, and his colleagues could sort out the practical details in Växjö with Olsson.

'But I would like to say hello to my officers,' HNC had said, and quarter of an hour later he was marching into the investigation's main premises.

What the fuck's going on, Bäckström had thought when he heard the commotion out in the corridor and caught a glimpse of the first camouflaged figure. Has war broken out, or what?

Nylander had stopped in the doorway and nodded towards everyone, like an oil tanker rising between two waves. Then he had taken Bäckström aside and even patted him on the shoulder.

'I'm relying on you, Åström,' HNC said. 'Make sure you get him as soon as possible.'

'Of course, boss,' Bäckström said, nodding back towards his own reflection in his superior's sunglasses. Cheers, Chinny.

'You can go ahead and arrest him this weekend,' Nylander said, when he and the county police commissioner were back at the airport. 'The lads who are going to do the job are confined to barracks already.'

'I'm afraid it may take a little longer than that,' the county police commissioner yelled, because the helicopter's engines were warming up and he could hardly hear his own voice. Why do they live in barracks, he wondered. Don't they have homes of their own?

'You got his DNA,' Nylander said. 'What are you waiting for?'

After lunch Bäckström wandered into Olsson's office. It was high time someone knocked a bit of sense into the little cretin's head. The red lamp was on, but Bäckström wasn't in the mood and just knocked and went in.

Olsson had company in the form of three officers of the NRRU, with whom he didn't seem entirely at ease. Wearing camouflage, and so similar that they were almost interchangeable, given that two of them were completely bald and the third clearly cropped his hair as closely as he could, none of the three moved a muscle when Bäckström walked in.

'Ah, there you are, Bäckström,' Olsson said, getting up quickly. 'Excuse us a moment,' he said, and pulled Bäckström out into the corridor.

'What on earth have they sent us?' Olsson said, shaking his head nervously as soon as he closed the door behind them. 'What's happening to the Swedish Police?'

'The search,' Bäckström said sternly. 'High time to search her room at her father's place.'

'Of course,' Olsson said with a pale smile. 'I just haven't got round to it, as I'm sure you understand, but if you could ask Enoksson to come and see me at once, we'll get it sorted out.'

'And I want us to interview her mother and father as well,' said Bäckström, who wasn't about to miss an open goal.

'Of course,' Olsson said again. 'They should have got over the worst of the shock by now. Well, enough for there to be some point to it, I mean,' he added in clarification. 'So you've given up the idea that she was killed by a completely unknown madman?'

'She was killed by someone she knew,' Bäckström said curtly. 'It remains to be seen just how mad he was.'

Olsson merely nodded. 'Ask Enoksson to come and see me at once,' he repeated, sounding almost imploring.

Enoksson was wearing a white lab coat and plastic gloves when Bäckström walked into the forensics lab, but as soon as he caught sight of Bäckström he pulled off the gloves and put them on the big laboratory table, then pushed a chair towards his visitor.

'Welcome to our humble abode,' he said with a smile. 'Would you like some coffee?'

'Just had one,' Bäckström said, 'but thanks anyway.'

'So what can I help you with, then?' Enoksson said.

'Drugs,' Bäckström said. Olsson can sit there sweating for a bit longer, he thought. 'My colleague, Lewin, has got an idea that he might have been high on something. How can we find that out?'

According to Enoksson, there was at least a decent chance. They had probably found enough blood on the windowsill to investigate the matter. He wasn't sure about the perpetrator's semen, but he would look into it. The strands of hair they had found were also a possibility. 'If they came from the perpetrator's head, the National Lab ought to be able to tell if he used cannabis, for instance. At least if he was a regular user.'

'What if he only took something just before he attacked Linda?'

'Doubtful,' Enoksson said, shaking his head. 'What drug have you got in mind?'

'Amphetamine, or something like that.'

'Ah. Yes, several of us were struck by that particular detail,' he said, without being more precise about what he meant. 'I promise we'll look into it. As far as Linda herself is concerned, we actually got the results back from the lab this morning.' He leafed through a pile of paper in front of him on the laboratory desk. 'Here it is,' he said, holding up the document.

'I'm listening.'

'Zero point ten parts per thousand in her blood, and zero point twenty in her urine, which in plain language means that she was at most mildly intoxicated when she was at the club, and pretty much sober when she died.'

'Nothing else?' Bäckström said. If I'm in luck, they took something together, he thought.

'Nothing,' Enoksson said, shaking his head. 'The test for so-called prescription drugs in her blood has come back negative, and there were no traces of cannabis, amphetamines, opiates or cocaine metabolites in her urine. Linda seems to have been completely clean, if I can express myself the way our colleagues in the drug squad usually do.'

Oh well, you can't have everything, Bäckström thought. 'One more thing,' he said. 'If you've got a moment?'

'Of course.'

'Who is he?' Take your time, Bäckström thought. Olsson's absolutely fine where he is.

'I thought that was your job, Bäckström,' Enoksson said evasively. 'You mean, the shoe-rack and all that? That it must be someone she knew?'

'Yep.'

'I see what you're thinking, but he seems pretty crazy too. Would Linda really have known someone like that?'

'Think about it,' Bäckström said generously. They never learn, he thought.

'Well,' Enoksson said, suddenly looking extremely embarrassed. 'This really is a terrible business. It's really got to me, and I thought I'd seen almost everything.'

'I know,' Bäckström said happily. 'Our mutual friend Lo must have a lot to do.'

'I suppose I'm starting to get old, but if you can't even bear to look at the pictures of a crime scene, then you probably shouldn't apply to join forensics. You don't get any decent pictures that way, and we're still the ones who are supposed to take them.'

Who the fuck would want to work in forensics, Bäckström thought.

'And I suppose only a very few among us are granted the blessing of our Lord's guidance and solace.'

'So you've heard, then,' Bäckström said with a grin. 'Thanks for the tip.'

'Yes, it's bad.' Enoksson sighed. 'What happened to the confidentiality of the confessional? The deeds of men may be fragmentary – and that's not a direct biblical quote, by the way, but a play on the text of chapter thirteen of Paul's first letter to the Corinthians, as any good Smålander could tell you – but do we police officers really have to hold all the fragments up for general view? Follow me, and you'll see what I mean.'

He got up, went over to his computer and starting tapping at it as if he were a computer geek forty years younger. 'This is one of our most popular internet newspapers,' he said, showing Bäckström the screen. 'And here you can read all the gruesome details that not even the evening papers dare to print. "Strangled by her dad's tie." That's the headline, and the article contains pretty much everything we discussed at yesterday's meeting. Including the shoes. But they seem to have missed the shoe-rack. Probably not interesting enough for them.'

You're a proper little philosopher, you are, Enok, Bäckström thought.

'Oh yes, one last thing,' Bäckström said. 'Olsson wanted to talk to you. I think it's about the search of the victim's father's house.'

This is going like clockwork, Bäckström thought. He had gone straight down to his friend Rogge and told him it was high time to interview Linda's parents, and that this should be done in the usual exhaustive way.

'In that case I'd better do it myself,' Rogersson said.

'Then we have to sort out the people she knew. Drag in anyone who ever said hello to her and stick cotton-buds in their mouths. That way we won't have to take samples from the whole town. Mum, dad, friends, fellow students, family friends and acquaintances, their neighbours, her teachers at college, people working here in the station, every single bastard in trousers at the club on Friday night. Even the ones who prefer skirts even though they've got something sticking out of the front. You know what I mean.'

'I know,' Rogersson said. 'Mind you, we can forget about her mum, can't we? As far as getting a sample goes, I mean? And no matter what, you're probably going to have to give our colleague Sandberg some reinforcements.'

'Any suggestions?'

'Knutsson, Thorén, or both. Neither of them is likely to win the Nobel Prize, exactly, but at least they're both fucking thorough.'

You take what you're given, Bäckström thought. Wasn't that what Jesus said when he shared out the fish and bread to his mates?

'Have you got a moment?' Anna Sandberg asked quarter of an hour later, looking enquiringly at Bäckström as he sat in majesty behind the piles of paper on his borrowed desk.

'Of course,' Bäckström said generously, gesturing towards the only unoccupied chair in the room. Who could say no to a pair of decent tits, he thought.

'I understand I'm going to get some back-up,' Anna said, sounding pretty much like her colleague and boss, Superintendent Olsson, a short while ago.

'Exactly,' Bäckström nodded. So can I possibly have a smile, please?

'But you're going to keep me in charge of the profiling of Linda and her acquaintances? You're not thinking of replacing me, I mean?'

'Of course not,' Bäckström said. 'You can borrow Thorén and Knutsson. Decent lads. Keep them on a short leash, and if they start causing trouble, just let me know and I'll deal with them.' Bloody hell, don't tell me we're going to have to have a debate on equality as well, he thought.

'In that case I'm happy,' Anna said, standing up. 'You've completely dropped the idea that she was the victim of an ordinary madman?'

'I don't know about dropped,' Bäckström said vaguely. 'One more thing. That pocket diary you promised me. You haven't forgotten?'

'I'll get it for you right away,' Anna said as she left.

What the fuck's she so miserable about?

A perfectly ordinary black pocket diary, in a slightly less ordinary red leather cover with the owner's name, Linda Wallin, embossed in gold in the bottom right-hand corner. A present from her father, Bäckström thought, as he started to leaf through it in a hunt for male acquaintances.

Half an hour later he was finished. The calendar contained everything that ought to be there. Short notes about meetings, lessons, lectures and exercises out at her college. Some times referring to her shifts in the police station, starting on the weekend of midsummer. Regular visits to see her mum in town. Short entries made during a trip to Rome together with a friend and classmate, Kajsa, at the beginning of June. Nothing particularly private, definitely nothing revealing, and the man mentioned more than anyone else was her father, usually just 'Dad'. After the trip to Rome he was 'Papa', but just a fortnight later he was back to 'Dad' again. Otherwise mainly her friends, and in particular her closest girlfriends, Jenny, Kajsa, Anki and Lotta.

The penultimate entry was for Thursday 3 July. A week old now, and Linda had written that she would be at work from 09.00 to 17.00, and that she and Jenny evidently had plans for the evening. *Party?* The last notes, which, judging by the handwriting and the pen used to make them, seemed to have been made at the same time as those for Thursday, gave the time of her shift on Friday, 13.00–22.00, then a line through Saturday and Sunday to indicate that she had the weekend off.

If only something hadn't got in the way, Bäckström thought, suddenly feeling inexplicably gloomy. Pull yourself together, lad, he thought, and straightened up in his chair.

In January there were a total of four entries about someone called Noppe, but as Bäckström already knew that this was her nickname for her ex-boyfriend, who was already out of the investigation thanks to his DNA, he didn't pay any particular attention to the fact that this Noppe had evidently incurred Linda's wrath, because he was granted the only negative emotional comment in the entire book. *Noppe's always been a little shit!* his ex-girlfriend declared on Monday 13 January.

Okay, Bäckström thought. Really there was just one thing he was wondering about. Not that it was particularly exciting, but it was probably just as well to deal with it before he stopped for the day and headed back to the hotel. Probably best if she comes to me. I am her boss, after all, he thought, reaching for the phone.

'Thanks for lending it to me,' Bäckström said amiably, passing the diary back to officer Sandberg.

'Did you find anything interesting?' she asked. 'Anything I missed, I mean?'

What the fuck's wrong with her? Still sulking, Bäckström thought. 'There's just one thing I'm wondering about.'

'What's that?'

'Saturday 17 May. The Norwegians' national day,' Bäckström said, nodding towards the diary.

'Right,' Anna said hesitantly, and leafed through to the relevant page. '*Ronaldo, Ronaldo, Ronaldo, magical name,*' she read.

'Ronaldo exclamation mark, Ronaldo exclamation mark, Ronaldo exclamation mark. Magical name, question mark,' Bäckström corrected. 'Who's Ronaldo?'

'Ah, I get it,' Anna said, suddenly smiling. 'It must be that footballer. That Brazilian, the one who's so good. I think he was playing in some Europa League final that day. I'm sure our colleagues in forensics have checked it out. I'm pretty sure he got three goals, if I've got it right. I think I said at our first meeting that Linda was one of the best players in the women's football team at police college. The match was shown live on television. She must have watched it. I doubt if there's any more to it than that.'

'Hmm,' Bäckström muttered. Bloody hell, you're suddenly very talkative, aren't you? Sadly, his next thought found its way out before he had time to stop it.

'It couldn't simply be that she was a dyke, could it?' Bäckström said. Shit, he thought, but it was already too late.

'Sorry?' Anna said, looking at him with her eyes wide open. 'That she was what? What did you call her?'

'Pretty girl, no blokes, interested in football, loads of female friends. She couldn't simply have been, well, a lesbian?' Bäckström clarified. Or whatever the hell they call themselves, he thought.

'Oh, come on, Bäckström,' Anna said with feeling, and evidently without any regard to their relative status. 'I play football as well. And I've also got a husband and two children. Whatever that's got to do with anything,' she said, looking at him angrily.

'In cases like this, the victim's sex life always has something to do with it,' Bäckström said, and when he saw that she wasn't going to back down he raised his hand in a defensive gesture. 'Forget it, Anna. Just forget it.'

'Yes, let's hope we can,' Anna said crossly. She picked up the diary and left.

There's something that doesn't make sense, Bäckström thought, pulling out a pen and a sheet of paper. *Ronaldo! Ronaldo! Ronaldo!* and then, immediately below, *Magical name?*

Fuck knows what, though, Bäckström thought, staring at what he'd just written. Besides, it was high time for him to make his way back to the hotel, have a little lie down before dinner, and maybe squeeze in a beer or two.

'I found this in her diary,' Bäckström said, shooting the note over to Rogersson a couple of hours and several beers later. 'From 17 May this year.'

'*Ronaldo, Ronaldo, Ronaldo, magical name,*' Rogersson read. 'Must be that football player, mustn't it? Some match she saw on television. She was interested in football, wasn't she? What are you wondering about?'

'Oh, bollocks,' Bäckström said, shaking his head. Bollocks, he thought.

# 25

## *Växjö, Friday 11 July*

The morning meeting on Friday mainly focused on an old police notion which turned out to be right more often than the even older theory about the murderer's usually showing up at the victim's funeral. Considering everything their perpetrator had come up with when he killed Linda, it didn't seem entirely out of the question that he might have committed other crimes in conjunction with that one. Interesting crimes in the vicinity of Linda's murder, in both time and space, which – in an ideal world – could have been committed when he was on his way to see Linda, or making his escape afterwards.

From the police database Detective Inspectors Knutsson and Thorén had dug out every reported crime and police report, and even ordinary parking tickets, that had been recorded from Wednesday 2 July up to Tuesday 8 July. The results were fairly meagre, even when the parking tickets were taken into account. A lot of motorists were on holiday and had taken their cars with them. And a lot of traffic wardens were also on holiday. There was no more to it than that, and in the area where Linda's mother had her flat there hadn't been a single parking ticket issued during the week in question.

In terms of other crimes, a total of 102 had been reported to the police in Växjö during that same week. There were 13 bicycle thefts, 25 thefts or cases of shoplifting, 10 burglaries from flats, houses, offices and business premises, 10 cars broken into, 5 cars damaged, 2 cars stolen, 4 cases of fraud, 1 of embezzlement, 2 cases of breach of trust reported by the same person, 3 cases of tax offences, 10 serious driving offences, of which 5 were drunk-driving, and a total of 17 different offences involving violence.

Of the latter, 8 were physical abuse, 7 unlawful threats or threatening behaviour, and 1 a case of violence against a public official. Half of them were marital rows and minor skirmishes, a further 25 per cent were between people who knew each other, and the remaining 25 per cent took place in and around bars. And one murder, of course, the murder of trainee police officer Linda Wallin, early on the morning of Friday 4 July.

This town's just like Chicago, Bäckström thought with a sigh. 'Anything interesting, then?' he asked, trying hard not to sound as uninterested as he felt.

'The one that's geographically closest to the crime scene is one of the car thefts. An old Saab was stolen from a car park on Högtorpsvägen, out in Högstorp, to the south of that patch of woodland just east of Linda's block. Basically, it was stolen about two kilometres south-east of the crime scene. Close to route 25, the Kalmar road,' Knutsson said.

'The most stolen cars in the country,' Thorén added. 'Old Saabs, I mean,' he clarified.

The problem was that it wasn't reported stolen until Monday, three days after the murder.

'Maybe the bastard camped out in that patch of woodland. Took the chance to get a bit of a tan and do some swimming while he was at it,' Bäckström suggested, and managed to get a few smiles from his colleagues.

'Obviously, we checked to see if the date the report was made matches the date of the theft. Erik called the owner and spoke to him,' Thorén nodded towards Knutsson.

'According to him it was there over the weekend. He'd spoken to a neighbour who saw it,' Knutsson said. 'He was a retired pilot, by the way, the owner, I mean, not the neighbour. He was away in the country and it was his old car. Mostly just sat in the car park. He's got a new Merc now. Not that that's got anything to do with the case. But you never know,' Knutsson said, nodding gravely towards Bäckström.

Yes, Bäckström thought. What the hell has that got to do with anything? 'And that's it?'

'Yes,' Thorén said.

'If you like we can look further afield,' Knutsson said helpfully.

'Bollocks to that,' Bäckström said. We've got more important things to do. 'Well, what are you sitting here for?' he went on, looking round his investigative team. 'The meeting's over. Did I forget to say? Go and do something useful, and if you haven't got anything better to do, try to catch some of the people we want DNA samples from.' He stood up. Completely useless, he thought. And it was hot too. Unbearably hot, and at least eight hours to the first cold lager of the day.

The same morning Enoksson and one of his colleagues searched Linda's room in her father's house outside Växjö. Superintendent Olsson had gone along, despite Enoksson's trying to steer him away from the idea without being too blunt.

'You're probably needed here instead,' the forensics chief had said. 'There's no need for you to worry, Bengt. My colleague and I can sort this.'

'I think it would probably be best if I come with you,' Olsson had decided. 'I've known him for a while, after all, and I can take the opportunity to have a bit of a chat, find out how he's feeling.'

Living somewhere like this would do nicely, Enoksson thought as they walked into the entrance hall of the manor house where Linda lived with her father. Or used to live, he thought. When she wasn't in town staying with her mother because she was working late or wanted to go out and have fun in the centre of Växjö.

'Henning Wallin,' Linda's father said as he came to meet them. He merely nodded at them, and didn't seem to notice Olsson's outstretched hand. 'Linda's father. But you know that already.'

She took after her father, Enoksson thought. Tall, thin build, blond, and in spite of the drawn look to his face he looked considerably younger than his sixty-five years.

'Thanks for letting us come,' Olsson said.

'To be honest, I don't understand what you're doing here,' Henning Wallin said.

'It's a purely routine procedure, you understand,' Olsson explained.

'Of course,' Henning Wallin said. 'I realize that, and if I want to know anything else I suppose I can always read the evening papers. You wanted to see Linda's room? Here's the key.' He handed it to Enoksson. 'The last door on the lake side of the corridor down there,' he said, tilting his head in that direction. 'Lock up when you leave, and I want the key back.'

'You haven't—' Olsson began.

'If you need me, I'll be in my office,' Henning Wallin said.

'Just what I was going to ask,' Olsson said. 'You haven't got a couple of minutes?'

'Two minutes,' Wallin said. Then for some reason he looked at his watch, before heading upstairs to the first floor, without looking back, and with Olsson two steps behind him.

The door to Linda's room was closed and locked. Probably by her father, who had given them the key. The curtains over the two windows facing the lake were closed, and the room was in semi-darkness.

'What do you think about drawing the curtains?' Enoksson's colleague said.

'Okay, there's not much point us bothering with the electrics,' Enoksson declared. Because someone's already been here and cleaned up, he thought.

'Linda had quite a bit more space than all my kids put together,' his colleague said as he opened the curtains and light flooded the room. 'And it looks like she kept it tidy too,' he added. 'My eldest daughter's room doesn't usually look like this.'

'Yes,' Enoksson said. 'Her father's supposed to have some old housekeeper, so we'll need to talk to her.' Not just tidy, he thought. The wide bed could well have been made up with fresh sheets, and Linda's desk was almost pedantically neat. The cushions on the sofa were arranged exactly like the photographs in interior design magazines. This is no longer Linda's room, Enoksson thought. It's a mausoleum to her memory.

'Well, did you find anything interesting?' Olsson asked in the car two hours later, on the way back to the police station.

'How do you mean?' Enoksson asked.

'Well, anything personal, I suppose,' Olsson said vaguely. 'She doesn't seem to have had a journal, according to her dad. At least not that he knew of,' he added.

'No, not that he knew of,' Enoksson said. 'I realize that.'

'And I find it very hard to believe that he'd lie about something like that,' Olsson said. 'I dare say the simple answer is that she didn't. I've got two kids, and neither of them keeps a journal. Did you check her computer, by the way?'

How does he keep it up? Enoksson thought.

'Actually we did,' his colleague replied, since Enoksson didn't seem to have heard the question. 'We did check her computer. We've checked for prints and looked at the hard drive, so that's done.'

'So did you find anything interesting?' Olsson persisted.

'In the computer, you mean, boss?' Enoksson's colleague said with a smirk, seeing as Olsson was safely hidden in the back seat.

'Yes, I mean in her computer.'

'No,' Enoksson said. 'Nothing interesting there either. Will you excuse me for a moment, Bengt,' he said, pulling out his mobile to call his wife, but mainly to shut his boss up.


'Well, Enok,' Bäckström said, nodding encouragingly at Enoksson. 'Did you find a journal?'

'Nooo,' Enoksson replied with a thin smile.

'And her dad didn't even think she had one?'

'His very words,' Enoksson agreed. 'He suggested that we ask Linda's mother. He had no intention of doing so. He's hardly said a word to her since the divorce ten years ago, and before that they seem to have done little but argue.'

'Yes,' Bäckström said with feeling. 'Women can be remarkably difficult.'

'Not my wife,' Enoksson said with a smile. 'So you're speaking for yourself, Bäckström.'

Well, who else is going to, Bäckström thought.

*

In the afternoon the personnel office up in Stockholm called Bäckström. Considering that the weekend was upon them, they wanted to point out that both Bäckström and Rogersson were close to the ceiling for overtime.

'Just thought we should let you know before the weekend,' the personnel assistant said. 'So you don't end up working without getting paid if all hell breaks loose.'

'Believe it or not, we arrest people whether it's a weekday or the weekend,' Bäckström said. Unlike you and all the other lazy bureaucratic fuckers.

'Surely nothing happens at the weekend? And it's summer, the sun's shining,' the personnel woman persisted. 'So take some time off, Bäckström. Why don't you go swimming?'

'Thanks for the tip,' Bäckström said, and hung up. Swimming, he thought. I can't even remember how to swim.

Rogersson, on the other hand, had no objections.

'I was thinking of taking a couple of days off anyway,' he explained. 'Thought I might take the car and head back to Stockholm. Come along – we can go out on the town. I suspect the lager tastes a fuck of a lot better in Stockholm than it does in this shithole.'

That's because you're not getting it for nothing any more, Bäckström thought. 'I think I'll stay,' he said. 'Mind you, you could do me a favour.'

'What do you mean, a favour?' Rogersson said, glaring at him suspiciously.

'Here are the keys to my flat,' Bäckström said, handing them over before Rogersson had time to raise serious objections. 'If you could pop in and take care of Egon. Give him a bit of food and so on. It's all on the side of the pot. It's important that you follow the instructions.'

'Anything else?' Rogersson said. 'Do you want me to give him your love, sit down and have a chat with him, maybe take him out for a change of scenery?'

'A bit of food will do fine,' Bäckström said.

Once he had got back to his hotel room and restored his hydration levels, he called Carin. Strangely enough she didn't answer, even though she had called him several times during the day, and he wasn't the sort who left messages on people's answer machines. Instead he had a couple more beers, interspersed with a few crafty shorts, to help him think things through. In the absence of any better ideas, he eventually made his way down to the bar. Even his colleagues were notable by their absence. Hans and Fritz were probably sitting in one of their rooms discussing the case, while little Svanström probably had her legs wrapped round Lewin's waist, thinking about other matters entirely. All the things they have in their little heads, Bäckström thought, then ordered a large cognac to help him think even better.

At roughly the same time as Bäckström was trying to improve his thinking with the help of fermented and distilled grapes, a memorial event in memory of Linda Wallin took place. A week after her death, the day she would have turned twenty-one if she had still been alive. A couple of hundred citizens of Växjö walked from the Town Hotel to the building where she was murdered, the route that had been the end of her earthly wandering. It wasn't the season for torches, but they had created a memorial garden outside the door to the building, with candles and flowers and a large portrait of the victim. The district governor made a short speech. Her parents were far too upset to attend, but a number of police officers who were working on the case took part in the procession, and considerably more were making sure that they and the other mourners weren't disturbed. Bäckström and his colleagues had declined to take part, purely as a result of a policy decision that had been taken some years before. Members of the National Crime Unit should restrict themselves solely to activity motivated by their work. More or less as the short ceremony came to an end, Bäckström left the hotel bar.

He returned to his room and called Carin again – still her answer machine – and just as he was putting the phone down he had the first constructive idea of the evening. It'll just have to be a standard porno, he thought, and how the fuck am I going to manage that in the best and most discreet way, so it doesn't end up on the bill for my room?

It only took him four seconds to come up with the answer. Must be the cognac, he thought as he went back down to reception, borrowed the key to Rogersson's room, threw himself on his colleague's neatly made bed and tuned in to one of the two adult channels that seemed most promising according to the screensaver. Then he drank one of the beers he had brought with him, as well as the last of the bottle of Baltic vodka he had also brought along, plus two half-bottles of wine which for some unknown reason were cluttering up Rogersson's minibar. This is the life, he thought, now so far gone that he had to put his hand over one eye to be able to focus on the frantic motion of the female lead's backside on the television screen. And round about then he must have simply passed out, because when he woke up a merciless sun was beating down on his stomach, since he'd forgotten to draw the curtains. It was almost ten o'clock in the morning, and on the television screen the same backside was still bouncing about, just as it had been when he had lost consciousness the previous evening.

After a quick shower and a change of clothes he went down to the restaurant to get some breakfast. The room was practically empty. The only people in there, at the back in their usual corner, were his colleagues Lewin and little Svanström. Where the fuck have the vultures gone? Bäckström thought as he piled up a serious helping of scrambled egg and sausages. Bearing in mind the previous evening's events, he complemented this with a few anchovy fillets and a handful of headache pills that the obliging hotelier had put out beside the salty fish.

'Is this seat free?' Bäckström asked, sitting down. 'Is it just my vain hope, or did someone put out some rat poison last night?' He gestured to all the empty tables.

'If you mean the journalists, I presume you haven't seen the news,' Lewin said.

'What?' Bäckström speared two anchovy fillets on his fork and folllowed them with three headache pills which he rinsed down with several deep gulps of orange juice. He sighed audibly.

'There was evidently some big wedding banquet last night down in Dalby outside Lund, and just as the newlyweds were about to take their first dance the bride's ex-boyfriend showed up with an AK4. He emptied the whole magazine,' Lewin explained.

'So what happened?' Bäckström said. Brilliant sausages they have here, he thought. The moment he put his knife in them, big pearls of fat practically leapt into his mouth.

'The usual,' Lewin said. 'I called our colleagues in Malmö, and according to them the bride, bridegroom and bride's mother are dead, with twenty more guests taken to hospital to be patched up. Stray bullets, shrapnel, ricochets, and various bits of flying decoration.'

'Gypsies,' Bäckström said, more as an optimistic statement than a question.

'Sorry to have to disappoint you,' Lewin said, suddenly sounding very tired. 'Pretty much everyone involved seems to have been local. Including the gunman, who was a section leader in the territorial army. He's still on the loose, by the way.'

Ah well, you can't have everything. Anyway, whatever happened to good old Swedish humour?

'Anything else you're wondering?' Lewin added.

'Where are Hans and Fritz?'

'Probably at the station.' Lewin got up and put his napkin down. 'Eva and I have both got the day off, so we thought we'd head off to the coast for a swim.'

'Good luck. Both of you,' Bäckström said. And don't forget to let your wife and husband and kids know how you get on, he thought.

In the absence of anything better to do, Bäckström looked in at the office after lunch. The atmosphere was flat, but what else could he expect seeing as he wasn't there? Knutsson and Thorén were in position in front of their computers, tapping away like two over-excited woodpeckers.

'How's it going, boys?' he asked. After all, I'm still their boss, he thought.

According to Knutsson, things had gone quiet for the weekend, but the DNA programme was proceeding according to plan. In total they had now taken samples from about fifty people. They had all volunteered, no one had made any fuss, and half of them had already been discounted. The experts were hard at work at the National Forensics Lab, and Linda's murder was top of the priority list.

'We'll get the rest of the results next week,' Thorén said. 'And we're gathering more all the time. We're going to get him, especially if you're right, Bäckström.'

What? Bäckström thought. Of course I am. What's the problem? 'What are you thinking of doing this evening?' he said. I haven't got much fucking choice, after all, he thought.

'Get a bite to eat,' Thorén said.

'Somewhere quiet,' Knutsson clarified.

'Then we were actually thinking of going to the cinema,' Thorén said.

'They're showing a really good classic at the screen here in town,' Knutsson explained.

'Bertolucci, *1900*,' Thorén said.

'Part one,' Knutsson clarified. 'That's by far the best one. Part two feels a bit slow in places. What do you think, Peter?'

They've got to be poofs, Bäckström thought. In spite of what they and everyone else says about all the women they've had, they must be poofs. Who the fuck else would come all the way to Växjö and go to the cinema?

When Bäckström returned to the hotel, after a short stop at a terrace bar on Storgatan for two large glasses of beer, he called Rogersson on his mobile.

'How's things?' he said.

'Damn fine, if you're asking me,' Rogersson said. 'But little Egon isn't so great. Do you want the long or the short version?'

'The short,' Bäckström said. What the hell does he mean?

'In that case, he's turned up his toes. No more swimming for him.'

'What the hell do you mean?' Egon!

'He was floating belly up, and when I poked him he didn't move a fin,' Rogersson said.

'What did you do?'

'I flushed him down the toilet,' Rogersson said. 'What would you have done? Sent him for a post-mortem?'

'But what the hell did he die of?' Bäckström said. He had more than enough food, after all, he thought.

'Maybe he was depressed,' Rogersson said with a chuckle.

Bäckström spent Saturday evening holding a wake for Egon, and on Sunday he slept through breakfast and devoted his remaining energy to a late lunch. The worst of his grief had subsided, and that afternoon he made a fresh attempt to contact Carin, but all he got was the same cheerful message on her answer machine.

What the hell's going on, Bäckström thought, as he opened yet another of the cans of beer that he had brought with him. It's like people don't care about anything any more, and definitely not about a simple policeman. And that was the last can.

# 26

Early on Monday morning, France's national day, 14 July, the head of the National Crime Unit called the county police commissioner in Växjö.

The county police commissioner himself had got up early, eaten breakfast and then sought out the restful shade at the back of his beautiful summer house. He had unfolded a comfortable chair beside the solid stone foundations and settled down to read the morning paper in peace and quiet as he sipped on a glass of homemade raspberry cordial with plenty of ice. Down on the jetty his wife lay sunbathing, flat as a Dover sole. They're not the same as us, the county police commissioner thought affectionately, and at that moment his mobile rang.

'Nylander,' Nylander said abruptly. 'Have you found him yet?'

'The investigation is progressing rapidly,' the commissioner replied. 'But when I last spoke to my colleagues, they hadn't found him yet, no.'

'There's a maniac on the loose in Skåne armed with an automatic rifle,' the Head of National Crime said. 'I've sent all my forces down to catch him. Without any warning, we've hit red alert, and because you and your colleagues haven't managed to get your arses into gear I'm going to have to redeploy them when they're needed in Växjö.'

'Yes, I hear what you're saying,' the commissioner said, 'but right now it's actually—'

'Have you even bothered to check whether it could be the same man?' HNC interrupted.

'I'm not sure I quite understand what you mean.'

'It's not that bloody difficult to understand,' Nylander growled. 'It's not that bloody far between Växjö and Lund, and in the world I live in, this is undeniably a remarkable coincidence.'

'I'm sure someone here will have checked to see if there was any connection,' the commissioner said. 'But if you like—'

'Is Åström there?'

'Here?' He must mean Bäckström, the commissioner thought. Although goodness knows what he'd be doing at my place in the country. 'No, Bäckström isn't here. I'm out in the country. I'm on my mobile.'

'In the country,' HNC said. 'You're out in the country?'

'Yes,' the county police commissioner began, but before he could say anything more Nylander had hung up.

Knutsson and Thorén evidently hadn't spent all weekend at the cinema. After the Monday morning meeting they came into Bäckström's office and showed him their latest findings.

'We were thinking about what you said, Bäckström. About not being able to rule out the possibility that we're looking for a fellow officer,' Knutsson said.

'Yes, or someone training to become an officer,' Thorén added.

'What are you getting at?' Complete idiots, Bäckström thought.

According to Knutsson and Thorén, the basic idea had some substance. Among American serial killers there were several who had managed to entrap their victims by pretending to be police officers. The most famous example in modern criminal history, they went on, was Ted Bundy.

'It must be an unbeatable tactic if you want to win a girl's trust,' Knutsson said.

'Saying you're a police officer,' Thorén clarified.

'Yes,' Bäckström said. 'But why not start with people who actually are police officers? So we don't have to worry about whether a fraudulent officer managed to pay a visit to a future officer in the middle of the night,' he added sourly. Fucking morons, he thought.

Even among real police officers there was a fair bit to go on. Going back in time, there was the renowned Hurva Man, a former officer named Tore Hedin, who had murdered eleven people, and the whole thing had started when he was suspended from duty for using his handcuffs on his girlfriend.

'You probably remember that case, Bäckström. It must have been after you started, 1952,' Knutsson said innocently.

'How about looking at Växjö in the present day instead?' Bäckström replied curtly.

'In that case, here are ten names of current and future officers,' Thorén said, handing him a list.

'Six of them were at the same club as Linda the night she was murdered,' Knutsson said. 'Three current officers, and three in training, two of whom have already contacted us and given a DNA sample. They've been discounted already.'

'They're the ones whose names have been crossed out, with a tick in the margin,' Thorén explained.

'We put them on the list just to make sure,' Knutsson said.

'Doesn't matter,' Bäckström said. 'What about the others? Why haven't we got samples from them?'

The reasons weren't clear, according to Knutsson and Thorén. The most likely explanation, emerging from the short interviews their colleague Sandberg had conducted with them all, was that they were still in the club after three o'clock, when the perpetrator showed up in Linda's flat. The third trainee had said that he had left the club just before four o'clock. He was alone and went straight home. Nice and sober, of course. The three current officers, on the other hand, had stayed until the club closed. They had split up outside and each gone home alone. There was no mention of their level of sobriety, nor any other details, but by then it must have been closer to five o'clock than four.

'Fuck me,' Bäckström said with feeling. 'Are they all poofs, then, or what?'

'How do you mean?' Thorén asked.

'That's what it says in the interviews, anyway,' Knutsson said. 'What they said, I mean.'

'Four police officers going home alone from a nightclub? Are you thick, or what?'

'One of them was actually still in training, the one who went home first,' Thorén corrected. 'But I understand what you mean.'

'Yes, that's never happened to me,' Knutsson said. 'But then this is Växjö, of course.'

'Yes, so it is,' Bäckström said. 'You haven't shown Sandberg this list, have you?'

To judge from their simultaneous and immediate headshakes, they hadn't, and the main reason was probably because the remaining four names on the list were not unknown to the internal investigation unit.

'So what have these lads been up to, then?' Bäckström asked, glancing intently at the list. No one I know, he thought.

A bit of a mixed bag, according to Knutsson. The first of the four worked as a uniformed officer in the neighbouring district, but had also had a number of secondments to the police college in Växjö as a shooting instructor. A couple of years ago one of his female students had reported him for sexual harassment: letters and phone calls with the usual offers. The complaint had been withdrawn just a month later, and the female student had left the course. When the internal investigators contacted her, she refused to cooperate and the investigation was dropped. But the instructor was still there, and as recently as May he had been at the shooting range with Linda and her fellow students.

'He's supposed to be highly regarded, both as an officer and as an instructor,' Knutsson said. 'Mind you . . .' He shrugged.

The complaint against the second officer was even older. Around the time of his divorce five years ago, his ex-wife had reported him for physical abuse. But that complaint had also been withdrawn, and the investigation eventually abandoned.

'But he was suspended for a month or so,' Thorén said, 'while the investigation was still going on. Then it looks like he got compensation from the force with the help of the union. They're divorced, by the way. Him and his ex-wife.'

'So what's he doing these days?' Bäckström said. Women are all the same, he thought.

'Well, he's back at work, of course,' Knutsson said, with a look of surprise.

'Next one,' Bäckström said. Good to hear, he thought.

The third officer did voluntary work as a sports coach for local youngsters: football, ice hockey and handball. In his younger days he had been a promising sportsman, and had played football and ice hockey professionally. One of the teams he coached was a girls' football team, with players aged from thirteen to fifteen. The parents of one girl had reported him for exposing himself in front of their daughter on several occasions. Sometimes in the changing room after training, and also when he and the girls and some of the parents had spent a week away at a training camp.

The whole thing had developed into a big story, even ending up on the front of the evening papers. The legal evidence was fairly meagre, however, and that case was ultimately dropped as well. The girl who had identified him stopped playing football, and she and her family had moved to another town. The officer coach gave up training, despite a groundswell of support from the other youngsters and their parents. After that he had been on sick leave for eighteen months before returning to work. Nowadays he worked in the police station in Växjö, where he only had administrative duties.

'Looks like a really sad story,' Thorén said. 'They took his service revolver away from him because they were worried he'd shoot himself when his wife took the kids and left.'

'What about the last one?' Bäckström said. So that's how it went. His wife took the kids and left, he thought.

'Seems to have been one of our simpler colleagues, if I can put it like that,' Knutsson said. 'To be brief, two years ago he was reported by his then fiancée. She worked in a hairdressing salon in Alvesta some twenty kilometres from here, and she doesn't seem to have been the only one, to put it bluntly. His fellow officers called him Randy Karlsson, or Randy Kalle.'

'His name's Karl Karlsson, by the way,' Thorén explained.

'So what was she so upset about?' Bäckström asked. Sounds like a good bloke, he thought.

'According to the report, our colleague Karlsson used to handcuff her when they were going to be intimate, and apparently he used his service cuffs,' Knutsson said.

'Oh, that's terrible,' Bäckström said with a grin. 'Didn't he have a pair of his own?'

According to Knutsson and Thorén, that wasn't clear from the preliminary report, where only his service handcuffs were mentioned. The hairdresser had moved to Gothenburg, where apparently she had her own salon and a new fiancé. The oddest thing about the story was that officer Karlsson followed her six months later, and now worked for the police in Mölndal, on the outskirts of Gothenburg.

'I spoke to a colleague I know in Gothenburg, and he knew perfectly well who Randy Karlsson was. He works in the patrol cars, and is still known as Randy Karlsson, or Randy Kalle. It doesn't look like he's calmed down at all,' Thorén said.

'What's he been doing this summer? Apart from shagging around,' Bäckström said.

'Holiday since midsummer,' Thorén said.

'Get a DNA sample. Doesn't sound like Linda's type, but better one too many than one too few. And those four who were at the club, plus the other three, the shooting instructor, the wife-beater and the flasher. Get samples from them all, and I don't give a damn what little Sandberg thinks. And one more thing,' Bäckström said before they had the chance to escape from his room. 'Make sure we get a sample from that fat little Polack as well.'

'Lewin is working on that,' Thorén said. 'He had an idea of going through a prosecutor.'

Lewin, Bäckström thought. Little Svanström must have livened him up a bit.

After the unpleasant conversation with the head of the National Crime Unit, the county police commissioner had sat deep in his own thoughts for a long time. Nylander seemed completely unbalanced, he thought. As he reflected on the matter, he strolled down towards the jetty and looked at his wife.

'You're not going to fall asleep in the sun, are you, my dear?' he said thoughtfully. 'You've got cream on, haven't you?'

She seems completely exhausted, poor thing, he thought.

Then he had called his colleague, Olsson, to find out about any potential links between the tragedy in Skåne and his own ghastly case up in Växjö. Olsson said it was quite a coincidence, because he had been about to call his boss to say that he had been in touch with their colleagues down in Skåne to look into that. He was expecting to hear from them later that day.

'Good to hear,' the commissioner said. Olsson's a rock, he thought as he hung up. One of those rock pillars on Gotland, even though he was from Småland. Standing firm no matter what the wind and weather threw at him, the commissioner thought, feeling almost poetic as he did so.

Bäckström summoned officer Sandberg to see him, even though he was starting to get thoroughly fed up with her by now. He nodded towards the free chair.

'Please, sit down,' he said. 'I want us to get DNA samples from the police officers who were in the club, and the trainee who hasn't already given one as well.'

Naturally, Sandberg had objections. Women are all the same, Bäckström thought, and on closer inspection this one was starting to look a bit saggy as well. In more than one place.

'But none of them left the club before half past three at the earliest,' Sandberg said. 'If you read my interviews. Besides, I was there as well, and I spoke to all of them during the evening. Several times, and when I left at four o'clock all three officers were still there, and the trainee had only just left. He came and said goodbye before he went.'

'Yes, of course,' Bäckström said. 'But I don't see what that's got to do with anything?'

'According to what was said at the morning meeting, you and Enoksson both seem to believe that the perpetrator arrived at Linda's flat at three o'clock,' Sandberg said.

'But we don't actually know that,' Bäckström said. 'The only thing our esteemed medical officer can say is that she must have died between three o'clock and seven o'clock.'

'But if he made his escape at five o'clock, when the newspaper arrived?' Sandberg persisted. 'Considering everything he did. How could he have had time for all that?'

'We don't know that either,' Bäckström said. 'It's what we believe. Make sure we get samples from all of them. Voluntarily, of course, and as soon as possible.'

'I hear what you're saying, Bäckström.' Sandberg was glowering at him sullenly.

'Good,' Bäckström said. 'Then there are three more men we need samples from.' Our colleagues in Gothenburg can take care of the randy fucker there, he thought.

'Who?' Sandberg said, looking at him cautiously.

'Andersson, Hellström and Claesson,' Bäckström said. 'Are the names familiar to you?'

'I'm afraid we may run into problems,' Sandberg said. 'I hope you realize that there's a serious risk of Claesson's committing suicide if you drag him into this case.'

'That's why it's an excellent idea to give him the chance to prove himself innocent as soon as possible,' Bäckström said. 'Then he won't have to hear a load of small talk in the corridors.'


After a light lunch of a green salad, fish, sun-dried tomatoes and a bottle of mineral water, the county police commissioner had finished thinking and called an old acquaintance who worked in the constitutional protection group of the Security Police.

'This isn't an easy thing to discuss,' he began. Ten minutes later he had told the whole story. 'He seemed completely unbalanced,' he concluded.

His acquaintance said that it was good that he had got in touch. Without breathing a word about why, he said it was both professionally justified, interesting in and of itself, and significant from the perspective of constitutional protection.

'The best thing would be for you to write a few lines covering what you've just told me,' he said. 'Naturally, anything you wrote would be strictly confidential, so there's no need for you to worry about that at all.'

'I'd rather not,' the commissioner said, sounding as dubious as he felt. 'I had hoped that this conversation would suffice.'

'I certainly appreciate that,' his acquaintance said, sounding almost jovial. 'Well, never mind, then. This informal conversation will be sufficient.'

'If things get complicated, naturally I shall stand by everything I've said.'

'Of course, of course. I wouldn't dream of expecting anything else,' his acquaintance said, sounding, if it were possible, even more jovial than before.

After they ended the call, the county police commissioner went back down to the jetty to reassure himself that his wife hadn't fallen asleep in the sun. She hadn't. But she had turned over.

His acquaintance, on the other hand, switched off the recording device attached to his phone, pulled out the memory chip containing the conversation, took it to his secretary, and asked her to produce a certified printout.

# 27

The next day they finally managed to get hold of a DNA sample from Linda's neighbour, the librarian, Marian Gross. No one in the investigating team actually thought he could be the perpetrator, but this was a matter of principle. No one, and least of all someone like Gross, could be allowed to get away with anything just by kicking up a fuss. Detective Superintendent Jan Lewin had spoken to the prosecutor who was in charge of the existing inquiry into Gross. He had pointed out the legal openings that the old case still offered, and she hadn't been the slightest bit difficult to persuade. On the contrary, she had expressed surprise that the matter hadn't already been taken care of. So now it was simply a matter of going to pick him up, and if he didn't want to provide a sample voluntarily they would take one anyway.

Von Essen and Adolfsson were given the task, and after the customary preparatory kick Gross had opened the door of his own accord, put on his shoes and accompanied them to the police station. And just like the last time, he hadn't said a word all the way there.

'Well, Gross,' Lewin said, looking at him amiably. 'The prosecutor has decided that we need a DNA sample from you. As far as I understand, we can do it two ways. Either you put this little cotton-bud in your mouth yourself and wipe it against the inside of your cheek, or we call a doctor who will come and stick a needle in your arm while my colleagues supervise the procedure.'

Gross hadn't said anything. Merely glared at them sullenly.

'I shall interpret your silence to mean the latter,' Lewin said, still sounding just as amiable. 'Okay, boys, take Dr Gross down to one of the cells while we're waiting for the doctor to arrive.'

'I demand to be allowed to do it myself,' Gross shouted, reaching for the test-tube containing the cotton-bud on Lewin's desk. When it was over, he declined Lewin's offer of a lift home, and quickly left the police station.

A few hours later he sent a courier to hand in a complaint of gross judicial misconduct directed at the prosecutor, Detective Superintendent Olsson, Detective Superintendent Jan Lewin, acting Police Inspector von Essen and Police Constable Adolfsson. The receptionist had put it in the internal mail for onward passage to the police complaints office. Everything was pretty much back to normal.

Taken as a whole, the work of gathering DNA samples was going much better than expected. One of the younger members of the investigative team who was interested in statistics had pinned up a large chart on the notice board where they could follow developments. The total number of samples taken from residents of Växjö and the surrounding district was already over a hundred. Half of them had been checked by the National Forensics Lab and eliminated from the inquiry. No one except Gross had put up any serious resistance. A couple of local hooligans had even been in touch themselves to volunteer samples.

The only clouds in the forensic sky were their fellow officers.

The three who had been in the nightclub had refused at first. After individual meetings, two of them had fallen into line, while the third had contacted his union representative and was still refusing. And, if what he said was true, he was considering reporting Bäckström and his colleagues from National Crime to the judicial ombudsman, if only to force them to learn some of the legal basics. The trainee officer was more straightforward. In spite of several phone calls to both his home and his mobile, they simply hadn't managed to get hold of him. They had left a number of messages, but he hadn't got back to them yet.

Olsson was worried about the three officers Bäckström wanted to get DNA samples from because of their past behaviour. From his own personal point of view, Olsson had no problem with the officer who had hit his wife or the shooting instructor who had harassed his student with grubby suggestions. Not if he were speaking confidentially to Bäckström. 'Just between us, I'd happily have seen them both dismissed from service,' he said.

What the hell has that got to do with you and me? Bäckström thought.

But the former sports coach was an entirely different matter. Olsson knew him personally, and was prepared to vouch for him. He was innocent, the victim of a miscarriage of justice.

'I don't want his death on my conscience,' Olsson explained. 'He's still seriously depressed, as I'm sure you can understand.'

'Of course, who isn't?' Bäckström said. 'But I thought it was commonplace for youngsters to lie about sexual abuse?'

Olsson was the first in line to agree with that. It was quite true, and the fact that his colleague and good friend had been accused even though he was innocent – assuming the girl had made everything up – simply proved the rule. However, in this instance it looked as though her parents were behind the whole business, which increased the seriousness of the whole affair. 'I hope you appreciate that, Bäckström.'

'Of course,' Bäckström said. 'I'm sure we all hope we can find a perpetrator that we're happy with. Was there anything else?' I wonder if we ought to get a sample from you as well, he thought.

Olsson did have something else on his mind: the maniac from Dalby who was still on the loose, even though the NRRU had cordoned off the area and was systematically conducting a thorough search, metre by metre.

'You don't think he could be our man?' Olsson said, looking at Bäckström hopefully.

'I saw that the same idea has occurred to our beloved evening papers,' Bäckström said. 'With reference to someone in a position of authority inside this building. If that's what you're asking, I'm not the one they spoke to.'

'Of course not,' Olsson assured him. 'But what do you think about the hypothesis itself, I mean?'

'I think that the person in a position of authority inside this building is as stupid as his friends in the press,' Bäckström said.

★

That evening Carin called and asked why he hadn't been in touch. She'd been away for the weekend, visiting her aged mother, but he could have left a message on her machine.

'Things have been a bit busy lately,' Bäckström said evasively. What does she mean, visiting her aged mother? Blimey, Bäckström thought.

'Anything you'd care to tell me about?' she asked, sounding just as she always did when she asked that question.

'Well,' Bäckström said, 'it's mainly a personal matter. My pet died. I asked a friend to look after him while I was on this case, but it didn't go well.'

'Oh, I am sorry,' Carin said, sounding upset. 'Was it a dog or a cat?'

What the fuck does she take me for, Bäckström thought. Only old women and poofs have cats.

'A dog,' Bäckström lied. 'Quite a little character. Very lively. His name was Egon.'

'That's so sad,' Carin said, and judging by the tone of her voice she was both fond of animals and a deeply empathetic person. 'A little dog, and such a cute name. I appreciate how upset you must be. Can you bear to talk about it? About what happened, I mean?'

'He drowned,' Bäckström said. 'If you'll excuse me . . .'

'I understand, you can't talk about it,' she said.

'Let's speak tomorrow,' Bäckström suggested. 'Call me if you feel like getting something to eat.' Crazy women, he thought.

Bäckström had avoided Rogersson for a couple of days, since there was considerable evidence to suggest that he had murdered little Egon. Rogersson, on the other hand, didn't seem to have noticed that Bäckström was avoiding him. He was his usual self. That's what they're like, real psychopaths, Bäckström thought. They don't think of anyone but themselves. Although Rogersson did seem to be a slightly more complicated sort of murderer, seeing as he'd just knocked on Bäckström's door. A very gentle knock for Rogersson, probably because of his guilty conscience, Bäckström thought. And as a conciliatory gesture he had brought a crate of cold beers and an almost full bottle of whisky.

'So you're sitting here moping,' Rogersson declared, and since

Bäckström wasn't the sort to hold a grudge they had gradually and in the usual manner managed to normalize their relationship and restore the camaraderie that had always existed between them.

'Here's to Egon,' Rogersson proposed.

'Cheers, mate. Here's to Egon,' Bäckström said solemnly. And he stood up and raised his glass.

The day after his second wake for Egon, he finally caught a glimpse of a suspect worthy of the description. It's almost enough to make you a bit religious, Bäckström had thought as he felt the familiar tingling.

# 28

Before the Wednesday morning meeting, Thorén had called his colleague in Gothenburg and asked for his help in getting a DNA sample from their fellow officer, Randy Karlsson. His friend had promised to do what he could and get back to him as soon as he had done so, then called Randy Karlsson on his mobile, and got through to him straight away.

In spite of the early hour, Randy Karlsson was already at a terrace café in Marstrand, looking at girls. Thorén's acquaintance had asked how the summer had been so far, seeing as he always thought it best to start cautiously no matter what subject you wanted to talk about. Brilliant, according to Randy Karlsson. He'd spent his holiday travelling round the west coast. He had started in Strömstad in the north, and had worked his way down through Lysekil, Smögen and a few smaller places that he'd already managed to forget the names of. And now he was sitting by the water in Marstrand, a few kilometres north of Gothenburg.

'It's incredible,' he said happily. 'You wouldn't believe the number of girls. There's no end of them. And the weather . . . talk about saving time!' He didn't have any problem providing a DNA sample voluntarily. He had already done so on numerous occasions in relation to various paternity disputes in Sweden and elsewhere, and he had always been okay. 'It's great,' he said, sounding even happier. 'I haven't got caught once. It looks like I'm immune to that shit.'

To save time they had agreed that Karlsson – as soon as he had a gap in his packed schedule – would visit the local police station in

Marstrand and provide the promised sample there. Whatever the point of that was, Thorén's acquaintance thought when he hung up.

Adolfsson and von Essen didn't attend the morning meeting, because they had been appointed as the team's DNA-sampling specialists, and had begun the day in a particularly successful way. First they managed to get hold of the shooting instructor, who was an old acquaintance of Adolfsson's, being a member of the same hunting party. Bolstered by this success, they had gone to find the officer who had been at the nightclub and was refusing to cooperate. He was sitting at home polishing the text of his complaint to the judicial ombudsman, but once Adolfsson and von Essen had talked some sense into him he had made the right decision.

'What do we do next?' Adolfsson asked. After all, Gustaf's still the boss, he thought.

'Now we deal with the trainee who seems to be refusing to answer his phone,' von Essen said. 'Then we'll have got everyone who was at the club with Linda.'

At the meeting they had first discussed the current state of the case, then mainly talked about the DNA samples. For once, everyone there seemed to be in complete agreement. If they didn't find him any other way, sooner or later their perpetrator would get caught in their DNA net. The only person to express any doubt was Lewin.

'There are risks in this sort of thing,' he said cautiously, nodding towards the chart on the notice board saying how many samples had been taken.

'How do you mean?' Olsson asked.

'There's a risk that you lose control of an investigation,' Lewin said. 'It's happened before, and it'll probably happen again, and in spite of the fact that we've got the perpetrator's DNA we still haven't found him. I can give you half a dozen recent examples off the top of my head.'

Speak for yourself, bloody conspiracy theorist, Bäckström thought. Personally, he was happy to get samples from the whole world if necessary.

'What do you think, Bäckström?' Olsson said.

'I've heard that before,' Bäckström said curtly. 'And from the same person, strangely enough,' he added, harvesting a number of smiles. 'This is all about discounting people who don't have anything to do with the case as quickly as possible, and if you ask me there's no better way of keeping control of an investigation.' You look after your own business and I'll deal with the rest, he thought, glowering at Lewin.

Everyone else round the table nodded in agreement, and Lewin made do with a shrug of the shoulders. Then they changed subject, to discuss the reward that Linda's father wanted to announce.

'He's called me and the county police commissioner,' Olsson said, stretching himself up for some reason. 'But I'm concerned it might send the wrong message . . . at this early stage, I mean, because it's not even a fortnight yet . . . to announce a reward.'

What a load of crap, Bäckström thought. If he didn't want to have to sit here half the day it would be just as well to do something about it now.

'It's like this,' he said. 'If it's someone she knows we'll get him anyway, whether or not he's said anything to someone who might consider telling us for a bit of money. And if it's a complete nutter, as some people seem to think, then he probably hasn't got anyone he could tell, so we'd have nothing to gain from a reward whenever it was offered. If it's your standard junkie, then all his friends probably know about it by now, so it might speed things up a bit. Either way, sooner or later we'll find out anyway.'

'Should I interpret that to mean that you don't think it would actively harm the investigation?' Olsson said carefully.

'What sort of money are we talking about?' Interpret it whatever fucking way you want to, you poof.

'Her father suggested a million kronor. To start with,' Olsson said, and the room suddenly fell silent.

'What?' Bäckström said. Her dad must be mad. Give me the money instead, he thought.

'What does it cost to get a fix in this town?' Rogersson asked suddenly, nodding towards one of the officers who usually worked in the Växjö drug squad.

'Depends what you want,' the officer said. 'Same as in the big city, I guess. Five hundred or more if you want heroin. You can get amphetamines for a couple of hundred. Hash costs next to nothing if you take a trip to Copenhagen.'

'Christ, we'll be deluged with a load of crazy junkies trying to sell a load of crazy stories. No reward,' Bäckström said, getting up. 'Well, if there's nothing else, I suggest we try to get some work done.'

After lunch Bäckström shut himself away in his room and switched on the red lamp so he would be left to think in peace. I ought to get them to put a bed in here, he thought. He'd stopped stretching out on top of his desk years ago, and he didn't even have a decent cushion in the room. Maybe I ought to fix up somewhere closer than the hotel, he thought, but these encouraging thoughts were interrupted by a discreet knock on the door.

'Come in,' Bäckström roared. And I'll rip you to shreds, you colour-blind bastard, he thought.

'It's not that I'm colour blind,' Adolfsson said apologetically. 'Nor my colleague here either,' he said, nodding towards von Essen, who was standing just behind him. 'But there's something we'd like to talk to you about, boss. Could be of interest, actually.'

This lad's going to go far, Bäckström thought, pointing amiably at the only spare chair in the room. 'Take a seat, lad,' he said. 'And get another chair from the corridor,' he said to von Essen. If you don't want to sit on the floor, you stuck-up bastard.

'So what is it?' he said encouragingly to Adolfsson.

'There was something that struck us,' Adolfsson said. 'What Enoksson said that woman at the forensics lab told him. That our perpetrator didn't have standard Nordic DNA. The fact that we're looking for a darkie, basically.'

'Adolf's thoughts often fall into this pattern,' von Essen said lightly as he examined his fingernails.

'I'm listening,' Bäckström said, giving von Essen the evil eye. And you can shut up, he thought.

'It's about her colleague at police college, the one who was at the same club as Linda the night she was murdered, the one we

haven't managed to get a sample from. His name's Erik Roland
Löfgren.'

'Erik Roland Löfgren? He sounds really exotic.'

'He seems to live in town, mainly. We've tried to get hold of the
young man at his home address, to offer him a little cotton-bud, but he
wasn't there,' von Essen said, apparently not having noticed
Bäckström's evil eye.

'Okay, shut up, von Essen,' Bäckström said in his most polite voice.
'Go on,' he continued, nodding to Adolfsson.

'It's actually better than it sounds,' Adolfsson said, passing a photograph to Bäckström. 'This is the picture on his ID card at college. So it
isn't all bad news,' he added, looking quite pleased with himself.

Black as night, Bäckström thought, looking at the photograph. And
at that moment he started to feel the familiar old tingling. 'So what do
we know about him, then?'

He was in the same class at police college as Linda, twenty-five
years old, adopted from French west Africa at the age of six, ending up
with Swedish parents and getting a couple of older Swedish siblings
into the bargain.

'His adoptive father's a senior consultant at Kalmar Hospital, the
mother's head of a high school somewhere in Kalmar. The finer sort
of folk, to be blunt. Not like some poor sods who have to grow up out
in the middle of nowhere,' Adolfsson said. He was the son of one of
the biggest farmers in the area, and grew up on the family farm outside Älmhult.

'What else do we know?' Bäckström asked. Six years old when he
arrived from deepest Africa, and probably only someone like Brundin
could work out the sorts of things he learned there. This just gets
better, he thought.

'Decent grades – nothing outstanding, but good enough for someone like him to get into police college,' Adolfsson said. 'If you get what
I mean, boss.'

'So what are his interests, then?' Bäckström gave von Essen a warning glance as he sat there looking up at the ceiling.

'He's got a weakness for the ladies, and he's evidently brilliant at
football,' Adolfsson said.

'Plays in the college team,' von Essen added. 'Supposed to be their best player. So although he prefers Roland, everyone just calls him Ronaldo, presumably after that Brazilian who plays professionally.' Von Essen looked as if he preferred rather more cultured activities.

'Everyone calls him Ronaldo,' Bäckström said slowly, and because the penny from the diary had already dropped inside his head, the whole room was suddenly tingling now. 'Okay, this is what we're going to do, lads.' To emphasize the point he leaned over his desk and looked them in the eyes one at a time.

'Number one,' he said, holding up a stubby index finger, 'not a word about this to anyone but me. This building's leaking like a fucking sieve. Number two, I want you to find out everything you can about him and his contact with Linda. Without anyone working out what you're doing. Number three, don't do anything that could alarm him. Leave him alone. Don't try to track him down, because we're going to find him anyway.' When it's time, he thought.

'Understood, boss,' Adolfsson said.

'Sure,' von Essen said.

As soon as Adolfsson and von Essen left, he called in Knutsson and Thorén. He explained what it was about, and how they were going to proceed.

'Not a problem for me,' Knutsson said.

'It'll be nice not to have to read everything we're doing in the papers,' Thorén agreed.

'Okay, let's get going.' Finally, we're getting somewhere, Bäckström thought.

'You don't think he could have taken off already?' Knutsson said. 'If it is him, I mean.'

'Bearing in mind that he doesn't seem to be at home and isn't answering his mobile,' Thorén added.

'And that's why I thought we could start by taking a look at his call register,' Bäckström said. Fucking morons.

A good boss must be able to delegate, Bäckström thought, putting his feet up on his desk as soon as he was alone in the room. And he must be able to make decisions as well. Like picking the right automated message for his phone, sneaking back to his hotel room, having a cold beer and spending a couple of hours in the land of nod. In an emergency, if everything kicked off, his faithful associates would just have to call him. After all, he was their boss.

# 29

After the meeting on Thursday morning everything was looking very promising. The business of collecting DNA samples in Växjö and the surrounding district was still going better than expected. Almost three hundred men had volunteered to provide samples, and about half of them had been discounted already. And the investigation into Linda's classmate Erik 'Ronaldo' Löfgren had got going nicely. Adolfsson had already called Bäckström to say that he and von Essen had got hold of a fair amount of good information that they would present later that day. Even Hans and Fritz seemed to have made a bit of progress.

'I think we've worked out that business of the football match,' Knutsson said.

'Not with anyone in this building, I hope?' Bäckström said.

'Absolutely not,' Thorén said, looking almost shocked.

'That would be stupid. We checked with one of our own experts,' Knutsson explained. 'With an officer we both know and trust.'

According to the officer in National Crime's information division, 28-year-old living legend Ronaldo had acquitted himself with honour on Saturday 17 May when he and his teammates at Real Madrid played a La Liga match against their sworn arch-enemies, FC Barcelona. But he hadn't scored three goals. He scored one, and set up another, and after the match he was picked by the international television audience as man of the match, as on so many occasions before.

'But that's not the real point,' Knutsson said.

'Everyone down here who thinks this is anything to do with him has got it all wrong,' Thorén clarified.

'So what is the point, then?' Bäckström asked.

According to the analyst in the information division who had analysed the phrase, the most likely interpretation of the words *Magical name?* was that the person who had written the message had been asking a question, and that this question ought to be understood as rhetorical.

'And what the fuck does that mean in everyday language?' Bäckström wondered.

'A question where the answer is obvious,' Knutsson explained.

'For instance, you know the old classic, Bäckström?' Thorén said. 'About the Pope. Does the Pope wear a pointed hat?'

'I get it,' Bäckström said. Are Hans and Fritz cretins? he thought.

And the rhetorical question didn't only refer to the person known to the whole world as Ronaldo, or at least to the part of that world interested in football, but to a whole collective of people with the same name.

'What the fuck does that mean?' Bäckström said, throwing out his hands. Those bastard academics are going to be the death of the whole damn force, he thought.

'More than one person called Ronaldo,' Knutsson explained. 'The football player Ronaldo, man of the match, and another Ronaldo who had accomplished something of similar quality, and who probably has some sort of connection to the match in question.'

'Okay, now I get it,' Bäckström said. 'Why couldn't you say that? Linda sat and watched the game featuring everybody's favourite Ronaldo on television, while her very own Ronaldo was playing a game with her on the sofa they were both sitting on. Am I pushing my luck here, or am I to understand that he did it three times?'

'That's one way of putting it,' Thorén said flatly.

'According to the analyst we spoke to, that's the most likely interpretation, yes,' Knutsson said. 'Although he might not have expressed himself in quite those terms.'

'So send the bastard on a course so he learns to talk like normal people,' Bäckström said. 'Anyway, how are you getting on with any calls to and from his mobile?'

'We're making progress,' Thorén said.

'Although that sort of thing takes time, of course,' Knutsson added.

'When?' Bäckström asked.

'The weekend,' Thorén replied.

'Tomorrow at the earliest, Sunday at the latest,' Knutsson clarified.

'I'll be in touch,' Bäckström said, pointing to the door.

When Bäckström was sitting in the staff canteen eating lunch, officer Sandberg came over to him and asked if she could sit down.

'Sure,' Bäckström said, nodding to the empty chair. Soon she'll look as saggy as all the other women, he thought.

'Can I speak freely?' Sandberg said, looking at him.

'I always do,' Bäckström said with a shrug.

'Okay, then,' Sandberg said, and took a deep breath.

'I'm all ears,' Bäckström said, 'but I can't hear anything.'

'I don't believe in this business of getting DNA samples from a load of fellow officers,' Sandberg said in a rush.

'I think it's going very well. The two younger officers we've borrowed are proving to be very efficient.'

'I didn't think people like that existed before I became a police officer. At least I hoped not. Now I know I was wrong.' Sandberg looked solemnly at Bäckström. 'For me—'

'You don't become a police officer,' Bäckström interrupted. 'You just are a police officer. Adolfsson and that Essen are police officers. There's no more to it than that. Is there a particular officer you're worried about?' This is starting to be fun, he thought.

'We've been able to discount all the officers we've had the results back for.'

'Yes, it must be quite a relief for them,' Bäckström said with a grin.

'I just can't go up to Claesson and ask him to volunteer a DNA sample. Not with everything he's been through and the state he's in.' Sandberg shook her head.

'Was there anything else?' Bäckström said, looking pointedly at his watch.

'Well, what do you think?'

'That everything will sort itself out. I'll ask Adolfsson or someone else to do it,' Bäckström said, getting up from the table. Suck on that, you little bitch, he thought as he put his tray on the trolley.

'How did you get him to agree to an interview?' Bäckström said two hours later, as he was sitting in the car with Rogersson, on their way to see Linda's father.

'I called and asked if we could come out and talk to him,' Rogersson said.

'And there were no problems?'

'No, not the slightest,' Rogersson said, shaking his head.

The interview with Linda's father took almost two hours. They sat in his office on the first floor of the manor house, Bäckström letting Rogersson direct the conversation and contenting himself with throwing in the occasional question. They talked about Linda's interests, her social life, her friends, and whether there was anyone or anything that her father thought they ought to know about. They carefully avoided two subjects. The first was the question of whether or not she had left a journal or any other personal documents in the house, and the second was how her father himself was feeling.

After an hour or so he asked them if there was anything he could offer them. Coffee, or anything else?

'If I weren't on duty, I'd ask for a cold beer,' Bäckström said with a faint smile. 'Rogersson here will be happy with a soft drink, seeing as he's got to drive us back.'

'I'm sure that can be arranged,' Linda's father said, getting up from the sofa he was sitting in and opening an antique cabinet that stood in one corner of the office. 'Not everything's what it seems,' he added when he saw Bäckström's look of surprise.

The cabinet contained a large number of bottles and glasses of various sizes. And a small fridge containing ice, mineral water, soft drinks and beer.

'I think I'll have a beer,' Henning Wallin said. 'I suggest that you gentlemen keep me company. If it comes to it, you can always walk back to Växjö. Or I can ask my man to drive you.'

'Sounds good,' Bäckström said. You're going to get through this, he thought. Even though you look like an apple core that's passed through someone's bowels. And even though you took half your face off when you tried to shave this morning.

'Do you recognize this man?' he asked, passing Linda's father the photograph of Erik Roland Löfgren. High time we got to the point, he thought.

Her father looked carefully at the picture. Then nodded.

'They were in the same class, weren't they? I think they call him Ronaldo.'

'Did Linda know him well?' Rogersson asked.

'No, I don't think so. She would have mentioned it if she did. I've only met him once.'

Rogersson nodded to him to go on.

'He came out here some time in the spring,' Henning Wallin said. 'I remember saying hello to him. I was going out to dinner in town. I seem to remember that they were going to watch some football match. Linda has ... had ... a huge number of channels on her television.'

'But you definitely remember him?' Rogersson asked.

'Yes,' Henning Wallin said. 'He's the sort of person you remember. At least if you're the sort of dad I am,' he added. 'But I can see what you're getting at. I'm pretty sure Linda didn't have any sort of relationship with him. I'm not really bothered about anything else.'

'You didn't find him unpleasant or threatening or anything?' Rogersson said.

'No, if anything rather ingratiating,' Henning Wallin said. 'Not the sort of person I would have wanted as a son-in-law,' he added, suddenly shaking his head and pressing his thumb and forefinger to his eyes.

'I'm not going to ask how you're feeling,' Bäckström said. 'I've also lost someone ... someone close to me ... the same way you lost Linda. So I do know how you feel.'

'Have you?' Linda's father looked at Bäckström in surprise.

'Yes,' Bäckström said sombrely. 'That's why I won't ask. Is it all right if we carry on?'

'Yes,' Henning Wallin said. 'I'm all right now. Before I forget: I've offered to put up a reward. Do you think that would be any help?'

'No,' Bäckström said, shaking his head.

'Why not?'

'Because I know we're going to catch him anyway,' Bäckström said, giving him his police look.

'Good,' Henning Wallin said. 'Well, if it turns out that a reward would be useful, just let me know.'

'I've got a list here, of people Linda knew or had met,' Rogersson said. 'Do you know any of them?'

Henning Wallin looked through the list of people Linda knew. He had nothing to add that they didn't already know, and the only one he had much to say about was Marian Gross.

'He's that neighbour, isn't he? I remember Linda talking about him. She said he was a particularly dirty old man. He must have moved in after my time.'

'You lived there? In the building where it happened?' Rogersson asked.

'It belonged to me,' Henning Wallin said. 'I gave it to Linda's mother in the divorce. Then she turned it into a residents' association. Money was always her main concern.'

'But you never lived there yourself?' Rogersson repeated.

'No. One of my Swedish companies had an office there for a while, but I hardly ever set foot there after I bought it. You don't think it could have been him? Gross, I mean?'

Rogersson shrugged. 'We're checking everyone we have reason to check,' he said.

'We're not discounting anyone until we're absolutely certain,' Bäckström emphasized. 'And whoever's left will be going to prison. For life.'

'When will that happen?' Henning Wallin asked.

'Soon,' Bäckström said. 'I couldn't borrow your sh— your toilet before we go, could I? Beer in the afternoon is clearly too much for an old policeman,' he lied.

'You can use my bathroom,' Henning Wallin said. 'First door on the left.'

'I think we're almost done,' Rogersson said when Bäckström had disappeared to ease the pressure. 'There's nothing on your mind that we haven't discussed? Anything you'd like to add?'

'Just get the bastard who did it,' Henning Wallin said. 'I can sort out the rest myself.'

'We're working on it,' Rogersson said.

'You're not too drunk to drive?' Bäckström asked fifteen minutes later when they were on their way back towards Växjö.

'No,' Rogersson said. 'I'm not usually after just one beer. Incidentally, I had no idea you had a daughter who was strangled.'

'That's not what I said,' Bäckström retorted. 'I said someone close to me.'

'If it's Egon you're thinking of, then I didn't strangle him. He looked like he'd drowned. Although I thought he was a goldfish.'

'I was thinking of Gunilla,' Bäckström said. I bet he did something to Egon, he thought. Why else would he keep talking about him?

'What bloody Gunilla?' Rogersson said, irritated.

'You know, Gunilla. From the Gunilla murder,' Bäckström explained. 'She was strangled.'

'What the hell . . . she was a prostitute, wasn't she?'

'She was a very nice girl,' Bäckström said. 'I met her a few times out on the street when she was looking for business and was still in one piece. Anyway, it worked. Didn't you see how Linda's old man perked up when he heard he had a fellow sufferer with him? By the way, have we got any evidence bags in the car?'

'There's everything in this damn car,' Rogersson said. 'In the glove compartment,' he added.

'Goody good,' Bäckström said, opening one of the plastic bags and with some difficulty extracting a bloody paper handkerchief from his pocket.

'So that's why you wanted to go to the toilet,' Rogersson said.

'Yes, certainly not because I needed to,' Bäckström said happily. 'He'd thrown it in the bin in the bathroom.'

'Do you know something, Bäckström?' Rogersson said. 'You're crazy. One day the devil's going to get you. And he'll turn up in person to pick you up.'

# 30

Adolfsson and von Essen were waiting in Bäckström's office when he got back to the police station. Adolfsson flew up from his chair when Bäckström walked in. His partner made do with a polite twist of his head and torso to indicate a generally benevolent attitude.

'I hope you don't mind, but we let ourselves in and sat down, boss,' Adolfsson said. 'We didn't want to stand in the corridor where anyone could see us.'

'Sit down, Adolf, it's okay,' Bäckström said cheerily, sitting down himself and putting his feet up on the desk. This lad's going to go very far indeed, he thought.

Erik Roland Löfgren had been questioned on Friday evening, the day Linda was murdered. The interview had been conducted over the phone, and the officer who had called him on his mobile was Anna Sandberg. According to the report, the interview lasted twenty minutes. It had focused upon three related questions, and the summary of what was said covered just two pages.

'Löfgren says he and Linda were in the same class at police college here in Växjö, but they didn't see each other privately. If they did meet outside college, it was in conjunction with various social events linked to the college, apart from a few occasions when they bumped into each other at restaurants and in other social settings in Växjö.

'He goes on to say that he didn't know Linda very well, but he thought her a nice, cheerful girl, interested in sport and well regarded by everyone on the course. As far as he knows, she never had a relationship with anyone from the college or with anyone he knew. According to Löfgren, she seemed to spend most of her time with girlfriends.

'About the night in question Löfgren says he arrived at the club at ten o'clock on Thursday evening in the company of two friends from police college, and left at approximately quarter to four on Friday morning. He walked straight home and went to bed, because he had promised to visit his parents at their summer house on Öland that weekend and he needed to get some sleep before the drive. While he was at the Town Hotel he noticed that Linda was there, but they only said hello very briefly as he was with a group of his friends. There were a lot of people in the club and Löfgren doesn't remember seeing anything of interest during the evening. He also says that he is extremely shocked at what has happened to his classmate. And that's the summary of what he had to say,' von Essen finished, nodding to Bäckström.

'There's also an appendix to the report,' Adolfsson said.

'I'm getting to that,' von Essen said calmly, 'I'm getting to that. The interviewer, officer Sandberg, added an appendix to the report. She writes the following, and I quote: "The undersigned was also at the nightclub of the Town Hotel on the evening in question . . . I informed the head of the preliminary investigation, Detective Superintendent Bengt Olsson, of this fact at 1500 hours today . . . I can confirm that Löfgren approached me and my party during the evening, and that he said goodbye just before four o'clock in the morning, when he said he was going to go home and sleep because he intended to visit his parents at their summer house that weekend. I have also met Löfgren previously, when I gave a lecture on domestic violence at the police college as part of my duties. Signed, Anna Sandberg."'

'So what do we think about this, then?' Bäckström asked them.

'Well, the bit about him hardly knowing her isn't true, sadly,' Adolfsson said.

'Never mind,' von Essen said, patting him lightly on the arm. 'You can't win them all, and if you do lose one there are a thousand more fish in the sea. Adolf here was rather keen on our victim,' he explained. 'He used to flirt with her when she was in reception.'

Bäckström chuckled. 'Maybe we should get a sample of your DNA as well, Adolf?'

'I've already dealt with that with Enoksson,' Adolfsson said, sounding rather abrupt for once.

'What for?' Bäckström asked curiously. What for? he thought.

'Because I was the one who found her. I was at the crime scene, in various rooms. Not that I was standing there drooling over her, but I did touch her to check if she was dead,' Adolfsson said. 'So I suggested to Enoksson that he take a sample. Voluntarily.'

'And he did as you said?'

'Yes.'

'Wise man,' Bäckström said. 'But to get back to the subject. How well did our little Ronaldo know the victim, then?'

'According to what he told a couple of his friends, he'd slept with her,' Adolfsson said. 'I'm afraid it's probably true. Do you want the details, boss?'

'Well,' Bäckström said, 'never mind the details. All women are crazy. Actually, while we're on the subject of women, our colleague, Sandberg. What's she like?'

'She's not one of my favourites,' Adolfsson said. 'And I don't regard her as my colleague either, seeing as you're asking, boss. She's married to another officer, and I'd prefer not to say what I think of him. He works in the neighbourhood team in Kalmar, which probably says it all.'

'The fact that we're both a touch reserved about our colleague Sandberg is possibly because she reported us both for using excessive force in the course of our duties,' von Essen explained. 'She said we'd assaulted one of her little charges during an arrest. Some time back in the spring.'

'So what had he done?' Bäckström asked.

'Not him, her,' Adolfsson said. 'She tried to bite the baron in the neck when we were trying to get her in the car, and considering that she was HIV-positive, I thought it best to gag her.'

'I didn't know you kept gags in the car,' Bäckström said. 'Sounds practical.'

'I took my jacket off and tied it round her head,' Adolfsson said.

'Even the traitors in police complaints didn't have any objections.'

'Okay, this is what we're going to do, and not a word to anyone outside this room,' Bäckström said. He took his feet off the desk and leaned forward.

# 31

## *Skåne, Saturday 19 July*

At the start of the week the Head of National Crime had flown down to Skåne to personally lead the hunt for the most dangerous criminal in the country. The madman from Dalby, a mass-murderer, and – in the world where people like Nylander were obliged to live – in all likelihood also a serial killer. To be close to the search area in and around Dalby, where his troops in the rapid-response unit had been deployed, he had taken quarters in the Grand Hotel in Lund.

At first they had had the poor taste to put him in an ostentatious suite, but when he explained in very clear terms about the operational circumstances of his visit they had swapped the suite for a normal double room with en suite bathroom. These wretched civilians haven't got a clue about heightened states of alert, Nylander thought.

Unfortunately, though, late on Saturday evening a small incident occurred in his hotel room.

Nylander was tired after having spent more than fifteen hours out in the field. The heat had been troubling and there had been some difficulties about obtaining adequate supplies. As he was going to bed, when he was unloading, or possibly loading, his service revolver – the specific details were never made public – a shot unfortunately went off and hit the mirror in his bathroom. Because no great damage seemed to have been done, Nylander brushed his teeth, put the pistol under his pillow, where he always kept it when he was away from home on official duty, and went to bed. He was on the point of falling asleep when he was woken by someone knocking violently at his door.

Unhappily, the errant bullet appeared to have ended up embedded in the television of the next room. His hysterically inclined neighbour had rushed straight to reception, screaming out loud, wearing nothing but a pair of boxer shorts embellished with pictures of Donald Duck. The hotel staff had immediately called the police and told them that there had been 'a series of shots fired in the room of the head of the National Crime Unit'. Just two minutes later the first patrol car arrived from Lund Police, and just to be on the safe side the rapid-response detail from the Malmö force was on its way.

After that the situation got out of hand. Even though Nylander himself calmly and systematically explained what had actually happened, and even suggested that everyone went back to their own business, he was ignored. The local officers were simply not professional enough to handle the situation. Instead they took his service revolver into safe keeping and dragged him to the police station in Lund for questioning, even though it was the middle of the night. After the interview they finally drove him back to the hotel.

'Unfortunately I shall be obliged to write a report about this matter,' Nylander said, fixing his eyes on the head of the Malmö rapid-response detail when they dropped him off outside the entrance to the hotel.

'Go ahead, Nylander,' the officer replied, in a broad Skåne accent. 'As long as you promise to keep your hands above the covers.'

The following morning they found the sought-after madman. He was in a fisherman's shed outside Åhus, and the fact that he was found by the owner of the shed rather than by Nylander's rapid-response unit was in all likelihood explained by the fact that he was in the wrong place, in terms of the area being searched. To judge by the smell and the number of maggots, he had evidently been there for several days.

'Looks like the bastard put the gun in his mouth and fired,' the head of Nylander's unit said.

'Get a DNA sample from him and let our colleagues in Växjö know,' Nylander said. Backwoods policemen, he thought. You had to do everything yourself.

# 32

## *Växjö, Sunday 20 July*

Late on Sunday evening Knutsson and Thorén knocked on the door of Bäckström's hotel room. Their colleagues in Stockholm had finished their preliminary investigation into the mobile phone belonging to trainee police officer Erik Roland Löfgren.

'What, they've been working over the weekend?' Bäckström said in surprise.

'I suppose they want the overtime, like everyone else,' Knutsson replied.

'So is he still here, or has he scarpered?' Bäckström asked. Hope the fucker's scarpered, he thought, suddenly feeling the familiar tingling again.

'Judging from the call log, he's been on Öland since the middle of the week,' Thorén said. 'Before that, it looks like he was in Växjö.'

'The most recent search locates him close to a phone mast in Mörbylånga,' Knutsson clarified. 'His parents have a summer house nearby, so he's probably there sunbathing.'

'So have you found anything interesting?' Bäckström asked. Cretins, he thought. Why would someone like Löfgren want to go sunbathing?

'I think so,' Thorén said, looking pleased with himself.

'What, then?' Bäckström said. 'Unless it's a secret?'

'Officer Sandberg seems to have tried calling him several times,' Thorén said. 'The first time on the day Linda was murdered.'

'Yes,' Bäckström said with a sigh. 'Which isn't so bloody strange

considering that she was the one who questioned him over the phone.'
Utter cretins, he thought.

'That's what we thought to start with,' Thorén said.

'Until we thought about it a bit more,' Knutsson explained.

'Really?' Bäckström said sourly. Who the hell do they think they are?

According to the interview report that Sandberg had written and signed, she had questioned trainee police officer Roland Löfgren between 19.15 and 19.35 on Friday 4 July.

'She called his mobile. Probably from her own extension in the police station in Växjö, seeing as the call went through the station's exchange,' Thorén said.

'I'm not that stupid,' Bäckström said. 'So what's the problem?'

'For one thing, the conversation's a bit short,' Knutsson said, giving Bäckström a crafty glance. 'It ends after just four minutes. At 19.19.'

'So what?' Bäckström said. 'That could just mean he asked her to call the landline instead. Bad reception, battery running out. How the hell should I know?' Christ, how stupid could you get? 'Have you checked his landline?'

'It's being done,' Thorén said. 'It's a normal Telia connection, to his student lodgings. In some big house on Doktorsgatan in the centre of Växjö, owned by a doctor with a private practice here in town. Probably one of his dad's old friends. The account is under his father's name, not the boy's, which makes getting permission to see the records a bit tricky.'

'Well, they'll just have to get it sorted,' Bäckström said. 'What's the other problem?'

'Well, to put it briefly,' Knutsson said . . .

To put it briefly, the problem was as follows: at 19.20 someone had made another call from the police station exchange to Löfgren's mobile, but he didn't answer. Another five incoming calls had been logged, all from the same number, and all of them – to judge by the length of the call – had gone straight to voicemail. The last of the calls was made just after midnight. During the following fifteen days, a total of ten more calls had been made to Löfgren's mobile from the police station exchange. All of them apparently unanswered.

As if this weren't enough, Sandberg had also called him from her official police mobile on five occasions, and those calls also seemed not to have been answered. Finally she had also called him one more time from her personal mobile.

'That was on Thursday afternoon, just after lunch,' Knutsson said. 'And they actually seem to have talked to each other that time. The call lasted nine minutes.'

'Weird,' Bäckström agreed. What the fuck's she playing at? Wasn't that when she had a go at me in the canteen?

'Yes, definitely a bit weird,' Thorén said.

'Pretty mysterious, if you ask me,' Knutsson said.

'Let's sleep on it,' Bäckström said. What the fuck's going on?

'One more thing,' Bäckström said, before they had time to disappear through the door. 'Not a word about this to a single damn soul.'

'Course not,' Knutsson said.

'Very hush hush,' Thorén agreed, winking with his right eye and holding his right index finger to his lips.

'What?' Bäckström said. Are the bastards freemasons as well?

'Very hush hush,' Knutsson repeated. 'Like that film about cops in Los Angeles in the fifties. *LA Confidential*.'

'One of the characters says that, very hush hush,' Thorén explained. 'It's a good film. Based on a book by James Ellroy. You should see it, Bäckström.'

There's no other explanation. They have to be poofs, Bäckström thought just before he fell asleep. Since the rest of humanity had got hold of television and video, only poofs still went to the cinema. Poofs and old women, of course. Not even kids went to the cinema any more, Bäckström thought, and that must have been when sleep caught up with him, because when he opened his eyes it was already light outside and the same merciless sun was searching for gaps in the curtain, trying to get into his room.

Today I'm going to make glue out of the bastard, Bäckström thought as he stood in the shower, letting the cold water prepare him for yet another new day in his life as a murder detective.

# 33

## *Växjö, Monday 21 July*

Detective Superintendent Jan Lewin had taken to reading the *Småland Post*. He still had to read at least one newspaper to stay informed about the media view of the world in general, and the murder of Linda Wallin in particular.

Obviously, Linda's murder dominated the news in the big local morning paper, but they also had room for other stories, some small comfort amidst all the human misery, and on this particular Monday morning this came in the form of an article about what was probably the largest strawberry in the world.

There was a picture of the strawberry on the front page, with the classic matchbox alongside for scale, from which it was possible to deduce that the strawberry was the size of a cauliflower, or perhaps a man's fist. Inside the paper was a lengthy interview with the man behind this horticultural feat, Svante Forslund, 72, and a slightly shorter one with his wife Vera, 71.

Svante Forslund had been retired for almost ten years, after a career as a biology and chemistry teacher at the high school in Växjö. He and his wife now spent all year in what had once been their summer cottage outside Alvesta. The Forslunds' great hobby was gardening. Their plot was almost an acre in size, and contained most of what could be grown for both culinary and visual delight. Flowers, herbs, medicinal plants, fruit and all other forms of greenery. Potatoes and every other root vegetable, and other nutritious things. Obviously also beehives, to guarantee the pollination of their private paradise. And, last but not least, there were numerous varieties of *Fragaria ananassa*, because strawberries in particular were Svante Forslund's great passion in life.

The strawberry in question was a recent American hybrid, *Fragaria monstrum americanum*, the American monster strawberry. Forslund had noticed this particular strawberry during the week after midsummer, and even then it had been considerably larger than others in the same row.

Forslund had immediately decided to embark upon a special growth programme. Other strawberries on the same plant had been removed to avoid any competition for nutrients, a special watering and feeding regime had been introduced, and the plant had been given particular protection from insects, grubs, birds, hares and deer. A fortnight later, when Forslund estimated that his strawberry had reached its optimal size, it had been picked, photographed, and ended up in the paper.

Aside from the purely horticultural interest, Svante Forslund also saw huge economic potential in his giant strawberry. Professional strawberry cultivation in Sweden currently occupied 2,350 hectares, and in Forslund's opinion it would only take a couple of years of systematic focus on his giant American strawberries for annual fruit production to increase by some 400 per cent. From the same area and with considerably lower watering and fertilizer costs than was currently the case.

His wife Vera had also had her say, and she was far less enthusiastic. In summary, she thought her husband's monster strawberry was both watery and tasteless, and, to put it bluntly, she wouldn't dream of using it in the kitchen. In Vera Forslund's world, a proper strawberry should taste like they did when she was little. Her own favourite was a local variety that produced a dark red and fairly small fruit with firm flesh, a sweet taste, and a pronounced flavour of the wild variety. She had inherited the plants from her parents, and although her husband was a latter-day Carl von Linné, even he had been unable to classify their origins. Nevertheless, their fruit still formed the main ingredient of the famous strawberry tart that she always made for her children, grandchildren, and friends each summer, and the readers of the

*Småland Post* could make for themselves by following the accompanying recipe: a base of thinly sliced sponge, a few splashes of homemade strawberry liqueur, a large quantity of jam made from the same strawberries, a lot of whipped cream, thinly sliced strawberries all round the sides and a particularly fine whole strawberry to crown the creation.

It sounded simple and tasty. Rather like the tarts his mother used to make when he was a child, Lewin thought, deciding to cut out the article and add it to the rest of the material he was collecting from his trip to Växjö.

# 34

The voluntary DNA sampling programme in Växjö and the surrounding district seemed to be a real success. They now had almost four hundred samples. The National Forensics Lab had set aside resources for the Linda murder and almost half of those who had submitted samples had been discounted from the investigation.

'What about our fellow officers and those students?' Olsson asked.

'It's going okay,' Knutsson said, looking at his files. 'We've had eight samples. All of them voluntary. The first four we received have already been discounted. There are just two we haven't got.'

'Yes, and I've promised to sort out Claesson's, so it's on its way,' Olsson said. 'No need to worry. I'll take care of it myself,' he added quickly.

'Right, so that leaves one student that we don't have a sample from,' Knutsson said, pretending to consult his notes. 'Let's see. He was in the same class as Linda, and was in the nightclub on the night in question. An Erik Roland Löfgren, according to college records.'

'I've tried to reach him by phone. Several times,' Sandberg said.

'How are you getting on?' Bäckström asked. Just tell us what the fuck you're up to.

'Well, it's the middle of the holidays, but I did eventually manage to get hold of him at the end of last week,' Sandberg said. 'He was with his parents at their summer house on Öland, but he promised to get in touch as soon as he gets back to Växjö.'

'That's very generous of him,' Bäckström grunted. 'So when can we expect to see him, then? When the college term starts in the autumn, perhaps? The simplest solution is surely to ask our colleagues in Kalmar to go over to Öland and take a sample.'

'I promise I'll chase him up again,' Sandberg said. 'I promise. Don't let's forget that this is about people volunteering. I mean, he's not a suspect, after all.'

'Just get it sorted,' Bäckström said. 'Explain to our little student what this is all about. Otherwise I'll go and get him myself, and then we'll be talking blood samples rather than cotton-buds.'

'I'm sure it'll sort itself out,' Olsson said. 'It'll be fine. Don't let's get wound up about such a small detail.'

'I'm not at all wound up,' Bäckström said. 'Just tell the fucker that if he wants to join the police, he'd better stop acting like a common criminal under suspicion of committing some sort of crap. Just a bit of kind-hearted advice. And if there's nothing else, then I at least have a lot of work to do.'

That afternoon Olsson asked to talk to Bäckström in private. 'I could do with a bit of wise advice from an experienced colleague,' he said.

The flasher, Bäckström thought. You've asked for a DNA sample, and now he's hanged himself in his attic, and you want to have a good cry on Uncle Bäckström's shoulder.

It turned out to be a rather different problem. There was a lot of anxiety in Växjö after Linda's murder, particularly among young women, and, seen from a social point of view, this had actually diminished the quality of life of a large group of individuals.

'Do people actually dare to go out and have fun any more without running the  constant risk of being attacked?' Olsson wondered.

'Interesting question,' Bäckström said.

'It's many years since we in the police have been able to guarantee anything like that,' Olsson said. 'Our resources aren't even sufficient to cover the essentials any longer.'

If there are actually any essentials in a shithole like this, Bäckström thought. Badly parked cars and missing dogs? 'Yes, it's a bad situation,' he agreed with a sigh.

'There's a group of us who've been trying to come up with an alternative solution, and it was actually Lo who came up with the idea,' Olsson said.

'I'm all ears, I can assure you.' Bäckström nodded seriously and leaned forward. Our very own battery hen. I can hardly wait, he thought.

'Växjö Men Against Violence to Women,' Olsson said. 'Ordinary men, fellow human beings, fellow menfolk, if I can put it like that . . . someone in the group suggested that phrase, "fellow menfolk" . . . a fellow citizen, who happens to be a man, patrolling the streets in the evening and at night, whose very presence in the urban environment would raise the level of security. For instance, they could offer to escort single women home from a nightclub . . .'

What a fucking brilliant pick-up technique, Bäckström thought. Even Lo herself could probably find a short-sighted fellow manfolk that she could lure up into her bedroom and give an unsatisfactory ride.

'What do you think, Bäckström?'

'Sounds like a great idea,' Bäckström said. Christ, how stupid can you get? he thought.

'You don't think there's a risk that it could be seen as some sort of vigilante group?' Olsson said, suddenly seeming rather worried. 'Or, even worse, that frivolous individuals might exploit the plan to their own advantage?'

'I don't think there's much risk of that,' Bäckström said. 'Providing you have adequate supervision of those taking part, I mean.' And take care not to let in men like our colleagues Randy Karlsson and the flasher.

'Really,' Olsson said, looking both relieved and happy. 'I don't suppose you could let us have your thoughts when our little group holds its next meeting?'

'Of course I'd be happy to share my opinion. Goes without saying,' Bäckström said. 'If you think I might have something to contribute,' he added modestly. I can hardly wait, he thought.

Adolfsson and von Essen's investigation of Erik Roland Löfgren had evidently continued apace over the weekend. A number of troubling details were starting to pile up around the trainee police officer. According to what he himself had told several of his male classmates, he had been having sex with Linda all spring, right up to the end of term in the middle of June, but because he was the sort of young man who valued his freedom he had chosen to keep their relationship secret. According to Löfgren, Linda had started to get a bit too clingy and demanding for his taste. But there hadn't been any dramatic scenes, nothing of that sort; he had simply explained to her in a friendly way that in future she would have to take her place in the long queue of interested young women. How she reacted to this was unknown. Apparently she hadn't said a word about it to her girl-friends, and she didn't seem to have acquired a new boyfriend or lover, if that was what he had actually been.

'So what he told Sandberg during the interview wasn't true?' Bäckström said.

'No,' Adolfsson said, shaking his head. 'And it's not just idle boast-ing either. That young man seems to have gone through the women of this town like a bulldozer. We've spoken to several of them. He seems to have slept with half of Småland.'

'Her last known sexual partner,' von Essen said. 'Doesn't that usually give some sort of clue to the perpetrator in cases like this?'

'Good,' Bäckström exclaimed. 'This is better than good, this is serious shit.' That aristocratic poof obviously isn't a complete cretin after all, he thought. 'Good work, boys. If we're in luck, then it's no more complicated than this. So what do the women say? Does he normally fuck about with them?'

'What, the cosy smell of leather, latex and restraints? That's not the sort of thing people talk about in a town like this,' von Essen said, even though he too was born and bred in the Småland countryside. 'But he doesn't seem to carry the necessary equipment round with him when he's out having fun. If I can put it like that.'

Löfgren was young, well built, in good shape, charming and extremely attractive. Considering that he was only twenty-five years old, he also seemed to have accumulated a great deal of experience and consider-able talent in the area of sex. According to one of their female informants, he was also as well-endowed as the myth about black men demanded. And an obvious central protagonist in the nightmares of white men.

'Ronaldo's a proper sex machine,' she had said, smiling fondly. 'If you really want to fuck your brains out, you couldn't do any better. It's big. And very thick.'

Like a good shotgun, Adolfsson had thought when he spoke to her. It takes practice, talent, and a good stock of ammunition.

'A bit like you, Patrik,' the informant had suddenly said. 'But the problem with you is that you're very likeable as well. Do you remember the time you wanted to show me the hunting tower you were in when you shot your first elk?'

'If we could stick to the subject,' Adolfsson had said. Ideally to things I can actually include in my report, he had thought.

Unusual sex? Deviant sex? Kinky sex? Bondage? Sadomasochism?

'Not with me, at any rate,' the informant had said with a shrug. 'Mind you, if I'd wanted to do anything like that, I'm pretty sure he would have agreed. He certainly wouldn't have backed down. I don't think I would even have had to ask. He'd have worked it out anyway. Sex is his thing, after all.'

They hadn't got much further than that.

'I'd put money on him being a sick, sadistic bastard,' Bäckström said greedily. And it'll be obvious when we go through his wardrobe, he thought. The familiar tingling was much stronger now.

Bäckström had started to settle into his new existence at the Town Hotel in Växjö. The worst of his grief for Egon had subsided unexpectedly quickly, and in recent days he'd hardly spared him a thought. His hotel room was always freshly cleaned and his bed freshly made when he returned from his arduous daily activities at the police station. All he needed to remember before he left each morning was to throw the towels in a heap on the bathroom floor so the environmental extremists among the staff didn't get the idea that they could just hang them up again, and actually had to replace them with nice clean ones. It was probably high time to hand all his used clothes in again to be washed and ironed. Which was entirely in order this time, seeing as he had got them all sweaty in the course of his duties.

He had established his evening routine fairly quickly. First a cold beer as soon as he got in the door. Then a short nap, another beer in his room, then a bit of food. Before going to bed and falling asleep, a bit of instructional conversation with his colleague, Rogersson, a few more beers, and possibly one or two discreet little snifters. And, as a bit of spice to everyday life, the now regular conversations with his very own reporter from local radio. So that she got the chance to complain that he never seemed to have time to meet her, even though she had sworn blind that they wouldn't talk shop.

Like this evening, for instance.

'I've got a lot on at the moment,' Bäckström said.

'Promises, promises, Bäckström,' Carin sighed.

She must have heard about the super-salami, she's so damn keen, Bäckström thought, as he heard a familiar knock at his door. 'Got to go,' he said. 'There's something I need to deal with. Speak soon.'

Rogersson was carrying a whole six-pack of chilled lager, and was apparently in an extremely good mood.

'I've just been talking to our colleagues up in Stockholm,' he said, grinning with the whole of his skinny, pock-marked face. 'They told me an incredible story about Chinny that I think my dear colleague Superintendent Åström would appreciate a very great deal.'

'I'm listening,' Bäckström said. Just watch yourself, you old drunk, he thought.

The story that Rogersson told him included all the usual additional material that stories accumulate as soon as they get passed from one mouth to another. This particular story had passed through several mouths on its way from the bathroom mirror of the Grand Hotel in Lund to Rogersson's keen ears.

'Absolute carnage. Apparently he shot up half the hotel,' he concluded with a cheery grin five minutes later.

'He must have got his chin caught in the trigger guard when he was cleaning his gun,' Bäckström suggested. 'If it had been you or me, we'd be sitting in a cell down in Malmö by now.'

'Who says life's fair?' Rogersson said, shaking his head and pouring the last drops from the first can into his glass.

'Does Dolly Parton sleep on her stomach?' Bäckström agreed.

'Funny that there hasn't been a word about it in the papers,' Rogersson said.

'I'm sure that can be arranged,' Bäckström said with a grin. 'I'll have a word with our good colleague Åström and see if he can mention it to some of our more obliging vermin.'

# 35

The following morning the *Småland Post* ran a long article about a serious cultural argument that had broken out in town. Jan Lewin had immediately decided to cut it out and add it to his scrapbook.

The chief prosecutor and current member of parliament for the Christian Democrats, Ulf G. Grimtorp, had gone into battle against the populist and ultimately morally corrupting ideas that appeared to dominate the activities of the cultural department of Växjö Council.

One project in particular had incurred his wrath. It was designed to appeal to the town's migrant women. It was called the cycle-swimming programme, and was basically intended to teach young immigrant women to ride bicycles and swim. A three-week residential summer school had been arranged, in relaxing rural surroundings, with a private lake, instructors, bicycles and swimming aids. All fourteen participants had learned to both ride a bike and swim, and had graduated with top marks.

Three of them had been interviewed by the paper, and declared unanimously that the physical accomplishments they had acquired would also help them to advance in life in a purely intellectual sense. Freeing themselves from the usual patriarchal chains that restricted their lives and those of their fellow women. Gaining strength, freedom and self-respect, and therefore being able to fulfil the most basic requirements for being able to apply themselves to more traditional cultural interests and values.

The official from the council's cultural department, Bengt A. Månsson, who was responsible for this and other so-called special projects, described the cycle-swimming project as an almost un-precedented success.

'If you assume that this has nothing to do with culture, you haven't understood the first thing about what culture actually is,' project leader Månsson declared. They were planning to follow up this initiative during the winter with a project to teach women to ski and skate, the ski-skating project.

According to Mr Grimtorp, MP, this was utter rubbish. A feeble and transparent excuse for various radical left-wing male cultural elitists to go sunbathing in the company of young women at the expense of hard-working taxpayers.

'Two hundred thousand kronor,' Grimtorp thundered. 'And what does this have to do with culture?'

Money which in Grimtorp's decided opinion ought to have been earmarked for the work of Växjö Town Theatre, the local chamber orchestra, the library, and associated activities. Not to mention the fact that the project was also threatening the number of grants given to the many promising young glass-blowers, artists and sculptors in and around Växjö.

That Grimtorp seems a miserable sort, Jan Lewin thought, and for some reason he started thinking about the summer almost fifty years before when he had been given his first proper bicycle. A red Crescent Valiant. Probably the same Valiant as in the cartoon about Prince Valiant. He had asked his dad, and his dad had told him all about the noble knight Prince Valiant.

Prince Valiant had lived a very long time ago, in the days when there weren't any bicycles. So instead, Valiant had a horse. A powerful red stallion that seemed as obstinate and difficult to control as Jan's first bicycle. The horse was called Arvak, Jan's dad told him, and he was given that name in honour of another horse, Arvakr, from Norse mythology, the horse that pulled the sun across the sky, and must have had its work cut out during that summer almost fifty years ago when Jan learned to ride a bike.

He had read all about this and much more in the cartoon about Prince Valiant in *Allers Weekly Journal*. Jan and his dad had spent a whole evening going through a load of boxes and crates in the loft above the old cowshed at their place out in the country. They must have found a hundred old magazines, each containing a story about the noble knight Prince Valiant, and before Jan went to bed he and his dad would read one or sometimes two cartoons about his exciting adventures.

Mind you, it was all a bit odd, Jan thought. His dad had told him his bicycle was called a Crescent Valiant after Prince Valiant. But Prince Valiant had had a red horse called Arvak, seeing as there weren't any bicycles in those days, so why wasn't his bike called an Arvak Valiant instead of a Crescent Valiant? And who was Crescent?

Maybe Crescent was the prince's first name, Jan thought. Prince Crescent Valiant. He'd ask his dad in the morning, because he knew a lot about most things, but then he had fallen asleep and as far as he could remember almost fifty years later he had never got round to asking the question.

# 36

The same morning that the cultural argument was raging in the pages of the *Småland Post*, the CP group had emailed their analysis of the murder of Linda Wallin, with a profile of the perpetrator. And the head of the group, Detective Superintendent Per Jönsson, had announced that he and one of his colleagues would be arriving in Växjö just after lunch the following day in order to discuss their findings in person with the members of the investigating team.

Bäckström spent Wednesday morning reading through the twenty-page report, groaning and sighing in turn. But as far as the actual crime itself was concerned, they did seem to have worked out what every intelligent police officer could work out for himself, Bäckström thought.

That the perpetrator hadn't broken into the flat by force, that he already knew the victim, that intercourse appeared to have been initiated in a relatively straightforward way, particularly considering what happened later. That it started with the victim and the perpetrator having sex on the sofa in the living room, without any indication that it was forced intercourse on the part of the victim. Then they had moved into the bedroom, where the level of both violence and sexual activity had escalated rapidly, that the perpetrator had strangled her during or after the final anal assault, that he had gone into the shower, masturbated and washed himself off, and finally left the crime scene through the bedroom window.

After that it was time for the usual reservations that no murder detective worthy of the title had any use for, except for saving them up for nightmares. Such as the fact that it couldn't be ruled out that Linda might have forgotten to lock the door, or that the perpetrator had snuck into the flat or tricked her into letting him in. That he might have used force from the start by holding a knife to her throat – for instance, the knife that had been found at the crime scene – and had forced her to take off her jewellery, watch and clothes, and used threats to get her to take part in various sexual activities, from the sofa in the living room to the bed in the bedroom where she was strangled. Nor was it impossible that the perpetrator, in the worst-case scenario, could be someone she had never met before.

In light of the accompanying profile, and considering who the victim was, this seemed the most likely explanation. According to the profile, the perpetrator was a man between twenty and thirty years of age. He lived close to the crime scene, or used to live there, or had close links to it somehow. He probably lived alone; his previous relationships had been difficult; those around him thought him odd; he had difficulty maintaining social relationships, or even long-term friendships; he was unemployed or got short contracts doing some sort of simple work.

He was also seriously psychologically disturbed. His personality demonstrated clear chaotic and irrational elements. He had problems with his attitude to women. Based upon traumatic childhood experiences, he actually hated women, without either him or anyone around him necessarily being aware of the fact. But he most definitely wasn't an ordinary sexual sadist with well-developed sexual fantasies.

He had an explosive temper. Faced with the slightest problem he could completely lose control of himself, and he was quick to resort to violence. These characteristics were bound to have manifested themselves before, and strongly suggested that he already had a police record, with reference to various violent incidents, but also drug-related crimes. Last but not least, he was physically strong. Strong enough to overpower and strangle a twenty-year-old woman who was training to join the police, and in better shape than most people her age of either sex. He was capable of lifting twenty kilos more than his own weight when he was in the gym. And he was also agile enough to jump out of a window four metres above the ground.

He also leaves his shoes on the rack in the hall. Neatly placed together. And no one saw him creeping away, even though he wears size 55 shoes, Bäckström thought with a deep sigh.

In spite of this, Superintendent Per Jönsson appeared to have made a deep impression on the qualified majority of his audience when, after spending an hour presenting his findings, he opened the floor to questions.

'I dare say you have a number of questions,' Jönsson said, smiling warmly at the gathering. 'Please, go ahead. Feel free to ask about anything that's on your minds.'

Excellent, Bäckström thought. Maybe you could start by explaining why all the proper officers in National Crime think you're a bit of a worm.

'Well, if no one else wants to jump in, perhaps I could go first,' Olsson said, glancing imperiously round the table.

Great, Olsson, Bäckström thought. Start by asking the bastard why his colleagues at National Crime call the CP group the X-Files.

'I'd like to start by thanking you for taking the time to visit us down here,' Olsson began. 'But mostly for your extremely interesting presentation. No doubt many of my colleagues around the table would agree with me when I say that I'm quite sure that the analysis that you and your colleagues have provided will be of decisive importance in our investigative work.'

But not to any proper police officers, Bäckström thought. Because things can't be so bloody awful that we have to pin our hopes on little wormy Jönsson and his random ideas.

'One thing in particular struck me when I read your report,' Olsson went on. 'Your description of the perpetrator. I can't help but envisage yet another criminally inclined and socially excluded young man.'

'Yes, there's a lot to suggest that that's exactly the sort of man we're looking for,' Jönsson agreed. 'But of course it's far from conclusive,' he added quickly.

'You mean, bearing in mind the fact that the majority of the evidence suggests that Linda opened the door and let him in?' Enoksson said.

'Well, yes, although of course people do sometimes forget to lock their doors behind them when they get home,' Jönsson said. 'Or the victim might have been far too trusting and let someone in, someone who in hindsight she really shouldn't have.'

'Yes, how on earth are we going to work that out?' Enoksson said, sounding as if he were thinking out loud.

'I've got a question, if you don't mind?' Adolfsson suddenly said, even though he was sitting as far away as possible.

'By all means,' Jönsson said, smiling his most democratic smile.

'I was thinking about what the National Forensics Lab said. That the perpetrator's DNA could mean that we're looking for an outsider,' Adolfsson said.

'An outsider?' Jönsson said, staring questioningly at Adolfsson.

'Yes, not a Smålander,' Adolfsson clarified. 'Someone from else-where, if I can put it like that.'

'I understand what you mean,' Jönsson said, suddenly looking very cagey. 'I think we should be very careful about that sort of hypothesis. We're talking about research which is still in its . . . early stages, so to speak,' Jönsson said, stopping himself at the last moment from saying what was on the tip of his tongue.

'Because otherwise the profile fits a lot of migrants here in town pretty well,' young Adolfsson persisted. 'Very well, in fact. If you want to know what a uniform thinks.'

'I don't think we can get much further on that point,' Jönsson said. 'But, as I said, I think I'd be very careful about drawing that sort of conclusion. Any more questions?'

Quite a few, it had turned out. In total, it had taken three hours. Three more hours gone to hell, Bäckström thought when it was finally over.

'Fly carefully, Pelle,' Bäckström said, smiling his most jovial smile when Jönsson said goodbye. 'And don't forget to say hello to everyone working on the files.'

\*

That evening after dinner Bäckström had once again gathered the faithful in his hotel room. He had already briefed Rogersson, and just like Bäckström the detective inspector had felt the pleasant tingling once Bäckström had told him. Adolfsson and von Essen had also been invited, seeing as they had done a lot of the work, and it was always an advantage to hear things from the horse's mouth. Really it was just a matter of letting Lewin and little Svanström in on the secret, even though Bäckström knew in advance what Lewin would think about it.

Was I right, or was I right? Bäckström thought when Lewin knocked on his door ten minutes early so he would have time to talk to Bäckström alone. 'What can I help you with, Lewin?' he said, smiling amiably towards his guest.

'I'm not entirely sure that you can, Bäckström,' Lewin said. 'I've said it before, and I'll say it again. You can't run your own investigation within an investigation and exclude the majority of your colleagues.'

'So you'd rather keep on reading everything in the paper, then?' Bäckström said.

'Don't be silly,' Lewin said. 'You know I wouldn't. No more than you or anyone else. But if you ask me, and considering the choice we seem to have, I'd rather try to live with that and not carry on the way you seem to be going.'

'Do you know what?' Bäckström said, smiling cheerfully at his guest. 'I'd rather you listen to what Adolfsson and his partner, and our colleagues Knutsson and Thorén, have to say before you make your mind up.'

'If you think that'll change anything,' Lewin said with a shrug.

'Once you've listened to them, I'll let you decide how we proceed,' Bäckström said.

'Really?' Lewin said, surprised.

'Oh, yes,' Bäckström said. Suck on that, he thought.

First von Essen and Adolfsson presented the results of their work.

'He's the last sexual partner that we know Linda had, and he lied about it when he was questioned,' von Essen said. 'According to what he and other people say, he leaves the hotel alone, some time between half past three and four. If he walks quickly he can be at Linda's flat in five minutes, and he hasn't got an alibi for the rest of the night.'

'The shoes, the underpants?' Lewin said. 'What do his lady friends have to say about them?'

'Bearing in mind the fact that those details haven't been made public by those in charge of the case, we haven't asked,' Adolfsson said. 'But they're the sort of thing that pretty much every other Swedish man is wearing at this time of year.'

Lewin made do with a nod.

Then Knutsson and Thorén presented their findings, and even Lewin looked concerned when they discussed the first telephone conversation their colleague Sandberg had had with Löfgren.

'In light of what the report says, I don't see how she could have fitted all those questions into just four minutes,' Knutsson said.

'A very efficient woman,' Thorén said cheerfully.

'But we can't rule out the possibility that she called him on his land-line instead,' Lewin said.

'No,' Thorén said.

'Not yet,' Knutsson amplified. 'Telia are making a fuss about his landline, because the account's in his dad's name. Our usual contact there got cold feet.'

'So, what do you say?' Bäckström said, looking slyly at Lewin. 'How do you think we should proceed?'

'Well, it's certainly a bit tricky. There's something that doesn't make sense in all this,' Lewin said. 'I was going to suggest that I talk to the prosecutor first thing tomorrow. She seems competent, and pretty solid. I'm sure she'll decide that we can pull the lad in for questioning without any prior warning, and if he carries on being obstructive she'll just have to declare him a formal suspect so we can get a DNA sample regardless of whether or not he wants us to.'

'That sounds like a quite excellent suggestion,' Bäckström said with a smile. 'You fix the prosecutor, and I'll get one of the lads here to get in enough supplies for us to celebrate properly when the little bastard's finally behind bars.'

# 37

## Växjö, Thursday 24 July

As soon as Rogersson had told him about the massacre in the Grand Hotel, Lund, Superintendent Åström had whispered confidentially in the ears of three different journalists. In spite of that, not a single line had appeared in the papers about that unsettling event. Those bloody vultures can't be trusted to look after anything, Superintendent Bäckström thought angrily.

Instead the first evening papers of the day, as well as the normal morning papers, were full of the usual. The mass-murderer from Dalby had been relegated to the inside columns once they had polished off the teary interviews with the survivors. The Linda murder was back in the lead, and the crush around the breakfast buffet at the Town Hotel in Växjö had swollen considerably.

At the morning meeting they were able to announce more than four hundred DNA samples taken, and another fifty of the volunteers had been discounted from the investigation. One of these was Linda's neighbour, Marian Gross, and his departure was mourned by no one, least of all Bäckström, who already had a far better perpetrator up his sleeve. Besides, Superintendent Olsson had had an idea that boded well for their work.

Taking the CP group's profile as his starting point, Olsson had made a number of demographic calculations, and had come up with the idea that they wouldn't need to take DNA samples from any more than five hundred people in Växjö and the surrounding district to cover everyone who fitted the profile. And once he had spoken to a statistician from the town council, he had realized it was actually even better than that.

'He told me about something called mathematical expectation,' Olsson explained. 'That's some sort of numerical hocus-pocus, but if I've got it right, then we should only have to take samples from about half the five hundred, if we were to do it entirely randomly, that is.'

What the hell is he going on about? Bäckström thought. In his book, it would be enough to get a sample from just one person. 'If you'll accept an honest tip from an old policeman, might I suggest that you restrict yourself to so-called outsiders,' he said.

'Don't you worry, my dear Bäckström,' Olsson said, apparently in an excellent mood. 'I've been around a while, and know a bit about Pappenheimer bodies. *Ich kenne auch meine Pappenheimer,*' he added proudly in his best schoolboy German, acquired on the open university course he and his wife had been studying since they went on a wine-lovers' tour of the Rhine Valley the previous summer. 'Don't forget that you promised to come along to our meeting.'

'Don't worry,' Bäckström said. What the hell has Pappenheimer got to do with anything?

After the meeting Detective Superintendent Jan Lewin spoke to both the prosecutor and the head of the preliminary investigation, Superintendent Olsson. Bäckström was conspicuous by his absence, however, which didn't appear to bother Lewin at all.

'So there's something not quite right about this young man,' Lewin concluded when he had outlined the case.

'Enough to call him in without prior warning?' the prosecutor asked.

'Yes,' Lewin said. 'But if he still refuses, I'd like to get a sample anyway. If nothing else, then to rule him out.'

'If he carries on lying and behaving in this childish way, I'll remand him in custody. And while he's sitting there in his cell thinking things over, we can get both fingerprints and a blood sample,' the prosecutor said. 'This is a murder investigation, after all, and I'm not the least bit amused by what he seems to be up to.'

'But is that really necessary?' Olsson suggested, squirming in his seat. 'I mean, he's still one of our own trainees, and he's not remotely like the perpetrator identified by the CP group in their analysis. I'd much rather—'

'In that case, it's probably just as well that it's my decision,' the prosecutor interrupted. 'The CP group,' she snorted. 'That's usually nothing but complete fantasy. As far as I know, they've never helped solve a single case. Certainly never any of mine.'

In the afternoon Bäckström kept his promise and attended the meeting of the newly formed committee of Växjö Men Against Violence to Women. He was given coffee, carrot cake and biscuits, and the chair of the committee, psychologist and psychotherapist Lilian Olsson, had begun by warmly welcoming him.

'Well, you already know me and your colleague Bengt Olsson,' Lo said. 'Bengt has also agreed to be a deputy member of our little committee. But you haven't met the others before, so I thought perhaps that as our guest you could start by introducing yourself to the rest of the committee members: Moa Hjärtén; our second Bengt, Bengt Karlsson,' she said, smiling at a lanky blond fellow who smiled back just as warmly, 'and our third Bengt, Bengt Axel Månsson.' She gave a friendly nod towards a short, thin, swarthy man at the far end of the table.

'Thank you, Lo, for inviting me,' Bäckström said, folding his hands over his bulging stomach and smiling extra piously towards the three people who had just been named. Two poofs in trousers, and someone in a sort of pink shift. How practical that all the poofs seem to be called Bengt, he thought.

'Well, my name is Evert Bäckström . . . although my friends call me Evie,' Bäckström lied. He hadn't had a proper friend in his whole life, and had been known as Bäckström even when he was in primary school. 'What else can I tell you? Well . . . I work as a detective superintendent in the murder squad of the National Crime Unit . . . and, as so often before in my life, I have been brought here by extremely tragic circumstances.' Bäckström nodded sombrely and sighed. A little something for the poofs to suck on, he thought.

'Thank you, Evie,' Lo said, with warmth in her voice. 'Well . . . perhaps we should carry on with our other fellow menfolk. Please,

Bengt,' Lo said, nodding towards the short, thin, swarthy man who was cowering behind his coffee cup and carrot cake at the far end of the table.

'Thank you, Lo,' Bengt said, then cleared his throat nervously. 'Well . . . my name is Bengt Månsson, and I work with cultural matters at the council here, where I have responsibility for what we call special projects, and our new foundation will be part of that work as a subsidiary project.'

Quite a little sweetie, and bloody similar to that equalities bloke in the government. The one whose mother must have been with a horse, whatever the hell his name is, Bäckström thought. He tried not to overload his brain with names that didn't belong to crooks, bandits and decent fellow officers. 'Yes, that can't be an easy job,' he said. 'All those projects, I mean,' he added.

'No,' Månsson agreed, instantly looking a bit happier. 'There's a lot involved in it, and I spend a lot of time managing the costs so that they don't—'

'Well, perhaps we should move on to our second Bengt,' Lo interrupted, for some reason evidently reluctant to go into detail on that point, and nodding instead to the rudely truncated Bengt's colleague, who was blond and blue-eyed, twice the height of little Bengt, and in some peculiar way seemed to hang across both his chair and the table, whilst simultaneously beaming with warmth and empathy.

'My name's Bengt Karlsson, and I manage the men's helpline here in town,' big Bengt said. 'We offer advice and counselling, and even behavioural therapy for abusing men here in Växjö. Abusing, not abused,' he emphasized, 'and, as I'm sure you can imagine, I'm not short of work.'

I can imagine, given the number of crazy women around. Anyway, you used to be a thug, Bäckström thought, because when it came to that sort of diagnosis he was just as confident as a country doctor distinguishing patients with mumps from those who just had swollen adenoids.

'Just little me left, then,' twittered the woman in the pink shift.

You're not that fucking little, Bäckström thought. You're three times the size of little Lo, if that's any comfort.

'Well, my name's Moa, Moa Hjärtén. And I'm sure you're wondering what someone like me does, Evie?'

You're in charge of the women's helpline, the victims of crime helpline, and all the other bastard bleeding heart helplines in the world, Bäckström thought, nodding encouragingly at her to go on.

'Well, I'm in charge of the women's helpline here in town, and chair of the crime-victims' helpline . . . and let's see, what else . . .'

Was I right or was I right?

'Well,' Moa went on, 'I also run a private home where we offer sheltered accommodation for women who've been raped and abused. And beyond that I don't really have too much time.'

Congratulations, Bäckström thought. If you're running it privately, you can't be entirely stupid.

Then the newly founded association was granted the opportunity to enjoy Superintendent Bäckström's expertise as one of the country's foremost experts in really violent crime. As his colleague Olsson had explained to him before, there were two things that the group was particularly concerned about: that they would be regarded as vigilantes, and that they would attract men with frivolous, unclear or possibly even criminal motives.

Bäckström did his best to reassure them.

'To summarize what I have already said, I don't think you need to worry about that,' he concluded. Although he was a Spiritual Man, he might have started to sound a touch pompous towards the end. 'And as far as the second matter is concerned, I have no doubt that you are already sufficiently good judges of character to be able to separate the wheat from the chaff.' And you, my dear fellow, I shall personally ensure that we take a good look at, he thought, smiling in a specially friendly way at committee member Bengt Karlsson.

After the meeting the committee met representatives of the media, but Bäckström had declined, pleading the National Crime Unit's policy on such matters.

'However much I might want to participate, I'm afraid I simply can't,' he said, still wearing the same pious smile as two hours earlier at the start of the whole thing.

Lo and her friends were full of understanding, and Bäckström returned to the investigation's main office to make his own small contribution.

'Can you have a look at this bastard,' he said, handing over a note with Bengt Karlsson's name and description.

'Of course,' Thorén said, surprised. 'Pardon me for asking, but why do you want to look him up? Isn't that . . .'

'Very hush hush,' Bäckström grinned, holding his right index finger to his lips.

As soon as he had got the go-ahead from the prosecutor, Lewin had sent von Essen and Adolfsson to Öland to pick up aspiring police officer Löfgren. Going by the most recent call he had made on his mobile, he was in all likelihood still at his parents' summer house outside Mörbylånga. Because Adolfsson was going, Bäckström had lent them his car. And given them a couple of pieces of advice.

'If you type in the address in the computer the bastard car finds its own way there,' Bäckström said. 'And if you have to hit the fucker, make sure you do it outside the car to save getting blood on the seats.'

'A new record,' Adolfsson said one and a half hours and 170 kilometres later, as he pulled up at the entrance to the Löfgren family's place in the country. A large wooden house, painted yellow, rather grand, with crunching gravel paths, large shady trees and a splendid view of the Kalmar Sound. And, on the lawn in front of the house, the very person they had come to pick up. Wearing running shoes, shorts and a sleeveless T-shirt, and busy stretching his long, muscular legs.

'What can I help you gentlemen with?' Löfgren asked amiably.

'We'd like to talk to you,' Adolfsson said, equally amiably.

'It'll have to be tomorrow. I'm about to go for my daily run,' Löfgren said, and set off with a wave in completely the wrong direction for Växjö.

Von Essen set off after him out of reflex, and to his credit managed to keep Löfgren within sight for several hundred metres before the student was swallowed up by the undergrowth and his pursuer was left standing there, doubled over and gasping for breath.

'Twenty-five degrees in the shade, and still you can't stop yourself from trying to keep up with a black man,' Adolfsson said, leaning back comfortably in one of the garden chairs when his partner returned to the house.

'Have you spoken to the parents?' von Essen asked, nodding towards the house.

'Doesn't look like anyone's home.'

'Let's call Lewin,' von Essen decided.

'What do you mean, ran off?' Lewin said over the phone five minutes later.

'What do you mean, ran off?' Olsson repeated another ten minutes later.

'Ran off. So he just ran off?' the prosecutor asked on her mobile after another fifteen minutes.

'He just ran off,' Lewin confirmed. 'So what do we do now?'

'What do we do now?' Olsson repeated when Lewin called him for the second time in half an hour.

'The prosecutor decided that we should sleep on the matter, and if we don't get hold of him tomorrow she's going to issue a formal arrest warrant,' Lewin said.

'So why the hell didn't you run after the fucker and beat him to death?' Bäckström roared. He was just as red in the face as von Essen had been two hours earlier, even though Bäckström hadn't got out of his chair all afternoon.

'We didn't actually have the chance, if you see what I mean, boss,' Adolfsson said.

'You don't really want to jeopardize any future interview by shooting someone just like that,' von Essen suggested in the conciliatory tone of voice that was part of his noble birthright.

Watch yourself, you fucking poof, Bäckström thought, glaring slyly at his aristocratic colleague. Personally, he wouldn't have had a moment's hesitation in calling out the dogs and the helicopters, and closing off the damn bridge to that island, he thought.

# 38

## *Växjö, Friday 25 July*

Over breakfast the following morning, Bäckström read the *Småland Post* for the first time in his life. The main local paper had devoted a good deal of coverage to the newly established association, Växjö Men Against Violence to Women, and what had particularly captured Bäckström's attention was the photograph of the association's committee that covered half the front page. In the centre stood the chairperson, Lo Olsson, with Moa Hjärtén to her right and Superintendent Bengt Olsson to her left. On the flanks stood little Bengt Månsson and big Bengt Karlsson, twice his size. They were all looking seriously into the camera as they held each other's hands.

What a load of idiots, Bäckström thought happily.

But the paper didn't appear to share Bäckström's opinion. The association was described in glowing terms, and was even honoured by a mention in the editorial, in which the editor-in-chief, in an unusually poetic turn of phrase, described the police as 'an inadequate and poorly maintained fence trying to hold growing levels of criminality at bay'. The editor also declared that private law-and-order initiatives like this not only were desirable, but also should be taken very seriously indeed. 'Even those of us living in such a predominantly peaceful town as Växjö have to realize that the battle against ever increasing levels of crime is actually our shared responsibility,' he concluded.

Where the hell do they get all this shit from? Bäckström thought, putting the paper in his pocket so that he could laugh to his heart's content as soon as he was shut inside his office.

*

Lewin, as was so often the case, had spent the night in Eva Svanström's bed, but after she had fallen asleep he had lain there for another hour, worrying about what young Löfgren was actually up to. As soon as he got to work, he pulled out various files relating to the investigation, read them carefully, and then, after further thought, decided that he had probably worked out what was really going on. But because he had occasionally been wrong before, he called in von Essen and Adolfsson and asked them to check something for him.

'There's an old tip-off that I'd like you to follow up for me. I did mention it at our morning meeting on Sunday 6 July, and it probably isn't that exciting, but I'd still like you to have a word with the informant for me. His name's Göran Bengtsson. Here are all the details,' Lewin said, giving the note to von Essen.

'Gurra Yellow and Blue, yes, we know him,' von Essen said, shaking his head.

'Sorry,' Lewin said. 'What did you call him?'

'Gurra Yellow and Blue, or just Yellow and Blue. That's what he's known as in town,' Adolfsson explained. 'Partly because he's politically tainted, as it's so politely termed, and partly . . .'

'. . . because of the brown colours of the political palette, if I can put it like that,' von Essen interjected.

'He and his friends got a serious going-over when they tried to celebrate the Swedish Flag's Day here in Växjö a couple of years ago,' Adolfsson went on. 'A load of thugs from the Anti-Fascist League and similar groups showed up, and Gurra and his friends got badly beaten up. Before we got the situation under control, they'd beaten him just as yellow and blue as his beloved flag.'

'He says he saw Linda with a fucking big ni— a fucking big man,' Lewin corrected himself, 'at about four o'clock on the morning of the murder.'

'Yes, that's not a particularly rare observation on his part, and our student Löfgren is far from being the only black man here in Happy Valley,' von Essen said. 'Not these days, anyway.'

'I'd still like you to go and talk to him. And I'd like you to show him some photographs, starting with Löfgren,' Lewin said, handing over a

224

transparent folder containing photographs of nine young black men, one of them Löfgren. 'Then I'd like you to move on to Linda, and it's important that you do it in that order.' He handed them another plastic folder holding nine photographs of young blonde women, including one of their murder victim, Linda Wallin.

As von Essen and Adolfsson were ringing on the door of Yellow and Blue's basic one-room flat in the centre of Växjö, Erik Roland Löfgren the police student stepped up to the reception desk in the police station on Sandgärdsgatan. He had with him a lawyer from Kalmar, who happened to be an old family friend, and he appeared in the nick of time. The prosecutor had just decided to issue a formal arrest warrant as a result of his absence.

Gurra Yellow and Blue was sitting at his computer playing a game that he had downloaded from the home page of the American organization White Aryan Resistance. Some of the computer geeks at WAR had put together a more ethnically focused variant of the old classics Desert Storm I–III, and Yellow and Blue was on a roll when von Essen and Adolfsson paid him a visit.

'New top score,' Yellow and Blue said, his cheeks glowing with excitement. 'I wasted three hundred and eighty-nine blunt-nosed fuckers in just half an hour.'

'Have you got a few minutes for a chat?' Adolfsson asked.

'Always happy to help the cops,' Yellow and Blue said. 'It's the duty of every Swedish citizen. It's war now. We've got to close ranks if we don't want the blacks to win.'

Löfgren wasn't quite as enthusiastic as he sat in the interview room with Rogersson, who was leading the session, and Lewin as the official witness. To start with, he had been just as formal as his aged legal representative, who was three times his age.

'Why do you think we want to talk to you, Löfgren?' Rogersson began, after the usual introductory remarks for the recording's benefit.

'I was hoping you could tell me,' Löfgren said with a polite nod.

'You haven't worked it out for yourself?' Rogersson asked.

'No,' Löfgren said, shaking his head.

'In that case I'll tell you,' Rogersson said. 'I can understand that you must be curious.'

Löfgren made do with another nod, suddenly seeming more watchful than curious.

'Hell, I've called loads of times and asked what the hell happened about my tip-off. It's obvious the nigger did it,' Yellow and Blue said. 'One of your colleagues must be protecting him. The police force is crawling with blacks working as officers now. Check them out, and you'll get the killer.'

'What did you do when you saw them?' von Essen asked.

'I said hello to that Linda. I recognized her, didn't I? I'd seen her down at the cop shop.'

'So what did you say, more precisely, I mean?' von Essen persisted.

'I asked if she didn't have anything better to do than go home and suck on a stick of liquorice,' Gurra said, smiling gleefully at them. 'Yes, and then I said something about the risk of HIV as well. Hell, those liquorice cowboys are walking biological bombs, when you think about all the shit they're carrying.'

'Then what happened?' Adolfsson asked.

'The nigger went mad and started running at me, and his face was really dark blue, and I thought that you wouldn't even want to touch that one because you'd die of herpes. At best. So I ran off.'

'And it was then about four o'clock in the morning, and the incident took place on Norra Esplanaden, some five hundred metres from the Town Hotel?' von Essen said.

'Affirmative,' Yellow and Blue said. 'Circa four o'clock, by the roundabout next to the health centre.'

'We've got some pictures we'd like you to take a look at,' von Essen said. 'Do you recognize any of these men?' He laid out the photographs of Löfgren and the eight others.

'In the interviews conducted by one of my colleagues, you deny categorically that you had a sexual relationship with Linda,' Rogersson said. 'The way you describe it, she was an ordinary classmate.'

'We were in the same class at college. But you already know that.'

'Yes,' Rogersson said. 'We know that. And we also know that you had sex with Linda. Why didn't you mention that?'

'I don't know what you're talking about,' Löfgren replied stubbornly. 'I never had any sort of relationship with her.'

'It's a simple question,' Rogersson sighed. 'Have you ever slept with Linda. Answer yes or no.'

'I don't understand what that has to do with anything,' Löfgren said. 'Anyway, I don't talk about things like that. I'm not that sort.'

'According to your friends, you're precisely that sort,' Rogersson said. 'We've spoken to a number of them, and according to them you recently spent several months boasting about all the times you fucked Linda.'

'Rubbish,' Löfgren said. 'I never talk about that sort of thing, so that's complete rubbish.'

'Complete rubbish, you say,' Rogersson said. 'If you've never slept with her, then all you have to do is answer no.'

'You don't seem to understand what I'm saying,' Löfgren said.

'I understand exactly what you're saying,' Rogersson said. 'And I know that you lied when you were being questioned by the police, and now I'm hearing with my own ears how you're trying to avoid answering a simple, straightforward question.'

'Which doesn't have anything to do with anything. I didn't kill Linda. If you think I did, you're mad.'

'Assuming that you're innocent, then you won't mind providing a DNA sample so we can discount you from the investigation,' Rogersson said, gesturing instructively at the test-tube containing the cotton-bud that was sitting beside the tape recorder.

'I've no intention of doing any such thing,' Löfgren said. 'Seeing as I'm innocent, and you haven't got a shred of evidence. What this is all about, and this is exactly what it is, is you trying to get rid of a future black officer.' Löfgren looked as upset as he sounded. 'That's what this is about. The rest is just bullshit.'

'And I'm telling you that you're lying, and the fact that you're lying to the police in a murder investigation which just happens to concern one of your classmates is enough to make me and my colleagues suspicious of you,' Rogersson said. 'For us, there's nothing more to it than that.'

'And that's enough for you,' Löfgren said heatedly. 'You're not even listening to—'

'Not just for us,' Rogersson interrupted. 'The prosecutor is just as curious as we are.'

'Pardon me for interrupting,' the lawyer said, 'but it would be interesting to hear the prosecutor's opinion of this.'

'It's very simple,' Rogersson said. 'If Löfgren continues lying and refusing to provide a DNA sample, she will consider him a formal suspect and he will be remanded in custody.' Rogersson exchanged a glance with Lewin, who nodded.

'In that case, I would like it noted in the records that I don't share her opinion,' the lawyer said.

'Noted,' Rogersson said. 'And I presume you are aware that if you wish to pursue the matter further, it isn't the police you should turn to. One final question for you, Roland, before we arrest you—'

'I've got an alibi,' Löfgren interrupted. 'Is that something your generation ever learned about? What an alibi is, I mean?'

'It was him,' Gurra Yellow and Blue said, smiling triumphantly and holding up the photograph of Erik Roland Löfgren.

'There's no rush, Gurra,' von Essen said. 'Take your time.'

'I tend to think they all look the same,' Adolfsson said. 'How can you be so sure?'

'You're talking to an expert,' Yellow and Blue said. 'I'm as good at niggers as Eskimos are at snow, or those Lapp bastards are at reindeer. Take this one, for instance.' He waved the picture of Löfgren. 'Typical blue nigger. Africa, if you ask me. But not just any Africa, because we're not talking Eritrea or Sudan or Namibia or Zimbabwe, and we're definitely not talking Masai. We're not even talking Kikuyu or Uhuru or Watutsi or Wambesi or Zulu or—'

'Hang on, hang on,' Adolfsson interrupted, holding up his hands to stop him. 'What part of Africa *are* we talking about? Never mind all the niggers that we're not talking about.'

'If you ask me, we're talking west Africa, Ivory Coast, maybe.

Basically old French west Africa, the Frogs' niggers,' Yellow and Blue said, nodding like a man who knew what he was talking about.

'Thanks for your help,' von Essen said. 'Just one more question. If you wouldn't mind taking a look at our pictures of girls as well.'

'Come off it, Count,' Yellow and Blue said. 'Try listening to what I'm saying. I've spoken to her, when I was in the cop shop, I told you. It was her. I'm a hundred and ten per cent sure.'

'Which one of these was it, then?' Adolfsson asked, nodding towards the photographs of Linda and the other eight young women.

'Tell me,' Rogersson said. 'Tell me about your alibi.'

'I wasn't alone when I left the hotel. I was with someone, and we went back to my place,' Löfgren said. 'I was with that person until approximately ten o'clock that morning.'

'When you were questioned you said you went home alone,' Rogersson said. 'So that was a lie as well? Okay, give me a name. What's the name of the person you went home with?'

'I've already told you. I don't discuss names,' Löfgren said.

'That's not much of an alibi, then,' Rogersson sighed. 'Not from what I've ever learned about alibis, anyway. From the little I remember, the teachers kept going on about the fact that it was important to know who was providing the alibi.'

'I don't discuss names,' Löfgren repeated. 'Is that really so hard to understand?'

'So what do you say now, lads?' Yellow and Blue said, holding up the photograph he had picked out.

'And you're absolutely sure it was her?' von Essen said, exchanging a glance with Adolfsson.

'What do you mean, absolutely sure? I'm a hundred and ten per cent sure, I told you. I've spoken to her more than once down at your very own cop shop. She was a proper little bitch, if you want to know what I think.'

'There's something funny about what you're saying,' Rogersson said, looking at Löfgren sceptically.

'What do you mean, funny?' Löfgren said. 'I don't see anything funny in any of this.'

'Your friends say you boasted to them about all the times you fucked Linda. In your own words. All the times you fucked Linda, as well as plenty more even worse phrases that I don't intend to embarrass either you or your legal representative with by repeating.'

'That's up to them,' Löfgren said. 'I haven't said anything.'

'But when it comes to leaving the Town Hotel, on the other hand, you told them that you went home alone. There's even someone who saw you going home alone. You said you were going home to get some sleep.'

'So what? I don't have to sit here and defend what other people have said. Besides, it looks like someone wants to talk to you,' Löfgren said, nodding towards the door, which was slowly opening after a discreet knock.

'Have you got a couple of minutes, Lewin?' von Essen asked from the other side of the door.

'This trick's as old as the hills,' Löfgren said to his lawyer. 'One of the lecturers at college told us . . .'

'Two minutes,' Lewin said, getting up and going out, carefully shutting the door behind him.

'I think we have a small problem,' von Essen said.

'I thought we might have, ever since first thing this morning,' Lewin said with a sigh.


'What did I say?' Löfgren said triumphantly, patting his lawyer on the arm. 'Five minutes, not two. What did I say?'

'Excuse me for interrupting, gentlemen,' Lewin said, looking at Rogersson for some reason. 'Have I got it right if I say that you're refusing to give the name of the person you claim could provide you with an alibi?'

'Good that you finally get it,' Löfgren said. 'Absolutely right. That's actually your job, not mine.'

'Well, it's good to know that we agree on something, at least,' Lewin said. 'In that case I would also like to inform you that the time is now 14.05 on Friday 25 July, and that the prosecutor has decided to remand you in custody. This interview is thereby suspended, and will recommence at a later point. The prosecutor has also decreed that we should take your fingerprints and a DNA sample.'

'Hold on a moment,' the lawyer said quickly. 'Wouldn't it be better if I could have a few moments to discuss matters alone with my client, so that we can try to find a more practical solution to this little problem?'

'I suggest that you take the matter up directly with the prosecutor,' Lewin said.

'Bloody hell, Lewin, you were suddenly in a hell of a hurry,' Rogersson said sourly five minutes later when they were alone in the room.

'So would you have been,' Lewin said.

'What for?' Rogersson said. 'If you'd given me another hour I'd have got the name of his so-called alibi out of him, if there is one, and got him to stick the cotton-bud in his mouth.'

'That's what I was afraid of,' Lewin said. 'That we'd end up having to deal with a hell of a lot of paperwork.'

'I don't actually understand what you mean,' Rogersson said.

'Let me explain,' Lewin said.

'I can hardly wait,' Rogersson said with a crooked smile, leaning back and making himself comfortable. 'Bloody hell,' he grinned five minutes later. 'When are you thinking of telling Bäckström?'

'Now,' Lewin said. 'As soon as I can get hold of him.'

'I want to be there,' Rogersson said. 'Then we can both try to hold the fat little bastard down before he starts attacking the furniture.'

This is going to be a wonderful day, Bäckström thought. Only ten minutes before he had seen Adolfsson and von Essen go past in the corridor on either side of a crestfallen Löfgren, clearly heading towards the cells. As if that weren't enough, Thorén had turned up in his office with the results of the check on committee member Bengt Karlsson, from Växjö Men Against Violence to Women.

'This Karlsson looks like he used to be a really nasty piece of work. Not a very nice person at all,' Thorén said.

'How do you mean?' Bäckström said. Not that I know what I'm going to do with him, seeing as the black guy's already locked up, he thought.

'He's got a total of eleven offences on record,' Thorén said. 'And his speciality seems to have been abusing women he was seeing.'

'Right man in the right job,' Bäckström declared happily. And definitely the right man to use to take the wind out of little Lo and that idiot Olsson's sails, he thought.

'The only problem is that the most recent entry is nine years old,' Thorén said.

'I suppose he's learned his lesson,' Bäckström said. 'He probably wraps a towel round his fist before he hits them now. Dig up all the shit you can find,' he concluded, seeing Lewin and Rogersson standing in the doorway looking like two egg-bound hens. 'Come in, lads, come in. Young Thorén here was just leaving.'

'So, tell me,' he said eagerly as soon as Thorén had closed the door behind him. 'Did you get him to talk himself into a corner? I saw Adolfsson and that stuck-up poof he drags around with him taking him off to the cells.'

'Sorry to disappoint you, Bäckström,' Lewin said. 'But both Rogersson and I are fairly convinced that Löfgren isn't the man we're looking for.'

'I love it!' Bäckström said, chuckling happily. 'So what the hell's he been locked up for, then?'

'I'll get to that,' Lewin said. 'But you should probably start getting used to the idea that he's innocent.'

'What for?' Bäckström said, leaning back in his chair.

'He's got an alibi,' Rogersson said.

'An alibi,' Bäckström snorted. 'Who the fuck would give him an alibi? Martin Luther King?'

'He doesn't want to say,' Lewin said. 'So we thought we'd lock him up before he had time to change his mind.'

'But Lewin's worked it out anyway,' Rogersson said happily.

'So who are we talking about, then?' Bäckström said, leaning forward and peering at them through narrow eyes.

'We think this is what happened,' Lewin said. 'Young Löfgren leaves the Town Hotel at quarter to four in the morning. He makes a big deal out of the fact that he's leaving alone, to go and get some sleep. He stops and waits a couple of blocks away for the woman he secretly arranged to meet while they were inside the club. She shows up just after four, and they both go back to Löfgren's flat and get on with the sort of thing people usually get on with in circumstances like that.'

'So who is she?' Bäckström said, even though he had already guessed the answer.

'Our colleague Anna Sandberg, according to a witness that we've spoken to,' Lewin said.

'I'll kill the little bitch!' Bäckström roared, getting up from his chair with a jolt. 'God help me, I'll—'

'No you won't,' Rogersson said, shaking his head. 'You're going to sit down, nice and quietly, before you give yourself a stroke or something worse.'

Whatever the hell that might be, Bäckström thought, sinking back on to his chair. She has to die.


Trainee police officer Löfgren was allowed to leave the holding cell in Växjö police station before the door had even had time to close properly. An hour or so later he was in the car with his lawyer, on his way back to his parents' summer house on Öland. He had also sworn to the prosecutor that he would be there for the foreseeable future, and would answer his phone if the Växjö Police needed to talk to him for any reason. The prosecutor had even given him a few words of advice before he left. Without going into detail, she had suggested that he might like to take some time to think about his plans for his future career. Löfgren had left behind him a set of fingerprints, a cotton-bud containing his DNA, and, as an extra bonus, a couple of strands of hair. All of it in all likelihood completely worthless to the current murder investigation.


While the local custody officer took care of the practical details concerning Löfgren's prints and cotton-bud, Lewin was busy tidying up after himself and his colleagues. First he had exacted a promise of silence from those most closely involved in Bäckström's secret operation, and then he had sat down with officer Sandberg to have a serious chat with her.

Bäckström had eventually calmed down. The worst of his anger had passed even though he was still up to his neck in the wreckage of the promising case that his useless – not to say criminally incompetent – colleagues had utterly ruined. For once Bäckström felt deeply miserable, because he had been so sorely and unfairly maltreated. He was surrounded by idiots, and it was high time he found something better, he thought as he stepped out into the shimmering heat outside the police station, on his way to the soft bed in his air-conditioned hotel room, with a stop to buy some drink on the way.

He began by forcing down the two chilled lagers that were already in his minibar, mainly to make room for the ones he had just bought. However, the customary pleasant sense of wellbeing failed to settle over his mind and body. Things might just be so bad that that little Sandberg bitch had sabotaged not only his investigation, but also his inner peace, he thought. In the absence of any better options, he switched on the television and lay there half watching a cultural discussion programme which the listings said would deal with the murder of Linda Wallin, but was actually just the usual poofs blowing smoke up each other's arses.

Shipwrecked-Micke, famous from both ordinary *Shipwrecked* and *Celebrity Shipwrecked*, and a second-year student at the Institute of Drama in Malmö, had applied for funding for a drama-documentary about Linda's murder. The cultural department of Växjö Council had turned him down flat, but he had managed to find a private investor willing to support the project. The script was pretty much ready, and the role of Linda would be played by a young woman called Carina Lundberg, better known to most people in Sweden as Big Brother-Nina. She had taken part in *Big Brother* and in *Young Entrepreneurs* on the new financial channel, had spent some time at theatre school, and was now making a name for herself in the cultural offerings of the state-funded broadcaster. She and Micke had known each other for a long time, and she trusted her director implicitly, even though the role of murder victim was far from easy. She was particularly anxious about the lesbian scenes, especially the ones in which she and her female co-star would be wearing police uniform.

What the fuck's she saying? Bäckström thought, turning the volume up and sitting up on the bed.

'Of course, a lot of young female police officers are dykes,' Nina explained. 'Almost all of them, actually. I've got a friend in the police, and she told me.'

'I've set it up as a classic triangle drama,' Micke explained. 'You've got Linda and the woman she loves, who's also a police officer, called Paula, and then there's the man, the killer, full of hate and jealousy and rejection. His castration anxiety. It's Strindberg, it's Norén, it's . . . classic male drama, basically.'

'Yes, it certainly sounds like it,' the presenter chimed in enthusiastically. 'And of course that's what this is all about. Another castrated man.'

Boiling these cretins down to make glue would be doing them a favour, Bäckström thought, switching off the television just as his phone rang, even though he had made it very clear to reception that he didn't want any calls.

'Yes,' Bäckström grunted.

Fucking hell, he thought as he hung up.


Bengt Karlsson, committee member of Växjö Men Against Violence to Women, had piqued Detective Inspector Peter Thorén's interest to the point where, even though it meant breaking the promise of confidentiality he had given Bäckström, he had felt obliged to let Knutsson into the secret. Mind you, it probably doesn't matter much, considering what Bäckström was doing to that poor student, Thorén thought.

Bengt Karlsson was forty-two years old. Between the ages of twenty and thirty-three he had collected a total of eleven convictions for violent behaviour against seven different women of his acquaintance aged between thirteen and forty-seven when the crimes were committed. The convictions were for aggravated abuse, physical abuse, unlawful threats, unlawful compulsion, aggravated sexual abuse, sexual exploitation and sexual harassment. These had led to

Karlsson's being given seven different terms in prison, totalling four and a half years, of which he had served approximately half.

'An interesting character,' Knutsson agreed when he had read through the summary Thorén had produced from all the various registers and databases and electronic paraphernalia that the judicial system had at its disposal these days.

'But why does he stop?' Thorén asked. 'The last conviction was nine years ago. Since then there hasn't been a single complaint against him.'

'Maybe he changed his modus operandi?' Knutsson suggested. 'Do you remember that thief who moved on to blowing up cash machines? He must have managed about a dozen before we worked it out. And all the while he was going round schools giving lectures about how he'd managed to break away from his criminal past.'

'He might have moved away from women he knows, ones he lives with or has gone out with, to women he doesn't know at all?' Thorén said, as if he were thinking out loud.

'Quite possible,' Knutsson said. 'Extremely possible, in fact. But there's something else that's struck me. Do you remember that lecture out at the Police Academy back in the spring, from that FBI officer?'

'I remember the one,' Thorén said. 'Nothing but sex crimes. That was the FBI bloke's speciality, if I remember rightly. Seemed to be pretty much the only thing in his head. Sex crimes.'

'Then maybe you remember what he said about the sort of sex offender who plays cat and mouse with the people trying to investigate him? Who gets a really big kick out of standing very close to the people chasing him?'

'Not really,' Thorén said. Could it really be that simple, he thought, and at that moment he felt the tingling sensation that his older colleague Detective Superintendent Bäckström had felt about trainee police officer Erik Roland Löfgren.

'We need a DNA sample,' Knutsson said. 'That man definitely has to be tested. God knows how we're supposed to manage that without the rest of the committee and Superintendent Olsson finding out.'

'It's already sorted,' Thorén said, not without a certain degree of pride. 'It turned out that a sample of Karlsson's DNA was already on record down in Malmö. He got caught up in some routine search in conjunction with the Jeanette murder five or six years ago. Mind you, that one's still unsolved, so he must have been okay.'

'So why didn't they get rid of the sample?' Knutsson asked.

'That's not the sort of thing you throw away just like that,' Thorén said indignantly. 'The National Forensics Lab obviously discarded their sample, because they had to, but our colleagues in Malmö kept a copy of the results in their files relating to the case. I've already got hold of it and faxed it through to the National Lab.'

Bäckström was still lying in bed, with a couple of extra pillows stuffed behind his back, looking like a perfectly ordinary overweight patient in a cardiac ward. She deserves no better, the little bitch, he thought, as he gestured towards the minibar with a fat, limp hand.

'If you'd like a chilled lager, Anna, there's one in the minibar,' he said. Suck on that, you criminal little bitch, he thought.

'You haven't got anything else?' Anna Sandberg asked. 'I've finished work for the day, and I'm staying over in town. I could do with something stronger.'

'Whisky, vodka, on the shelf over there,' Bäckström said, pointing. What the fuck's going on?

'Thanks,' Anna said, pouring a measure almost worthy of Rogersson himself in her glass. 'Do you want one?' she asked, waving Bäckström's own bottle of whisky enquiringly.

What the fuck's going on? Bäckström thought again. First she sabotages my investigation, then she comes bursting into my room, and a minute later she's offering me my own whisky.

'Maybe just a little one,' he said.

Police Constable Anna Sandberg had come to apologize to Bäckström. She had made a damn fool of herself – her own words – and Bäckström was the first stop on her hike to Canossa. In so far as she had anything to say in her own defence, it was that Löfgren had promised over the phone that he would behave like a gentleman and immediately provide a DNA sample. Entirely voluntarily, and obviously completely unnecessarily, but, in light of what had happened, the simplest solution for both of them.

The reason she hadn't been to see Bäckström to lay her cards on the table when Löfgren, in spite of his promise, had refused to come up with the goods was simply yet another example of human frailty. Partly because she had kept hoping that Löfgren would come to his senses, or at the very least help her out of a tricky situation, but largely because she had no idea what Bäckström and his colleagues were planning. Her chat with Lewin had changed all that.

'There are quite a few people I need to talk to. You, Bäckström, and Olsson, and my husband. Not least my husband,' she said, shaking her head and taking a deep gulp from her glass.

What? Bäckström thought. Women really aren't right in the head. 'Are you stupid? Surely you're not thinking of telling Olsson about this?'

Evidently that was exactly what she was thinking. It was just as well to take the bull by the horns, get to grips with the shame and, if it came to it, leave the police force and do something else instead.

'That's none of my business,' Bäckström said. 'But I can't see why you want to tell Olsson.'

'Before he works it out for himself,' Sandberg said sternly. 'I'm not going to give him that satisfaction. Nor anyone else, for that matter.'

'Correct me if I'm wrong,' Bäckström said, 'but I'm talking about Detective Superintendent Bengt Olsson. The Ritual Killer detective from the backwoods of Småland, who ends up deep in troubled thought every time he gets up from the toilet and finds he's holding a piece of paper in his hand.'

'So you don't think I should tell Olsson?' Sandberg asked, suddenly looking much happier.

'No,' Bäckström said, shaking his head. 'Nor anyone else. Lewin and Rogersson have already talked to anyone who knows anything, so they'll just shake their little heads if you try to talk to them. Forget it.' Women are just crazy, he thought.

'What about my husband?' Sandberg asked. 'He's also in the force, but of course you know that.'

'Does he get turned on by hearing stuff like this, then?' Bäckström asked with a look of mild distaste. But, considering her husband was a neighbourhood officer, there was every reason to fear the worst, he thought.

'I find that very hard to believe,' Sandberg said.

'Well, then,' Bäckström said with a shrug. 'What you don't know can't hurt you.'

Anna Sandberg nodded thoughtfully. 'Can I have another?' she asked, indicating her empty glass.

'Sure,' Bäckström said, holding out his own. 'Get me one as well. Just a small one.'

It's a shame little Lo isn't here. She could have picked up a few tricks from an old professional, Bäckström thought. Sandberg already looked like a different, better person. Even her tits had perked up and were starting to look like their old selves. After just a couple of stiff drinks and few wise words, he thought.

'Well, bollocks to all that, Sandberg,' Bäckström said, raising his glass. 'No one becomes a police officer. It's just something you are, and a real police officer never shops a colleague.' Even if it's a woman who should never have been allowed to join the force in the first place.

That evening, after the now customary dinner in the hotel restaurant, Bäckström and Rogersson returned to Bäckström's room, to talk through the case in a relaxed setting, and work out how best to proceed now that young Löfgren had faded from the investigation. Eventually both the lager and the spirits had run out, and Bäckström was so far gone that he wasn't in a fit state to accompany Rogersson down to the bar to round off the evening. He spent Saturday catching up on his sleep, and naturally the lazy and unreliable hotel staff took the opportunity to exploit his tardiness by not bothering to clean his room or replace his dirty towels.

# 39

During the night between Saturday and Sunday, while Bäckström was lying asleep in his unmade bed in the Town Hotel, another woman was attacked, right in the centre of Växjö, and just a few hundred metres from the hotel. The victim was a nineteen-year-old woman who was walking home alone after a party. When she opened the door to the building she lived in on Norrgatan at about three o'clock in the morning, an unknown man attacked her from behind, shoved her into the lobby, knocked her to the floor and attempted to rape her. The victim screamed and fought for her life. Several neighbours were woken by the noise and the perpetrator ran from the scene.

Within fifteen minutes everything was in motion. The victim had been taken to hospital. The crime scene was cordoned off, duty officers and forensics experts were on the spot questioning witnesses and looking for evidence. Three patrol cars were driving round looking for anything suspicious in the neighbourhood, reinforcements were on their way, and the phones of the team investigating the Linda murder were starting to ring. Detective Superintendent Olsson had his phone glued to his ear out at his summer house as he tried to pull his trousers on with his free hand, while trying to remember where he had put his car keys. Detective Superintendent Bäckström was still sleeping soundly. He had learned from previous experience to switch off his mobile phone and unplug the telephone in the room at night.

When he came down to breakfast on Sunday morning and Rogersson told him what had happened, it was pretty much all over, and it was already apparent that some of the details were distinctly unclear.

'I spoke to Sandberg a short while ago,' Rogersson said.

'What did she say?' Bäckström asked.

'That there was something funny about the victim,' Rogersson said. 'Sandberg thinks she might have made the whole thing up.'

Little Sandberg, bloody hell, Bäckström thought. It's amazing, the things you hear, he thought.

That evening Bäckström called his very own radio reporter, but just like the previous weekend he only got through to her answer machine. Aged mother, Bäckström thought, and in the absence of any better options he ordered food and beer up to his room and lay there channel-surfing for half the night, until he finally fell asleep.

Jan Lewin had started dreaming again.

Sweden, the mid-1950s. The summer of Jan Lewin's seventh birthday, before he started school that autumn, and when he got his first proper bicycle. A red Crescent Valiant.

Grandma and Grandpa's summer cottage out on Blidö in the Stockholm archipelago. Mum, Dad, and him. The sun shining day after day in a cloud-free sky. A proper Indian summer, his dad says, and for once his dad's summer holiday never seems to end.

'Why's it called an Indian summer, Daddy?' Jan asks.

'That's just what it's called,' Daddy replies. 'When it's an unusually long, hot summer.'

'But what's that got to do with the Indians?' Jan persists. 'Why do people call it an Indian summer?'

'I suppose they normally get better weather than us,' Daddy replies, then he laughs and ruffles Jan's hair, and it seems a good enough answer.

That summer his dad taught him to ride a bike. Gravel tracks, clumps of nettles, ditches. The smell of creosote. Daddy running behind him, holding on to the saddle while Jan clutches the handles in his sweaty little hands and pedals as fast as he can with his skinny, sun-tanned legs.

'I'm going to let go now,' Daddy shouts, and even though Jan knows that he has to pedal and steer at the same time, it just doesn't work. Either he pedals or he steers, and sometimes Daddy isn't in time to catch him. Scraped knees, bruised shins, burning nettles, sharp thistles and thorns.

'Let's try again, Jan,' Daddy says, ruffling Jan's hair, and off they go again.

Steer and pedal, steer and pedal, and Daddy lets go and again he doesn't get there before Jan falls off. And when he turns round he doesn't see his dad about to help him up. He sees his colleague Bäckström, standing there grinning at him.

'How fucking stupid can anyone be, Lewin?' Bäckström says. 'For fuck's sake, you can't just stop pedalling because I'm not pushing you.'

Then he had woken up, padded out into the bathroom, and let the cold water run as he massaged his eyes and temples.

# 40

## Växjö, Monday 28 July

At the week's first morning meeting of the investigative team, the head of the preliminary investigation, Detective Superintendent Bengt Olsson, was able to announce that they had set a new Swedish record. The Olssonian DNA-sampling offensive in Växjö and the surrounding district was rolling on unchecked, and during the weekend they had passed five hundred voluntary samples, not to mention a bloody paper handkerchief and an apple-core. Their future colleague, trainee police officer Löfgren, had been discounted from the investigation with the help of the usual cotton-bud, while their mentally troubled colleague Claesson had been dropped thanks to his own healthy eating habits, and without his having any idea of what had happened.

Unfortunately, Detective Superintendent Jan Lewin took the opportunity to tell them how the previous record had been set. He and National Crime had been involved on that occasion as well. Another murdered woman, up in Dalarna. Close to five hundred samples had been obtained in that case, but sadly the Petra murder was now several years old, still unsolved, and practically abandoned. Then Lewin had made the mistake of deciding to add a far too lengthy personal observation on the subject.

'I remember my first murder investigation involving a young woman,' he said, sounding as if he were talking out loud to himself. 'It's almost thirty years ago now, so a lot of you sitting here weren't even born then. The Kataryna murder, as it was called in the papers. In those days we'd never even heard of DNA, and we all knew that if we were going to solve our cases we almost always had to do it the old-fashioned way, without a lot of forensic help and scientific methods. Forensics was something they did in court once us ordinary officers had found the man who did it.'

'Sorry, Lewin,' Bäckström interrupted, pointing at his watch. 'What do you think about getting to the point before lunch? Because the rest of us have quite a bit to do.'

'I'm getting to that,' Lewin said, unconcerned. 'In those days our clear-up rate for murder cases was over seventy per cent. Today we manage to solve less than half, in spite of all the new technology and all the new methods. I can't believe that our cases today are that much more difficult than they used to be.'

'So what do you think it depends on?' Sandberg suddenly asked. 'You must have given it some thought.'

'Oh yes, I've certainly given it some thought,' Lewin said. 'Take this business of DNA, for instance. When it works, then obviously it's a tremendous resource. If you find good DNA evidence, like in this case, and if you find the person who left the evidence.'

'So what's the problem?' Sandberg persisted.

'If it's good DNA, then there's a risk that you get so carried away that you neglect everything else. 'All the good old-fashioned and systematic police work.'

'You mean, to catch the person who did it you can't just run about like headless chickens?' Sandberg said with a smile.

'Yes, that's one way of putting it,' Lewin said.

The final point on the programme that morning was Sandberg's presentation of what they now knew about the assault early on Sunday morning.

'So many of the details are so vague that I can't help feeling she might have made it all up,' she said.

'But why would she have done that?' Olsson said. 'That's surely not the sort of thing anyone would make up?'

'I'm getting to that,' Sandberg said, suddenly sounding very like her twenty-years-older colleague, Detective Superintendent Jan Lewin.

There were no witnesses who saw either the attack inside the lobby of the building, or even a glimpse of the perpetrator. There was absolutely no forensic evidence, even though Enoksson and his colleagues had literally hoovered up everything from the alleged crime scene and in its immediate vicinity. All they had was the victim's own story, about an assault that she managed to fend off by putting up fierce resistance. She claimed to have both bitten and scratched her assailant. There was also her description of the attacker.

'There's nothing wrong with the description,' Olsson insisted. 'I think it sounds very good. What is it she says? A single attacker, about twenty years old, well built and in good shape, approximately 180 centimetres tall, black baseball cap, black T-shirt, baggy black jogging trousers, a pair of those white running shoes, tattoos on both arms. Some design with curling black snakes or dragons on both upper arms, stretching down past the elbows almost to his wrists. And he threatened her in English, but with such a thick accent that she's sure he wasn't English or American. Probably eastern European or something like that. It's no secret, at least not to those of us based here, that that's often exactly what they look like. It's actually starting to be quite a problem.'

'Yes, it's a fantastic description,' Sandberg agreed. 'Considering what she was going through at the time, she certainly made sure she got a good look.'

'I agree with you, Anna,' Bäckström grinned. 'She seems to be a very alert young lady. And it matches the profile we got perfectly. And it looks like she's also found the time to appear in both the evening papers and on television, to say how terrible it was. She'll probably be presenting the weather on TV3 soon, or flashing her tits on that farm where they make that programme.'

'Thanks, Bäckström,' Sandberg said for some reason. 'That's one of the things that's been bothering me. Normally girls who've been subjected to something like this can't even bear to look at themselves in the mirror. They can hardly talk, even to those closest to them. They just want to be left in peace.'

Bäckström had risen from the ashes left by trainee police officer Löfgren, had already identified his next prey, and quickly jumped back into the flames again. Immediately after the meeting he took young Thorén aside to find out how he was getting on with committee member Karlsson.

'You were absolutely right, Bäckström. Mr Karlsson doesn't seem like a very nice person,' Thorén said, before giving a quick outline of his findings.

'We need a DNA sample from the bastard,' Bäckström said keenly.

'Already sorted,' Thorén said, and explained about their colleagues' previous efforts in Malmö.

'Why the hell didn't you tell me that before?' Bäckström asked crossly. 'Is it a secret or something?' Running round like headless chickens, he thought.

'Sit down, Lewin, sit down,' Bäckström said warmly, gesturing towards the visitor's chair in front of his desk. 'How are things going with your own little constructions? Are you starting to make any sense of them?'

'I'm sure they'll work out,' Lewin said neutrally.

He also had two concrete proposals that might offer a step in the right direction. First, to interview Linda's mother again. The two interviews that had already been conducted hadn't been sufficiently thorough, in Lewin's opinion. If he wanted to be critical, they didn't really provide anything that they wouldn't have been able to find out without talking to her. And he also wanted them to have another go at trainee police officer Löfgren.

'You know I always listen to you,' Bäckström said generously. Even though you were on the point of fucking up half the force with that black bastard, he thought.

'My suggestion is that we get Rogersson to interview Linda's mother,' Lewin said. 'Rogersson's extremely thorough when it comes to that sort of thing.'

'Yes, it's odd, isn't it?' Bäckström agreed. 'Even if he drinks like a Russian and keeps running to the toilet.'

'I've never noticed that,' Lewin said curtly. 'But you're probably better informed than me on that point, Bäckström.'

'There's been some talk, if I can put it like that,' Bäckström said with a grin. 'What about the black? Who's going to deal with him?'

'If you mean young Löfgren, I was actually thinking of talking to him myself,' Lewin said. 'I have a feeling he might be more willing to talk now that he's no longer a suspect.'

'Bound to be. It'll be a breeze this time,' Bäckström agreed. And you, Lewin, will probably end up getting the Nobel Prize sooner or later.

# 41

Linda's mother was at her summer cottage out on Sirkön, in the middle of Lake Åsnen, some twenty kilometres south of Växjö. She had a female friend staying with her, and according to her Linda's mother was concentrating on surviving from one day to the next. However, she understood that the police were keen to talk to her, and was willing to oblige as best she could.

'Thank her from me,' Rogersson said. 'I'll be there with one of my colleagues in about an hour.'

'Do you need any directions?' the friend asked.

'I think we'll be okay,' Rogersson said. 'If we get lost I can always call again. Do tell her how grateful I am that she's prepared to talk to us.'

Bäckström had decided to keep his friend Rogersson company. He felt like getting out of town for a bit. Preferably in a comfortable, air-conditioned car, where he and Rogersson could talk crap in peace and quiet about all the non-present idiots who were otherwise ruining his life. Besides, he was also a bit curious about Linda's mother.

'Down there on the left is the lake,' Rogersson said half an hour later, nodding towards the blue water shimmering between the birch trees in the sun. 'It's only another ten kilometres or so to Sirkön. Classic territory for people like you and me, Bäckström.'

'I thought all the strong spirits were made in Skåne?' Bäckström said, already feeling much brighter in spite of the undeserved slings and arrows that had struck him recently.

'Swedish criminal history,' Rogersson explained. 'One of our most notorious disappearances of the past century. Up there with Viola Widegren from 1948. This was where little Alvar Larsson disappeared from his parents' home on a cold and windy April morning in 1967.' He sounded almost ceremonial. 'I read an interesting article about the case in the *Nordic Crime Chronicle* a few years ago. Didn't sound like a murder. He probably just tumbled into the lake and drowned while he was outside playing.'

'I don't believe that for a minute,' Bäckström said. 'Of course he was murdered. By one of those paedophiles. There must be loads of them down here. Sitting in their little red cottages downloading kiddie porn from the internet.'

'But hardly in 1967,' Rogersson said. 'From the internet, I mean.'

'Well, they'd have got up to some other shit back then,' Bäckström said. 'Sitting in their outside toilets wanking over a pile of old newspapers with pictures of Scouts skinny-dipping. How the fuck should I know?'

'You seem to know almost everything, Bäckström,' Rogersson said. 'But I think what I appreciate most about you is your view of humanity. You're a truly warm person, if I can put it like that.'

What the fuck's got into Rogersson? Bäckström thought. He's acting seriously hungover. I just hope Linda's mum's as generous with the beer as her dad was.

A little red cottage with white woodwork, an old guardian tree shading the little patch of gravel in front of the house where they parked the car, flagpole, lilac arbour, outside lavatory at one end, jetty, boathouse and sauna, and its own little strip of beach down by the lake. Neatly raked paths through the large garden, where two carefully placed boulders marked the edges of the trimmed lawn.

In short, the very picture of the Swedish summer idyll, and obviously they all sat outside, round the table in the lilac arbour. No beer, of course, but an equally unquestionable jug of homemade blackcurrant cordial with plenty of ice and tall stemmed glasses, probably from some local glassworks for a price that would buy several crates of ordinary export-strength lager. And if you and your eyes weren't somewhere else entirely, you'd be a damn fine woman,

Lotta Ericson, Bäckström thought. Forty-five years old, but under normal circumstances I'm sure you look considerably younger than that.

'Just say if you find this is getting the least bit difficult for you,' he said in his very gentlest voice.

'I don't think it'll be a problem,' Linda's mother said, and if it hadn't been for her eyes, he'd almost have said she sounded chirpy.

I wonder how much Valium they've stuffed into you since you woke up, you poor thing, Bäckström thought.

During the following three hours Detective Inspector Jan Rogersson gave convincing proof of the thoroughness that his colleague Lewin had attested to. First he had asked her about Linda. About her childhood and upbringing. About the years in the US, about the divorce and what it had been like when the two of them returned on their own to Sweden.

'A happy, carefree little girl, who liked everyone, and everyone liked her, and I suppose it was always like that with Linda, even when she was older . . .

'A difficult period in our lives . . .', 'getting used to a new environment . . .', 'Linda made new friends, started a new school . . .', 'I got a new job as a teacher while I was still studying . . .', 'when I met my husband I was working as a secretary . . . that's how we met . . .', 'then, once we were married and I had Linda and we moved to the US, I was mostly just a trophy wife . . .', 'I was terribly bored, although Henning took to it like a fish to water. The person Linda and I saw least of was probably her dad . . . in fact, we hardly ever saw him . . .

'But of course, in a financial sense I was very privileged. We might have had a prenuptial agreement, but the first thing he did before Linda and I moved back to Sweden was give me the building where . . . where it all happened . . . and we lived there until Linda suddenly . . . that was when she was already in high school . . . decided that now that her father had deigned to come home, she wanted to live with him out in the country . . . although as soon as she wanted to be back in town she'd live with me again . . .'

Boyfriends?

'The first one was probably a little black boy who was in the same class as Linda when we lived in the States . . . Linda was only seven, the same as him . . . his name was Leroy, and he was so sweet you just wanted to eat him all up . . . that was probably the first time Linda fell in love . . .'

After that? Boyfriends that she had a sexual relationship with?

Not many, according to her mother, albeit with the proviso that Linda always kept very quiet about things like that. The longest relationship Linda had been in had lasted about a year, and came to an end about six months ago.

'The son of some family friends. One of the few families that I still see since I divorced my ex-husband. Another very nice boy, went by the name Noppe, although his real name's Carl-Fredrik. I think Linda simply got fed up with him. It got too much for her once she'd started at police college.'

Was Linda ever difficult, did she ever argue, did she have any enemies, could there even be anyone who wished her harm?

Not in her mother's world. Not when it came to her beloved daughter, because when she was at her worst she was probably like most teenage girls were most of the time – Lotta had realized that from friends with daughters the same age – but Linda wasn't often like that. Bad sides? Linda could be very stubborn. And she could be a bit naïve. A bit too trusting, believing people were better than they really deserved.

During his twenty years as a murder detective, Rogersson had conducted hundreds of interviews with close relatives of murder victims. So it was no surprise that Linda's mother herself was the last point on his list of questions, and no surprise at all that she reacted the same way all the others before her had. Why did he want to talk about her? She didn't have anything to do with Linda's murder. She was a victim as well. Someone had snatched her only daughter from her, and she was expected to live on with nothing but her grief to cling to.

Rogersson gave her the usual answers. That this was about finding Linda's murderer. That he had absolutely no suspicion that Linda's mother might have had anything to do with the crime, but that the actual point of someone like him and his questions was that he sometimes uncovered things that the mother of a murdered daughter might not notice, precisely because her grief stopped her from seeing them. She took it better than most of them did.

Had she seen any new men since the divorce from her husband? Had any of them ever shown any interest in her daughter? Had she ever met anyone who could possibly want to harm her by attacking her only child?

Naturally, she had seen other men since the divorce. Several, in fact, but they had mostly been short or even fleeting relationships, and the most recent of them had been several years ago now. Someone she worked with, someone one of her friends worked with, someone else she met through work, even the divorced father of one of her former pupils. And several brief encounters with other men, mostly when she was on holiday abroad. She had actually fallen for one of those, and had kept in touch for a while. But it hadn't led to anything, and had dwindled to phone calls, then emails, with increasingly large gaps between them, before finally silence.

Must have been gay, Bäckström thought. Blind and gay.

The thought that one of these men could have murdered her daughter was completely impossible to imagine. They just didn't belong in that context, that wasn't the sort of man she ever met, most of them had never met Linda, and at least a couple of them didn't even know that she had a daughter.

'She must have been attacked by a complete maniac,' Linda's mother said. 'As I said, Linda thought the best of everyone. She could actually be very naïve at times.'

'What the hell were we doing out there?' Bäckström asked in the car on their way back to the police station. 'That didn't give us anything at all.' Suck on that, you pedantic bastard, he thought.

'There was nothing wrong with that cordial, considering that it was just cordial,' Rogersson retorted. 'For a while I got the impression that there was something she suspected, or was still trying to work out. Something on her mind.'

'And what the hell would that have been?' So Rogge isn't just an alcoholic, Bäckström thought, he's got second sight as well.

'I haven't the faintest idea,' Rogersson replied. 'Just a feeling, really.

I've been wrong before.' He shrugged. 'Right now her head must be complete chaos. I wonder how many tranquillizers they're pushing into her.'

'If you ask me, she was completely gone,' Bäckström said. Like most women, just considerably better looking, he thought.

'And that might well be a good enough reason to go back and talk to her again,' Rogersson said.

'Well, if nothing else, she's a damn fine woman,' Bäckström declared. 'Once she's back to normal, I mean. Let me know when you're going again and I'll tag along.'

# 42

Even though trainee police officer Löfgren was a changed person, almost accommodating, and even though he seemed to be telling the truth in all important respects, Lewin still thought he had shown his better side the first time he had met him, when he mostly sat there and messed them about.

Now that Erik 'Ronaldo' Löfgren had been eliminated from the murder investigation, his gentlemanly reservations about discussing his sexual relationship with Linda seemed to have vanished. The first time had been in the middle of May, at Linda's father's house out in the country. The plan had been to watch a football match on television together. But rather more than that had actually happened, and they had carried on for more than a month, until the end of term at police college when everything had come to an end. They had met on their own on four or five occasions, all of them with the exception of the first in Löfgren's lodgings in Växjö. On one occasion they had gone to the cinema, and on another they went to a coffee shop, but mostly they had sat and watched television and DVDs, just relaxing or having sex with each other.

'So which one of you ended it?' Lewin asked.

That wasn't entirely clear, according to young Löfgren. It was probably coming to an end of its own accord anyway, but if someone had taken the initiative, then it was probably him.

'Things weren't really going anywhere,' Löfgren said with a shrug. 'Linda was a great girl, lovely, and really quite pretty, and there was nothing exactly wrong with the sex either, but it wasn't brilliant. It wasn't like I was moping about at home when she wasn't there or anything. So I suggested we could maybe rewind a bit and just be ordinary friends again. Not even fuck-buddies, in fact.'

What sort of sex had they had? What sort of sex did Linda prefer? And who had taken the initiative and made the decisions, if there was anything like that in their relationship?

Ordinary sex, normal sex, not too much, and not too little, in Löfgren's estimation, and the one responsible for anything happening was him.

'She was in good shape and all that. And she used to come, as long as I worked at her. I was in the driving seat and she used to ride along, if I can put it like that. It wasn't bad, it just wasn't brilliant. I know I shouldn't talk about her like this now she's dead, but seeing as it seems to be so important for you . . . Maybe a six, six and a half maybe, out of ten, but some of that's because she was pretty good-looking. She wasn't very experienced, and . . . and I know this sounds harsh . . . she didn't have that glint in her eye.'

'I understand that you're an experienced man when it comes to women, and that's why I'm going to ask this question.' Lewin nodded thoughtfully towards Löfgren, though really he felt like picking up his chair and smashing him over the head with it. 'You never got the impression that Linda was really after slightly harder sex? If you really wanted to get her going, I mean?'

'No,' Löfgren said in surprise. 'I would have noticed if she had been. I mean, if that was the case, then she would have got it. I'm absolutely sure she just wanted to go through the basic programme, so that's what she got.'

Linda's previous boyfriends, her relationship with her parents, friends of either gender?

They hadn't really talked much about that sort of thing. Although she mentioned her ex-boyfriend. A complete disaster in bed, according to what Linda had told Löfgren. As far as friends were concerned, they had mostly talked about her female friends. Which wasn't so odd, in Löfgren's opinion, seeing as he knew a lot of them and had even slept with a couple.

'Did Linda know that?' Lewin asked.

'No. Are you mad, Lewin? No one knew about it. That's the first rule. Never tell girls that sort of thing. Only girls are allowed to tell other girls that sort of stuff. It's a typical girl thing. I mean, if I slept with the girlfriend of one of my friends, I wouldn't be stupid enough to tell him. You'd find yourself looking for new kneecaps.'

'So Linda might well have known that you'd slept with two of her friends?' Lewin summarized.

'If she did, she never mentioned it,' Löfgren said sourly. 'But sure.' He shrugged his shoulders. 'Girls talk a fuck of a lot, after all.'

According to Löfgren, there was one person who seemed to have meant more to Linda than everyone else put together. Her dad.

'Talk about a daddy's girl,' Löfgren said. 'Everything seemed to revolve about her damn father. It looked like she got everything she ever wanted, without even having to ask. It was pure Beverly Hills. I don't know if you've met him, but they're . . . or rather, they were . . . pretty damn similar. If they'd been the same age, you would have thought they were twins. He used to call her all the time as well. One evening when she was round mine, he called her mobile three times. And they used to talk constantly, even though they didn't really have anything to say. Hello darling, hello Daddy, I forgot to say, darling. All that sort of thing, if you get what I mean.' Löfgren pretended to hold a phone to his ear.

'You didn't like Linda's father?'

'I don't think I had a problem,' Löfgren snorted. 'It was more like he did.'

'I thought you only met him once?' Lewin said.

'Once was more than enough,' Löfgren said. 'I could tell right away what he thought of me. About people like me, I mean.'

'What do you mean?'

'Black men,' Löfgren said. 'In his world, nothing else mattered. Someone like me was fucked from the start. It was probably no coincidence that he lived in the US for years. Linda's dad was a real racist.'

'But Linda wasn't like that?'

'No, her thing seemed to be that you should like people like me. I'm sure she really did as well. Really liked people like me precisely because that was who we were. And how great do you think that makes you feel?'

'Did you and Linda ever talk about that?' Lewin asked. Can't have been very nice if it's true, he thought.

Once, according to Löfgren. He had actually said what he thought of her father, that he thought he was racist.

'She got furious,' Löfgren said. 'Mind you, she agreed with me, but all she kept saying was that it wasn't the old man's fault. Some sort of generational thing, and that he was really the kindest man in the world, and for him it was all about individuals, all that bullshit.'

'What about her mother, then?' Lewin wondered. 'What did she think of her mum?'

'Not much, if you ask me,' Löfgren said with a crooked smile. 'They used to argue like crazy all the time. I heard them going at it over the phone once. Complete cat-fight.'

'I thought Linda used to live at her mother's quite a lot?'

'When she was in town, yes, and when she knew her mum wasn't at home. Otherwise she used to go back to her dad's. Sometimes she'd even get a taxi from town to take her out there, even though it must have cost – what? – five hundred kronor or so?' Löfgren shook his head.

'So why was she so angry with her mum, then?'

'I think it was all to do with her dad, because he was pretty much god,' Löfgren said. 'She used to go on about her mum leaving her dad, that she'd only been interested in his money and all that. That her mum had betrayed her dad, and that it was her mum's fault he had a heart attack, all that sort of thing.'

'Did you ever meet Linda's mother?' Lewin asked.

'Once,' Löfgren said with a smile. 'I met her when Linda and I and a group of other friends were out in town one evening. Back in the spring. Before we got together. I only said hello. To her mum, I mean.'

'What sort of impression did you get of her?'

'She seemed really okay, actually. She's a teacher, apparently.'

'Anything else that struck you?' Lewin asked. You're holding something back, he thought.

'Okay,' Löfgren said with a grin. 'I thought she looked bloody good. I mean, she must be at least forty, but, well . . .'

'So explain it to an old man,' Lewin said.

'Talk about having a glint in her eye!' Löfgren said. 'If you ask me, Linda's mum was a clear ten. If you get what I mean. I wouldn't have said no if she'd asked.'

'I think I understand what you mean,' Lewin said.

'That's what was so weird,' Roland said. 'With Linda and her mum, I mean. They weren't at all alike. Linda was a lovely, sweet girl, a good friend. But her mum . . . Talk about a really cool woman! The sort of woman who could take you places you'd never been before.'

'Really?' Lewin said, nodding thoughtfully. Really? he thought.

# 43

The association Växjö Men Against Violence to Women had received a very positive welcome in the local media, and even though it was summer and height of the holiday season some fifty men had already said they would like to take part. In practical terms, this was considerably more than they really needed. Växjö's nightlife, particularly in summer, wasn't exactly hectic, to put it mildly, and in order to balance their resources with demand, they had divided the volunteers across the days of the week. They had even decided that the association's fellow menfolk would patrol the town's streets and squares in teams of two. This offered other advantages besides ease of planning, partly because it increased the security of the menfolk themselves, and partly because it acted as an extra control in case some joker managed to get through the eye of the association's needle.

They had also adapted to the weather, and had a load of T-shirts printed bearing the word MENFOLK in red lettering across the wearer's chest and back. This meant that the wearers were easily recognizable by those they were there to help and protect, while offering a means of authorization that didn't have to be fished out of a pocket if anything ever happened.

Communications had been set up in the simplest possible way, with the Menfolk on the same shift making sure they had each other's mobile numbers before they headed out into town. And of course there was also a special emergency number to the police, in case they ever found themselves in a dangerous situation. And, finally, they had also had the foresight to place an order with a local clothing company for rainproof jackets with detachable linings, bearing the same logo, in plenty of time before the autumn, when rather different weather could be expected. Last but by no means least, and particularly not in parsimonious Småland, there had been so much interest from different sponsors that they would really have needed to wear overalls to have room to promote them all.

Against this background, it was especially unfortunate that a regrettable incident that could easily have ended in tragedy occurred during the very first week. On Tuesday night two of the association's committee members who, together with two other pairs, were patrolling the central area between the Tegnér Cemetery, the health centre, the fire station and the cathedral tried to mediate between half a dozen youngsters who were arguing outside McDonald's, at the junction of Storgatan and Liedbergsgatan.

All of those involved came from immigrant backgrounds, and all of them apart from the two that the dispute was actually about were boys or at most young men. Committee member Bengt Karlsson had first attempted to lower the tension by talking to them, which was the introductory step in the three-step model of conflict resolution – conversation, intervention, immobilization – that they had chosen to follow.

In spite of this, two of them had started fighting anyway, eagerly cheered on by the rest of them, regardless of gender, and at this point Karlsson and his partner had been forced to proceed directly to step three of the CII model and try to separate the two opponents. The effect of their action had been immediate. The two fighting men had immediately forgotten their differences and along with their supporters had turned on the two Menfolk as one. If Karlsson's partner hadn't already rung the emergency number on his mobile, things could have ended very badly indeed.

Within a couple of minutes one of the other Menfolk teams had arrived at a run from the railway station, and tried to help as best they could in accordance with the recommended method. At roughly the same time a patrol car containing von Essen and Adolfsson had also arrived. Because of the stretched resources within the Växjö Police, they had had to pull on their uniforms and do an extra shift in the station's rapid-response unit. First out was Police Constable Adolfsson, and, although it is unclear exactly what he and his partner did, within the space of a minute and a half they had separated all those involved and Adolfsson had got the two most active of them on the ground.

'Just stop it,' Adolfsson had said, 'and the rest of you stand still until my partner's booked you all.'

After another fifteen minutes' discussion, and after getting the names of all six immigrant youths and four Menfolk, Adolfsson had raised his hand and dismissed the gathering.

'You go that way,' he said to the youngsters, pointing north towards Dalbo, which was the best bet, being Växjö's own little ghetto.

'And you go that way,' von Essen said to the Växjö Menfolk, pointing towards the hospital.

'But we're supposed to be patrolling the centre of town,' one of the Menfolk protested. 'Why would we want to be going south?'

'I suggest you take the long way round,' von Essen said diplomatically. 'How's your nose, by the way?'

The visible, physical injuries to all involved were fortunately restricted to one of the Menfolk, whose nose was bleeding after being punched by one of the men he was trying to help. Regrettably, in the heat of the fight, he had also ended up in Adolfsson's clutches, and immediately found himself flat on the ground with a very sore back and neck.

'If you like we can drive you to the hospital, or take you home if you'd prefer,' Adolfsson said. 'Or we've got a first aid kit in the car. Just lean your head back and take some deep breaths.'

'It isn't easy, as I'm sure you can appreciate,' von Essen said in a conciliatory tone, handing a compress to the injured Manfolk, 'telling the difference between the good guys and the bad when they're all brawling in a heap, if you see what I mean.'

The injured Manfolk understood exactly. He didn't have any complaints at all. He'd never dream of pressing charges against the teenager who had happened to punch him on the nose, and he had no intention of making a complaint against Police Constable Adolfsson, who was only trying to help him.

'A nosebleed isn't the end of the world,' he said with a brave smile. 'It was just an unfortunate misunderstanding.'

# 44

Work on the investigation was still going according to plan. With regard to the DNA sampling of potential perpetrators, things were going so well that the only thing spoiling this forensic party was perhaps Bengt Karlsson's test results. They had been sent back by return of fax from the National Forensics Lab, and an overworked and sullen technician had attached a question, wondering whether the team working on the investigation were having trouble reading these days: *As has already been made clear in previous notifications from the National Forensics Lab, the DNA tested in this sample does not match the DNA profile of the perpetrator in this case.*

Unfortunately Olsson happened to be standing by the fax machine when this message appeared, and he had passed it on to Adolfsson with the instruction that it be added to the computer database along with the other results.

'I see that the name has been concealed. Adolfsson, do you have any idea who this might be?' Olsson wondered curiously, his own secret effort with Claesson's apple-core still fresh in his mind.

'It's that walking disaster, Bengt Karlsson. The one from that association,' Adolfsson replied.

'Who in the name of God decided to drag him into this?' Olsson asked heatedly.

'Talk to Bäckström. He's bound to know,' Adolfsson said with a shrug.

Olsson had gone directly to see Bäckström and asked him how on earth anyone could have come up with the idea of investigating Bengt

Karlsson's DNA. According to Bäckström, there was a very simple answer to that question. A quick glance at their own records ought to be enough for even an ordinary civilian to realize that it would be a dereliction of duty not to check someone like Karlsson. Bäckström was in one of his most diplomatic moods, hence the conscious decision to avoid the phrase 'backwoods police', about which backwoods police were a little sensitive, even though a backwoods police officer like Olsson ought to have realized that ordinary civilians, unlike ordinary backwoods police officers, were fortunately unable to get in the way of the activities of proper police officers.

According to Olsson, Karlsson's case was an entirely irrelevant subject under current circumstances. After his most recent conviction, Bengt Karlsson had, voluntarily and entirely on his own initiative, participated in a very successful project organized by the outpatient department at Sankt Sigfrid's. They had used the most recent scientific developments in behavioural modification to try to break the pattern of criminal behaviour in those who were persistent abusers of women, and Karlsson had been their most successful case ever. He was a completely different person now, through and through. He had gone from being a clenched fist to an open embrace, and for many years now he had been one of the most active advocates of efforts to help abusing men to find their way back to a normal, functional life.

'I appreciate that you have trouble accepting this, Bäckström, but Bengt Karlsson is now one of the kindest men there is. He just wants to embrace the whole world,' Olsson concluded.

Maybe, although it looks like he missed Linda, Bäckström thought.

'I want to know what you think, Bäckström,' Olsson said seriously. 'What do you think, deep down?'

'A leopard never changes its spots,' Bäckström said with a grin.

Sadly, even his colleague Lewin had started to behave more and more oddly, even though he worked for the murder squad and ought to have known better. He had begun to go round asking his colleagues peculiar questions, which obviously illustrated the dangers of ending up in a mess of structural worries, Bäckström thought.

First Lewin had had a long conversation with Rogersson, mostly about Linda's mother rather than the victim herself and querying a load of strange details, such as where mother and daughter had actually lived since they got back from the USA after the divorce some ten years before.

'According to what she's said in interview, she's lived at the same address the whole time,' Rogersson said. What was so odd about that?

'I'll check with Svanström,' Lewin said. He was very discreet about his private life, and would never dream of calling her Eva in front of other men when she herself wasn't present.

'You do that, Lewin,' Rogersson said, grinning for some reason. 'Go and have a word with little Svanström. Was there anything else?' he added, making a show of glancing at his wristwatch.

There was one more thing, Lewin said. Would Rogersson mind calling Linda's mother and asking one more question? 'I think it would best if you do it, seeing as you've already met her.'

'The question,' Rogersson prompted. 'What do you want to know?'

'If you could call and ask if she's ever had a dog,' Lewin said.

'A dog,' Rogersson said. 'You want to know if she's ever had a dog? Any particular sort of dog, or will any old dog do?'

'Just something that occurred to me,' Lewin said evasively. 'Just call her and ask if she's ever had a dog.'

'I wonder why he wants to know that?' Bäckström said when he and his friend were sitting in his hotel room and had just embarked upon their usual preparations for the weekend. 'You don't think he's just hit the wall? Lewin's always been a weird bastard. I've hardly ever seen him with a proper beer in his hand, not in all these years.' There was something about some bastard dog, Bäckström thought. Oh, what the hell.

'He's probably just hit his head against the wall while he's been banging little Svanström,' Rogersson grinned, shaking his head.

'So has she ever had a dog?' Bäckström asked, still thinking about this little detail. 'Linda's mum, I mean?'

'No,' Rogersson said bluntly. 'She's never had a dog. She doesn't like dogs. Nor cats either, for that matter. Linda used to have a horse, apparently, but that was out at her dad's. We didn't get any further than that.'

In spite of backwoods policemen sticking their oar in, in spite of Jan Lewin's peculiarities, and in spite of the fact that the notorious wife-beater Bengt Karlsson had evidently managed to find a simple way of pulling the wool over the eyes of people like Olsson nine years ago, Bäckström was in an excellent mood all weekend. And when he was standing in the shower on Monday morning, he even burst into song.

'I'm going to test the whole world's DNA . . . I'm going to keep on testing DNA all day,' he sang as the cold water splashed over his fat body and he carefully scrubbed under his arms and in other nooks and crannies to prevent any unpleasant odours later in the day.

Police hunk of the year, he thought as he inspected the end result in the mirror. Watch out, ladies.

# 45

## Stockholm, Monday 4 August

On Monday morning the National Rapid-Response Unit conducted a major exercise around the Kronoberg block that contained police headquarters on Kungsholmen in Stockholm. Neighbouring blocks were cordoned off, but 'for practical reasons and out of consideration for the people living there' local residents and people already in the area weren't evacuated. So there were plenty of spectators to watch what was happening, and within just a few minutes the first camera teams from the usual television channels were in place.

In total, four members of the unit, wearing black overalls and black face masks and with the usual weapons, abseiled down from the roof of the block closest to the road. When they reached the ninth floor they – to judge by the muffled explosions – set off small explosive devices around the windows, knocked them out and clambered into the building. The phones in the national police headquarters were extremely busy, a special press officer was already in place, and the representatives of the media were told that this was an entirely normal exercise within the frame of the so-called 11 September Project.

The National Rapid-Response Unit was practising in case there was ever a coup aimed at the top leadership of the Swedish Police, but more detailed information could not be revealed for obvious reasons, because further disclosure would have negated the whole point of the exercise.

The media were apparently happy with this explanation. All the television channels showed footage of the exercise, but mainly because they were good images in a time of news drought. A representative of the rapid-response unit was interviewed, and explained in general terms what they were doing.

'We conduct exercises all the time,' he said. 'And it's in the nature of the beast that some of our exercises involve people and targets that mean they can't always be concealed from the general public. Unfortunately this is unavoidable, and naturally we can only apologize if we alarmed anyone unnecessarily. We did consider evacuating local residents, but because that's a different sort of exercise, and one that is principally the domain of the regular police, we decided against it.'

And with this the matter was put to bed. People from the highways agency, overseen by uniformed police officers, cleaned up fragments of glass from the lawn and street in front of police headquarters, the uniformed officers removed the cordons with the help of the highways agency, and everything returned to normal. The weather had been just the same as it had been throughout this remarkable summer. Between twenty and thirty degrees in the shade, from early morning to late in the evening.

# 46

## *Växjö, Monday 4 August*

For the investigating team, the week began peacefully, in an almost academic atmosphere. During the morning meeting Enoksson ran through the latest forensic results from the National Forensics Lab and the other experts they had approached.

The fingerprints that had been secured at the crime scene had now been examined. Five of them belonged to people who hadn't yet been identified. One of these sets ought reasonably to belong to the perpetrator, and they also had an idea of which set was the most interesting. But because they weren't entirely sure, they had run all of the prints through the national police fingerprint register, without getting any matches. Of course this could simply mean that none of the prints belonged to the perpetrator and that he was still in the register.

Ten pubic hairs, two strands of body hair, and several strands of head hair belonged to the perpetrator. The DNA results left no room for doubt on that point. Other forensic tests on the hairs, blood and sperm had contributed additional information about the perpetrator they were trying to find.

'That idea that he may have dabbled in various drugs turns out to be pretty accurate,' Enoksson said. The head hairs had contained traces of cannabis. Because it looked as though the killer hadn't cut his hair for a couple of months – medium length dark blond hair with no trace of grey, and possibly the most common cut for Växjö men who weren't too old – they were able to hazard a guess at his pattern of consumption.

'He doesn't seem to have been a particularly frequent user. According to the expert I spoke to at the National Lab, maybe once every two or three weeks, something like that. Definitely not a heavy user.' Enoksson shrugged his shoulders. 'Besides, it looks like he had rather more strings to his bow. Tests have found traces of stimulants in the blood he left behind, even though there wasn't much of it. In this sort of context, I mean. So that's really not bad.'

'So, someone who smokes hash now and then, and also uses amphetamines, if I've understood correctly,' Lewin said.

'Yes,' Enoksson said. 'Although I'd prefer to say that he uses both, because there are various ways of taking hash and amphetamines. Administering the dose, as medical doctors usually say. In other words, we've got someone who consumes cannabis between once a month and once a week, and he probably does so by smoking hash and/or marijuana. That's the most common method of consumption, especially among infrequent users, but of course there are other ways, as I'm sure many of you are aware.'

'What about the amphetamines?' Lewin prompted.

'Same reservations there,' Enoksson said. 'Amphetamine or some other general stimulant. There are a number of closely related products on the market. He could have injected it, eaten it, or even drunk it. According to the lab, he doesn't seem to have been a frequent user of that either. If our friends in Linköping had to hazard a guess, they reckon he consumes this sort of thing in roughly the same way he consumes cannabis. Every now and then, in which case the most usual method would be either eating the tablets or crushing them up in liquid and drinking it.'

'Doesn't sound like your usual junkie,' Bäckström declared contentedly. 'He's never had to give his fingerprints to the friendly local police, he only takes drugs now and then, and he's got the same sort of haircut that normal men have.'

'Doubtless, Bäckström, doubtless,' Enoksson said. 'But on the other hand, he does seem to use both cannabis and general stimulants. As far as his fingerprints are concerned, we can't rule out the possibility that we haven't found his, although I personally doubt that. And then there's the biggest problem: what he did to Linda. So I don't think we can say that he's that normal.'

'Fish or fowl. That's the question,' Olsson said, nodding solemnly.

'Neither, if you ask me,' Enoksson said drily. 'I've actually saved the most interesting thing till last. Oh, yes.' He was evidently delighted when he saw the looks on the faces of his audience. 'This'll give you something to get stuck into.'

On the sill and frame of the window they had found traces of fibre. A pale-blue fabric which, according to the experts at the National Lab, probably came from a thin sweater. The structure of the fibre, its thickness and other properties, indicated the sort of sweater that was thin enough for someone to wear at least during the evening in the sort of weather that currently prevailed in Växjö and much of the rest of Sweden without getting heatstroke. And it was far from a common sort of fabric.

'This is no ordinary sweater,' Enoksson said. 'The fibres we're talking about are a blend, fifty per cent cashmere and fifty per cent another highly exclusive variety of wool. According to the lab, we're talking about a top that would cost several thousand kronor in the shops. Maybe more than that if it was a particularly exclusive brand.'

'That almost sounds like the sort of thing Linda could have been given by her father,' Sandberg said hesitantly. 'That couldn't be how they got there? Your fibres, I mean.'

'That she could have hung it out to dry, or to air?' Enoksson said.

'That's what I was thinking,' Sandberg said. 'Typical female thinking. Ever think of that, lads?' she asked, looking at her colleagues round the table.

'Well, the top wasn't found in the flat,' Enoksson said. 'And there were also traces of blood on a couple of the fibres we found on the windowsill. It remains to be seen if the perpetrator borrowed it from Linda or her mother, and in that case what he did with his own top, assuming he wasn't bare-chested to start with. Elementary, my dear Watson.' Enoksson nodded towards Olsson.

'We ought to be able to find that out,' Bäckström said, nodding in turn towards Rogersson. 'And if it's his own sweater, it sounds like the sort of thing it might be possible to track down.'

'If he actually bought it,' Olsson said doubtfully. 'If we're talking about the sort of person described by your colleagues in the CP group in their profile, then he probably stole it from somewhere.'

'Precisely, Olsson,' Bäckström said. 'I quite agree with you. If he didn't steal it, or just grab it from a washing line somewhere, he probably found it on the beach when he was on holiday in Thailand. When you're dealing with a proper murder case, you have to make the best of things.'

'I understand what you mean, Bäckström. I take that back,' Olsson said with a faint smile.

And you're humble as well, you little poof, Bäckström thought.

The first part of the search for the exclusive sweater was done by phone. First Rogersson called Linda's mother and asked her. She was entirely sure. She had certainly never owned a top like that. Pale blue just wasn't her colour.

What about her daughter? Had Linda ever owned a pale blue cashmere top? Her mother couldn't recall ever having seen anything like that, although Linda had loads of clothes. To be on the safe side, she suggested that Rogersson talk to Linda's father. If she'd been given it as a present, it was bound to have been from him.

'A pale blue cashmere top?' Henning Wallin said. 'Not something I've ever given her. Not that I can remember, anyway. Blue was certainly her colour, but not light blue, exactly.'

The conversation ended with Henning Wallin suggesting that he would talk to his housekeeper about it. She ought to be able to say, and whether the answer was positive or negative he promised to get in touch as soon as he had spoken to her. 'Is it important?' he asked.

'Could be,' Rogersson said. 'At this stage, most things are important.'

'That sweater,' Rogersson said to Bäckström an hour later.

'I'm listening,' Bäckström said. Right now a cold beer would be great. Who the hell could bear to talk about sweaters in this sort of heat, he thought.

'It doesn't look like it was Linda's. I spoke to her dad, who spoke to his housekeeper, who called me and went on about how she's sewn and mended and washed and ironed and folded and hung up and brushed and rubbed and scrubbed everything for Linda and her dad for the past ten years.'

'And?'

'She can't recall any pale blue cashmere top ruining her life with its presence,' Rogersson said. 'But their household martyr does seem to have had a lot of valuable stuff to look after.'

'What about her mum, then?'

'Wrong colour. Completely the wrong colour for her. Not a chance,' Rogersson said. 'So we can forget her.'

Wrong colour? Bäckström thought. Women are completely mad. Personally he had a favourite sweater that had blue, red and green horizontal stripes. He had found it when he had been on a murder case up in Östersund a few years ago; some lazy rich bastard had left it in the hotel restaurant, and Bäckström had taken pity on it. Besides, it had been cold enough to freeze the arse off an Eskimo when he was there, even though it was only the beginning of August.

Detective Superintendent Lewin didn't waste a thought on the presumed pale blue sweater. He was too old to run around trying to find things that way. Everyone who knew what it was really about knew that you had to differentiate between big and small, and that you had to look very carefully in order to be able to tell which was which. This business about where Linda's mother had lived, for instance. Besides, he had the best possible help for that sort of practical search.

'I understand exactly what you mean, Janne,' Eva Svanström said. 'I don't understand why Bäckström and the others all assume this is just about Linda. I've thought that all along. Maybe he wanted to see the mother? I pulled up her passport photo just out of curiosity, and if she looks the way she does on the picture, I find it hard to believe she had any shortage of men in her life.'

'Don't let's get carried away now . . . Eva,' Lewin said, seeing as they were alone. Personally, he would rather she called him Jan than Janne regardless of whether they were alone or in company.

Most of the evidence suggested that this was about Linda,

according to Lewin. Linda was the victim, and the hideous abuse that had been directed at her seemed to be aimed at her specifically. It was extremely personal, and extremely private. That her killer covered her with the sheet at the end, careful to cover her face and body, was an expression of severe guilt, angst, and the fact that he couldn't bear to look at her.

In the world Lewin lived in, that was also a clear sign. It was the sort of thing the usual sex maniacs he had investigated never bothered with. There it was all about exposing the victim in a sexually provocative way, to the limits of what was physically possible. To violate her even more after death, to shock the people who found her, and the people who would be looking for him. But mostly to give succour to their own fantasies as events unfolded, and to store memories for future use. And the pattern of behaviour shown here didn't fit the married men, ex-husbands, and all the various categories of boyfriends who, in a fit of jealousy, drunkenness or simple rage, had attacked their girlfriends and wives, hitting and beating them to death, because then the crime scene was usually transformed into a slaughterhouse.

Then there were the details as well. Small but not uninteresting, and they all pointed to Linda rather than her mother. The mother hadn't lived in her flat for the past month. As soon as her summer holiday began, she moved out to her cottage in the country. On the few occasions when she had been in town, she had had errands to run. Instead, Linda had lived alone in her flat. For almost three weeks in a row, with all the possibilities this opened up for meetings, contacts and ordinary coincidental encounters.

'You just want to make absolutely sure this isn't anything to do with the mother,' Eva Svanström said, smiling at him in the way his mother sometimes had when he was a young boy and needed comforting.

'Yes,' Lewin said. 'That would be good, actually.'

'Okay,' Eva said. 'So, this is how it looks.'

Around ten years ago, at the time of her parents' separation, Linda and her mother had left the USA and moved back to Växjö. Linda's mother had been born and raised in Växjö, and, with the exception of the four years in the States, had lived there all her life. The same thing with her daughter. She was born in the maternity unit in Växjö Hospital. When she was six years old, she moved to the USA with her parents. Four years later, just in time for the start of the autumn school term, she moved back to Växjö with her mother and moved into the house on Pär Lagerkvists väg that her mother had received in the divorce.

Linda's mother had been registered at that address ever since. Nor was there anything to suggest that she might have lived anywhere else, with the exception of the time she spent in her summer house out on Sirkön, which she bought the year after she returned to Sweden, and where she spent her summer holidays, weekends and other breaks.

Linda had also been registered at the same address until she reached the age of seventeen, and she attended Växjö High School. Then her father had moved back home as well, bought a large manor house south of Växjö, and just a few months later was joined there by his only daughter. During the first year Linda seemed to have lived a fairly nomadic existence, and had a room both in her mother's flat in town and with her father out in the country, where she was registered as living. After she left school, learned to drive and got her own car, given to her by her father, she seemed to have preferred the countryside to the town, and spent less and less time staying at her mother's.

Svanström had found no trace of 'men' connected to the flat, at least not in the official sense. Only Linda and her mother had ever been registered at the address in question.

'I see,' Lewin sighed.

'You don't seem very happy,' Svanström said. 'It would be good if you could explain why. It would make things easier for me. If I knew what you were looking for, I mean.'

'I don't actually know,' Lewin said. 'What about the others registered in the building? What about their living arrangements?'

According to Svanström, they all seemed to have lived there just as long as, or even longer than, Linda's mother, with one exception. The only occupant who had arrived in the past ten years seemed to be Marian Gross the librarian, who had bought his flat and moved in at roughly the time the building was transferred from rented to private flats a few years ago.

'But you've already turned him inside out by now,' Svanström said.

'Anyway, didn't his DNA mean that he's been eliminated from the investigation?'

'If Gross bought his flat, that must mean that someone else sold it to him,' Lewin said. 'And moved out.'

'Not on this occasion,' Eva Svanström said. 'Believe it or not, I've checked that as well, even though it took quite a while. He actually bought it from another occupant who lived there when Linda and her mother moved in, and still lives there, so the simple explanation is that she had two tenancies. I noticed that she ran some sort of accountancy business, so I'd guess that she used the flat that Gross bought as an office. It seems to be quite tricky, in purely legal terms, to use a domestic flat as an office. Especially if it's managed by a small housing association. She must have made quite a bit of money from it as well.'

'Margareta Eriksson,' Lewin said suddenly.

'That's her name,' Svanström said. 'Do you know what, Janne? Sometimes I wonder what you need me for. That's the same Margareta Eriksson who came forward in the papers, isn't it? That story about the perpetrator trying to break into her flat the same night Linda was murdered?'

'Yes, that's the one,' Lewin said. He was finally starting to feel that he was beginning to make sense of his thoughts. A bit of structure to his world.

'Mind you, I still don't understand what you're looking for,' Svanström declared.

'Nor me, frankly,' Lewin said. 'Do you know what, Eva? Could you call Margareta Eriksson and ask her about it?'

'But you still don't know why?' Svanström asked.

'A complete shot in the dark,' Lewin said with a weak smile. 'A shot in the dark at an unknown target,' he added.

'Well, if it will make you happy,' Eva said with a shrug.

# 47

The peace and tranquillity came to an abrupt end just after lunchtime, and the gentle search for meaningful structures and a pale blue sweater suddenly transformed into something completely different. Raised voices, people running down corridors, doors slamming, von Essen and Adolfsson suddenly showing up in the investigation's office with holsters, weapons and tense faces, taking Sandberg and Salomonson away with them, getting an unmarked police car out of the garage and putting the blue light on top as soon as they emerged on to the street, heading towards Kalmar as fast as they could.

Two hours earlier a rape had taken place on an island called Björnö, ten kilometres north of Kalmar, and unlike their own week-old attempted rape case there wasn't the slightest doubt that this one was the real thing, and the very worst sort. The victim was a fourteen-year-old girl. Together with her sister, who was two years older, and a friend of her sister's of the same age, after breakfast she had gone down to the beach to sunbathe and swim.

After an hour or so on the beach the fourteen-year-old victim had set off to buy ice-cream and soft drinks from a nearby kiosk. Hardly a surprise, seeing as she was youngest. When she was heading through the strip of woodland along the shore, the perpetrator had suddenly attacked her from behind, pulled her into the undergrowth, beaten her half unconscious, and raped her. When she didn't come back after half an hour her older sister and her friend started to get worried and set off to find her. Hardly a surprise either, after the Linda murder and all the coverage in the media. After just one hundred metres they had found the younger sister. The perpetrator was sitting astride her. They had started screaming and the perpetrator had run off.

Half an hour later the victim was on her way to hospital in Kalmar, the police had arrived, the crime scene had been cordoned off and they had started questioning the first witnesses. A dog patrol was on its way, expected to be there within fifteen minutes. In short, there was a great deal of activity, and the police patrols that were heading into the area also had a decent description to go on. According to both the older sister and her friend, the man they were looking for was remarkably similar to the man described by the girl in Växjö just a week before. They had noticed his tattoos in particular. Thick blue swirls, which might be snakes or possibly dragons, on both arms, from his shoulders down to his hands.

'This doesn't feel right at all,' Anna Sandberg said when she and her colleagues stepped inside Kalmar police station, thinking mainly about her own case in Växjö, which she had decided to write off as a fictitious report as recently as that morning.

'You mean the tattoos?' Salomonson said.

'Yes,' Anna said. 'It doesn't feel right at all.'

'Don't get hung up on that,' Adolfsson said consolingly. 'Every self-respecting thug has tattoos like that these days. Their bodies usually look like old Oriental rugs.'

'It's all sorted now, so you can relax, Janne,' Svanström said, waving a bundle of papers encouragingly at Lewin as he sat slumped in his chair behind a desk groaning with piles of entirely different papers.

'I'm all ears,' Lewin said, leaning back in his chair.

'It wasn't quite as straightforward as I thought,' Eva Svanström said. 'According to what Margareta Eriksson told me a short while ago, this is what happened, and she seems to know what she's talking about. Besides, she's also chair of the management committee.'

About three years previously, more or less at the same time as the transfer from rented flats to a residents' association was being concluded, Margareta Eriksson had sold her flat on the first floor to Marian Gross, who moved into the building. At the same time she bought the flat at the top of the building where she now lived from her neighbour, Lotta Ericson, Linda's mother. And finally Linda's mother had moved down to the ground floor into the flat that she had lived in ever since, the flat where her daughter was murdered almost a month ago. That flat had originally been office premises, then had been sub-let, and in the end had stood empty while the transfer to a residents' association was going on. And it was owned by Linda's mother and not the association.

'Margareta Eriksson evidently wanted more space, even though she's single,' Svanström said. 'She wanted a couple of rooms as an office for her accountancy business, and she had also sold her house in the country and had quite a bit of antique furniture that she wanted to keep, and needed more space for.'

'While Lotta Ericson was happy with a smaller flat because her daughter had moved out,' Lewin said.

'Exactly,' Svanström said. 'So what do you need me for, then?' she said with a smile.

'There are actually a couple more things,' Lewin said.

'I might have guessed,' Svanström said. 'If we take it from the beginning: if you're wondering whether Margareta Eriksson with a k and two s's and Lotta Ericson with a c and one s are related, the answer's no.'

'So you've worked that out?' Lewin said.

'It wasn't exactly difficult,' Eva Svanström said. 'I realized that when I looked into the details of the way they had moved flats. Margareta Eriksson spells Eriksson with a k and two s's, the normal spelling, or at least the most common, and that's been her name since she got married. Lotta Ericson, on the other hand, was originally called Liselotte Eriksson, with a k and two s's. Full name Liselotte Jeanette Eriksson. When she married she became Liselotte Wallin Eriksson, and when she moved to the USA she changed the spelling to Ericson with a c and one s. She's always been known as Lotta, ever since she was a child. When she got divorced and moved back home she got rid of the Wallin, then a year or so later she applied to change her name. For the past eight years her full name, according to the official register, is Lotta Liselotte Jeanette Ericson.'

'I see,' Lewin said.

'You think the perpetrator rang on the wrong door at first?' Svanström said.

'Yes, I was starting to wonder. Because of what Margareta Eriksson said in the paper, and the fact that she and Linda's mother have the same surname. But it's actually thanks to you. You were the one who said it could have been an old flame popping up again.'

'To meet Linda,' Svanström said. 'And he got it wrong and rang on the door of the flat they used to live in. Are you sure about that? She wasn't exactly eighteen years old then, was she? When her mum lived on the top floor, I mean.'

'To meet Linda, or Linda's mother, or both of them. I really don't know any more,' Lewin said, shuffling in his chair. 'But it probably doesn't matter.'

'If I was going to show up at the home of an old flame . . . in the middle of the night after three years . . . I think I'd probably try to call first,' Eva Svanström said.

'Telephones. That's actually the next thing I was going to ask you to do,' Lewin said. 'I think we should find out if Lotta Ericson has changed her number.'

'Now that we've already got started.'

'Exactly,' Lewin said. 'Exactly.' What's wrong with another shot in the dark? he thought.


'What do you think about that rape in Kalmar?' Bäckström asked as he stuck his nose into Rogersson's office.

'Bloody awful business,' Rogersson said.

'Has it got anything to do with us, or with Linda, I mean?'

'Not the slightest.'

'Then you think exactly the same as me.'

'I'll just have to try to live with that,' Rogersson said with a grin.

'I asked Hans and Fritz as well. Separately, just to make sure.'

'And?'

'Hans didn't think there was a connection but still thought it sounded interesting. He suggested that we ought to talk to our colleagues in the VICLAS unit.'

'And what about Fritz?' Rogersson asked.

'He didn't think there was a connection, but we should probably follow it up, and maybe have a word with our colleagues in VICLAS.'

'How exciting. Where do they get it all from?'

'Then I asked Lewin too,' Bäckström said.

'And what did he think?'

'Do you want his exact words?'

'Of course.'

'With the proviso that Rogersson had only heard a description of the Kalmar case over the phone from officer Sandberg, he still thought it highly unlikely that the perpetrator was the same one as in the Linda case.'

'Sounds like Lewin,' Rogersson said. 'On to something else entirely. What do you think about giving up on this and heading back to the hotel to squeeze a couple of cold beers before dinner?'

'I think that's an excellent proposal,' Bäckström said.

'Turn on the news on TV4,' Rogersson said when they were sitting in Bäckström's hotel room two hours and two cold beers later.

'What for?' Bäckström said in surprise, as he reached for the remote.

'I thought I might check to see if my office is still in one piece,' Rogersson said.

'What a fucking story,' Bäckström said five minutes later as he switched the television off. 'The windows those crazy fuckers blew out were the ones to Chinny's operations centre. Chinny must be mad if he agreed to an exercise like that.'

'I spoke to the lads at work this afternoon,' Rogersson said. 'They thought the same as you. And that was where the shoe was chafing.'

'Oh, so that's it,' Bäckström said.

'What a fucking story,' he repeated after another five minutes.

'Supposed to have been just like the Grand Hotel in Lund,' Rogersson said. 'Seems he's got a taste for bathroom mirrors.'

'Or he got it all wrong. Maybe he's just trying to commit suicide. With that fucking chin it can't be easy for him, after all. Maybe he just can't quite get it together.'

'How do you mean?' Rogersson said.

'Every time he looks in the mirror he fires a bullet at his forehead, only he keeps aiming at the mirror,' Bäckström said.

# 48

The dreams were coming more frequently now. About that summer almost fifty years ago when he got his first proper bicycle and his dad taught him to ride it. Although that night the dream hadn't been about his red Crescent Valiant but about his dad and his mum.

A strange summer when his dad's holiday never seemed to end. Eventually he had asked him. 'How long is your holiday, Daddy?'

At first his dad had looked a bit odd, then he had laughed and ruffled Jan's hair and everything was back to normal again. 'As long as I need to teach you to ride your bike,' Daddy had replied. 'That'll take as long as it takes, and I don't suppose my job will run away from me.' Then he had ruffled his hair again. Once more than usual.

It really had been an Indian summer, because his dad became more and more like an Indian with every passing day. Thin, suntanned, his skin stretched tight over his face. 'You look like a real Indian,' Jan had said to him.

'That's not so strange,' Daddy replied. 'With all this lovely weather we've been having.'

One night he had woken up. He must have heard a noise. He had padded slowly down the stairs and when he reached the hall he saw that his dad and mum were sitting on a chair in the kitchen. Mummy was sitting in Daddy's lap, facing the other way with her arms round his neck, her head buried in his chest. His dad had one arm round her waist while he gently stroked her hair with the other. 'It'll be all right,' he was muttering. 'It'll be all right.'

And neither of them had noticed him, and he had crept back to his room in the attic and eventually fallen back to sleep.

When they were having breakfast the following morning everything was back to normal again. 'Are you ready, Jan?' Daddy asked, putting his coffee cup down. 'Shall we take a turn on the Valiant?'

'Always ready, Daddy,' Jan replied.

And then he woke up.

# 49

## *Växjö, Tuesday 5 August*

The fourteen-year-old rape victim from Kalmar had survived. Her condition was described as critical but stable, and the report indicated that she would have died if her sister and her friend hadn't shown up at the last minute and frightened the perpetrator away. It was also confirmation of what the media had suspected from the very start. That a serial killer who raped young women was on the loose in Småland. Right in the middle of idyllic, summertime Sweden.

First he had murdered Linda. A few weeks later he had attacked another woman, and the fact that he failed on that occasion was, according to the newspapers, the most likely explanation for why he had attacked a third victim just a week after that. The pressure inside him had built up to the point where the risk of getting caught was the least of his worries.

A professor in criminal psychology from Stockholm University, described as the country's leading expert on serial killers, was able to give numerous examples of the police's inability to identify sequences of violent crimes at an early enough stage. The police lacked perspective, staring themselves blind on details, and there were failures in their internal communications. One hand 'couldn't see' what the other was doing. They didn't pick up the whole picture, the pattern, the most obvious signs.

'They simply don't see that the emperor isn't wearing any clothes,' the professor said on the sofa of TV4's breakfast show.

'How do you mean?' the presenter asked.

'Well, that he's naked,' the professor clarified.

For the first time that summer the media were openly critical of the police, and the police in Växjö in particular. In spite of a wealth of evidence, they still hadn't managed to solve the murder of Linda Wallin. Even worse: according to several anonymous police sources, they hadn't managed to make any progress at all in the investigation. Even though a month had passed since the murder, the investigation was still stuck exactly where it had started.

The nineteen-year-old woman the perpetrator had attempted to rape the weekend before also popped up again. The police had simply refused to take her story seriously. Instead of hunting for the perpetrator they had bullied his victim, and a fourteen-year-old girl had had to pay the price for that incompetence. The editorial columns of the papers were all talking about a scandal and the team investigating the Linda murder suddenly found themselves devoting most of their time to dealing with problems that the majority of them regarded as complete fantasies.

The previous day, the county police commissioner in Kalmar had contacted his counterpart in Växjö and raised the idea of establishing a joint unit. One murder and two rapes within the space of a month, with the interruption of the most recent incident sadly suggesting that the perpetrator might well strike again soon. The county police commissioner in Växjö was dubious, but promised to raise the matter with the leader of the preliminary police investigation into the Linda murder and get back to him.

Detective Superintendent Olsson raised the matter as the first item at the morning meeting on Tuesday, and declared himself willing to consider various options.

'What do you think?' he asked, looking around those present. 'Personally, I'm starting to lean strongly towards the possibility that the same man was involved in both rapes, since the descriptions given by the witnesses are almost identical.'

'What about the Linda case, then?' Bäckström asked grouchily. 'Did he do that as well?'

'The problem there is that we don't have a description,' Olsson said carefully.

'Yes, but that's pretty much the only thing we don't have,' Bäckström said. 'And we're soon going to find the man who did it. If there's anyone here who seriously believes that Linda would have let that tattooed thug into her flat at three o'clock in the morning, would they please raise their hand?'

'Sorry to interrupt,' Lewin said, clearing his throat carefully. 'What about the latest victim? Did they find any traces of semen?'

'Yes,' Sandberg said.

'In that case, it will soon be fairly obvious whether there's a connection to Linda,' Lewin pointed out.

'Yes, it will,' Sandberg agreed, already seeming a bit brighter.

'As far as the two rapes are concerned, I don't really see how we could help our colleagues in Kalmar, other than letting their witnesses look at the same photographs that we've shown our own victim. If they haven't already done that, of course,' Lewin said, clearing his throat again.

'It's already been arranged,' Sandberg said, now even happier.

'Well, then. That all sounds splendid,' Lewin said. 'Sounds like a textbook example of collaboration between different forces.'

'But what do you think personally, Lewin?' Olsson persisted. 'About whether there's any connection, I mean?'

'I don't usually like to give an opinion on things like that,' Lewin said. 'But, since you're asking, I don't think the man who murdered Linda is the same man who raped that poor girl in Kalmar, and that will be made clear when our colleagues in Kalmar get their DNA results. I don't think we need concern ourselves with any other possible connections.'

'Well, let's hope so,' Olsson said, shaking his head anxiously. 'I sincerely hope that you're right.'

At the end of the meeting, he directed Sandberg, Salomonson, von Essen, Adolfsson and a couple of others to begin work at once, in collaboration with their colleagues in Kalmar, on finding out if there were any links between the Linda murder, the attempted rape in Växjö and the rape in Kalmar. And in the meantime he would contact the

VICLAS unit and the CP group to make sure that they didn't neglect the analytical angle.

Once the afflicted had gone off to hunt for possible links and relative calm had descended again, Bäckström mustered his remaining troops.

'Well, then,' he said. 'How are things going with the list of DNA samples? Have we got enough cotton-buds?'

Lewin returned to his office, and was soon joined by Eva Svanström.

'The information about the mother's phone numbers will take a few days. I've spoken to Telia, and the files they've got immediate access to only go back a couple of years,' Svanström said.

'But the information's there somewhere?' Lewin asked, suddenly feeling the old anxiety again.

'Of course,' Svanström said. 'But the person I spoke to said it would take a few days to dig it out.'

'Oh, well,' Lewin said. A few days isn't the end of the world, and it's probably completely irrelevant anyway, he thought. Like most shots in the dark.

# 50

## *Alnön, outside Sundsvall, Tuesday 5 August*

Lars Martin Johansson was into the last week of the longest holiday of his life.

For almost two years now he had been on leave from his post as operational head of the Security Police in order to lead one of the most secret investigations in Swedish history, and now that task was nearing its conclusion. What remained could be done perfectly well by his staff, and in the week before midsummer Johansson had left the motherland and headed off round Europe with his wife. His wife liked travelling – new people, new places, new impressions – whereas Johansson preferred a good book, a phone that never rang and proper mealtimes.

Regardless of their different motivations, they usually returned to Sweden in the best of moods. In accordance with a promise made several years ago, which had since developed into something of a tradition, they were now spending the last week of their holiday with Johansson's older brother on his farm on Alnön, an island outside Sundsvall. Peace and quiet, good food and decent drink, unfussy and generous hosts who really did mean what they said when they told you to make yourselves at home. And, most important of all, Johansson thought: was there any country on this planet that in any real and positive sense could possibly stand comparison with Sweden? Not anywhere, he thought, with a deep sigh of contentment, before promptly falling asleep in his chair.

Johansson had three mobile phones these days. One private, one for his usual job, and one that was so secret that it was hardly ever used. For safety's sake, it was also red, and Johansson himself had programmed the ringtone. Apart from the volume, it was the same siren that the police emergency vehicles used, and he was as proud as punch of it. After installing it he had demonstrated it to his wife by calling it, so that she had the opportunity to appreciate his technological abilities. But the first time she heard it ring properly, its installer carried on snoring gently in his chair.

The Germans have probably made a cash offer for the whole of Småland, Johansson's wife Pia thought. She worked in a bank as a fund-manager. She put down the book she was trying to read and answered the phone.

'Hello?' I don't suppose I'm allowed to say what my name is, because I'd probably end up in prison, Pia thought.

'Enchanté,' a smooth voice said on the other end of the line. 'I presume you're the person I think you are,' the voice went on. 'However, no matter how much I might like to carry on this conversation, I'm afraid I must ask to speak to your dear husband.'

'Who should I say is calling?' Pia asked.

'No name, I'm afraid,' the smooth voice said. 'Just tell your dear husband that Pilgrim's old associate would like to exchange a few words with him.'

'And if I ask what this is about, I suppose I end up in prison?' Pia said.

'If I were to answer that, *I* would end up in prison,' Pilgrim's old associate countered, in a tone that sounded almost affronted.

'I'll go and wake him up,' Pia said. They're like children, she thought.

'Who was that?' Pia asked curiously ten minutes later when her husband had concluded his muttered conversation, which for some reason he had conducted at the far end of the large terrace. He put the red mobile down and sank back on to his chair with a sigh.

'An old acquaintance,' Johansson replied vaguely.

'One of those secret little rascals. With no name,' Pia said.

'More or less,' Johansson said with a shrug. 'He works in the cabinet office as a special adviser, helping the Prime Minister with odd bits and pieces, and his name's Nilsson.'

'Ah,' Pia said. 'Our very own grey eminence. The Swedish answer to Cardinal Richelieu.'

'Pretty much,' Johansson said. 'Something like that.'

'So what did he want?' Pia asked.

'Nothing much, just a chat,' Johansson said.

'And now you've got to go to Stockholm?' Pia said, having been through all this before.

'If you don't mind. But I'll be back tomorrow.'

'Sounds like an excellent idea,' Pia said. 'You can stop by the house and pick up a few things I need if we're going to that party at the weekend.'

'Of course.' Johansson's thoughts were already elsewhere and he didn't want to get caught up in any lengthy discussions.

'To begin with I almost thought he was drunk,' Pia said. 'That's how he sounded.'

'I dare say he was just in a good mood,' Johansson said neutrally. 'It's only twelve o'clock, so he probably hasn't had time for lunch yet.'

'Yes, perhaps he was just happy. A nice, happy little fellow,' Pia said.

'I can't quite picture that,' Johansson said, shaking his head firmly. 'So what do you think?' he asked, looking at his watch. 'About lunch, I mean?'

# 51

## Stockholm, Tuesday 5 August

Johansson changed into a linen suit and a dark blue cotton shirt, with his tie in the top jacket pocket for the time being, then took a taxi to the airport, where he caught the mid-afternoon plane from Sundsvall to Stockholm. His driver from the Security Police picked him up and drove him straight to the palatial home of the special adviser in Djursholm.

'Welcome to my humble abode!' the special adviser said, throwing his arms out in welcome as soon as Johansson stepped through the front door. 'I hope you don't mind sitting inside.'

'The cooler the better,' Johansson said, even though he was a devoted sauna enthusiast. So this is where you live, he thought as he glanced discreetly at the intricate pattern of the parquet floor, the dark wood panelling and the ornate plasterwork on the ceiling high above, careful not to miss a single Persian carpet, Dutch oil painting or Venetian chandelier on the way.

To begin with they settled down in the library to deal with practical matters, so that they could dine in peace and quiet. Everything was sorted out within ten minutes.

'When can you start?' the special adviser asked.

'On Monday,' Johansson said.

'That sounds quite splendid,' the special adviser said, his round face beaming like the sun. 'Well, at last we can get to more important matters. I haven't eaten a bite since lunchtime.'

'You have a very beautiful home,' Johansson commented

as they were walking to the dining room. 'Was it your parents'?'

'Are you crazy, Johansson? I come from extremely humble circumstances,' the special adviser declared. 'I'm an old Söder lad, born and bred on the hills of Södermalm. I bought this place from a poor chap for whom things weren't going too well.'

'But things seem to be going quite well for you,' Johansson said.

'Quite splendidly,' the special adviser agreed happily. 'And richly deserved, if you ask me.'

It being the middle of the week, the special adviser hoped that his guest would excuse the fact that he was being fobbed off with such a simple meal. But of course they both earned their daily bread working for a left-wing government, so simple customs ought perhaps to be the order of the day, notwithstanding the fact that there was every reason to celebrate Johansson's impending appointment, and perhaps no less reason for his employers to celebrate their wisdom in choosing Lars Martin Johansson.

'I'm afraid you'll just have to make do with my way of doing things,' the special adviser said with a sigh. 'Make the best of things, basically. Isn't that what you policemen usually say?'

In the world that the special adviser had lived in for almost his entire adult life, the most important thing was to meet other people halfway, and for both parties to be equally content as they carried on along their chosen path. Taking this existential motto as his basis, Johansson's host hoped that he had found a solution which his guest might appreciate, and ought certainly to be able to reconcile himself with.

'I've heard that you come from a family of old foresters up in Norrland, so what could be more fitting than to start with a variation on the age-old Swedish schnapps table,' he declared, gesturing towards a corner of the dining room in which an aged housekeeper was standing, dressed in a stiff black dress and white apron, with a carafe of schnapps already in her hand.

'Well,' Johansson said. 'My mother's family were more like crofters, whereas my father's . . .'

'Now then, my dear Lars Martin,' the special adviser interrupted. 'Don't let's allow false modesty to cloud our gaze and muddy the otherwise so clear prospects. Let us instead hasten to the buffet to partake of a couple of sturdy drinks and swathe our ravaged souls in the silken and velvet mantle that we so richly deserve.'

'Sounds good,' Johansson said.

Different sorts of sturgeon, the special adviser explained when, after the prefatory drink, consumed as they stood to attention, they finally sat down at the table laden with dishes and filled glasses. Poached sturgeon, cold braised sturgeon, fried sturgeon, smoked sturgeon, cured sturgeon, salted sturgeon, and sturgeon caviar with potato blinis were indicated by instructive gestures with his fork.

'Only second-hand car salesmen eat Russian caviar,' he declared as he shovelled a prodigious quantity of sturgeon caviar into his maw. 'Normal people eat sturgeon caviar.'

'The vodka was quite excellent,' Johansson said, turning the tall crystal glass in his right hand with the mien of a connoisseur. But you're wrong about my brother, because he prefers whitefish roe even though he does sell cars, he thought.

'It's superb, isn't it?' his host sighed contentedly. 'I took the opportunity to grab a few bottles when I was visiting Putin last week.'

The dinner progressed simply. The special adviser and his guest made the best of things, as faithful public servants should, while the chilly star of necessity shimmered from the crystal chandelier high above their bowed heads. The sturgeon had been followed by stuffed quail with a lukewarm timbale of root vegetables and then a simple slice of goat's cheese from the Camargue, before a lemon and lime sorbet cleansed the palate in advance of the concluding coffee, cognac and chocolate truffles. Each course was accompanied by wines which the special adviser had himself selected from his extensive cellars: a red Bourgogne from the fine year 1985, then a potent fortified red from the Loire with no given vintage.

'Wine is without doubt a drink that is best produced in France,' the special adviser declared with satisfaction, sticking his long nose deep into his glass.

'My wife and I drink a lot of Italian wine,' Johansson said.

The special adviser squirmed in his chair. 'If you'll accept a piece of friendly advice, Lars, I think you perhaps ought to avoid taking that sort of risk. Considering your health, if nothing else,' he said.

'So, how is Nylander?' Johansson asked once they had returned to the library to conclude the meal with a double espresso and some of the special adviser's 1990 Frapin.

'Better than he has been for a long time,' the special adviser said. 'His own room, three meals a day, little red, green and blue pills, and someone to talk to.'

'Is he in a private home?' Johansson asked carefully.

'A private home?' the special adviser snorted. 'There have to be some limits! First he tries to transform the police force in our relatively respectable banana monarchy into the sort of thing one can scarcely find in a common banana republic. Then he locks himself inside his office and refuses to come out, so that that poor football player in our already hard-pressed government is forced to ask his own little private army to blow off half the front of the building before they can drag him away to the tender mercies of a secure psychiatric ward. That sort of thing doesn't come cheap.'

'Ulleråker?' Johansson hazarded.

'Precisely,' the special adviser said emphatically. 'And not a day too soon, if you ask me.'

'So what happened, exactly?' Johansson asked curiously.

'That's not entirely clear,' the special adviser said, shrugging his bottle-shaped shoulders. 'It's supposed to have started with him taking a shot at the mirror in his private bathroom.'

'Imagine, the peculiar things people come up with,' Johansson said, nodding phlegmatically in the typical Norrland way.

'Maybe he got his chin caught in that curved bit round the trigger when he was cleaning his gun,' the special adviser speculated.

'The trigger guard, you mean?' Johansson said.

'Whatever,' the special adviser said with a dismissive hand gesture. 'I'm just trying to give him the benefit of the doubt,' he muttered.

After another hour of small talk, and a couple more glasses of the special adviser's admittedly remarkable cognac, Johansson's host had suggested that they play a game of billiards before addressing a light supper. But Johansson had heard terrible horror-stories about precisely that, and he declined the offer.

'I don't play billiards,' he said, shaking his head apologetically.

'If you like, I could teach you,' the special adviser said, looking at him hopefully.

'By all means, but I'm afraid it will have to be another time,' Johansson said. 'I really should think about going.'

Then Johansson thanked his host for the splendid dinner, ordered a taxi, and went home to his and his wife's apartment on Wollmar Yxkullsgatan, empty for the summer. And pretty much as soon as he got into bed, he fell asleep.

That one doesn't seem particularly sane either, he just had time to think before Morpheus took him into his welcome embrace.

# 52

*Växjö, Wednesday 6 August*

While the team investigating the Linda murder were having their usual morning meeting, Detective Superintendent Olsson marched in and announced that their colleagues in Kalmar had caught their rapist. The manager of an immigration centre outside Nybro had recognized one of his charges from the description given on local radio. He had phoned the police in Kalmar immediately, but they were already on their way. They had received the test results from the National Forensics Lab an hour before, and for once they were fortunate enough for the sample to match one of the 0.05 per cent of the country's male population whose DNA was already in their register.

A seventeen-year-old asylum-seeker from Moldova had arrived in Sweden a month before. A sample of his DNA had been taken just in case he got up to any mischief during the months that it usually took for a deportation decision to be made. Now he was sitting in one of the cells inside Kalmar police station. Denying everything, according to the interpreter, but at least now he would get to stay in Sweden longer than almost anyone else with the same background. He was innocent of Linda's murder. His DNA profile didn't match.

'Of course, we all suspected that,' Olsson declared. 'But I'd put money on him being behind our attempted rape.' He gave an encouraging nod towards Anna Sandberg.

All six officers who had been detailed to work with the Kalmar Police and follow up the rape case were now restored to the investigative team. The work that remained could be finished off in the usual way with the telephone, internal police internet and fax. There were more important things for them all to be doing.

'So we'll proceed on a broad front, relentlessly,' Olsson said. 'By the way, how are we getting on with our DNA samples?'

Beyond all expectation, according to Olsson's colleagues. They had now passed six hundred voluntary samples, smashing the old record. Four hundred of these had already been eliminated from the investigation.

'We're working along two lines,' Knutsson said with a quick glance at Lewin. 'We're trying to get people who live in the vicinity of the crime scene, and we're also trying to find people who fit the CP group profile and sample them systematically.'

'So there's certainly no question that we're working randomly,' Thorén clarified.

'Well, sooner or later he'll get caught in the net,' Olsson said, looking confident.

Over their habitual beer back at the hotel, Rogersson was able to tell Bäckström that their former boss had now found a new placement.

'Huddinge. Forensic psychology in Huddinge?' Bäckström suggested, having been to the hospital several times over the years in the course of his duties.

'Ulleråker,' Rogersson replied. 'Apparently he comes from somewhere round there, so it makes sense for him to be close to his wife and kids. Apparently he did his degree in Uppsala.'

'So how's he getting on?' Bäckström asked curiously.

According to Rogersson's source, things were going very well. By his second day there Nylander had been entrusted with certain responsible tasks, and now pushed the patients' book trolley around the various wards.

'Apparently he's happy as a pig in shit,' Rogersson said.

Bäckström contented himself with a nod of agreement. Wonder who's looking after Brandklipparen? he thought. Why am I wondering that? Oh, what the hell.

'Cheers, mate,' he said, raising his beer glass. 'And cheers to Chinny as well,' he added. Nylander was quite an entertaining bloke really, and he felt he had to say something.

Thursday's *Dagens Nyheter* included a long essay by university librarian Marian Gross, which the paper also picked up in its news pages and editorial, even though the same article had been refused on various grounds by the *Småland Post* in Växjö a few days before. Gross was upset, partly about the incompetent manner in which the police were managing the investigation into Linda's murder and partly on a purely personal level, because of the extreme abuse they had subjected him to.

Without any concern for himself and the risks he might be exposing himself to, he had volunteered as a witness to help the police. Anything else was out of the question, as it would be for every normal, functional human being living in a democracy under the rule of law. Himself a refugee from Poland during the time of the Soviet empire, he if anyone was well aware of what it was like to live in a dictatorship. He also had a personal involvement. He had known both the victim and her mother. Both of them delightful people, and the best neighbours you could wish for, according to Gross. Because there were strong reasons to suppose that he was the only person to have seen Linda's killer and be able to give a description of him, the way the police had treated him was both inexplicable and deeply insulting.

On two occasions they had used force to enter his home and drag him off to the police station, they had made insulting racist remarks, they had subjected him to drawn-out interrogations, and forced him to provide a DNA sample even though they didn't have a shred of evidence against him. And afterwards they had the gall to claim that he had provided the sample voluntarily and at his own request.

When the results of the test were known, it had taken him and his legal representative numerous telephone calls and letters before the police had deigned to tell him that he had been discounted from the investigation. In other words, that he had nothing to do with Linda's murder. Which had been obvious to him and every intelligent human being from the start, but not to the police in Växjö and their henchmen from National Crime in Stockholm.

Nor was Gross the only person who had been maltreated. A large article in the news section of the same paper revealed that a senior source in the police had told them that in connection with the Linda investigation, DNA samples had been collected from almost a thousand men in the Växjö district. The great majority of these were ordinary, decent, hard-working individuals. All of the test results which had been received back so far had proved, not unexpectedly, that the donors were innocent.

Three of them had been interviewed by the paper, and one of the three who had voluntarily provided a DNA sample was, remarkably, a woman. All three of them were unhappy, and the voluntary nature of the collection that the police kept talking about didn't match their own experiences. None of them had thought they had any other option, to put it simply, and so as not to attract further harassment they had chosen to do as the police requested. But to suggest there was anything voluntary about it was a very poor joke.

Most upset of all was the woman, because she had no idea what it was all about. Everyone knew by now that the person who killed Linda had to be a man, so what the police wanted with her DNA was a mystery. At least it was to her. The same question had obviously been fired at the press officer for the Växjö Police, but she had declined to comment. Those in charge of the investigation into the murder of Linda Wallin would not be commenting on any of the steps that had been taken. In purely general terms, that would affect the nature of their work, and in the worst-case scenario it could jeopardize or even ruin a potentially successful investigation.

The expert the paper turned to instead was not inhibited by these police restrictions. According to him there was only one reasonable explanation. The woman who had 'volunteered' to be tested probably had a son whose DNA the police were interested in, but evidently hadn't been able to get hold of. According to the woman herself, this much was actually true. She did have a son, but how he could possibly help them to solve Linda's murder was, if possible, even more of a mystery to her than her own involvement had been. According to his mother, he had never hurt a fly in his whole life, and also happened to have been living in Thailand for the past two years.

'I just don't think the police know what they're doing,' she said at the end of the long interview.

Sadly she didn't seem to be alone in this opinion. The editorial of the *Dagens Nyheter* recognized the sweet smell of injustice and could also see clear signs of the same confusion and desperation that had characterized the police hunt for the murderer of Prime Minister Olof Palme some twenty years before. Perhaps this wasn't so strange, really, seeing that several of the officers sent from the National Crime Unit to investigate Linda's murder had also played an active part in that investigation as well.

The Kalmar paper, the *Barometer*, also dealt with the Linda case in its editorial, albeit from a slightly different perspective from that of their colleagues in the capital city. According to the *Barometer*, this was fundamentally about a clash of two police cultures. On one side were the Växjö Police, with their local knowledge and contacts, knowing their Pappenheimers, preferring to work on the details and investigate things thoroughly. On the other side were their colleagues from National Crime, who lived in a computerized world, were used to practically unlimited resources, and were far from opposed to attacking problems on as broad a front as possible.

The *Barometer* also appeared to have sources inside the police. According to one of them, tensions within the investigative team had arisen at a fairly early stage, and this was obviously not beneficial to the investigation, regardless of who was right or wrong. To conclude: they were worried, although it was still too early to throw in the towel, and with luck the perpetrator would eventually be found, even though it was now over a month since Linda had been murdered.

That day the morning meeting of those leading the investigation went on right up to lunch. Most of what they discussed was what they had read in the papers that day. Detective Superintendent Olsson had even asked about the Palme investigation. Admittedly, he was asking purely out of personal curiosity, and it certainly wasn't intended as criticism. But none the less . . .

'Well, Bäckström, I dare say you were involved, of course,' he said, for some reason.

'Yes,' Bäckström said, with all the authority of someone who had worked on murder cases for almost all of his police life. 'The problem was that none of the people in charge listened to what I said.'

'I conducted a few interviews,' Rogersson said with a shrug. 'And if you gentlemen will excuse me, I've got several more waiting for my attention now as well.' Then he gave a curt nod and walked out.

'I was there as well,' Lewin said. 'Which probably isn't so strange, seeing as pretty much everyone working in crime in Stockholm in those days got caught up in the Palme investigation one way or another. And no one listened to me either, if anyone here is wondering.' Then he too excused himself and left the room.

But Bäckström didn't have any choice. He was left sitting there, watching as yet another morning of his valuable time ran into the sand, until he was finally able to put an end to the nonsense and make sure that at least he got a bite to eat.

Rogersson had evidently not only been conducting interviews. He was already sitting in the canteen when a grouchy Bäckström arrived at the same table with the dish of the day and a low-alcohol beer in the absence of the real thing.

'Are you sitting comfortably?' Rogersson asked as soon as Bäckström had sat down.

'Yes.'

'All hell's broken loose up in Stockholm,' Rogersson said, leaning forward across the table, lowering his voice and nodding excitedly at Bäckström.

'Don't tell me. Chinny's turned up with his little book trolley in HNC's office on the eleventh floor?' Bäckström said as he spread plenty of butter on a stale slice of white bread.

'I spoke to one of the lads at work,' Rogersson said. 'Do you know who's taking over from Chinny?'

'No. How the hell would I know that?'

'Johansson,' Rogersson said. 'Lars Martin Johansson. You know, the one the uniforms call the Butcher of Ådalen.'

'You mean that Lapp bastard? Fucking hell, that can't be true?'

'Reliable source,' Rogersson said.

And also a remarkable source, considering that the government meeting at which the acting head of the Security Police, Lars Martin Johansson, had been appointed as the new head of the National Crime Unit just an hour ago was still going on, and not even the most well-informed journalist had the faintest notion of his elevation, which would be made public in a couple of hours' time when the press release from the Justice Department was distributed.

On Friday evening Bäckström gathered his core team for dinner at the hotel. They started in Bäckström's room, to be able to discuss the case in peace and quiet, and just for once Lewin, Knutsson and Thorén had all said yes to Bäckström's generous offer of a beer. Little Svanström didn't drink beer, but she was perfectly capable of going to her room for a glass of the white wine from the bottle she evidently kept in the minibar.

'Then at least I can keep you company,' she said.

Bäckström was furious. He wasn't the sort who was prepared to take a heap of crap and put up with a load of backstabbing from a bunch of hillbilly cops who were too cowardly to say it to his face. Several times that day he had thought about going up to the police commissioner's office and banging his fists on his desk.

'With all due respect, Bäckström, I don't think that would be particularly constructive,' Lewin said.

'Really?' Bäckström said. Bloody traitor, he thought.

'I'm inclined to agree with Lewin,' Rogersson said, even though it was Bäckström's beer he was guzzling his way through. 'Anyway, as soon as we get the bastard behind bars, the talk will stop.'

Another one, Bäckström thought.

'It was someone she knew,' Lewin said. 'Someone she let in of her own free will, because she liked him, and I'm also pretty sure that she had sex with him of her own free will, at least to start with. Until it got out of hand.'

'So where do we find him?' Bäckström asked. In one of your bastard constructs, he thought.

'We're going to find him,' Lewin said. 'There can't be that many to choose from, can there? Sooner or later we're going to find him.'

Then they went down to the restaurant to have dinner, and because Bäckström had started to thaw out he even managed to persuade the others that they should have another drink before the meal.

'The schnapps is on me,' he said, having already worked out how to deal with that little problem without having to surrender any of his hard-earned cash.

After that there were several more. Mostly for him and Rogersson, of course, but even Lewin, of all people, fell into line and had a couple. Hans and Fritz acquitted themselves reasonably well before they eventually headed out into town, and this time they evidently weren't thinking of enjoying the films on offer in Växjö.

Bäckström stayed in the bar together with Rogersson, and when they finally staggered back to their rooms for some well-deserved rest they were both fairly far gone. Bäckström had trouble with the plastic key to his room, but Rogersson had helped him and made sure he got in.

'Do you want one?' Bäckström said, gesturing in the direction of the minibar.

'I think I've had enough,' Rogersson said. 'I know, there's something I meant to say.'

'I'm listening,' Bäckström said, as he kicked off his shoes and lay down on his side to save time before he fell asleep.

'One of those bastard reporters called and had a go about us sitting here watching porn films all night,' Rogersson said. 'Do you know anything about that, Bäckström?'

'Not the foggiest,' Bäckström muttered. What the hell's he going on about? he thought. Porn films? Now?

'Nor me,' Rogersson said.

'So what did you tell him?' Bäckström muttered.

'I told him to go to hell, of course. What would you have done?'

'Told him to go to hell, of course,' Bäckström said. 'What do you think about getting a bit of sleep?'

★

On Sunday 10 August, Linda Wallin's family buried her in the presence of her parents, her two half-brothers from her father's previous marriage, and twenty or so other relatives and close friends. No journalists or police, however. Detective Superintendent Olsson had been sharply rebuked by Linda's father when he had called and offered their services. He had already made his own arrangements. The funeral service took place in the church where Linda had been confirmed seven years before, and she was buried in the adjoining cemetery, in the plot her father had bought on his return to Sweden for himself and coming generations. His own grief was already boundless, with no beginning or end, so the fact that his only daughter had ended up there before him could scarcely make it any worse.

# 53

## *Stockholm, Monday 11 August*

By seven o'clock on Monday morning, Lars Martin Johansson had already arrived at his new workplace. His desk was covered with piles of neat documents. One of them had a Post-it note from his secretary with the words *Immediate action?*

On the top of the pile was a memo from the Chancellor of Justice, CJ, then one from the Judicial Ombudsman, JO. Their contents were almost identical, and they were addressed to the county police commissioner of Kronoberg County Police Authority, with copies to the Head of National Crime for information and eventual comment. They had been prompted by the contents of the *Dagens Nyheter* newspaper on Thursday 7 August, and concerned the methods which were reported as having been used in the preliminary investigation into the murder of Linda Wallin, and, in particular, the use of so-called voluntary DNA samples. But last but by no means least, the memos from CJ and JO were both policy initiatives. In light of their origins, this was the second worst thing that could happen, and a fairly good omen of the worst.

Why are these on my desk? Why didn't they send them straight to Ulleråker? Johansson thought crossly, as he wrote on the Post-it note that he wanted to meet whichever one of all his lawyers was responsible for this matter immediately. But otherwise everything seemed exactly the way it had been for years in his elevated existence. Papers, papers, papers, and yet more papers, he thought.

# 54

## *Växjö, Monday 11 August*

When the investigating team gathered around the big table for the first morning meeting of the week, they had no idea of the dark clouds that were gathering above their investigation. On the contrary, they all seemed to feel that a merciful sun was finally shining down on them. A minute after they began Enoksson suddenly appeared and asked Bäckström if he could start. He said he had a number of interesting things to tell them, and because it was Enoksson rather than Olsson – who had made Bäckström very happy by not being there – Bäckström suddenly felt a hint of the familiar tingling somewhere nearby.

'Our colleagues in Kalmar have found a match for the Linda murderer's DNA,' Enoksson began, and observed with satisfaction the way everybody immediately sat up and took notice. 'Unfortunately they can't provide us with an identity, but I still think it's pretty encouraging.' Is this what it feels like to have an audience spellbound? he wondered.

Because Enoksson was a thorough and pedagogical man, he tried to make things easier for his audience by summarizing, with bullet points, what he was about to tell them, and just to make sure he handed round some photocopied notes that they could look at as he explained. The first point was about Linda's murder. The last was about the report he had received from the National Forensics Lab in Linköping just an hour ago.

Linda had been murdered between four and five o'clock in the morning of Friday 4 July, at home in her mother's flat on Pär

Lagerkvists väg in Växjö. On the afternoon of Monday 7 July the Växjö Police received a report that a ten-year-old Saab had been stolen a couple of kilometres from the crime scene on the morning of the day it was reported missing. The same car had appeared in their investigation on Friday 11 July, when, as part of the investigation into Linda's murder, they had checked other interesting crimes in the area. Because it had been deemed to be of little interest, it had been set to one side. But now there were good reasons to take another look.

'If I remember rightly, we thought at the time that if it had been stolen three days after the murder, then it was pushing the boundaries of anything that could have any connection with Linda,' Enoksson said.

No matter. It had been found on the Sunday, so it couldn't have been stolen on the Monday. It was hidden in the forest near a side road off route 25 between Växjö and Kalmar, about ten kilometres from Kalmar. It was found by the landowner early that morning when he was inspecting his property. The car's registration plates had been removed, and someone appeared to have made a half-hearted attempt to set light to it. Considering the state it was in, it looked pretty much like the usual easy way for the owner to avoid one last journey to the scrapyard, and this wasn't the first time the landowner had experienced this particular form of private initiative. In short, he wasn't remotely amused.

That afternoon he had called the police in Kalmar, but because they were short of staff it wasn't until Wednesday 9 July that a patrol from the neighbourhood police unit in Nybro was able to take a look at the problem. After checking the car and taking a quick look round the surrounding area, they found a pair of number plates in a ditch some fifty metres from the vehicle, back towards route 25. They had checked them out over police radio, and were told that the plates matched the car, and this was where things began to get really interesting.

The crime reduction division of the county police authority in Kalmar had taken to heart the Justice Minister's proposals to deal more firmly with everyday offences, and they were participating in a national trial to use modern forensic techniques in an attempt to raise the clear-up rate for car thefts.

There were also several indications to suggest that this particular vehicle had been stolen. The car had been started by someone ramming a screwdriver into the ignition, and the steering lock had been broken the usual way, by locking the car's wheels and then wrenching the steering wheel as hard as possible.

In the ashtray between the front seats their colleagues from Nybro had found a hand-rolled cigarette with a promising smell of *Cannabis sativa*, so they put the butt in an evidence bag and sent it off to the National Forensics Lab for DNA analysis, and had the car moved to the police compound in Kalmar in case any further forensic tests were required within the framework of the national trial.

After that, both car and cigarette butt had got lost in the police computer system. The police in Kalmar had no idea that the same car had been discussed in the country's highest-priority murder investigation for a whole minute. They had made do with sending a letter to the car's owner saying that they had found it, but he hadn't got in touch, and no one appeared to have given it another thought.

At the National Forensics Lab the submitted marijuana butt ended up at the bottom of the ever-expanding list of pending DNA samples. Regardless of the Justice Minister's political manoeuvrings, and regardless of the priorities of the crime reduction division of the county police authority in Kalmar, and with no intentional disrespect to a national trial, it had been set to one side and had to wait its turn, and only after a whole month did anyone have any time to deal with it.

Late in the afternoon of Friday 8 August the analysis was finished, and when the results were compared with other cases in the database the warning lights began to flash. Unfortunately all of those most closely involved, from both the Växjö and Kalmar forces, had already gone home, and out of respect for confidentiality and various other reasons of the usual personal variety it wasn't until Monday morning that Enoksson and his colleagues were given the happy news over the phone by an expert at the National Lab.

'That's pretty much it,' Enoksson concluded. 'We've got officers on their way to Kalmar to bring the car back here. We thought that would be the easiest option. What else? Oh yes, a message from our colleagues in Kalmar.'

'What do they want?' Bäckström asked, although he already knew the answer.

'The usual,' Enoksson said. 'That if we need any more help solving Linda's murder, we only have to ask.'

'I don't think that will be necessary,' Bäckström said. 'Okay, comrades,' he went on. 'Now we've something to get our teeth into, and if there's ever been a car theft that's ever been more thoroughly investigated anywhere in the kingdom of Sweden than this one, then I promise to throw in the towel.' Dream on, losers, he thought.

# 55

In the county police commissioner's office one floor above, no one had any idea of the enthusiasm pervading the murder investigation downstairs. On the contrary, the county police commissioner was seriously concerned, and, as was so often the case, his fears were shared by his colleague Detective Superintendent Olsson, who was both faithful and wise.

Early that same morning his secretary had called him at his summer house, even though he was on holiday, with the sole purpose of informing him that he had received letters from both CJ and JO. This was something he had previously been spared, despite having worked in the police for almost twenty-five years and having in that time accumulated increasing numbers of fellow officers to keep in line. Accepting that he had no choice, he got in his car at once and made the roughly hundred-kilometre one-way trip to the police station in Växjö. But first he had checked on his beloved wife. As usual, she was lying down on the jetty sunbathing, and as usual she just waved at him dismissively when he, as usual, reminded her to use sun cream.

Once he was in the car he called his faithful squire Olsson, and, bearing in mind the sensitive nature of the matter, was careful to stress the importance of their having the chance to discuss the matter privately first, and that it would be advantageous to withhold all information for the time being from their colleagues from National Crime.

'I completely agree with you, boss,' Olsson concurred, promising to talk to Bäckström at once and ask him to take charge of the morning meeting in Olsson's absence, but without going into the reasons.

After discussing the situation in peace and quiet over a cup of coffee, it turned out that they agreed on much more than just that. The information in the newspaper article had admittedly, and entirely as usual, been both seriously spun and violently exaggerated, but Olsson had still attempted on several occasions to get their colleagues from National Crime to hold back.

'I suppose in part I see it as them having a completely different culture of policing from the one we have down here,' he explained. 'And it really does seem like they've never had to take the cost of things into consideration. It's very much get up and go, if you know what I mean.'

As far as the response to JO and CJ was concerned, he promised to look into the precise details. His boss had no need to worry himself with that at all.

'If it comes to it, I'll just have to give them a stiff talking to,' he said, straightening his back.

Olsson's a rock, the county police commissioner thought, wishing it were possible to ask him to call the newly appointed head of the National Crime Unit for him as well. That was a conversation he probably ought to get over and done with more or less immediately; he had been getting wound up about it since early that morning. What is it the others call him? he thought. The Butcher of Ådalen?

He himself had only met him on a couple of occasions, but that was more than enough to appreciate how he had earned the nickname. A big, coarse Norrlander who seldom said anything, but had a way of looking at people that certainly didn't contribute to the peace of mind of those under observation. Some sort of distant country cousin with no background, education or even the slightest hint of legal training, the county police commissioner thought, a shiver running down his spine.

Maybe it would be best if I called him myself after all, the county police commissioner thought, and without thinking about it he tapped in the same mobile number as the one his old classmate had used only a week before.

'Johansson,' a voice snapped abruptly at the other end of the line.

*

HNC Lars Martin Johansson wasn't the only person getting a telephone call. At roughly the same time as the county police commissioner called him, the head of the CP group, Inspector Per Jönsson, called his colleague Bäckström down in Växjö to offer his services in light of the DNA match he had just heard about. An excellent opportunity to pay back, in a subtle way, the various shameless remarks that Bäckström had spewed out the last time they met, Jönsson thought.

'I don't really see what the problem is,' Johansson interrupted after having to spend far too long listening to the county police commissioner's tirade. 'Your people are leading the investigation, aren't they? I thought our people were only there to help.' Which was probably bad enough, considering that one of them was Bäckström, but I'll deal with that little nightmare later, Johansson thought.

'Well, yes,' the county police commissioner conceded. 'The preliminary investigation is being led by one of my most reliable colleagues, a very experienced officer from regional crime here.'

'Good to hear,' Johansson said. 'Tell my guys to behave properly, otherwise they'll be in serious trouble. If you want me to recall them, I'll need that in writing.'

'Oh no, definitely not, definitely not, they're doing an excellent job,' the county police commissioner protested. In spite of the heat, his hands felt cold and clammy.

'Okay, then,' Johansson said.

What an extraordinarily primitive person, the county police commissioner thought.

'Correct me if I'm wrong, Pelle,' Bäckström said, evidently in an extremely good mood. 'You're calling to ask if you and your playmates down among the X-Files can help me and my team with something that we haven't yet had time to work out for ourselves?'

'Well, if you say so, Bäckström,' Jönsson replied stiffly. 'I'm calling to offer our analytical expertise with regard to the DNA traces on that car you found.'

'In that case I understand correctly,' Bäckström said. 'You're calling to ask if you can help us with something we haven't yet had time to work out for ourselves.'

'Okay, if you prefer to put it like that.'

'Negative. I repeat: negative,' Bäckström said loudly and switched off his phone, which he had learned was unquestionably the most effective way to finish a conversation, especially if you happened to be talking to someone like Jönsson. That'll give the little worm something to think about, he thought.

# 56

The following day the larger of the two main evening papers contained long reports about Linda's funeral – GRIEVING FOR LINDA – and to judge by both the text and the pictures, they had had to rely on external sources for the underlying information. The text was sympathetic but fairly basic, and could have been written about almost any funeral. It was illustrated with grainy shots of a cemetery taken from a distance, showing what could have been any random group of mourners. Neither the reporter nor the photographer was familiar to the paper's readers. They both had blandly anonymous names, and there were no by-line pictures of them alongside the article, which was unusual since it covered a whole page of the main news section.

The big scoop was on the opposite page, and as a banner across the top of the front page – MURDER COPS WATCHED PORN ALL NIGHT. Although the article didn't actually say so, any idle browser who didn't read every word would none the less get a good idea of what had happened: while Linda's family and closest friends, paralysed with grief, had been laying her to eternal rest, the officers from National Crime who were supposed to be catching her killer had been sitting in their hotel watching porn films.

'I don't understand a fucking thing about all this,' Rogersson said as they got into their car to drive the half kilometre between the hotel and the police station. 'Hell, I haven't watched any porn.'

'Well, never mind that,' Bäckström said soothingly. 'No one cares what those fucking muckrakers make up.'

Bäckström's memory had cleared considerably since the last time

Rogersson mentioned the matter, and now he just had to maintain his story. Seeing as this was one of the things he was best at, he wasn't particularly worried. Pretend to think about something else, shake his head if anyone asked, and if necessary get upset at all the crap people chose to dwell on if the person asking wouldn't take no for an answer.

Someone who evidently did care was Lars Martin Johansson. He had taken a copy of the evening paper into his room to read over morning coffee, and had quickly worked out what was really going on. For some reason he had Bäckström in mind when he summoned the chief superintendent responsible for the murder squad.

'Sit,' Johansson said, pointing first at the chief and then at a chair as the man slunk into his office. 'A question. Who sent Bäckström to Växjö?'

It was unclear, according to the other man. But he was sure of one thing. It hadn't been him. He had been on holiday and if he hadn't been on holiday Bäckström would have been the last person he would have picked to lead National Crime's contingent down in Växjö. And he had, in fact, tried to guard against any such eventuality before he disappeared on leave.

'He was supposed to be going through a number of cold cases,' he said defensively.

Johansson didn't say anything. Instead he merely stared at his visitor, and the stare he used was very similar to the one that the county police commissioner in Växjö had had in mind the day before.

'If you ask me, boss, I'm pretty sure it must have been Nylander himself who took the decision,' the chief added, clearing his throat nervously.

'Paper and pen,' Johansson said, nodding towards his victim. 'I want to know the following . . .'

# 57

By Monday afternoon the stolen car had been safely installed in the garage of the police station. Enoksson and his colleagues had set to work immediately, and just twenty-four hours later they were able to inform the investigating team of their initial findings. They had secured a number of fingerprints from inside the car. Two of these matched the most likely of the five sets of prints of unknown origin that had been found at the scene of the murder. They had also found some blue fibres on the driver's seat. These had been sent to the National Forensics Lab, but according to their own preliminary evaluation – they had a comparison microscope in the forensics unit of Växjö Police – there were good grounds to believe that they were the same exclusive cashmere fibres that had been found at the crime scene.

Then they had found all the other stuff as well. The stuff that you always found if you examined a suspicious vehicle closely enough. Sand, gravel, dust and fluff on the floor, masses of hairs and fabric fibres on the floor mats and seats, old receipts and other pieces of paper tucked away in the glove compartment and all sorts of other places. In the boot was a jack and the usual set of tools, a set of red children's winter overalls, and an old child's car seat. Outside the car, tossed into a thicket a few metres away, their colleagues in the Nybro police had found an empty ten-litre petrol can. But they hadn't found any traces of blood, semen or other circumstantially interesting bodily fluids.

The thief's modus operandi was also fairly obvious. The screwdriver jammed into the ignition, the broken steering lock, the hand-rolled joint found in the ashtray, the attempt to set fire to the vehicle to destroy any evidence. All of this suggested a classic example of a car thief: a drug-user with a long criminal record and numerous run-ins with the police and the criminal justice system. Even the fact that he failed to burn the car because he didn't have enough petrol fitted the theory, because they were almost always messy, disorganized, and high.

Two things spoiled this picture in the world that Enoksson inhabited, but he could live with the first of these. The blue fibres from the expensive top could be explained by the fact that the perpetrator had stolen it. Which left one fact that was hard to swallow – his fingerprints weren't in the police database. If he was the person that all the other evidence suggested, then they should have been there, and even if he was the exception that proved the rule it had still taken almost thirty years for this exception to crop up in Enoksson's police career.

'You don't think that could be a red herring?' Olsson speculated. 'I mean, apart from those blessed missing prints, he's an almost perfect match for the profile we were given.'

What the hell is he going on about? Enoksson thought in amazement. 'I'm confident these are the perpetrator's prints,' he said. 'What would be the point of giving us misleading evidence that doesn't lead anywhere? Leaving aside the fact that neither I nor anyone else can imagine how on earth he might have gone about it in purely practical terms. He seems to be fairly familiar with the rest of the details in the profile provided by our colleagues in Stockholm.'

'You don't think that's something he picked up along the way somewhere? That he's only just moved here and isn't in our register yet?' Olsson suggested.

'Possibly,' Enoksson said, looking sceptical. 'But why on earth would Linda let someone like that into her flat in the middle of the night?'

'Assuming that she did,' Olsson said, suddenly seeming quite pleased with himself. 'We mustn't forget that we don't actually know how he got into the flat.'

'That's something I've given some thought to,' Lewin put in slowly.

'Oh?' Olsson leaned forward.

'Actually, no,' Lewin said, shaking his head. 'Forget it. I'll get back to you. It was just an idea.'

The interviews with the owner of the car and anyone else who might have anything interesting to contribute had just resulted in more question marks and the usual unclear details. The retired pilot who was listed as the car's owner – Bengt Borg, sixty-seven years old, yet another Bengt in the Linda investigation's database of characters – hadn't used it since he had driven it back from the country approximately two years ago. He had another, considerably newer car that he used on a daily basis. After his retirement he and his wife had moved out to their summer cottage outside Växjö, and regardless of the time of year they seldom used their flat in town. The old Saab had been left standing in the car park pretty much ever since.

One of his grown-up daughters used to use it, but she had had a car of her own for the past few years. This daughter was thirty-five years old, worked in customer care at Växjö airport, and had a seven-year-old daughter who was due to start school that autumn. It was her overalls and car seat that had been found in the boot of the car, and if her grandfather were to hazard a guess, he thought these objects probably gave a good indication of when the child's mother had last used the stolen car. The child's car seat was for a very young child, and the label on the red overalls indicated that they were intended for children up to three years old. Four years ago fitted fairly well with his memory.

The most obvious thing would have been to ask the daughter. The problem was that she, her husband and the daughter had gone to Australia to explore that exciting continent for two months. According to her father, the pilot, it wasn't a bad idea, as Australia was in the southern hemisphere and its relatively cool winters were preferable to the almost tropical heat that had been tormenting him and other Smålanders for the past couple of months.

'But if it's important, I can try to get hold of her,' he offered help-fully. 'Otherwise she'll be home next week. My grandchild's starting school this autumn, of course.'

Detective Inspector Salomonson had thanked him for the offer, but thought that they would manage. 'There's no one else you know of who might have borrowed it?' he asked.

No, according to the pilot. He did have another daughter, but she didn't drive and had no licence. For the past few years she had been living in Kristianstad, where she worked as a lawyer. She didn't visit her parents very often, and from her father's description Salomonson understood that it was the airport worker rather than the lawyer who was his favourite.

'And I don't have any other children or grandchildren,' he declared. 'Not that I know of, anyway,' he added, looking very pleased with himself.

Why did he think that the car was stolen on the morning of 7 July, Salomonson wondered.

To be honest, the car's owner wasn't altogether sure on that point. To begin with he hadn't even registered that it wasn't standing in its usual spot in the car park out in Högstorp when he had called to collect something from the flat. When he noticed that both sets of keys were hanging on their normal hooks in the cupboard in the hall, he had started to wonder. So he had gone back out into the car park to check once more, in case he had left it somewhere else and had simply forgotten. And it was while he was doing this that he had bumped into his next-door neighbour and had mentioned it to him. His neighbour was sure he had seen the car parked there over the weekend. Hadn't he already explained all this when he reported the car missing? The simplest solution would be to talk directly to the neighbour, but he had gone hiking in the Lapland fells, and, from what he had said, wouldn't be back for another fortnight.

'There's one thing I don't understand,' the pilot went on, looking curiously at Salomonson. 'Why are you so incredibly interested in who stole that old wreck?'

'It's a new initiative we're pushing here in Växjö,' Salomonson said, trying to sound as believable as he could. 'We're trying to focus more on so-called everyday crimes.'

'I would have thought you had more important things to be doing,' the pilot said, shaking his head. 'That's the impression you get from the papers, anyway. Sometimes you can't help wondering where this country's heading.'

In the absence of any better options, two days had been spent knocking on doors in the area. They started with people who over-looked the car park, then carried on through the rest of the block. Half of the doors they knocked on stayed closed. They all received notes through the letterbox, and at least a few of them contacted the police. Evidently one or more of them contacted someone other than the police, because a number of journalists began calling the police station, and even showed up in the area to conduct their own inquiries. The news that the police were looking for a stolen car in connection with the Linda murder had reached most of the media within the space of a few hours.

One of the many neighbours who had been questioned did have some information for them, but in light of what she told them they would probably have been better off without her. Rogersson had set her aside when he looked through the reports that reached his desk, attaching a note to it with a paperclip: *Confused old lady. No action. JR.*

It was Anna Sandberg who had questioned her. Mrs Brita Rudberg, ninety-two years old, a widowed pensioner living in the building closest to the car park. Her flat was on the first floor, with a balcony that offered an excellent view of said car park. Every morning that summer she had got into the habit of going and sitting on the balcony for a while until it became too hot to stay there, and she remembered that day very well. It was around six a.m. on Friday 4 July, which was when she usually woke up during the summer. When it got darker outside she usually slept a bit longer, but even in the middle of winter she never woke up any later than half past six.

To begin with Sandberg had thought the witness was both charm-ing and compos mentis, even though she was ninety-two and clearly had no idea about the murder that had taken place a month ago, still less that the car she was being questioned about had been stolen. How could she be so sure that it was Friday 4 July?

'I remember it very well,' Sandberg's witness said, smiling at her. 'That's my birthday. I turned ninety-two,' she added. 'I had bought a slice of cake from the patisserie in town the day before to have some-thing to celebrate with, and I remember that I sat and ate it with the cup of coffee I always have first thing. I even said hello to him. He was doing something to the car and I remember thinking that he was probably heading off to the country, seeing as he was up so early.'

'Can you describe him, the man who was doing something to the car, the man you said hello to?' Sandberg said, and without realizing it she started to get the same tingling that Bäckström felt every now and then, even though he was usually completely wrong.

'I got it into my head that it was the son,' Mrs Rudberg said. 'At least it looked very like him. He's very good-looking, you know. The way men used to look when I was young.'

'The son?' Sandberg asked.

'Yes, that pilot's son, the man whose car it is,' Mrs Rudberg explained. 'He's got a son who's very similar to the man I said hello to. Dark, handsome, slim as well.'

'Did he say hello back?' Sandberg asked. 'When you said hello, I mean?'

Now the witness seemed less certain. He might have nodded, but she wasn't entirely sure. But she was fairly sure that he had looked at her. More than once, even.

Did she remember what he was wearing? She wasn't sure about that either. He was probably dressed the way most young men his age seemed to be when the weather was warm and they were going to the country.

'Those casual trousers, and one of those casual shirts,' she said, suddenly seeming very hesitant.

'Short or long trousers?' Sandberg persisted, trying to sound calm and friendly and not pushing for an answer.

The witness would prefer not to have to say, but if she had to choose then she would say short, considering the heat if nothing else. She wasn't sure of the colour either. Neither of the short, or possibly long, trousers, nor of the casual top. All she had was a notion that the trousers and top had been dark. They certainly weren't white, because she would have remembered that.

His shoes? Had she noticed them? Even more hesitant now. Shoes weren't the sort of thing anyone looked at, were they? If there had been something peculiar about them, then she would have noticed.

They were probably those rubber shoes that all the youngsters seemed to wear these days.

Barefoot? Could he have been barefoot? No, definitely not. Because she would certainly have noticed that, and even though she had never learned to drive she did at least understand that you should never drive a car barefoot.

'Rubber shoes,' Mrs Rudberg repeated, with a nod. 'The sort youngsters always wear these days.'

But she was absolutely sure of two things. First that it was her birthday, the day she turned ninety-two, Friday 4 July, at about six o'clock in the morning. And second, that he had spent about ten minutes fiddling with the car before getting in and driving away. And, considering the way he was dressed and the time of day, he was obviously heading out into the country to see his wife and children. She was also almost certain of a third thing. If it wasn't the pilot's son, then it was someone very like him. Dark, handsome, slim, good-looking in the way that men used to be.

Did she remember anything else about that morning, Sandberg asked, hoping she would mention the cloudburst that had hit Växjö just after seven o'clock and lasted until almost eight o'clock.

'Nooo. Such as what?' Mrs Rudberg looked at her hesitantly.

'Anything else that happened during the day?' Anna prompted.

Nothing, according to the witness. She didn't read the papers, she seldom watched television or listened to the radio, and certainly not the news programmes. She hadn't had many close friends for many years now, and most days in her life were almost identical.

After another three attempts Sandberg had told her about the thirty millimetres of rain that had fallen in less than an hour, constituting the sum total of the precipitation that had fallen on Växjö in the past month.

Mrs Rudberg had no memory of the cloudburst, or even of any rain at all. That was probably because she had already left the balcony to have a little lie down on her bed by the time it started. 'Yes, because otherwise I'm sure I would have remembered. After all, it's been so dry this summer.'

# 58

'If you ask me, the old woman's completely dotty,' Rogersson said the next day when the investigating team were discussing her testimony and that of the other people in the area.

'Why do you say that?' Olsson said. For the past few days he had been back in his place at the head of the table.

'To start with, the pilot doesn't have a son, he's never had one, doesn't want one and won't even entertain the idea of one. All he's got is a son-in-law. He's a flight officer for SAS, and he's in Australia with the pilot's younger daughter, to whom he's been married for years. They left Sweden on Wednesday 18 June, two and a half weeks before Linda was murdered. They're due home about a week from now, so the kid can start school. Anyway, he got cross when I phoned and went on about his son. Wondered what the hell we were up to. He'd already explained to one of my colleagues that he had two daughters, a granddaughter and a son-in-law, but no son.'

'The other daughter,' Lewin said. 'What about—'

'Thank you, Lewin,' Rogersson interrupted. 'She's thirty-seven years old, works as a lawyer in Kristianstad and for the past fifteen years has been living with her partner, who is also a lawyer and whom she met when they were both studying law in Lund.'

'What do we know about him?' Lewin asked.

'Well, we know that he's a she, and I'm sure you don't want to hear what the father said when I began to ask him about her.'

'Mind you, that business about the birthday is quite striking,' Lewin persisted.

'That's what I thought, as did Anna, who was the one who spoke to her,' Rogersson agreed. 'Until we discovered that the old woman was born on 4 June, not 4 July. At least she was if we're to believe her ID number.'

'Maybe she was celebrating some other anniversary? Who knows, maybe she makes any excuse to have a bit of cake. The old bag's probably one of those sugar addicts,' Bäckström said, laughing so much his stomach was bouncing.

'Point taken,' Lewin said with a sigh. 'What about the description, then?'

'You mean the way he was so similar to the son that doesn't exist?' Rogersson said. 'Well, seeing as I had nothing better to do, I've spoken to the old woman's optician. He wasn't exactly impressed, let me say. I'm no expert, but I got the impression that she's practically blind. He also told me to remind her that she's overdue for a check-up. She hasn't been to see him for the past six years.'

'I don't think we're going to get any further, are we? What do you think, Lewin?' Bäckström said with a grin.

After the meeting, Eva Svanström went to Lewin's office to console him.

'Don't worry about those two. Bäckström's never been right in the head, and Rogersson drinks like a fish, so I dare say he was just hungover as usual. I don't know how many times I've said this to you.'

'You came to console me?' Lewin said with a smile.

'And what's so wrong with that?' Svanström said, sounding the way she usually did again. 'But that's not the only reason. I've got something to tell you.'

What's so wrong with a bit of consolation? Lewin thought.

About three years ago, at roughly the same time as she moved from one flat to another in the building she lived in, and her daughter moved back to her father's, Linda's mother had changed her phone number. Normally people took their existing number with them when they moved the way Lotta Ericson did, but for some reason she got a new one. Ex-directory. Up until then she had been in the phone book, like most other people.

The old number had reverted to Telia, and after the usual quarantine period it had been re-allocated to one of their new customers, a female anaesthetist who had transferred from a post at the university clinic in Linköping to a better position at the hospital in Växjö. Her name was Helena Wahlberg, she was single, forty-three years old, and lived on Gamla Norrvägen, approximately half a kilometre north of the crime scene, in a part of town that was conveniently called Norr.

The old open-access number now also became ex-directory, which wasn't so strange given the nature of the new customer's work. Svanström had tried to get hold of her at the hospital, but it turned out that she had been on holiday for the past month. She was due back at work on Monday, and the only thing that was significant about all this – and even this was probably just an irrelevant coincidence – was that her holiday had started on Friday 4 July, the day Linda was murdered.

'Do you want me to request a list of calls to and from her number?' Svanström asked.

'I think we should wait,' Lewin said. 'The easiest thing would be for me to call and ask her first. But there is something else I'd like to ask you to do,' he added.

In spite of the fact that their 92-year-old witness had evidently got her birthday wrong by a whole month, Lewin still wasn't inclined to let go of her. The explanation for this lay in his own background, which could be regarded as a common police affliction. And possibly also in his nature, although that was something that he hadn't considered at all, even though the woman on the other side of the desk did so pretty much every time she thought about him.

'My old grandmother – she's dead now, but if she was still alive she'd have been about a hundred – well, according to the population register she was born on 20 February 1907, but we always used to celebrate her birthday on 23 February.'

'Why did you do that?'

'According to the story we told as a family, the priest was supposed to have been drunk when he was entering her name in the church register, and simply wrote the wrong date. Admittedly, it's only a few days rather than a month, but there's something about June and July that bothers me.'

'It's fairly easy to get them mixed up,' Svanström agreed.

'That's why a lot of old lawyers emphasize the difference when they speak. To avoid any confusion. I remember how surprised I was the first time I heard one of them do it. We had a dotty old lecturer in criminal law at the Police Academy. His weird way of pronouncing July was pretty much the only thing he taught us. That lawyers pronounce July weirdly. Otherwise it was mainly the usual nonsense about making sure you held on to your sword tightly when you took a swing at a criminal. The fact that the police had switched to batons several years before seemed to have escaped his notice. On one occasion he devoted an entire lecture to the legal consequences of hitting someone with the edge instead of the flat of the blade, until one of us summoned up the courage to mention batons.'

'How did he take it?'

'He got angry.'

'It's probably easiest if you just ask her. The witness, I mean.'

'Maybe I should.' Maybe I should have a word with her optician as well, Lewin thought. The problem with officers like Rogersson, however fundamentally decent they were, was that they preferred to see reality in black and white.

When Eva got up to leave, he was suddenly struck by the elusive thought that had crossed his mind a couple of hours before.

'One more thing,' Lewin said. 'Something that struck me during the meeting. What Enoksson said about anyone stealing a car in that way probably being an habitual thief. I don't think that's necessarily true.'

All you needed was a bit of technical expertise, he said. A car mechanic, or even just someone interested in cars, good with their hands generally. Or maybe the perpetrator picked it up from someone else. Maybe he worked in the remand system, youth custody, something like that.

'Or the police,' Svanström said.

'Yes, maybe,' Lewin agreed. 'Although I wouldn't have the faintest idea what to do, and I've been in the police for almost thirty years.'

'Someone who knows what they're doing, but didn't necessarily end up in our database when they learned how to do it,' Svanström summarized.

'Exactly.'

'So we're basically talking about the exact opposite of that disgusting librarian Gross. Someone who isn't particularly cultured.'

'Exactly,' Lewin repeated. Definitely not someone like Gross, he thought.

Once Svanström had left, naturally he couldn't resist. Without having any idea that he was confirming Eva Svanström's most recurrent thought about him, he dialled the home number of the female anaesthetist. She wasn't yet back at work, but people were surely just as likely to come home before the end of their holiday as to wait until the very last day? At least, that was what he usually did.

'I can't answer right now, but if you leave your name and number, I'll get back to you as soon as I can,' the voice on the answer machine said.

Lewin hung up. That must have been her voice on the machine, he thought. She sounded just like a forty-something female anaesthetist. Correct, well-meaning, alert. Single, according to the population register, and an acting consultant at Växjö Hospital according to the taxation records that the conscientious Eva Svanström had dug out from their computers.

# 59

About a week earlier Bäckström had deputed two younger colleagues from Växjö Police to try to trace the origin of the blue cashmere fibres that for the sake of simplicity he had decided to call the fabric line of inquiry. The fact that they were both women was no coincidence. It was pretty much in the nature of the task, and Bäckström thought it was excellent that the little things had something to do, so that they didn't cause any serious trouble for him and the real police officers.

Nevertheless they appeared to have taken the task seriously. According to the National Forensics Lab, they were probably dealing with a thin pale blue sweater, and the officers searching for it had spoken to everyone who might, in the light of their professional experience, be able to help them find it. They had spoken to fashion designers, fashion journalists, fashion photographers and fashion experts generally, to manufacturers, wholesalers and representatives of a large number of boutiques selling more exclusive clothes. One of them had even begun by talking to her aunt, who was almost obsessed with what she wore.

Assuming that they were dealing with a man's jumper, there were ten possible designs to choose between. The most likely, a V-neck sweater with long sleeves made in Britain, Ireland, America, Italy, Germany or France, had a price tag of between two and twelve thousand kronor, depending on the label. If it had been bought in a sale, or possibly at a factory outlet, or anywhere other than a boutique, the price would have been lower. But anything under a thousand kronor was unlikely, and would have been a serious bargain, according to the people they had spoken to.

But it didn't appear to have been sold anywhere in Växjö or the surrounding area. None of the shops there had stocked a man's sweater of that sort in recent years. All they had, or had had in the past, were a few for women, but to judge from the available delivery notes and stock figures none of them had been the right colour. Which left some twenty shops and department stores in Sweden, almost all of them in Stockholm, Gothenburg or Malmö. Unless it had been bought abroad. That was just as likely, according to the people they had spoken to, and, considering the price, often a better buy. Both supply and demand were considerably larger abroad than they were in Sweden. But that was about as far as they had got.

Which left the possibility that it had been stolen. With the help of the police computers they had brought up lists of all thefts of exclusive clothes reported by importers, wholesalers, warehouses, department stores and boutiques in the south of Sweden in recent years. Then they had looked through all the normal household burglaries, thefts and lost property reports which had found their way into police files. No men's cashmere sweaters.

'I'm afraid it doesn't look like we're going to get much further than that,' one of the two fabric detectives said when she and her colleague reported to Bäckström.

'It's not the end of the world,' Bäckström said with a cheery smile. 'The main thing is that you girls have had some fun while you were at it.'

Women have no sense of humour. A couple of proper attack-dykes, Bäckström thought when they left his office a minute or so later. He glanced at his watch, which already showed almost three o'clock. It was Friday and high time for the first beer of the weekend. But certainly not for that little poof Olsson, who was suddenly standing in his doorway, wanting to talk to him.

'Have you got a couple of minutes, Bäckström?' Olsson asked.

'Of course,' Bäckström said, smiling warmly. 'We've got a long way to go before we can think of calling it a day.'

Olsson was evidently up for spending half the evening discussing the voluntary DNA samples, unless Bäckström managed to put a stop to him at an early stage. Olsson was worried, and the county police commissioner shared his concerns. So to settle his anxieties he had decided to go round and, in true democratic spirit, find out what the key members of his team thought about the matter.

'We're actually getting close to seven hundred voluntary DNA samples now,' he said, having just received the current figure from Thorén.

'Yes, it's going very well,' Bäckström agreed enthusiastically. 'We'll soon have the bastard. Any time now.' So there, you little coward, he thought.

'I'm sure you're right, of course,' Olsson said, even though he didn't seem to have been listening to what Bäckström said. 'The problem is that both JO and CJ are on to us. I'm not particularly concerned about what gets written in the papers, of course, but I have tried to take account of the criticism.'

'Yes, well, you are the head of the preliminary investigation,' Bäckström emphasized cheerily.

'What do you mean?' Olsson was looking at him suspiciously.

'Well, you'll be the one sitting up to your ears in shit if they get it into their heads to cause trouble for someone, and that can't be much fun,' Bäckström said, smiling his most sympathetic smile.

'Well, of course that's not the main reason why I think we should adjust our approach on this matter, at least for the time being,' Olsson said nervously.

'What about proceeding on a broad front, relentlessly?' Bäckström asked innocently.

'Naturally I've taken that into consideration, Bäckström, but I'm also starting to get a definite sense that the investigation is starting to point in a more focused direction, if I may say so.'

'So you're giving up the idea of getting DNA samples from the whole town?' Bäckström said brightly. 'In that case, I—'

'What I mostly had in mind was the car,' Olsson interrupted. 'That we should suspend the DNA sampling programme in order to focus hard on the line of inquiry offered by the car.'

'You mean that hundred-year-old who's forgotten when she was born?'

'Ninety-two,' Olsson said. 'Maybe not her, exactly, but we're far from finished with the door-to-door enquiries out in Högstorp, and Enoksson and his colleagues usually have something to offer us once they've finished their examinations. What do you think, Bäckström?'

'I think we should send in the heavies to deal with the old woman. Maybe the Sala League.'

'The Sala League?' Olsson said. 'I'm afraid I don't quite understand.'

'Charming characters, very busy in central Sweden back in the thirties,' said Bäckström, who had garnered all his esoteric knowledge from the *Crime-Police Yearbook*. It was the only book he read, mainly to check that he was mentioned in sufficiently flattering terms in the case descriptions that certain of his half-demented colleagues insisted on sharing with the general public. And all at no cost, seeing as he usually stole a copy from work.

'Yes, I know that. But what have the Sala League got to do with our witness?' Olsson was looking doubtfully at Bäckström.

'Nothing, sadly,' Bäckström said. 'Besides, they're dead now, but back in the thirties they gassed an old woman to death before robbing her. They got a sum total of six kronor and thirty öre that she kept hidden under her mattress. A lot of money in those days, Olsson.'

'You're joking,' Olsson said.

'You never know,' Bäckström said. 'You never know.' Maybe we should let Rogersson loose on the old bag, he thought.

# 60

Bäckström's ultimate superior, Lars Martin Johansson, hadn't given a thought to looking at the time, even though it was already past three o'clock on Friday afternoon, and a nervous chief superintendent had been sitting outside with his secretary and sweating for the last half hour. He hadn't even read the editorial in *Svenska Dagbladet*, since he had spent the past hour trying to get to grips with what Bäckström and his colleagues had actually been doing down in Växjö for the past month.

'You can send him in now,' Johansson said over the intercom, and whether it was because it was almost the weekend or for some other reason, it took no longer than ten seconds before the chief superintendent was sitting in the visitor's chair on the other side of his large desk.

'I've read the files you gave me,' Johansson said.

'I'm listening, boss,' the chief said.

'I want someone in the finance office to take a look at them. I've indicated the main question marks in red,' Johansson said, nodding towards the folder lying on the desk between them.

'When do you want it done, boss?'

'It'll be fine if I can have it first thing Monday morning. It is the weekend, after all,' Johansson said generously.

'I'd better have a word with them at once. Before they disappear, I mean,' the chief said nervously, starting to stand up.

'One more thing,' Johansson said. 'I want to take a look at the investigation as well. If I've understood correctly, our colleagues in the CP group have copies of most of the files?'

'And when do you want those, boss?'

'Quarter of an hour will do fine,' Johansson said.

'I'm afraid they may already have finished for the day,' the chief said, glancing nervously at the time.

'I find that hard to imagine,' Johansson said. 'It isn't even half past three yet.'

'I'll see to it that you get them in quarter of an hour, boss.'

'Excellent,' Johansson said. 'You can give them to my secretary.'

# 61

Exactly one week after Queen Silvia's name-day, on Friday 15 August, a bolt of lightning struck the head of Detective Superintendent Evert Bäckström of the murder squad of the National Crime Unit. At least that's how he himself described it when he was telling his closest friend, Detective Inspector Jan Rogersson, about the undeserved nightmare that yet another crazy woman had landed him in.

'It was as if a bolt of lightning struck me in the head,' Bäckström said.

'You always have to exaggerate, Bäckström,' Rogersson objected. 'Just tell me what really happened. You were drunk, weren't you?'

It had begun the same way as usual, and very promisingly considering that it was the weekend and the overtime ceiling prevented him from even setting foot in his workplace before Monday morning. As soon as he had got rid of that little poof Olsson, he had left Växjö police station in his usual circumspect way and strolled slowly back to the hotel. Once he got up to his room he had undressed, put on a freshly laundered dressing-gown and opened the first chilled beer of the weekend, and when Rogersson eventually showed up, red-faced as a turkey ready for the chop, he was already on his third.

'Friday at last,' Rogersson said, easing the worst of the pressure straight from the can. 'Any special plans for the weekend, Bäckström?'

'You'll have to manage on your own tonight, young man,' said Bäckström, who had made use of the dead minutes between the second and third beers to call little Carin and ask her to dinner.

'Female company,' Rogersson said. In spite of everything, he wasn't a bad detective.

'First we're going to have a bite to eat out in town, then I thought I might let the super-salami have a bit of a work-out,' Bäckström said, emphasizing his point by taking a deep gulp of beer.

To start with everything went according to plan. Bäckström and his lady for the evening ate a reasonable dinner in a nearby place on Storgatan, and even managed a few drinks, although he was trying to hold back out of consideration for the finale to the evening. Eventually they ended up back at the hotel, and even though Carin for some reason kept saying that they should go to the bar she had finally accepted the offer of a little drink in his room. By this point the exact timings and other details weren't entirely clear. Certainly not clear enough for him to sit and go through them later with a number of humourless so-called colleagues from the internal investigation unit.

'There's something I wanted to show you,' Bäckström said, firing off his most charming smile before disappearing into the bathroom.

'As long as it doesn't take long,' Carin said through the door as she sipped from her glass, suddenly seeming a bit stand-offish.

Quicker than Superman in his phone-box, Bäckström had carried out a similar manoeuvre in his bathroom. Fastening a towel round his waist, he stepped out in all his glory and let the towel fall, simultaneously pulling in his stomach and thrusting out his chest. Entirely unnecessarily, of course, but sometimes you had to make a bit of extra effort. 'What do you think about this then, my dear?' he said.

'Have you gone mad? Put that nasty little thing away at once!' Carin cried from her seat on the sofa. Then she grabbed her handbag and jacket and marched out, slamming the door behind her.

Women aren't right in the head, Bäckström thought. What does she mean, little thing? What the hell's the woman saying? He put on his clothes again and went down to the bar, but the only person there was Rogersson, sitting leering in a corner. In the absence of anything better to do, he stayed and squeezed in a couple more shorts. Then, when he finally returned to his room, he called her to wish her good-night to show that he wasn't the sort to hold a grudge, but before he had the chance to open his mouth she hung up on him. Evidently she disconnected the phone, because he didn't get through to either her or her answering machine when he tried again. Just like that crazy bitch who lumbered me with little Egon.

# 62

On Saturday morning, taking Eva Svanström with him, Lewin got on the train and went to Copenhagen. A little surprise that he had been planning in secret, and it made her as excited as a young child.

'Why haven't you said anything?' she asked.

'Because then it wouldn't have been a surprise,' Lewin replied.

'This is going to be so exciting. I've never actually been to Copenhagen,' Eva said.

First they visited the Tivoli Gardens, where they went on the roller coaster and the roundabout. Then they took a gentle stroll down Strøget. They found a nice bar in Nyhavn and ate a proper Danish breakfast, with herring, pastries and all the usual trimmings. The sun was shining just as it was in Småland, but here it seemed quite bearable, and Lewin felt better than he had for ages. In fact he felt so much better that he finally felt able to mention what had been preoccupying him so much recently.

'Maybe we ought to do something serious with our lives, Eva,' he said, squeezing her hand.

'I'm fine,' Eva said. 'I've never been as happy as I am right now.'

'Let's think about it,' Lewin said, and then the moment passed, but perhaps that was just as well. Even if he never plucked up the courage to ask again.

'So what do you think about our new boss?' Eva said, preferring simply to change the subject than to make a big song and dance. 'That Lars Martin Johansson.'

'I've actually met him,' Lewin said. 'We were on a case together back when he was just an ordinary officer. Must be almost thirty years ago now. Before your time. The Maria murder. A woman was found strangled and raped in her flat out in Enskede.'

'Tell me about it,' Eva said, lacing her fingers between his. 'What's he like? Johansson, I mean.'

'As a police officer he wasn't bad,' Lewin said. 'His colleagues used to joke that he could see round corners. He had an unnerving ability to work out what was going on.'

'The policeman who could see round corners,' Eva repeated delightedly. 'Sounds a bit like one of those cop shows on telly. So what was he like as a person, then?'

'What was he like as a person? He was the sort who could pretty much step over a body without even worrying where he was putting his feet.'

'Ugh. That really doesn't sound very nice.'

'I might be wrong. We don't have much in common, him and me. Maybe I just didn't understand him.'

'Sounds like a complicated character, anyway.'

'Maybe the combination of being able to see things yet still be untroubled by the consequences frightened me,' Lewin said. 'Isn't that what they're supposed to be like, those supercops? Seeing everything, being able to work everything out, yet not sparing a thought for what happens to the people that it's ultimately all about?'

'Well, if the worst comes to the worst, we can always move,' Eva said. 'Apply somewhere else. I know the Stockholm force needs people. My old boss has even been in touch and asked me.'

'It's worth bearing in mind,' Lewin said, and for some reason he leaned over and smelled her hair, nuzzling gently between her right earlobe and cheek. That would be the worst that could happen, and things could never be any better than they are right now, he thought.

# 63

The night after they returned from Copenhagen Lewin dreamed again of that summer almost fifty years before, when he got his first proper bicycle. A red Crescent Valiant. And his dad had taken almost the whole summer off to teach him to ride it.

The hardest bit was always when they were almost home again. Worst of all was the gravel path leading to the house. The last twenty metres between the white garden gate and the red wooden porch.

'I'm letting go,' Daddy calls, and Jan squeezes the handlebars and pedals and pedals and slides over on the loose gravel. And this time he slid over badly, scraping his elbows and knees, and the whole idea of ever learning to ride a bike suddenly seems pointless.

'Up you get, Jan,' Daddy says, picking him up and ruffling his hair. 'Let's go and have some hot chocolate and a cheese sandwich, and find some plasters.'

And everything was back to normal again.

# 64

On Sunday Johansson stretched out on the sofa in the living room of his flat on Wollmar Yxkullsgatan on Södermalm in Stockholm. He had fixed himself a large gin and tonic with plenty of ice, and started to read through the files on the Linda murder. It looked as though it might take him all afternoon, but his wife was away staying with a friend and he had nothing better to do. Besides, this was pretty much as close as he could get, given his elevated position, to a proper murder case these days. Maybe I should apply for a job in that CP group? It looks like they need help with pretty much everything, he thought, as he glanced through the profile of the perpetrator.

What on earth are they doing down there? he thought four hours later when he had finished reading, done some thinking and put the files to one side. Any proper police officer ought to have worked this out last week.

# 65

## *Växjö, Monday 18 August*

By the Monday when the hunt for Linda's killer entered its eighth week, Bäckström was starting to feel rather tired of the whole business. They weren't able to take any more DNA samples, although even an idiot like Olsson ought to have realized that if they weren't going to catch him any other way, they would do so eventually if they carried on with that. Nor was there anything tasty for him to get his teeth into either. No juicy breakthroughs or promising thugs to get hold of. All they had was crazy hundred-year-olds who couldn't remember when they were born and thought the perpetrator looked like someone who didn't exist. Not to mention all the other so-called witnesses who hadn't seen, heard or thought anything, let alone the usual lunatics and head-cases with their premonitions and messages from the other side. What the hell was he doing here? It was entirely the wrong place for a proper policeman, and high time to pack up and go back to work in Stockholm.

Besides, the town he'd ended up in was fucking awful. To top it all, every newspaper, television channel and radio station now seemed to devote all its time to telling him and his colleagues how they should do their job. And of course the bosses were conspicuous by their absence when it came to standing up for the common foot-soldiers. Like, most recently, that bastard Lapp, whom even the biggest of the evening papers hadn't managed to find in order to get a quote out of him. If you could believe what they themselves were claiming, that is, and Bäckström thought that in this instance you probably could.

As if all this wasn't more than enough, his colleague officer Sandberg suddenly appeared in his office. She closed the door behind her, and just managed to whisper the reason why she was there.

'There's been a complaint about you this morning.'

'So what have I done this time?' Bäckström asked. 'Apart from just trying to do my job?' I expect I've exceeded the National Crime budget for the purchase of cotton-buds, he thought.

Attempted rape, according to the complainant. Sexual harassment, according to the colleague who had received the complaint and, for safety's sake, had put it in a little pile all of its own.

'Are you pulling my leg?' Bäckström said, although he had already worked out what was going on. Of all the crazy bitches on this planet, he thought.

Sadly not, according to Sandberg. The report claimed that late in the evening of 15 August, Bäckström had, in his room at the Town Hotel, done what he had actually done, and a number of other things that he hadn't actually done. The victim was a female reporter for local radio in Växjö named Carin Ågren, forty-two years old. The person who had filed the complaint was a close friend of hers, the coordinator of the women's helpline in town, by name Moa Hjärtén. The only positive was that they hadn't been able to get hold of the alleged victim, Ågren, and that, as was so often the case, there were no witnesses.

'I have no idea what you're talking about,' Bäckström said. 'I never touched the woman.' Which was entirely true, he thought.

'Not my case,' Sandberg said, shaking her head defensively. 'I just thought it might be useful for you to know about it.'

'I have a vague recollection of that Hjärtén woman,' Bäckström said. 'Is she the little fat woman who scuttles about in an old pink shift? I've met her here at the station. Evidently some close acquaintance of our colleague Olsson.'

'Well, I've told you now,' Sandberg repeated.

'Good of you, Anna.' Bäckström smiled his most relaxed smile. 'In this job you have to put up with a lot of crap.' And they haven't got any witnesses, he thought.

\*

The female anaesthetist hadn't been very easy to get hold of. As soon as she got back to work her services were required in the operating theatre, and it wasn't until later that afternoon that she had time to see Lewin. Assuming it was important enough. Assuming that it wasn't about anything that conflicted with her oath of confidentiality, and assuming that he came to her and not the other way round, seeing as he evidently didn't want to tell her what this was about over the phone.

But once he was sitting in her office at the hospital, the whole thing was remarkably painless, and far better than expected. White coat, stethoscope in her pocket. Short blonde hair, thin, in good shape, attentive blue eyes and a look in them that darted between alertness, insight and humour. An attractive woman, Lewin thought.

Without going into the reasons in any detail, Lewin quickly explained what was troubling him. Had she received any strange phone calls? He was particularly interested in any such calls she might have received the night before she went on holiday or early in the morning of the day her holiday began.

'This is about the murder of that trainee police officer, isn't it?' She looked at him inquisitively, and the activity behind her blue eyes was obvious.

'I didn't say that,' Lewin said with a faint smile. Almost too attractive, he thought.

And he really hadn't. She was the one who had said it, and she didn't expect an answer. But she was capable of working it out for herself. Twenty-four hours ago, when she had just got back from her holiday abroad, she hadn't had any idea of the Linda murder. After catching up on her old newspapers and taking a couple of trips to the staffroom at work, she now knew as much as everyone else.

'I've never met a real murder detective before. Least of all one from National Crime,' she told him.

'That must be nice,' Lewin said.

'So now that you're here, I'm almost pleased.'

'Thanks.' Where's this conversation going? Lewin thought.

'You seem to be made of the right stuff. Isn't that what you lot usually say? The right stuff,' she repeated. 'Anyway, I think I might be able to help you. Not that I understand why, but this is what happened.'

She seldom got calls from people she didn't know, and almost all the calls she did get had something to do with work. She had had a few wrong numbers, but she usually forgot those pretty quickly. And she'd never had to put up with any unpleasant calls since she moved to Växjö almost two years ago.

'No heavy breathing,' she explained. 'Hopefully because my number's ex-directory, and not because I'm too old.'

That was one reason why she remembered the call. The other was that she had had to agree to being on call on the Friday morning, before she left for Copenhagen airport, because the father of one of her colleagues had suddenly had a heart attack.

'The phone rang in the middle of the night, and I just assumed that my holiday was about to go up in smoke.'

In the middle of the night? She couldn't remember more exactly what time it was?

'According to the alarm clock beside the bed, it was 02.15,' she said, smiling at Lewin's look of surprise. 'I can see you wondering why I remember that,' she added.

Lewin smiled back. I suppose I could always ask you a few control questions about your date of birth, he thought.

Times were important in an anaesthetist's life, especially when it came to nocturnal phone calls, which she always assumed must be from work. Besides, she had an excellent memory for numbers, and, fortunately, a notepad and pen beside the phone. The first thing she did was note the time of the call. Then she had picked up the receiver and answered it.

'Because I was so sure it was work calling, that was a reflex,' she explained. 'And just to make sure they realized that they were about to sabotage my holiday as well as my beauty sleep, I did my best to sound like I was still asleep.'

'You didn't say your name when you answered?'

'No. All they got was a very sleepy and drawn-out hello, even though I was wide awake. I thought that would serve them right, I suppose.'

'So what did the person on the other end say?' Lewin asked. 'Do you remember?'

The person calling her was a man. He sounded happy, pleasant, sober, and to judge by his voice roughly the same age as her.

'First he said something in English. Long time no see, or something like that, then he said he hoped he hadn't woken me. I still thought it was someone from work trying to be funny. Because I was going to America on holiday. Then I suddenly started to wonder.'

'Why was that?'

'Because I assumed my holiday was going up in smoke, I was probably a bit short. I asked how many people, and what had happened to them this time,' she said. 'When they call at that time of night, it's almost always a car crash.'

'So what did he say?'

'He suddenly sounded rather taken aback as well. It was like he realized he'd got the wrong number. He asked who he was talking to, and then I asked him who he was trying to call, and it was round about then that I realized that it wasn't anyone from work, just a wrong number in the middle of the night.'

'Did he say anything else?'

'Yes. First he asked if this was the right number for Ericson. I thought that was a rather odd way of putting it, which is why I remember it so clearly. I actually remember thinking about that phone company there was all that fuss about, and that it might still have been someone messing around. By that time I was pretty annoyed, so I just said he must have got the wrong number. And then he apologized and all that, and it sounded like he really meant it, and I suppose I was fairly cheerful again because my holiday was safe. So I said it didn't matter, as long as he promised not to do it again.'

'And that was all?'

'No,' the anaesthetist said, shaking her head. 'He said something else, and because he said it in such a charming way, I remember it.'

'Try to be as accurate as you can,' Lewin said, checking that his little tape recorder was working properly.

'Okay,' she said. 'He more or less said that he didn't suppose it was the right moment to ask for a blind date. Yes. "I don't suppose this is the time to ask you out on a blind date", that's what he said. Or something like that, but before I had time to say anything he had hung up. A shame really, because he actually sounded charming and nice.'

'Happy, sober, nice, charming,' Lewin summarized.

'Yes. If he hadn't called in the middle of the night, who knows where it might have led. I remember I actually had trouble getting back to sleep. I suppose I was lying there fantasizing about him being as nice and charming and handsome as he sounded.'

'You were hoping he might call back?'

'Well, I'm not quite that desperate. Not yet, anyway.'

'And he hasn't called back?'

'Not while I was on holiday,' she said with a shrug. 'Just the usual boring messages.'

Maybe he had other things on his mind, Lewin thought. Otherwise he would probably have done so, if he's the sort I think he is. 'If you remember anything else, I hope you'll let me know,' he said, handing her his card.

'Of course,' she said, looking at the card before putting it in the top pocket of her white coat. 'And if you'd like me to show you the delights of Växjö, give me a call. After all, you've got my number.'

As soon as Lewin got back to the police station, he called an old friend and former colleague who now worked as an inspector with the Security Police, and also happened to owe him a favour or two. To begin with they chatted idly about this and that, and then, once they had got the social bit out of the way, Lewin got to the point.

Not a matter of national security, but a serious crime none the less. It was a matter of tracing a particular phone call, but for once he knew the exact time it had been made, and the number that had been called. What he wanted to know was the number from which the call had come, who that account belonged to, and – if it wasn't asking too much – who had made the call.

'I don't suppose I'd be wrong if I guessed that this is about the murder of that trainee officer?' his old friend said. 'Seeing as you're the one asking, and you want to know about a call made to a number in Växjö, I mean.'

'That's the one,' Lewin said. 'How long do you think it'll take?'

Assuming that Lewin's information was correct, and that the call was made at quarter past two on the morning of 4 July to the number given, it ought to be possible to find out almost immediately.

'I'll be in touch tomorrow,' his friend said. 'So keep your fingers crossed. As I'm sure you know as well as me, they nearly always use those pay-as-you-go mobiles these days, and then it's almost impossible to trace who made the call.'

'I've got a feeling we're not talking about one of those,' Lewin said. Not this time, he thought.

# 66

In police headquarters on Kungsholmen in Stockholm, four hundred kilometres north of Växjö, the Head of National Crime was feeling his blood pressure rise. The main reason for this, in purely objective terms, was the least important of all the cases that had accumulated on his desk. When the Bäckström circus rolled into Växjö, Lars Martin Johansson thought.

He was talking to a nice young woman from the finance department who had spent the weekend trying to deal with the red question marks that Johansson had highlighted in the documents she had prepared for him. Without success, unfortunately. There were still a number of peculiar invoices for everything from care of equipment and conference materials to the usual bar and restaurant visits with anonymous informants. All of them verified by Detective Superintendent Bäckström, and totalling almost twenty thousand kronor. There were also a number of unexplained cash withdrawals made by the same Bäckström to a total of almost twelve thousand kronor, plus the usual expenses for excursions of this nature, where the costs, not including wages and national insurance contributions, had now built up to about three hundred thousand kronor.

'What's this all about really? Just between you and me,' Johansson said, nodding to her encouragingly.

'Someone's had their hand in the cookie jar, and because this is strictly between us I don't think it's the first time. Besides, I also happened to recognize the name of the person verifying these expenses.'

'You've seen worse?' Johansson said, suddenly feeling brighter than he had in a long time.

'Much worse,' the finance woman said, with emphasis and feeling. 'I've seen plenty of peculiar invoices over the years.'

'What was the most peculiar?' Johansson asked curiously.

'During the most recent financial year, that would have to be two tons of hay. That was some time last winter, but it wasn't actually that expensive. A few thousand, if I remember rightly.'

'I think I can guess who authorized that invoice,' Johansson grunted.

'Apparently the rapid-response unit needed it for an exercise,' the finance woman said. 'After all, they do jump off things all the time, and I suppose they wanted something soft to land in. Mind you, Detective Superintendent Bäckström's laundry bill from Växjö isn't bad either. I even requested a breakdown of the costs. I've got a husband and three kids who are all complete pigs, between the two of us, but compared to Bäckström they're amateurs.'

'Tell me,' Johansson said eagerly.

The same day Detective Superintendent Bäckström arrived in Växjö, one of his colleagues handed in some laundry on his behalf to be washed by the hotel. These items had been returned a few days later. The relevant invoice was authorized by Bäckström and, according to a handwritten note, covered 'care of equipment occasioned in the course of duty'. According to the breakdown of costs requested by the finance officer – which for some reason had not been attached to the original invoice – this included, in absolute terms, the dry-cleaning of '27 pairs of men's boxer shorts, 2 pairs of men's long johns, 31 men's vests, 14 pairs of socks, 9 ties, 4 long-sleeved sweaters, 14 shirts, 3 pairs of trousers, 2 pairs of shorts, 1 jacket and 1 three-piece suit comprising jacket, waistcoat and trousers'.

'A waistcoat?' Johansson said, grinning like a small child. 'Does it really say that? A waistcoat?'

'A waistcoat,' the finance woman said, almost as delighted as her boss. 'I think I might even have seen it. Some sort of pin-striped brown thing, and Bäckström's not exactly renowned for changing his clothes every day, if you know what I mean.'

'Phenomenal!' Johansson said, sounding like he really meant it. 'Okay, this is what we're going to do . . .'

When Johansson met the chief superintendent who was Bäckström's immediate superior, the northerner was in a brilliant mood. The chief superintendent had no idea why he was there, had had nightmares about Johansson for three nights in a row, and had spent every waking moment since being summoned to it dreading this meeting. For him it was actually a near-death experience.

'Let's see, said the blind man,' Johansson said, leafing through a bundle of papers with a cheery look on his face. 'I don't suppose you want a cup of coffee?' He nodded enquiringly towards his guest.

'No, thank you, no, I'm fine,' the chief assured him. The man must be a full-blown sadist, he thought. Is he trying to force some sort of low-budget last meal on me? A cup of coffee and a biscuit?

There were three things Johansson was wondering about. Why had the chief superintendent sent these six officers in particular? Why had he appointed Bäckström to be in charge? And which one or more of them had spent at least one long night in the hotel watching the hotel's porn channels? Possibly the most basic thing on the long list of absolute no-nos covering all the things you really weren't supposed to do when you were on duty and your employer, the National Crime Unit, was footing the bill.

According to the chief superintendent, the matter was rather more complicated than that. To begin with, he hadn't personally sent any-one to Växjö. As he had already explained, with all due respect to his boss, he had been on holiday and the decision had been taken by Johansson's predecessor, Nylander. Why Nylander had chosen to appoint Bäckström head of the operation was also outside his knowledge, and as far as the porn films were concerned, the matter was still under investigation.

'I see,' Johansson interrupted. 'But surely you've given the matter some thought? I see that Jan Lewin is down there. Why isn't he in charge? Back when I knew him, he was a fully functional police officer.'

'He doesn't like being in charge,' the chief said. 'As I understand it,

Nylander asked his secretary to call Bäckström. Why him in particular remains unclear. Bäckström was given the task, and it was left to him to put together a group of officers who were available at the time. With the exception of Bäckström, who certainly has his idiosyncrasies, there's really nothing much wrong with any of the others. Lewin, for instance, is both very experienced and very competent. Must be one of the best murder detectives in the country.'

'Well, maybe,' Johansson said. I've seen better, he thought. 'That goes for Rogersson as well,' he went on. 'As I understand it, the invoice for the porn film was linked to his room.'

'But he himself was in Stockholm. He left the car he was using in the garage here on Friday evening, and signed it out again at lunchtime on Sunday, so it couldn't have been him,' the chief said.

'Find out which one it was,' Johansson said.

'I promise to do all I can,' the chief said.

'Just finding out who it was will do,' Johansson said. 'So I know who to kick out of this unit and replace.'

# 67

When Jan Lewin read the *Småland Post* the next morning the front page was dominated by a large picture of head of purchasing, Roy Edvardsson, forty-eight years old. Judging by the picture, he was a rather fat man in the prime of life, dressed in classic male attire for the Swedish summer: sandals with socks, knee-length shorts, a striped, short-sleeved shirt, and a check cap of the lighter variety out of consideration for the time of year. Edvardsson was leaning comfortably against his car, a Mercedes, radiating both confidence and material success. And he was born, raised and lived in Småland.

The reason for his appearance in the *Post* was a lengthy report about the fact that the National Food Administration had conducted an extensive investigation which had found that Smålanders were less likely than other Swedes to buy organic and environmentally friendly products when they bought their groceries. And this in spite of the notable efforts of the world's most famous Smålander, the author Astrid Lindgren, to liberate hens from their cages and give pigs a happy life all the way to Christmas.

The paper's reporter had gone out on to the streets of the town and conducted a rather smaller study in which she had asked people about their views on organic and environmentally friendly groceries and other products. The answers she received from a majority of those questioned appeared to support the National Food Administration's findings, and the reason for their negative opinion was unambiguous. Organic and environmentally friendly food was more expensive than ordinary food, even though it tasted pretty much the same as all food did these days.

But none of this covered Roy Edvardsson, 48, who, in spite of his job, was entirely unfamiliar with the question.

'Don't ask me about that,' Edvardsson said. 'I never do the shopping. I mean, I've been married for years now.'

I didn't think men like that still existed, Lewin thought, astonished, as he reached for the scissors so that he could add this little insight into Roy Edvardsson's life to his scrapbook of memories from Växjö.

# 68

Once he had finished breakfast, Lewin followed in his colleague's footsteps, and because he hadn't mentioned this to him each step pricked his conscience. First he paid a visit to the 92-year-old witness's optician, to determine, once and for all, the state of her eyesight.

He was a man in his sixties, and he had been supplying the witness with glasses for the past thirty years. In total that had amounted to two new pairs of glasses and a few minor repairs, so she wasn't exactly a big customer. The last time she had been to see him was about six years ago. The examination conducted on that occasion had shown that the glasses she had bought five years previously were still perfectly adequate. And those had been bought shortly after her eightieth birthday, and mainly because she needed new frames.

The witness was near-sighted, but she had been born with the problem and it didn't seem to have got noticeably worse over the years. Assuming that she was wearing her glasses, and that her sight hadn't deteriorated dramatically since her last visit, she ought to have practically normal vision, making her perfectly capable of recognizing someone at a distance of some twenty metres away from her, as Lewin asked. If she hadn't been wearing her glasses, then she couldn't have done so. It was out of the question. At that distance, without her glasses she could make out movement and differentiate between a person and a dog, but probably not tell a dog from a cat.

But there was a different problem with old people and their eyesight, which lay outside the area of optical medicine but was still a part of their daily life, which every conscientious practitioner had to take into account.

'Old people's eyesight is affected in a completely different way by their general physical and mental condition. They get a lot of dizzy spells and double vision, and they're more sensitive to changes in the light. They can also get quite confused generally, mixing things up, before it passes and they're back to normal again. They come to me and I try out new lenses on them and sometimes they even manage to read the bottom lines of the chart, then they come back and test the new glasses and all of a sudden they can't even read the top line because they slept badly or have had a row with their children or something.'

'But assuming she was the way she usually was, and was wearing her glasses, she ought to be able to see and recognize a person at that distance? Especially if it was someone she'd seen before?'

'Yes,' the optician agreed. 'But then there's the mental aspect. They get people mixed up, and think the person they see is someone they know, possibly because of some superficial similarity, and then they might describe the person they know and not the person they actually saw. I'm not a doctor, but I've seen and heard plenty of examples of this sort of thing over the years.'

Evidence pointing both ways, Lewin thought, sighing inwardly as a little while later he rang the doorbell of the flat where their witness lived. He had asked Eva to phone her beforehand, and hoped that was why she didn't bother to look through the peephole before she opened the door to him.

'My name is Jan Lewin, and I work as a detective superintendent for the National Crime police,' Lewin said, holding up his ID and smiling his most trustworthy smile at her. She seems lively enough, he thought.

'Come in, come in,' she said, pointing the way with her rubber-tipped stick.

'Thank you,' Lewin said. And compos mentis, he thought, feeling his hopes rising.

'I should be thanking you, superintendent,' Mrs Rudberg said. 'You're not just something the cat dragged in, are you? That lass who was here before, she was just an ordinary police officer, wasn't she?'

First they talked about her birthday, and it turned out that the witness had evidently encountered the same sort of priest as his old grandmother had. It had also taken a number of years before her parents had realized the mistake and told her.

'It must have been when I was about to start school that my father realized the priest had written the wrong date in the register,' she explained. 'But by then we had got a new priest, and he didn't want to change it now that it had been entered. So it had to stay as it was.'

For a while she had been annoyed that she was registered under the wrong month. But as she got older the extra month had mattered less, and when she reached retirement age she had even been grateful for the priest's mistake.

'I got an extra month of my pension,' she explained, smiling at Lewin. 'So I kept quiet and accepted it gratefully.'

The business about her birthday had never led to any practical problems. She had always celebrated 4 July as her birthday, and the fact that she hadn't explained about the priest's mistake to the female police officer she had spoken to was simply because it hadn't even occurred to her. It was 4 July at six o'clock in the morning that she had been sitting on her balcony. Like most other days this summer, but in honour of that particular day she had taken a piece of cake out to have with her usual morning coffee.

'I'd even laid a tray so I wouldn't have to keep running in and out. I have to think about my stick as well, you see,' she explained.

Which leaves one more problem, and how on earth am I going to deal with that? Lewin thought.

'And of course now, superintendent, you're wondering if I was wearing my glasses,' she said, fluttering her eyelashes at him over the frames.

'Yes,' Lewin said with a friendly smile. 'How are your glasses, Mrs Rudberg?'

No problems at all, according to the witness. The last thing she always did once she'd gone to bed in the evening was take off her glasses and leave them on the bedside table so she could find them easily the next morning. And the first thing she did each morning before she got out of bed was put them back on again.

'Superintendent, what would I be doing out on the balcony without my glasses?' she declared. 'My word! I doubt I would have even managed to find my way there.'

Which left the man she had seen doing something to the car out in the car park. This is going like a dream, Lewin thought.

Fairly short, dark, quick and agile. In good shape, as people said these days. Good-looking, the way men used to be when she was young. 'Mind you, in those days they didn't have to do any of that exercising to keep their bodies in trim.'

How old was he, Lewin wondered.

The age the men who looked like that had been when she used to look at them that way when she was a few years younger than they were. Men were always a few years older, weren't they? And that still seemed to be the case if she had understood correctly.

'He must have been about twenty-five; thirty, perhaps,' she concluded. 'Mind you, nowadays I think practically everyone looks like a youngster, so he could have been a little older.'

'And you thought he was someone you knew, Mrs Rudberg?' Lewin prompted cautiously.

'Yes, but I got that badly wrong.'

'How do you mean?'

'Well, I must have got him confused with someone else.'

'I see. So how . . . ?'

'I was talking to our caretaker the other day. He came in to help me with my fridge, it makes such a racket I can hardly sleep at night, and we talked about that car. It had evidently been stolen, because they said something about it on the radio, and I happened to mention what I had said to that policewoman, about it being him, the son, who had taken it and gone off to the country.'

'I see,' Lewin said, nodding encouragingly.

'But I must have got that badly wrong,' she repeated, 'because he doesn't have a son. So I must have got that completely wrong. My scythe hit a rock that made it sing, as my old father would have said.'

'So it was actually someone else that he reminded you of?' Lewin said.

'Yes, it must have been. I mean, if he hasn't got a son, then he hasn't got a son.'

'So your caretaker knew that your neighbour, the retired pilot who owned the car, didn't have a son, Mrs Rudberg?'

'If there's anyone who knows that sort of thing, it's him,' the witness said firmly. 'He knows everything about everyone who lives here. Of course he does. That pilot has two daughters. I know that for certain, and we were in complete agreement about that. And it wasn't either of them that I saw. I'm not quite that dotty. Not yet.'

'I appreciate that you've given the matter some thought, Mrs Rudberg,' Lewin persisted. 'You weren't thinking of someone else who lives here, someone else you know? Or someone that you may have seen before who resembled the person you saw?'

'No,' the witness said, shaking her head firmly. 'I've certainly given it some thought, but the only person who comes to mind is that actor. The one in *Gone With the Wind*. That Clark Gable, although without a moustache, of course.'

'Clark Gable, but without a moustache,' Lewin said with a nod.

'Although it could hardly have been him, I suppose.'

'No,' Lewin said. 'It doesn't seem very likely.'

'No, it doesn't seem very likely at all,' the witness agreed. 'Because he ought to be the same age as me by now, and anyway, isn't he already dead?'

'I think so,' Lewin said. 'I have a feeling he died quite some time ago.'

'So I could hardly have seen him, then.'

As Lewin walked back to the police station, the old sense of gloom had made itself felt again. The little over-stuffed flat, the family pictures, friends and relatives who belonged together and were all dead now. That special smell that's always in older people's homes, no matter how scrupulously clean they are kept, or no matter that their occupants might live another twenty years. A ninety-two-year-old woman who was healthy and alert for her age, and still managed to live in a flat on her own, make her own coffee, even carry a tray in one hand. No wheelchair, not even a walking frame, just the power and strength that could manage to get out on to the balcony with just a rubber-tipped stick.

Not even close to the ante-room of death that institutionalized care of the elderly had to offer all those less fortunate than his witness, many of them considerably younger than her. Linoleum floors, the television permanently stuck on the same channel, boiled fish and fruit soups, being fed with a spoon, a bed for the night with the back tilted to support a crooked back and ease tired lungs. And the only freedom on offer being an end to all of this. If you were even conscious of it being there, and that it was waiting patiently for you, utterly regardless of who you might have been when you still had a life to live.


'He was like Clark Gable?' Sandberg asked an hour later.

'But without the moustache,' Lewin said with a thin smile.

'I actually dug out a recent picture of the pilot's son-in-law. His name's Henrik Johansson, thirty-eight years old. He's the flight officer married to their younger daughter,' Sandberg said.

'What's he look like, then?'

'Not at all like Clark Gable, and you should know that you're talking to a woman who's seen *Gone With the Wind* on video several times,' Sandberg said. 'What do you think about a photo-fit picture? In the absence of anything else?'

'God help us,' Lewin said, shaking his head. Of Clark Gable? We could probably get away with just removing his moustache, Lewin thought, already feeling a bit livelier.


Olsson had asked to have a private conversation with Bäckström, the reason for which had already been divulged to Bäckström by Anna Sandberg the previous day.

'Yes, I heard about that,' Bäckström told him breezily. 'It's that crazy woman in the pink shift that I met at that meeting you invited me to. That's the only occasion I've ever met her, and I dare say there won't be another any time soon. Are you good friends, by the way?'

'Now you mustn't misunderstand me, Bäckström,' Olsson said, putting up his hands in the defensive gesture that had become something of a trademark for him. 'I just wanted to warn you, that's all. In case you should hear any unpleasant rumours.'

'Unfortunately I've had to get used to things like this over the years. Do you happen to know, Olsson, just how many of our fellow officers are currently the objects of one or more complaints from all the thugs and confused souls we're trying to keep in check?'

'Quite a lot, I dare say, sadly,' Olsson said.

'About two thousand,' Bäckström said emphatically. 'Fifteen per cent of the entire force, and practically all of them simply for trying to do their jobs. And do you know how many are actually convicted?'

'Not many,' Olsson said.

'Nice try, Olsson,' Bäckström said. 'One or two each year. Less than one per thousand officers out of all the officers whose reputations those people have done their level best to ruin.'

'Yes, it really isn't a good situation.' Olsson made a move to stand up.

'I should really have a word with the union and organize a charge of false accusation.'

'Against the alleged victim?'

'No, against that crazy bitch in the pink shift. Anyway, I didn't think you even had a victim. So think about whether or not we should report her. That woman in the pink shift, I mean.' Suck on that, you little prick, he thought.

'I don't think that will be necessary,' Olsson said, getting up.

'So how did Bäckström react? Did he have anything to say in his defence?' the county police commissioner asked five minutes later.

'He didn't seem to understand,' Olsson said with a sigh. 'He thought we should report Moa Hjärtén for making a false accusation. Says he's thinking about talking to the union.'

'Is that really necessary?' the commissioner groaned. 'By the way, have you spoken to the victim?'

'Only over the phone,' Olsson said.

'So what did she say, then?'

'She didn't want to talk about it at all, and she's not thinking of making an official complaint. But I'm absolutely convinced there's something behind this.'

'Yes, of course,' the commissioner said. 'There usually is, but we're still talking about a fellow officer here, and if the victim is refusing to make a complaint I don't really see what we can do about it.'

'Maybe you should have a word with Bäckström's new boss,' Olsson suggested. 'That Johansson.'

'You mean Lars Martin Johansson, our new HNC?'

'Yes, him. He's bound to find out about it sooner or later anyway.'

'I promise to give the matter some thought,' the commissioner said. What's happened to Olsson? he thought. I must have been completely wrong about the man.

That afternoon, just before he was about to head back to the hotel, Lewin's friend in the Security Police called back to give him the details of the telephone Lewin was trying to identify.

'You're in luck, Jan,' the officer said. 'It's a traceable mobile. Registered to Växjö Council, and if you can give me another day I'll be able to tell you who uses it. There are several hundred staff to choose from.'

'If you wouldn't mind, I'd obviously be very grateful. As long as it doesn't cause any problems for you,' Lewin said.

No problems at all, according to his old friend. The Security Police just happened to have an excellent contact in a strategic position inside Växjö Council, so all he needed was another twenty-four hours.

'Well, that sounds good,' Lewin said. 'Thanks very much indeed.'

'Don't mention it,' his friend said. 'I'll be in touch tomorrow to let you have the name.'

'Well, thanks very much, really,' Lewin repeated. Maybe, maybe not, although maybe after all, he thought, and he suddenly felt the old familiar gloom again. The feeling he usually got when he thought he was in the process of working out something that would soon have very real consequences for people of flesh and blood.

# 69

In his dreams things were usually even worse when he was feeling low. Naked anxiety that made his body swing, spin and fall, his legs twisting the sheets into a sweaty rope in the middle of the bed. Completely natural, seeing he was so utterly exposed to his thoughts, unable to defend himself by thinking about something else the way he could when he was awake.

But not this night.

Another Indian summer, almost fifty years ago. Jan Lewin has been given his first proper bicycle. A red Crescent Valiant. Named after the noble knight Prince Valiant, who lived so long ago that there weren't any bicycles, just horses.

For the umpteenth time Daddy is running behind him, holding on to the saddle and cheering him on.

He grips the handlebars, pedals as hard as his legs can manage, and at least he's stopped closing his eyes now when he knows he's about to fall off and scrape his knees.

And now there's just the worst bit left. The gravel path between the white gate up to the red wooden porch of the house, where Mummy must be frying pancakes because it's Thursday.

'Don't worry, Jan,' Daddy cries behind his back. 'I've got you. Don't worry. I've got you.'

Jan pedals and steers and manages better than usual, because Daddy's still holding on, and when they reach the house he brakes carefully, puts his left foot on the ground and clambers off.

And when he turns round he sees that his daddy is still standing down by the white gate, a smile on his suntanned face, far too far away to ruffle his hair, but of course he doesn't need to do that any more.

# 70

## *Stockholm, Wednesday 20 August*

The county police commissioner didn't have to call the Head of National Crime, because on Wednesday morning Lars Martin Johansson called him.

'I'll be brief,' Johansson said. 'It's about Bäckström. Unless you have any pressing need for him down there, I'm thinking of recalling him. I can send you some new people.'

'Ah, I see,' the commissioner said. 'Naturally, I'm grateful for all the resources you can spare, but of course if you need Bäckström for more important duties I'd have to accept that.'

'More important duties?' Johansson snorted. 'I'm thinking of recalling him so I can tear a strip off him, and once I've finished doing that I'm wondering if he actually ought to have any duties at all.'

'If it's that complaint you're worried about, I think perhaps we shouldn't be too quick to judge our dear Bäckström,' the commissioner said, trying to keep his voice calm and steady.

'I have no idea what you're talking about,' Johansson said. 'What complaint?'

At that point the commissioner had no choice but to explain about the complaint against Detective Superintendent Evert Bäckström which had been reported to the police authority in Växjö two days before.

'That sounds fairly remarkable, if you ask me,' Johansson said five minutes later, as soon as his long-winded colleague had finally finished. 'Correct me if I'm wrong, but you've received a complaint from the co-ordinator of the women's helpline in Växjö, to the effect that Bäckström subjected a female journalist of her acquaintance to what, according to my version of the criminal law, sounds like sexual harassment. Which the female journalist, for reasons unknown, refuses to talk about, still less file a complaint against.'

'Yes, that's a fairly comprehensive summary,' the commissioner agreed. 'And then there's the certified statement brought in yesterday by the person who filed the complaint.'

'I'm getting to that,' Johansson said. 'After you contacted the alleged victim and she refused to make a complaint, the woman who filed the report came in with some sort of document signed by her and someone else, purportedly the notes of a conversation which this woman had with the aggrieved party. One simple question. Who is the second witness?'

'He's the co-ordinator of the men's helpline here in town. His name's Bengt Karlsson. The co-ordinator of the women's helpline, the one who filed the complaint, is Moa Hjärtén, and—'

'Okay, now I really don't understand,' Johansson interrupted. 'I thought you said the aggrieved party had only spoken to Hjärtén. So what's this Karlsson actually put his name to?'

'Yes, it certainly is a little unclear.'

'Not in my opinion,' Johansson said. 'In my book, this sounds like a completely fabricated certified statement. It's not my place to give you advice, but if I were you I'd either try to make sense of this report, or write it off altogether before our dear Bäckström has time to cook something up with his friends in the union.'

'Really?'

'That man has the capacity to be quite astonishingly troublesome. You'd need a hundred dogmatic legal experts to match one Bäckström. Just so you're aware of the sort of person we're talking about here,' Johansson said.

'Obviously, I'm very grateful for your help,' the commissioner said.

'I'll ask Bäckström's boss to get in touch with the head of your preliminary investigation, so that they can sort out the practical details,' Johansson said.

\*

Bäckström's immediate superior had no objections. The report which the finance office had copied him in on was unfortunately both troubling and very pointed. But he had of course been on holiday when it all happened.

'I also heard through the grapevine that a complaint has been made against him, alleging that he exposed himself to a journalist,' the chief superintendent said with a blush.

'Yes, you get to hear a lot of strange things over the course of a life-time,' Johansson said.

'When do you want him back, boss?' the chief asked.

'As soon as possible,' Johansson said. 'By Monday morning at the latest, because I've got a gap in my diary that I thought I might squeeze him into.' To tear him off a strip or two.

'Do you have any preference about who we should send down to replace him, boss?'

'Anna Holt and that little blonde, whatever her name is, Lisa Mattei,' Johansson said. 'Admittedly, that's better than they deserve down there, but it's time to wave the flag and send the A-team out on to the ice.'

'I'm afraid that might be a problem,' the chief said nervously.

'There are no problems,' Johansson said. 'In my world there are only challenges.'

'Neither of them is working for me at the moment,' the chief explained. 'Anna Holt is acting superintendent of the national co-ordination office, and Mattei is on secondment to the analysis group to cover their holidays.'

'So much the better,' Johansson said. 'They could probably do with a bit of fresh air. Just get it sorted. Quick as you like. Oh, and one more thing, which you might like to think about if you want to carry on working for me here.'

'How do you mean, boss?'

'I never express wishes when I'm on duty,' Johansson said. 'I gave you an order. That's all there is to it.'

An hour later the chief superintendent had returned to his boss to say that everything had been done, and for some reason he had remained standing in front of Johansson's desk as he spoke.

'According to orders,' the chief superintendent concluded, swearing silently to himself that he hadn't been brave enough to click his heels as he said it.

'Thank you,' Johansson said, giving him a friendly smile. 'That's excellent.'

'Do you want to talk to them, boss? I can ask them to come in at once if you like,' the chief superintendent said innocently.

'Good,' Johansson said. 'Send them in at once.'

For reasons that remained unclear, Holt and Mattei weren't happy when they came in to discuss their new roles with Johansson, even though he had asked his secretary to organize coffee, Danish pastries and biscuits. Holt just shook her head when he offered her the plate. She had her hands full with her new job, and wasn't the least bit amused at having to clean up Bäckström's mess. Mattei admitted that it all sounded very interesting and exciting, but pointed out that as she was on leave from 1 September in order to complete her studies at university, she might have certain practical problems. Not least considering that she was already on secondment.

'There's almost a fortnight until then. A perfectly ordinary murder investigation. You girls will solve it in a week,' Johansson cajoled, taking another Danish pastry. 'Besides, it might be nice for you to get out into the fresh air. Put your ear to the ground, put one thing together with something else and come up with two, work out that it fits, go and get the suspect that evening, when it's just started raining and you have to turn up the collars on your coats when you get out of the car, and see him watching television, totally unsuspecting, already getting used to the idea that he might have got away with it. Then you ring on the door, you hear him heading towards it . . . We're from the police. There's something we'd like to talk to you about,' Johansson said, with a deep sigh of longing for a bygone age.

'That's all very well, Lars, but this really isn't about us, is it?' Holt said.

'So what is it about?' Johansson said warily.

'Really you'd like to be able to go yourself,' Holt said, as if she was talking to a restless child. 'But seeing as you can't go, you have to send us instead.'

'You're a proper little psychologist, aren't you, Anna?' Johansson said with a crooked smile. 'I may not have been expecting a standing ovation, but a discreet nod of approval might not have gone amiss.'

'Of course,' Holt said. 'Make the best of things, don't complicate things unnecessarily, and never trust coincidence. Lars Martin Johansson's three golden rules for every murder detective. Lisa and I are practically down in Växjö already.'

'Precisely,' Johansson said. 'Although in this particular instance, and bearing in mind that it's Bäckström you're cleaning up after, there's a fourth rule that you should also be aware of.'

'I'm listening, boss,' Lisa Mattei said, looking like the class swot who doesn't even have to put her hand up any more.

'Beware the demon drink, girls. A piece of advice from an old man who's been around the block a few times,' Johansson said, grabbing another biscuit from the well-stocked plate.

# 71

Holt and Mattei spent the next two days preparing for their trip to Växjö. Holt had made the practical arrangements in thirty minutes with the help of Bäckström's boss. Getting up to speed with the case that they were to investigate had taken some twenty hours, and to that extent everything was pretty much the same as usual. The only odd thing was the conspicuous absence of their boss throughout. Right up to Friday afternoon, when he suddenly appeared in the doorway of their office.

'I hope I'm not interrupting,' Johansson said as he sat down. 'So tell me. What do you make of it?' He nodded towards the documents on the table between them.

'What do *you* make of it?' Holt said, who had known Johansson for several years and had been through this before.

'Since you ask, Anna,' Johansson said, because he had known Holt just as long, and had been through considerably more, 'I think the whole thing seems pretty straightforward. It was someone she knew. Probably someone her mother knew as well, or at least had met. She let him in voluntarily, it all began consensually, then it got out of hand and he killed her.'

'That's pretty much what Lisa and I think,' Holt agreed.

'Glad to hear it. Seeing as we're talking about Växjö here, and since both the victim and her mother seem to be ordinary, decent, normal people, there can't be that many to choose from. Go down and arrest the bastard. We can't have someone like that on the loose. It shouldn't be much of a challenge to find him.'

'So why haven't they managed so far? To find him, I mean?' Mattei asked, looking curiously at her boss. 'They seem to have checked out a number of people already.'

'Bäckström, probably,' Johansson said with a sigh.

'What about Lewin, then?' Holt said. 'He's there too. And the others. There's nothing much wrong with any of them, as far as I'm aware.'

'They probably just haven't thought of him yet,' Johansson said, with another sigh. 'Because he's the sort of ordinary, decent, normal person that doesn't spring to mind in this sort of context. Or else they haven't had time, because they've been running round with those damn cotton-buds the whole time.'

'Considering what he did to the victim, there seem to be other sides to his character as well,' Holt said. 'Sides which aren't quite as nice.'

'That's just what I mean,' Johansson said. 'On this occasion all the safety barriers gave way, he lost control and things went the way they did. I had a case once, many years ago now. The Maria murder. She was a teacher too, just like Linda's mother. Have I ever told you about that one?'

'No, I don't think so,' Holt said. He's just like a child, she thought.

'Tell us, boss,' Mattei said, looking as interested as she actually was.

'Okay, if you really want me to,' Johansson said.


Maria had lived in Enskede outside Stockholm and worked as a teacher in a high school on Södermalm. Single, ordinary, decent, normal, friendly, well liked by her friends, acquaintances, workmates and pupils, and everyone else the police talked to. She didn't seem to have even the tiniest skeleton in her closet, not even a secret vibrator in the drawer of her bedside table. But still she was found raped and strangled in her flat. Even though it was the middle of the week, in the middle of winter. Even though she hadn't been out to a bar, and had just been sitting and marking essays when it happened.

'First we did all the things you always do,' Johansson said. 'Men she'd been seeing, ordinary friends and acquaintances, workmates, neighbours, anyone she might just have bumped into shortly before it happened. As well as the old classics that always show up whenever the police look into a case like this. All the usual suspects, from rapists to flashers, and anyone else who might have been in the area and had left a trail in police records in the past.'

'And what did that tell you?' Holt asked, even though she already knew.

'Nothing,' Johansson said. 'Then one of us started thinking about a mysterious car that had been seen a couple of days before it happened, and just twenty-four hours later the penny dropped,' Johansson declared, looking very pleased with himself.

I wonder who that could have been? Anna Holt thought, even though a child could have guessed the answer.

The car had been badly parked, in front of a driveway, and the second time it happened the owner of the driveway had called the police, annoyed, and filed a complaint against the car's owner. The complaint had been among the heaps of surveillance material, but because the owner was an ordinary, decent, normal man in his forties with no criminal record, no one had paid it any attention. Until 'one of us' in the investigating team started to think about what he was actually doing there.

'After all, the victim lived in an ordinary residential area. And he had been there late at night. The car's owner was married and had two children, and worked as an engineer for an energy company out in Råcksta, and they lived in a rowhouse in Vällingby on the other side of the city. Obviously, I wondered what he was doing there at that time of night,' Johansson said, finally deciding to take off his mask.

'So what happened?' Holt asked, even though she had already worked it out, and mostly to pre-empt her breathlessly listening younger colleague.

The usual tragic little story, according to Johansson. And in its most common form. 'I said he had a wife, didn't I? When we checked her out, it turned out that she worked with the victim, which, to put it mildly, was a remarkable coincidence. The perpetrator had met the victim when he picked his wife up from a staff party at the school. Eventually the victim had got fed up with him and his endless empty promises, and ended the affair. So he switched to watching her in the evening and at night, to see who her new man was. One evening he went up and knocked on the door, and unfortunately she let him in and things went the way they did. I suppose he just lost control.'

'Did she have a new man, then?' Holt asked.

'No, she didn't, but he had evidently got it into his head that she did, and that was presumably where it all started. Simple, basic police work,' Johansson said modestly, shrugging his shoulders. 'None of that modern hocus-pocus where you seem to need an entire laboratory to work out the most obvious things.'

'So what advice can you give us for our trip to Växjö?' Holt wondered innocently.

'I'm sure you and Lisa don't need any advice from an old man like me,' Johansson said.

'Just trying to be polite,' Holt said.

'Exactly,' Johansson said, evidently not the least bit put out. 'But seeing as you asked, I'd probably suggest you start by talking to Linda's mother.'

'Our colleagues have already interviewed her three times,' Holt said, nodding towards the files on the desk. 'One of them looked very thorough, if you ask me.'

'She's probably still in shock,' Johansson said with a shrug. 'I think she's trying to protect herself, in some subconscious way. Sooner or later I think she's going to work out what happened, if she hasn't already done so.'

'You think we should interview her again?' Mattei said.

'Definitely,' Johansson said. 'Anything else would be a dereliction of duty. Preferably before she gets it into her head to do anything stupid herself,' he added.


Johansson and his wife spent the weekend with good friends out at their summer house in Södermanland. They had had a very pleasant time, not getting home until Sunday afternoon, which had the fortunate side-effect of stopping Johansson from plaguing Holt with questions about their preparations for the Linda case. But no sooner had he got through the door of the flat on Wollmar Yxkullsgatan than he was calling her on her mobile.

'How's it going?' he asked.

'We're sitting on the train to Växjö,' Holt said. 'The signal's not very good.'

'Call me on my mobile as soon as you arrive.'

'Of course,' Holt said. She switched her mobile off with a sigh.

'Who was that?' Mattei asked.

'Who do you think?'

'That man's amazing,' Mattei sighed. 'Lars Martin Johansson. The man who can see round corners.'

'Mind you, I think he'd feel better if he could see his own feet,' Holt said. And I wonder what your relationship with your father is like, she thought.

'Watch what you're saying, Anna,' Mattei said, hushing her with a finger to her lips.

'You're worried he can hear what I say?'

'That man can hear what you and I are thinking.'

'Correct me if I'm wrong, but you seem very taken with him.'

'Taken!' Mattei giggled. 'I've got a huge crush on Lars Martin Johansson.'

'Well, I still think he needs to watch his weight,' Holt said. He ought to lose fifty kilos or so, she thought.

'I think's he's very sweet just as he is. Mind you, twenty or thirty kilos wouldn't hurt,' Mattei said with a twinkle.

When Holt and Mattei arrived in Växjö on Sunday afternoon, they were suddenly very busy. It didn't occur to Holt to call her boss and engage in pointless small talk over the phone, and when she did finally get a minute to herself, he got there before her.

'You haven't called,' Johansson said, sounding almost hurt. Even though it's almost nine o'clock in the evening, he thought.

'I've been pretty busy,' Holt said. And how can I say this without him having a heart attack, or a stroke, or both at once? she thought.

'That's okay,' Johansson said, because he wasn't the sort to bear a grudge, except when he felt like it. 'So how's it going?'

'Fine,' Holt said. 'It's already over.'

'What do you mean, over?' Johansson said.

'Bäckström and his colleagues caught the perpetrator this morning.

The prosecutor has already remanded him in custody, and tomorrow she's going to declare him a formal suspect on the grounds of reasonable probability.'

'Bäckström? Are you pulling my leg?' What's she saying? he thought.

'Bäckström and his colleagues.'

'Bäckström's never cleared up a case in his life,' Johansson snorted.

'If you promise to sit down and stop interrupting, I'll tell you,' Holt said.

'I'm already sitting down,' Johansson said. He had been lying on the sofa when he called, but was now sitting bolt upright. *Bäckström*, he thought.

'Good,' Holt said. 'Well, everything has pretty much happened during the course of the day, and, to be brief . . .'

'I'm listening,' Johansson said. What's going on? he thought.

'Yes, I rather assumed you were,' Holt said. 'But it would be good if you could stop interrupting me the whole time.'

When she ended the call with Johansson she took Lewin to one side.

'I've already congratulated you,' she said. 'Now, would you mind rewinding a bit for me and Lisa, and tell us what happened. Things must have changed dramatically since we last spoke.'

'Thanks,' Lewin said. 'Well, in broad strokes, this is how it was. I'm sure I don't have to tell you that things move fast once they start happening, so it's certainly not as if we've been holding anything back.'

'Tell us,' Anna Holt said.

# 72

As time passed, the murder of Linda Wallin was occupying less and less space in the columns of the *Småland Post,* and over the course of the past week they had made do with merely saying that there wasn't much to report about the actual investigation. No particular progress, and definitely no breakthrough. Yet it still didn't look as though the investigation had ground to a halt, or even noticeably slowed down. It was more like it had entered a 'calmer and more systematic phase', where the police were working 'on a broad front, with no pre-conceived ideas', all of this courtesy of the unnamed sources inside the investigation to whom the paper had spoken.

On Wednesday, however, local crime was back on the front page of the paper, with the tantalizing headline ARGUMENT OVER MUSKRAT SLIPPERS LED TO VIOLENCE.

The incident in question had actually taken place in January, six months before the murder of Linda Wallin, but because the investigation had been complex and protracted, the case had only just reached the district court in Växjö, where the previous day a 45-year-old man had been fined and given a suspended sentence for the physical abuse of his former partner, forty-two.

Jan Lewin read the article with interest. It was both entertaining and thought-provoking, and, having a professional interest and being able to read between the lines, he worked out what had happened.

At some point after New Year the accused and his partner decided to split up, and, because the flat was registered in her name, he was the one who had to move out. The *Småland Post* skimmed over the reasons for their separation, but Lewin none the less got the impression that she had got fed up and simply thrown him out.

In any case, it seemed to have been she who packed his things so that she finally had the run of her own flat, and when the accused had unpacked them in his new temporary abode, shared with a female work colleague, 33, who had evidently taken pity on him, he had discovered that his most treasured possessions were missing. A pair of sixty-year-old muskrat slippers that he had inherited from his father, who in turn had inherited them from the accused's grandfather.

The accused had gone to see his former girlfriend at once to ask her about them. When she told him she had thrown them out he had become violent, grabbing her by the arm, knocking her to the floor, slapping her face several times, and attempting to kick her as she lay on the floor. The neighbours had called the police, who had broken things up, hauled the man off to the police station, and taken the woman to hospital so that she could be patched up and her injuries documented. Then things had followed their usual course, and the reason it had all dragged on so long was that the stories of those involved had been different, there were no witnesses to the attack itself, and several accusations and counter-accusations had been made during the course of the investigation.

The accused worked as a salesman for a large car company in Växjö. His father had worked for the same company, from the mid-fifties until he retired forty years later, and his grandfather had sold agricultural machinery for a firm outside Hultsfred until he died just after the end of the war.

Apart from their interest in cars and tractors, the accused, his father and his grandfather also shared a common passion: hunting. A relatively large proportion of the trial in the district court had been devoted to exploring this, and amongst other things the accused and his defence lawyer had called two character witnesses to explain what the discarded muskrat slippers really meant to their friend and hunting partner. This certainly wasn't a matter of just any old slippers.

According to the story that was told in the accused's family, during the long years of the war his grandfather had shot some dozen muskrats in the ditches and wetlands around Hultsfred. He had skinned his prey himself, prepared the skins and then taken them to a local shoemaker, who made a pair of very comfortable, warm slippers out of them. They had been greatly appreciated by their owner, and were invaluable during the cold winters towards the end of the war.

The muskrat, *Ondatra zibethicus*, was very rare in the Hultsfred region. It was also very timid, very difficult to hunt, and no larger than a small rabbit. So it had been several years before the grandfather had killed a sufficient number to produce a pair of slippers. After his death they had been passed down to his eldest son, and then to his son. The story of how the slippers came to be made had been told countless times for more than half a century, in front of blazing fires in the snow-covered, masculine space of the hunting lodge. The tale certainly hadn't got any worse with the years, and now formed part of the oral hunting tradition in Småland. The slippers had even become part of our local cultural inheritance, according to the defence lawyer, who also concluded his cross-examination of the plaintiff with a remark about their fundamental significance for his client's mental wellbeing.

'And now you have the stomach to sit here and claim that these were just an ordinary pair of slippers!' the lawyer declared indignantly, fixing his eyes on the plaintiff.

It was actually considerably worse than that, it turned out, according to the unusually comprehensive report of the trial which the crime reporter of the *Småland Post* had chosen to share with her readers. The plaintiff was not only the former girlfriend of the accused. She had also spent many years working as a veterinary assistant, and even though she had never had any professional dealings with *Ondatra zibethicus* – fortunately – she none the less appeared to be in possession of considerable knowledge about muskrats.

The whole story was a typical male fabrication, she explained to the members of the court. If the grandfather really had told the stories that she had been forced to listen to so many times during the far too many years she had spent with his grandson, then he was as much of a liar as his descendant was.

The muskrat had migrated into Sweden, and Norrland in

particular, from Finland, but this hadn't happened until 1944, in other words a couple of years after her ex-boyfriend's grandfather, thirteen hundred kilometres further south, was supposed to have shot enough of them to make a pair of slippers, so the whole damn story was nothing but a pack of lies. For the sake of domestic harmony she had chosen to keep quiet about that fact for a good many years. But if anyone wanted her opinion, the most likely explanation was that the slippers had been made from perfectly ordinary rats, and certainly not muskrats, since the latter had only been sighted in Småland in recent years.

In short, according to the plaintiff, this was a pair of badly worn, fifty-year-old rat-fur slippers, impregnated with the sweat of three generations of male feet, and if anyone really wanted to talk about emotional symbolism, then that was her opinion of her ex-boyfriend's so-called muskrat slippers.

It was a shame she never applied to join the police, Jan Lewin thought as he pulled out his scissors to add the article to his scrapbook from Växjö.

# 73

Lewin had got to work on Wednesday morning before half past seven. Eva Svanström had some things of her own she needed to sort out, and to avoid having to listen to Bäckström's words of wisdom over his morning coffee Lewin had got up at seven and eaten breakfast in peace on his own. But in spite of all this, his colleague Sandberg was already at work when he arrived.

'You're in early, Anna,' Lewin said. Mind you, you don't look terribly awake, he thought.

'Later,' Anna said, shaking her head to warn him off. 'Our old lady called a little while ago, wanting to correct her statement.'

'Really? Well, we know she does get up early.'

'She wanted to change the bit about Clark Gable. It was Errol Flynn she had in mind. Not Clark Gable in *Gone With the Wind*. Apparently his face was too fat. The man she saw had a much thinner face, more like Errol Flynn. But still no moustache.'

Lewin smiled. 'It's a good job we didn't release a photofit picture, then.'

'Yes,' Anna said, looking at him hesitantly. 'Then she said something else. I don't know . . . ever since you explained about her birthday really being 4 July rather than 4 June . . .'

'She said something else?' Lewin prompted.

'She asked if we were absolutely sure that the pilot doesn't have a son,' Sandberg said.

'Not one that we've been able to find, at any rate,' Lewin said, shaking his head. 'Anything else?'

'She promised to call again if she remembered anything else. And she said to say hello to you as well. Seems you made quite an impression.'

'There's nothing else I can help you with?' Such as whatever's really worrying you, he thought.

'That's kind of you, but I don't think so. There are some things you just have to sort out on your own. But thanks anyway.'

She's told her husband what happened when she went to that night-club last month, and now her whole life has been plunged into chaos, Lewin thought. She's braver than me.


At the morning meeting Bäckström was unusually restrained, even though Olsson wasn't there. He had asked if anyone had any new ideas, now that a bunch of ignorant outsiders had wrested the cotton-buds out of the hands of the police. Lewin had taken the opportunity to remind everyone about his old ideas.

'At the risk of sounding like a broken record, I still think we know far too little about our victim,' he said.

'Imagine that,' Bäckström said, smiling his crooked smile. 'So, in concrete terms, what's really on your mind, if I might be so impudent as to ask?'

In Lewin's world, there was no harm in asking. In concrete terms, fresh interviews with Linda's parents and closest friends. And all the personal notes, possibly diaries, photograph albums and so on, that he was still missing and which, according to his firm conviction, definitely existed. Because they always existed.

Bäckström let out a deep sigh, and promised to take up the same old question with Olsson. And then, if no one else had anything to add, then he at least had more important things to be getting on with.

'Get out there and do something useful for a change, and I'll get the cakes in,' he said.

No one wants cake any more, Lewin thought as he collected his papers and went back to his office. And as far as the rest of it was concerned, it looked like he was going to have to sort it all out himself.

★

Just after lunch Bäckström's boss called him on his mobile, and, because he was taken by surprise, he answered. What? Go home to Stockholm to talk to some bastard Lapp? Bäckström thought, as he listened with half an ear to the torrent of words on the other end of the line.

'I can't hear you very well,' Bäckström said, holding his mobile at arm's length. 'Can you hear me? Hello? Hello?' As he should have done earlier, he finally switched the wretched thing off.

Forewarned is forearmed, he thought, and immediately switched it on again to call his union representative and explain about the miscarriage of justice of which he was the victim. It hadn't been difficult to wind the union guy up, seeing they were like peas in a pod anyway, and also happened to be related. Police officers were often fairly similar to one another, fortunately.

'That's bloody awful, Bäckström,' the union rep declared. 'Bollocks to this. It's high time we manned the barricades and put down a clear marker.'

He spent the rest of the day polishing his complaints against Moa Hjärtén and Bengt Karlsson, and as soon as he was finished he went to see Olsson and told him to make sure they were registered properly and, naturally, addressed as soon as possible with all available resources. Which was, of course, the least one could expect from the head of a preliminary investigation.

'Making false accusations, false certification, use of illegal documentation, violation of a public servant, grave defamation,' Olsson read.

'Exactly,' Bäckström said. 'The union's lawyer is going to get back to me if there's anything I've missed, but I suppose if that happens we can always add a little amendment.'

'But hang on a minute,' Olsson said, holding up his hands in his usual gesture. 'You don't think perhaps that this might be—'

'Correct me if I'm wrong,' Bäckström interrupted, glaring keenly at Olsson, 'but I hope you're not trying to suppress the reporting of a number of serious offences?'

'Of course not, of course not,' Olsson said. 'I'll see that this is addressed at once.' What do I do now? he thought once Bäckström had disappeared. And what choice do I actually have? He dialled Moa Hjärtén's number.

That gave the little bastard something to suck on, Bäckström thought as he shut the door behind him. As for him, it was high time for a chilled beer.

Jan Lewin spent the day going through the piles of paper on his desk one more time, without finding anything interesting. His contact in the Security Police hadn't been in touch, despite his promise, and when Lewin called him he just got his answer machine. Something urgent's probably come up, Lewin thought, feeling a pang of guilt about the fact that he was so impatient.

Just before it was time to leave off for the day, Eva came into his office and told him that in her inquiries concerning their 92-year-old witness she had made a minor discovery that probably wasn't at all interesting. The flight officer who had been married to the pilot's younger daughter for the past five years wasn't the biological father of her child. There was another man, thirty-five years old, the same age as the child's mother, but hardly the sort of person to make a police officer's mouth water, or even that of a civilian employee like her.

'He's lived here in town for ten years. Seems to be some sort of culture vulture, no criminal record, nor any mention of him in our files,' Svanström summarized, handing over the printouts about the child's hitherto unknown father.

Not a name that sets any alarm bells ringing, Lewin thought. But then why should it? And why is everyone in this case called Bengt? Bengt Olsson and Bengt Karlsson and the pilot, Bengt Borg. Plus at least twenty or thirty other witnesses and men who'd provided DNA samples who all shared the name Bengt.

'What's his job these days?' Lewin asked, mostly for the sake of saying something.

'The computer's playing up, so you'll have to wait till tomorrow,' Svanström said. 'When their daughter was born he seems to have been working for Malmö City Theatre. Like I said, seems to be some sort of culture vulture.'

Lewin sighed. Well, if no one else felt like doing it, he might as well make a serious attempt to talk to Linda's parents. Culture, culture vulture, he thought as soon as Eva had shut the door. What exactly am I hoping to find?

On Thursday morning the journalist Carin Ågren suddenly appeared in Växjö police station, to file an official complaint against Detective Superintendent Bäckström for sexual harassment. Because the officer of Växjö Police who received the complaint had been discreetly warned by Detective Superintendent Olsson the previous evening, he immediately set to work with all the conscientiousness that the matter demanded, and held a lengthy interview with the victim.

Now that little fat metropolitan bastard would have to hold on to his hat, he thought in delight as he read the printout of the interview back to Ågren and got it accepted and signed.

Detective Superintendent Olsson reached the same conclusion when he read the same interview an hour later. Since he was at heart a peaceful soul, and had already spoken to Bäckström's boss, who had promised to find a definitive solution to the Bäckström problem by the weekend at the latest, he decided to take some time owing and spend a couple of extra days at his house in the country. He had been working almost two months without a break, and it was high time that he recharged his batteries in advance of the coming week's renewed efforts. If anyone was going to say goodbye to that little nightmare from the regal capital city, someone else could do it, Olsson thought before heading out of town to his beloved wife and the relative tranquillity of the Småland countryside.

On Thursday afternoon Lewin's contact from the Security Police finally got in touch. After the introductory apologies – something had come up out of the blue and got in the way – he said that he thought Lewin would probably forgive him, seeing that he had a fair amount to tell him.

The person the mobile phone belonged to had been identified. He worked in the culture department of Växjö Council, and the council was listed as the account holder. On Monday 7 July the owner had reported his mobile phone missing, some time between Thursday

3 July and Monday 7 July. On Thursday 3 July the owner had taken a few days off, and he had a distinct memory of leaving the mobile in the desk drawer in his office. When he returned from his short break he couldn't find it. He had spoken to the colleague who was responsible for the council's phones. The mobile had been reported missing at once, and the account had been blocked.

None the less, it had been used to make two calls during that time. First, the wrong number that Lewin had been interested in, at 02.15 on Friday 4 July. And second seven hours later the same day. Both calls had been traced back to the mast they had been sent via. The first call appeared to have been made from central Växjö, while the second had been traced to a mast outside Ljungbyholm, about ten kilometres south-west of Kalmar. The second call had been made to another mobile, the sort of pay-as-you-go cell phone with an unknown user that was all too common in this sort of context. It hadn't been used since then.

'Well, that's about it,' Lewin's old friend said. 'I'll email you all the details, so it's over to you now.'

'Thank you, thanks very much indeed,' Lewin said, who knew what was coming. 'By the way, I don't suppose you could give me the name of our mobile user?'

'Oh, did I forget to mention that to you?' Lewin's friend was clearly having some difficulty concealing his glee. 'How strange. You're probably barking up the wrong tree, I'm afraid. I took a moment to look him up, and he doesn't appear in our register, or yours. Seems to be a perfectly ordinary, decent, honest citizen. Above all suspicion, not to mention all the horrors that people like you seem to enjoy wallowing in.'

'But I dare say he still has a name?' Lewin said, who had been through this before.

'His name's Bengt Månsson, Bengt Axel Månsson,' Lewin's contact said. 'You'll get all his details in the email. His passport photo is also fairly recent. Less than a year old, if I remember rightly.'

Once doesn't count, but twice is too many, Lewin thought. He hated coincidence, and had been told the same name by Eva Svanström just before he had left work the previous day. The father of the little girl who had a grandfather who used to be a pilot.

'Thanks,' Lewin said. 'I've a feeling this case is solved now.'

'If you say so, I believe you,' his colleague concurred. He had also been around a while, and had known Jan Lewin since they were at Police Academy together.

# 74

As soon as he had hung up, Jan Lewin did exactly what he always did in similar situations. First he closed his door and made sure the red light was on. Then he took a sheet of paper and a pen and tried to make sense of everything that was going through his head. It always got easier when he could see it on paper. And for once he didn't have to worry about either Olsson or Bäckström. Olsson had taken some time owing and gone out to the country, and there was really no need for Lewin to disturb him with the little he had to tell him. Bäckström's general absence was conspicuous, and with a bit if luck he was already packing for his return to Stockholm.

Which left the facts, Lewin thought. Which facts spoke for and against Bengt Månsson, Bengt Axel Månsson, thirty-five years old, responsible for so-called special projects in the culture department of Växjö Council, father to the daughter of the pilot's younger daughter, a person he had never met, spoken to or even glimpsed, who appeared nowhere in his investigation, and evidently not in any other police case either . . . What evidence was there to suggest that he either did or did not murder Linda Wallin? And where had he come across his name before Eva Svanström and then his old friend at the Security Police had given it to him? And then he had suddenly thought of his first proper bicycle. A red Crescent Valiant. And can it really be possible? he thought as he recalled the old article in the *Småland Post* about the local cultural dispute that had broken out in Växjö just a week or so after the murder, and which, all things considered, shouldn't have anything to do with his investigation.

Let's begin with the profile, and for once let's try to be a bit professional, Lewin thought, clearing his head of all extraneous thoughts. To suggest that Månsson didn't match the profile was a considerable understatement, even from the little that Lewin already knew about him. The only thing that didn't seem to be utterly wrong was that he lived on Frövägen in the part of town known as Öster, about two kilometres south of the crime scene. But half the population of the town lived within that radius, so it was of little help for anyone looking for a perpetrator. To put it mildly, there was nothing that matched, and according to the CP group's profile, Månsson was entirely unthinkable as the perpetrator.

Yet the fact that his mobile had been used to make the mysterious wrong number call to the anaesthetist indicated that he could have something to do with the murder. Of course, it could be the case that he simply called a wrong number, and so far there was nothing to suggest that he knew either Linda or her mother, but the coincidence of a call to that number at that time on that night was undeniably highly peculiar.

The idea that his mobile might have been lost or even stolen was also rather strange, considering the timing and the context. If someone had stolen it, why would they only have made two calls, one of which was the supposedly mistaken call to the number that the victim's mother had had a few years before? People who stole phones weren't usually so restrained. And suspected perpetrators seemed to be struck remarkably often by crimes in which perfect strangers for some reason chose to relieve them of possessions which might otherwise prove highly problematic for their owners.

Then there was the stolen car as well. It could be linked forensically to the perpetrator they were looking for. Bengt Månsson could not, admittedly, be linked directly to the car, but he was the biological father of the car-owner's grandchild, and if their 92-year-old witness had actually seen what she said she had, then the natural next step in the investigation was to present her with a set of photographs including one of Bengt Månsson.

The sooner the better, and with a bit of luck she didn't go to bed as early as she got up, Lewin thought.

First he spoke to Eva Svanström, who promised to arrange the practical details at once, then he talked to Anna Sandberg. Partly because she had actually found their witness, partly because he had a feeling that she needed something else to think about, and partly because he was, in practice, in charge in Olsson's and Bäckström's absence.

'I've got a feeling that you're absolutely right,' Anna Sandberg said, suddenly not seeming to spare a thought for her difficult domestic situation.

'Well, we'll find out soon enough,' Lewin said.

'That's him. Him, the son. That's what I've said all along,' Mrs Rudberg said an hour later when they were sitting at her kitchen table and she had just put her finger on the picture of Bengt Månsson.

'Like that Errol Flynn, who was in all those pirate films, but without a moustache,' the witness went on. 'He does look like him, doesn't he? But why on earth would a father deny that he has a son? Maybe he's illegitimate.'

Not the son, but the son-in-law. In the modern way that applied in today's Swedish society, Lewin had explained as gently as he could, however you were supposed to do that to a 92-year-old woman. And from Småland, he thought.

'Well, that's it then,' the witness said as soon as Lewin had finished. 'I don't know how many times I've seen him pushing the child in that pushchair.'

Which probably indicated that it was a few years ago, Lewin thought. But what difference would that make if you were close to a hundred years old yourself?

'That blue cashmere sweater,' Anna Sandberg suddenly said when they were sitting in the car on their way back to the police station. 'I've suddenly realized that it's exactly the sort of sweater a pilot might have bought on one of his trips abroad.'

'Not a bad thought,' Lewin agreed. The same thought had occurred to him even before their witness put her finger on Bengt Månsson, but naturally he wouldn't dream of saying so to Sandberg. It would have been both immodest and completely unnecessary.

'What do you think about going to see him and showing him pictures of various sweaters, and asking if he's ever had or bought or given away anything resembling any of them?' Sandberg asked, evidently keen to carry on.

'We should definitely do that,' Lewin agreed. 'But first we have to do something else.'

'Never wake a sleeping bear,' Sandberg said. 'Not too early, anyway.'

'Exactly,' Lewin said. 'First we find out as much as we possibly can about Månsson without having to ask anyone who might tell him about it.'

# 75

Bäckström had evidently decided to hold out until the very last minute, and under those circumstances Lewin felt he had no choice. Regardless of anything else, he had to inform him. Now that their witness had identified Månsson, it was no longer a question of random shots in the dark, or improbable coincidences. And, since Lewin had these days somehow ended up wandering the same nocturnal paths as his colleague Bäckström, he chose to tell him before breakfast on Friday morning, just the two of them, in Bäckström's room.

Bäckström was fresh from the shower, pink as a little piglet, his eyes only slightly bloodshot, and in an excellent mood.

'Sit yourself down while I get my trousers on,' he said. 'If you fancy a morning beer, there's one in the minibar,' he added generously.

Lewin declined the offer and instead gave him a brief summary of the situation. Bäckström immediately started firing on all cylinders, and even forgot about putting on his trousers.

'Fuck, Lewin,' he said. 'I think we've struck gold here.'

Who's this 'we'? Lewin thought, sighing deep inside. Then he suggested that they talk to the prosecutor as soon as they had put together a file about Månsson and his involvement in the murder inquiry. Everything suggested that this could be done that afternoon, and that they might even be able to go and pick Månsson up without any prior warning as soon as the prosecutor had taken the decision. The stolen car and the fact that their witness had picked him out ought to be sufficient grounds. Not least considering what this was actually about.

'He's supposed to be at work today, so the easiest thing would probably be to pick him up when he's leaving.'

'Not a chance!' Bäckström said, shaking his head. 'This bastard's
mine, and this is what we're going to do . . .'

I wonder how he became yours? Lewin wondered as he headed
downstairs shortly afterwards to get some breakfast.

As soon as Bäckström reached the police station he summoned the
faithful to his room and allocated the jobs. Lewin, Knutsson, Thorén
and Svanström, reinforced by Sandberg, would check out their
suspect, Bengt Månsson. Not a stone was to be left unturned.
Rogersson would take care of various unspecified tasks under the
direct leadership of Bäckström, whilst Bäckström himself would
manage and delegate the work, as well as obviously providing them
with encouragement and support. And of course they were given a
few words of advice to help them on their way.

'This has to be kept quiet. Not a word to anyone outside this room.
Don't forget what I said about little Olsson being best mates with
Månsson. I'm damn sure Olsson's mixed up in this one way or another,
and if we so much as whisper anything about this to him he'll scuttle
off and tell Månsson, and I don't even want to think what that bastard
might do.'

'I was under the impression that you were going home to
Stockholm, Bäckström?' Lewin said. And what a fine way with words
you've got, he thought.

'Forget it,' Bäckström said. 'No one's leaving this ship until we've
made it to shore.'

'It would still be interesting to know what you were thinking of
doing yourself,' Lewin persisted.

'I'm going to arrange a bit of discreet surveillance of our
perpetrator,' Bäckström said. 'So he doesn't disappear and kill anyone
else. Tell Adolfsson and that stuck-up toff that I want to talk to them
right away.'

'Of course, Bäckström,' Lewin said. Not a word to anyone outside
this room, he thought.

\*

'Månsson, Bengt Axel,' acting Police Inspector and Baron Gustaf von Essen said a short while later when he and Adolfsson were standing in Bäckström's office. 'Isn't he one of the town's beloved Fellow Menfolk?'

'Exactly,' Bäckström agreed. 'Crazed sex pests, the lot of them.' So the stuck-up little twerp's not completely stupid after all, he thought.

'In that case he was the one who got blood all over your uniform, Adolf. I remember taking his name along with everyone else's,' von Essen said, with a nod to his partner.

'So you've already beaten up the little fellow?' Bäckström said cheerily, fixing his gaze on Adolfsson. Was I right about this lad or what? he thought.

'Well, it wasn't quite like that,' Adolfsson said, and explained to Bäckström about his intervention in the brawl outside McDonald's on Storgatan about three weeks before.

'So what the fuck did you do with the uniform?' Bäckström snarled, staring at Adolfsson with unusually narrow eyes, even taking into account the fact that they happened to be in Bäckström's head.

'I wiped off the worst of it and hung it back up,' Adolfsson said, shrugging his shoulders. 'Haven't had time to hand it in. He didn't seem to be your average junkie, so it ended up back in my locker.'

'So what the fuck are we waiting for?' Bäckström said excitedly, jumping up from his chair, and five minutes later he was standing in front of Enoksson in the forensics unit, clutching the jacket of Adolfsson's uniform. First he made Enoksson swear to keep quiet, then he explained what it was all about. According to Bäckström, informing Olsson was out of the question. Unfortunately there were a number of mysterious circumstances which indicated that Olsson was at best to be regarded as a clear security risk, but it was probably considerably worse than that.

'With all due respect, Bäckström, I doubt things are quite that bad,' Enoksson said as he examined Adolfsson's jacket under a high-strength lamp.

'Well, bollocks to that right now, Enok,' Bäckström said in his usual polite way. 'Is there enough blood left on there?'

Assuming that it was Månsson's blood on the jacket, and that it

hadn't been contaminated with anything that Enoksson couldn't see –
but he didn't want to risk damaging it by subjecting it to further
examination at the moment – there was more than enough blood for
a DNA analysis and anything else that might prove to be of interest
given the context.

'When can we have the results, then?' Bäckström asked.

At the start of the following week, according to Enoksson, assuming that there were no legal hindrances of the sort that had been top
of the agenda for the past few weeks.

'Forget it,' Bäckström said. 'Do you think I'm prepared to risk him
slaughtering half of Växjö while we wait?'

'I'll see what I can do,' Enoksson sighed. 'From a purely technical
point of view, they ought to be able to come up with a preliminary
analysis within twenty-four hours, assuming there's nothing wrong
with the material we send them. But we mustn't forget that it's the
weekend, as well. Anyway, weren't you supposed to be going back to
Stockholm?'

'Weekend? We're not talking weekends, Enok, we're talking
murderers!' Bäckström blustered. And no one's going anywhere, he
thought.

'I'll be in touch in an hour or so,' Enoksson sighed.

As soon as Bäckström had grabbed Adolfsson's jacket and taken it off
to Enoksson, von Essen and Adolfsson had begun the surveillance of
their subject, Bengt Månsson. First they got a young female colleague
from the surveillance unit of Växjö Police to make a call to Månsson
at his office in the culture department, to find out if there was any
chance of getting some funding for a theatre project for young
immigrant women. While the conversation was going on, they parked
their unmarked car a discreet distance away, from where they had a
good view of the entrance to the premises of the culture department.
Quarter of an hour later their female colleague called von Essen on his
mobile to give a report. Not only was Månsson at his desk, he also
sounded 'really nice', and had been 'really interested' in the project.
He had even suggested that they meet up soon to discuss the idea in
person.

'So what kind of impression did you get of him?' von Essen asked.

'Horny,' the female colleague declared. 'Really horny. I think he wanted to check first to make sure I'm as nice as I sound. Let me know if there's anything else I can do to help,' she said, and giggled.

'So what did little Caijsa have to say, then?' Adolfsson said as soon as his partner had ended the call.

'She seems quite taken with Månsson,' von Essen said.

'She's quite taken with everyone,' Adolfsson said, suddenly sounding rather cross for some reason.

'Not quite everyone, surely?' von Essen retorted innocently. He had been at the same staff party as Adolfsson a couple of months earlier.

Enoksson had done his best, and in the end one of his old contacts in the National Forensics Lab had given in and promised to help. She had to work that weekend anyway, so with a bit of luck she'd be able to find time to do what Enoksson wanted. But he could forget all about twenty-four hours. Assuming she got the material within the next few hours, and assuming it was usable, and assuming nothing unexpected happened, the earliest he could have the report was Sunday morning.

After some more persuasion, and the promise of both overtime and time off in lieu, he had also managed to find a young colleague who was prepared to act as a courier to Linköping, a round trip of four hundred kilometres, even though it was already Friday afternoon. Once Adolfsson's jacket was safely on its way to the lab, Enoksson took several deep breaths and called Bäckström. Let's hope this means we can actually get rid of the fat little bastard some time soon, Enoksson thought, even though he was renowned, with good reason, as being a gentle soul.

'Sunday morning,' Bäckström groaned. 'So what the hell are they so busy with up there? Am I the only person doing any work in this fucking police force?'

'Sunday morning at the earliest,' Enoksson repeated.

'I'm not deaf,' Bäckström said, and hung up.

What's wrong with just saying thank you? Enoksson thought, as he called his colleague Olsson to explain what was going on. Olsson, after all, was still head of the preliminary police investigation. But, as on so many previous occasions, Enoksson had to make do with leaving a message on his answering machine. 'Yes, hello Olsson. Enoksson here. I didn't want anything in particular, but if you feel like it, call me on the usual number. Otherwise, have a good weekend.' Enoksson didn't actually have any more faith in Adolfsson's jacket than he had in the rest of Bäckström's theories. Mainly he just wanted to get home to his beloved wife and their domestic bliss out in the Småland countryside.

# 76

Adolfsson and von Essen had spent the rest of Friday watching Månsson, which like all surveillance jobs had mainly meant sitting and waiting for something to happen. Because they were both keen hunters there was nothing particularly difficult about this. Hunting was all about the ability to wait. The fact that Månsson had met them three weeks before didn't worry them much either. The idea, of course, was to see without being seen, and they estimated that the risk of Månsson's seeing them before they saw him was fairly negligible. Not that it would matter much in a town the size of Växjö, where people were always bumping into each other.

At about four o'clock on Friday afternoon Månsson had emerged from his place of work in the council offices on Västergatan, just along from the concert hall, in the company of a few other people who, to judge by their appearance and manner and the way they were dressed, were probably his work colleagues. Adolfsson had taken a few discreet pictures from a safe distance, and noted the time and place in their surveillance log. There was nothing whatsoever to suggest that their subject was remotely like the serial killer Bäckström had warned them about.

First Månsson and the others had sat down at an outdoor terrace on Storgatan, a few blocks away from their offices. There they had drunk beer, eaten fried chicken wings and chatted. Then the company had broken up, disappearing in different directions, each of them most likely just going home. Månsson had headed east on Shanks's pony, towards his home on Frövägen, and because that was a couple of kilometres away and he was obviously planning to walk, Adolfsson and von Essen decided to split up. Von Essen had followed him on foot, while Adolfsson took the car.

In spite of what the profile said about the killer, Månsson lived more than two kilometres from the place where he was supposed to have murdered Linda seven weeks earlier. But apart from that, the fact that he lived where he did was quite splendid, because one of their fellow officers from the traffic division happened to live in the building on the other side of the road. Månsson's flat was on the third floor, and their colleague's on the fourth floor of the building opposite, so things couldn't be better for anyone wanting to see what Månsson got up to. They had managed to get hold of their colleague before they left the police station, as soon as Thorén had given them a list of addresses associated with Månsson. The officer had been seconded to Öland for the weekend, but he had nothing against letting them borrow his flat as soon as they told him what it was about. Nothing special, just a bit of extra overtime helping the drugs unit, von Essen had explained. 'Great, let those junkies have it!' their colleague had said as he handed over the keys. Von Essen and Adolfsson were to make themselves at home: everything was where they might expect in the home of a 39-year-old bachelor who worked for the traffic division of Kronoberg District.

When Månsson disappeared through the door of the building he lived in Adolfsson was already in position in the flat opposite, and by the time Adolfsson saw Månsson's feet and legs come in through the front door of his flat von Essen had joined him.

'He hasn't got any curtains, either,' von Essen said happily.

'Culture vultures like him never have curtains,' Adolfsson explained, as he followed Månsson through his personal pair of Zeiss binoculars, enlarged twenty times.

As von Essen and Adolfsson were settling into their new abode, Bäckström called them to find out how things were going. The subject was at home in his flat, on his own, and right now he was watching the seven thirty news on television, Adolfsson told him.

'So he's not doing anything he shouldn't be?' Bäckström asked.

'Not apart from watching the news,' Adolfsson said.

'Call me if anything happens,' Bäckström said.

'Understood, boss,' Adolfsson said.

'I wonder what he's really doing?' Bäckström said, looking at Rogersson, who was dealing with their empty beer glasses.

'So what was he really not doing just then?' Rogersson asked.

'Watching television,' Bäckström said. 'Who the fuck watches television at this time of day?'

'Maybe he hasn't got anything better to do,' Rogersson suggested.

'I bet you he's got something new on the go,' Bäckström said.

Månsson sat and watched television for about two hours, and the longer he sat there, the more often he zapped between channels. Like most other people, he seemed to have twenty or so to choose from. Just after half past nine he spoke to someone on the phone for a few minutes. Then he went into the kitchen and lifted some side plates down from the cupboard above the sink, took various things out of the fridge, sliced a baguette and put it all on a tray, which he carried through and placed on the coffee table in front of the sofa in the living room. Then he went back into the kitchen.

'Things are heating up,' Adolfsson said to von Essen, who was lying on the sofa watching a film on their colleague's television.

'Has he rigged up a block and tackle from the ceiling?' von Essen asked, changing to TV4 so as not to miss the latest news.

'He's opening a bottle of wine,' Adolfsson said. 'And now he's fetched two glasses.'

'Aha!' von Essen said. 'Mark my words, Adolf, he's expecting female company.'

At ten o'clock a blonde woman in her thirties pulled up in a small Renault and disappeared in through the front door of Månsson's building. She had a large handbag hanging from her shoulder, and in her left hand a plastic bag which looked as if it contained a large wine box. Two minutes later she had reached Månsson's flat, and at ten past ten they were sitting on the sofa pulling each other's clothes off. After another five minutes they were having sex. Adolfsson took the opportunity to complement the surveillance log with numerous excellent photographs, and used the spare time to note the registration number and model of the visitor's car.

The sexual activities on the sofa continued until just after midnight, with some short breaks for food and drink. After an hour Bäckström called to ask what was happening, and Adolfsson gave him a quick update.

'He's got a girl there. They're hard at it on the sofa, although right now they're taking a break for some food,' he said.

'Has he tied her up yet?' Bäckström said eagerly.

'No, just the usual,' Adolfsson said.

'What do you mean, the usual?' Bäckström said suspiciously. 'No neckties, no knives?'

'Just normal sex. So far they haven't done anything I haven't done myself,' Adolfsson said. 'Mind you, Månsson seems fairly energetic for his age,' he added. He himself was ten years younger.

At fifteen minutes past midnight things calmed down. Månsson and his guest finished the plate of food. They drank the last of the bottle. His guest went into the kitchen and returned with a three-litre box of white wine while her host selected a film on one of his many film channels. Nothing remarkable, an ordinary romantic comedy, Adolfsson noted after a quick glance at the television section in the evening paper. At half past two they left the living room, heading for the bedroom which faced the other side of the building.

Adolfsson woke von Essen, who was lying on top of their colleague's bed snoring. Von Essen went outside to take a discreet look, and returned to confirm that the subject had evidently gone to bed. Then he took over from Adolfsson, who lay down on the same bed and fell asleep at once. Everything had been carefully noted, and the name and date of birth of the car's registered owner seemed to match Månsson's guest. Even if it didn't, they had numerous photographs of her in case there was ever any problem with identification.

For once, Bäckström was having trouble sleeping. First he and Rogersson had sat in his room talking, and when he finally managed to get rid of his parasitic colleague it was already two o'clock in the morning. Three hours later he woke up, and only after another little drink was he able to settle down and get back to sleep. But by seven o'clock he was awake again, and in the absence of any better options he wandered down to the dining room to get some well-deserved nutrition after a hard and trying night.

First he piled up his plate as usual with headache pills, anchovy fillets, scrambled egg and sausages, and after washing down the first of these with several large gulps of orange juice he finally started to feel like a human being again, and set about the sausages with some vigour. He also managed to grunt in the direction of Lewin, who nodded politely and even deigned to lower his morning paper a fraction, while little Svanström for some reason got an attack of the giggles that only got worse and worse until, red-eyed, streaming with tears and holding a napkin over her mouth, she got up from the table and rushed out towards the ladies' room.

What the fuck's got into her? Bäckström thought suspiciously as he crammed another little sausage into his mouth. 'What the fuck's got into her?' he asked, peering at Lewin, who didn't seem to have noticed that an hysterical woman had just left them.

'I have absolutely no idea,' Lewin lied, even though he had worked out the day before that Bäckström was probably the only person in the entire police station who hadn't read the report of the interview with Carin Ågren. And who was he to ruin the day for a fellow officer so early in the morning, notwithstanding the officer in question's personal failings and other human shortcomings?

Lewin excused himself and got up from the table, to make sure that Eva Svanström was kept at a safe distance from Bäckström for the rest of the day.

# 77

Månsson and his guest didn't appear to have had any trouble sleeping. It wasn't until almost ten o'clock in the morning that von Essen had reason to make any new notes in the surveillance log. First a naked Månsson appeared in his hallway and then disappeared into his bathroom. A couple of minutes later his similarly naked guest followed him, and evidently they were both very careful with their hygiene seeing as it was almost an hour before they emerged, Månsson with a towel wrapped round his waist and his female guest wearing a dressing-gown, and went into the kitchen to have breakfast.

By then even Adolfsson was up on his feet, freshly showered and busy making coffee and boiling eggs, mixing juice and making sandwiches. Then Bäckström called once more to hear how things were going.

'Well? Is she alive?' he said.

'In the peak of health, apparently,' von Essen asserted. 'Right now she and her host are having coffee, oatflakes with yoghurt, a crispbread sandwich with a lot of salad and a slice of low-fat cheese.'

'Fucking hell,' Bäckström said with distaste. 'Sick bastards. Let me know if he makes a move for her throat.'

Von Essen promised they would. Then he took the chance to grab a quick shower while Adolfsson took over the surveillance and note-taking. Activities in the flat opposite seemed to suggest that their subject was thinking of leaving it and heading somewhere unknown.

\*

Lewin and his colleagues had spent a day and a half trying to find a connection between Bengt Månsson on the one hand and Linda or her mother on the other. And they hadn't succeeded. Even though they had combed every accessible database with all the care, thoroughness and inventiveness they had picked up over the years, they hadn't found anything.

The most likely conclusion was usually depressing. There were no straightforward connections which had anything to do with their family circumstances, working lives, upbringing, education or accommodation. Nor any mutual networks, interests, hobbies, friends and acquaintances that could link them. Which left only more coincidental encounters, and what little consolation there was to be had from the fact that they all seemed to be ordinary, decent, normal people, and that Växjö was a small enough town for them to have been bound to bump into each other sooner or later.

Yet this was meagre consolation, and a nagging doubt was growing inside Lewin that everything he had believed would turn out to be wrong. Where would someone like Månsson have learned to hotwire cars and break a steering lock? Where would someone like him have picked up any druggie contacts? And how common were people like him, when it came to what this was ultimately all about? Raping, torturing and strangling a woman fifteen years younger than himself? The only real consolation so far was von Essen and Adolfsson's reports about his substantial sexual appetite, albeit a need that he appeared to satisfy within the frame of conventional sexual behaviour. On the one hand, on the other hand, Lewin reasoned, mainly to subdue his own anxieties.

At five o'clock that afternoon Bäckström rang Adolfsson and von Essen again, and his first question was why they hadn't contacted him. According to von Essen, the reason was that they had nothing to report that was important enough for them to trouble their esteemed boss, who was bound to be occupied with more important matters.

'Don't talk crap, Essen,' Bäckström interrupted. 'Just tell me what the bastard's doing.'

After they had finished breakfast, Månsson and his female guest had got dressed and packed a few things in a bag, which, suggested that they were planning to go on a short excursion, if nothing else then to enjoy this fantastic summer. When they reached the hall, however, something must have arisen, since they had suddenly pulled off all their clothes again and conducted various sexual activities on the hall carpet. The details of these were, however, unclear, as the surveillance team had only been able to observe the participants' naked legs and feet.

This somewhat unexpected interlude had been concluded relatively quickly, and just quarter of an hour later Månsson and his female guest had set off in her car. To judge by their behaviour, they were both in a very good mood. Adolfsson and von Essen had followed at a safe distance, and after ten kilometres or so the subjects had stopped at a beach on the northern shore of nearby Lake Helgasjön. There they had spent the whole afternoon lying on a blanket, chatting to each other, sunbathing and swimming. They had also enjoyed a simple picnic. Twenty-seven degrees, twenty-four in the water, and even von Essen and Adolfsson had taken turns cooling off as best they could with a few discreet swims at a safe distance from their quarry.

Then they had returned to Månsson's flat, stopping to buy some groceries on the way. They took farewell of each other in the road outside Månsson's block, and the guest had left. Månsson had returned to his flat, where he threw off his clothes and disappeared into the bathroom, emerging after half an hour with the same blue towel wrapped round his waist. After that he lay on the sofa in the living room reading the evening papers.

'First *Aftonbladet*, then *Expressen*,' von Essen stated in a neutral voice.

'And nothing else in all that time?' Bäckström asked suspiciously. 'No alfresco fucking while they were at the beach?'

Nothing like that, von Essen said, with a possible reservation for anything Månsson might have got up to while he was on his own in the bathroom.

What the fuck's the fucker really up to? Bäckström thought, glancing angrily at his wristwatch. Already six o'clock, and he hadn't had a single beer all day. But at least that was something he could put right fairly soon. Thorough as always, that morning he had sent Rogersson to restock their supplies in advance of what would probably be his last night in Växjö. Although if the lazy bastards up at the National Forensics Lab didn't manage to live up to their own promises, there would be nothing for it but to stay another night, he thought. Surrounded by cretins and mere incompetents as he was, it took a hell of a time to get the smallest thing done. The bastard Lapp that the socialists had put in charge of him and his fellow unfortunates would just have to console himself by shoving the party manifesto up his fat Norrland arse. No one could say that Bäckström was the sort who left a job half done, Bäckström thought, already feeling considerably brighter.

Bengt A. Månsson, A. as in Axel, seemed to be a man of fixed habits and regular routines. And a man with a fundamentally liberal attitude and a good deal of flexibility when it came to his choice of partner. Saturday evening had begun exactly like the day before. First he lay on the sofa watching television for a couple of hours. Then he made a couple of phone calls, after which he went out into the kitchen and prepared the usual tray at half past nine or so. Bread and various toppings, side plates, two wine glasses, and the three-litre wine box that his guest the previous night had evidently left behind. Wise man, trying to keep costs down. I wonder who gave him the bottle he shared with the blonde? Patrik Adolfsson thought. Born and bred in Småland as he was.

Half an hour later a woman appeared along the road outside his door. In contrast to the blonde, this one was brunette and considerably younger, which might explain why she arrived on foot rather than by car. Whatever, five minutes later she was sitting on the sofa in the living room together with her host, and after that things proceeded as per usual.

'Anything interesting to report?' von Essen asked from his seat at the kitchen table, where he was reading that morning's *Svenska Dagbladet* while Adolfsson covered the surveillance.

'Brunette, about twenty, much bigger tits than the blonde,'

Adolfsson summarized. 'And it looks like she's shaved down below, maybe because of the heat.'

'Let's see,' von Essen said, getting up from the kitchen table and taking the binoculars from Adolfsson without further ado. 'Looks less sophisticated,' he said.

'Maybe Månsson's tired of getting hairs in his mouth,' Adolfsson suggested.

'You're a true romantic, aren't you?' Von Essen handed back the binoculars and went back to reading the financial pages of *Svenska Dagbladet* in the hope that his investments might give him the chance to repair all the leaking roofs that he'd inherited from his parents.

'How are things?' Bäckström asked over the telephone an hour later.

'Same as last night,' von Essen summarized.

'Same woman?' Bäckström asked. What's happened to the check on her background? he wondered. He hadn't heard a peep from Lewin and his so-called colleagues all day, even though he'd asked them for both pictures and background of the woman in question.

'Different woman, brunette, about twenty, seems less sophisticated,' von Essen said, trying not to go into the sorts of details that might get a man like Bäckström excited.

'How many times has he been at her, then?'

'Three times in two hours,' von Essen said after a quick glance at the log. 'Mind you, they're at it again now, so there's every chance of more.'

'Fucking hell, what a sick bastard,' Bäckström groaned. 'And in this sort of heat as well.'

Von Essen and Adolfsson spent the rest of the night taking turns to rest on their colleague's bed. At seven o'clock in the morning Månsson's most recent female company left him. Alert and well, apparently, and probably because the poor thing worked as a nursing assistant or something, the baron in von Essen thought, while the acting police inspector made a note in the log. Månsson, on the other hand, seemed to be sleeping the sleep of the just, and he didn't even seem to have seen his lady friend out. By this point von Essen was starting to feel rather weary, and more than a little irritated by the sound of his partner's snoring that was issuing from the bedroom. High time something happened, he thought with a deep yawn, glancing at his watch just as their mobile phone began to ring.

'Has something happened?' von Essen said as he answered it.

# 78

## *Växjö, Sunday 24 August*

Half an hour earlier, Enoksson's phone had rung. Because he was a morning person, he had already read the paper and made breakfast, which he was about to serve to his wife, who was rather less of a morning person.

'Enoksson,' Enoksson said.

'Are you sitting down?' his contact at the National Forensics Lab asked, and at that moment he knew what she was going to say.

'Bloody hell,' he said two minutes later when she had finished. The age of miracles is not yet past, he thought, even though in his mind's eye all he could see was a little fat officer from National Crime in Stockholm.

'Has something happened?' von Essen asked.

'We're going to crucify the bastard and dunk him in boiling oil,' Bäckström snarled at the other end of the line, and at that moment von Essen knew that his waiting time was over. For this case, at least.

Bäckström and Rogersson joined the surveillance team within the space of half an hour, parking their car at the back of the building and behaving as surreptitiously as possible. Bäckström was wearing shorts, a Hawaiian shirt, sunglasses, sandals and socks, and could easily have been an extra in an old spy film set in the Caribbean. Rogersson, in contrast, looked the same as usual, but because he had entered the building sixty seconds after Bäckström he might as well have been invisible.

Von Essen quickly updated them on the current position. Månsson seemed to be in bed still. Probably asleep. Assuming he didn't jump from the balcony or either of the two small windows at the back of his flat, that left the main door to the building and the entrance to the cellar, which was also at the front.

'Okay, let's go up and get the bastard,' Bäckström said eagerly. 'Can anyone lend me a pair of handcuffs? I managed to leave mine behind.'

'With all due respect, boss, I wonder if this is such a good idea,' Adolfsson said.

'You're thinking about calling the rapid-response unit?' Bäckström asked. Typical. It's always the least likely ones who wimp out at the last minute. And this lad could have gone far, he thought.

Adolfsson hadn't had any notion of calling the rapid-response unit. But he did have some practical operational thoughts. Månsson would probably recognize all of them, with the exception of Rogersson. He certainly ought to recognize Bäckström, considering they had spent a couple of hours together in the same room, and Rogersson's irredeemably cop-like appearance didn't work in his favour in this sort of situation. Besides, Månsson had a peephole in his door, and if they just showed up and rang the bell in the hope that he'd open up he would have plenty of time either to cut his throat with a bread knife or to jump from the third floor.

'I've seen both of those happen before,' von Essen added. 'It was an extradition. First he cut his throat, then he jumped from the balcony. Probably wanted to cover his bets. Sad business. Here in town, too, of all places.'

'I'm still waiting for suggestions,' Bäckström said, glaring at his team.

'He seems fairly keen on women, to put it mildly, so I'll tell you what I think we should do,' Adolfsson suggested. 'It nearly always works with men like him.'

While Bäckström and his colleagues planned the only properly masculine element left in their case, Lewin, as usual, had taken care of everything that needed to be done. First he had called Olsson and left a message on his answering machine saying that he should call Lewin on his mobile as soon as possible, and preferably at once. Then he had called the prosecutor, who had actually answered, and promised to be there within an hour at the latest.

Then he had asked Anna Sandberg to take another officer with her and go to see Linda's mother, so that she didn't have to hear the news any other way, and certainly not via the media. And to make sure that she had someone with her who could help look after her. The same with Linda's father, and that task he had entrusted with full confidence to his colleague Knutsson. He had suggested that Henning Wallin might most easily be contacted over the phone, and if he had any particular wishes, then they could probably be accommodated.

While Lewin had been conscientiously organizing these pieces of police software and making sure that they all ended up in the right places, Bäckström and the others had been joined by a young female officer from the surveillance unit of the regional crime squad. She had introduced herself as 'Caijsa with a C, and both an i and a j', and two days before she had spoken to Månsson on the phone, pretending to be Houda Kassem, an immigrant from Iran who was interested in the theatre. As far as today's activities were concerned, she was thinking of suggesting a different role, seeing as Månsson had no idea what Houda looked like.

'I was thinking of going with the old market-research routine. Going round asking people what they think of the area. That always works with people like him.' Caijsa smiled at Adolfsson as she held up an ID card from a market-research company which was hanging from a chain round her neck.

'Sounds like an excellent idea,' Rogersson said before Bäckström had time to mess up something which was simple and obvious to any police officer with a brain.

'Well, he's up and moving now,' von Essen said from his position by the window. 'He's in the kitchen, wearing just a pair of skimpy briefs, drinking water direct from the tap. I think you have to watch those boxes of white wine, actually.'

'Okay, let's do it,' Bäckström said, pulling in his stomach and puffing out his chest, sending waves through his Hawaiian shirt. 'And for fuck's sake make sure you get handcuffs on the bastard, so we don't have a rerun of the hundred metres out in the street,' he added, for some reason glaring at Adolfsson and von Essen.

Caijsa had been absolutely right, and Månsson had even opened the door with a smile on his lips. The undramatic arrest that followed was over in fifteen seconds, from the moment von Essen stepped forward from one side holding his badge to the click of the handcuffs as Adolfsson quickly secured Månsson's hands behind his back.

'What's this about? There must be some mistake,' Månsson said, looking both upset and completely uncomprehending.

'The bastard's on his way in,' Bäckström snapped over Lewin's mobile phone. 'Get those lazy fuckers in forensics to wake up so they can make a start on his flat. We've got two patrol cars out in the road already, so soon we'll have a whole flock of vultures here.'

'Our colleagues from forensics are on their way,' Lewin said. 'Did everything go well otherwise?'

'He's not so fucking cocky now,' Bäckström said with a happy grunt.

I wonder if he ever was, Lewin thought.

# 79

Lewin also had to take care of the practical details during the afternoon, and he started with the prosecutor.

'I'm sorry I didn't tell you any of this until this morning,' he said. 'Before that, it was all rather vague hypotheses, and I didn't want to bother you unnecessarily in case they turned out to be no more than that. I do hope you don't object to having been kept in the dark.'

The prosecutor had no objections at all. On the contrary. She was just very relieved, and as soon as she received the definitive results from the National Forensics Lab confirming that it was Månsson's DNA in Linda's flat, she would formally arrest him. Until then, he would be remanded in custody, and if Lewin felt like it he was very welcome to accompany her to the cells while she informed him of her decision. 'And on a completely different matter: where's Olsson?'

'He's on leave this weekend,' Lewin said. 'We've been trying to reach him by phone. With a bit of luck he'll call us back.' I can't imagine what we might need him for, though, he thought.

'I'm afraid he doesn't look like much,' he said as they entered the custody corridor. 'Considering what he's done, I mean.'

'They don't usually, do they?' the prosecutor said. 'Not the ones I've seen, anyway.'

Månsson didn't look like much. He was sitting on his bunk inside the cell, and seemed almost detached. Just like everyone else the first time they had their identity taken away from them in the most tangible way possible in a democracy. First they had taken off the handcuffs and checked him in. Then they had removed all his own clothes and given him a set of official clothing: underwear, socks, trousers and shirt. And a pair of felt slippers that he could wear if he wanted to. Then he had had to sign a receipt for his possessions.

After a short wait a couple of forensics experts had arrived. Månsson had been photographed, his height and weight noted, and a set of fingerprints and palm-prints taken. The forensics experts had been joined by a doctor who had taken a blood sample, then taken samples of hair from his head, body and crotch, and finally examined him. All the samples had been put into small containers, labelled, sealed and signed. Just before he was left alone, for the first time he had said something without having been asked a question first.

'Can somebody please tell me what this is all about?'

'The prosecutor will be here shortly,' one of the forensics experts had said. 'I'm sure she'll give you all the information she can.'

'I'm not feeling very well,' Månsson had said. 'I'm on several medications and I didn't have a chance to bring them with me. They're at home. In the bathroom cabinet. For asthma and so on.'

'We can deal with that a bit later,' the doctor had said with a friendly smile. 'Once we're finished with all the rest of it.'

'He's very good-looking,' the prosecutor said once she and Lewin had returned to the main office of the investigation. 'You say he's got no criminal record at all? Considering what's happened, I mean.'

'Looks the way film stars used to once upon a time,' Lewin agreed. 'No criminal record,' he confirmed.

'Mind you, he's probably not feeling too great,' she said, and it sounded as though she was thinking out loud. 'Do you think he's going to confess, then?'

'I really don't know,' Lewin said, shaking his head. 'I suppose we'll find out.' As if it will make any difference, considering the rest of the evidence, he thought.

While all the others were rushing round like headless chickens, Bäckström took a turn around the police station to soak up all the congratulations he so richly deserved. They were all like happy young children suddenly. Even those two miserable fabric detectives who had been as sour as vinegar only last week started smiling and giggling when they caught sight of him.

'Good to see you, Bäckström,' one of them said cheerfully. 'Congratulations, by the way.'

'It's such a shame you have to leave,' the other one said. 'Mind you, maybe we'll get another chance? To get to know each other better, I mean.'

There's something not right here, Bäckström thought, but not knowing what it was he made do with a nod. Quick and manly. 'Yes, I dare say you can finish this off without me now,' he said. Backwoods cops and a load of women. It was more than time for a cold beer, he thought.

Rogersson was sitting in his office, looking rather miserable. 'I was thinking of heading home,' Bäckström said.

'I'll join you,' Rogersson said. 'I've just got to shift all the files and have a few words with Holt, then I'm ready to go.'

'Holt?' Bäckström said. 'Is that bitter little cunt already here?'

'I saw her in the corridor a while back,' Rogersson confirmed. 'Her and that little blonde who used to work for the Security Police, Mattei, I think her name was. Lisa Mattei. Her mum's some sort of inspector for them. A right bitch, if you ask me. They were having a chat with our little prosecutor. All these women will be doing a Mexican wave next.'

'See you in the hotel bar,' Bäckström said, getting up quickly. 'And make sure you stay sober, so you can drive.'

He took his usual discreet way out to avoid bumping into Holt. Maybe I should call the victim's father to tell him the happy news? he thought as he stepped into the street. But first things first.

While he was sitting quietly in his hotel room sipping the chilled beer that he so richly deserved his phone rang. It was Linda's father. Evidently that little sod Knutsson had already called him, trying to grab all the glory for himself.

'I heard you're heading back home,' Henning Wallin said.

'Things are a bit tricky right now,' Bäckström said, without going into detail. 'But I've personally put the man who killed your daughter behind bars, so you don't have to worry about him any more. We're going to make glue out of the bastard.'

'I'd still like to meet you,' Henning Wallin persisted. 'If only to thank you in person.'

'That might be a bit tricky, for purely practical reasons,' Bäckström said. 'I've already had a beer.'

'I can send my man to pick you up,' Wallin said.

'Well, perhaps,' Bäckström said, still slightly hesitant.

'There's something I want to give you,' Wallin persisted.

'Okay then,' Bäckström said.

An hour later Bäckström was sitting comfortably on the sofa in front of the open fireplace in Henning Wallin's enormous living room out at the manor house. Out of courtesy to his grieving host he had changed out of his Hawaiian shirt and shorts into something more suitable. In his hand he had a glass of the finest malt whisky, and life could certainly have been worse. Even Wallin seemed considerably brighter than he had done the last time they met. Amongst other things, he seemed to have regained control of his right hand while he was shaving.

'So who is he?' he asked, leaning forward and looking hard at Bäckström.

'Someone I've had my eye on for a while,' Bäckström said, holding up his right hand and rubbing his fingers with his thumb. 'You feel it in your fingertips. Nothing obvious, but because I've been in this game for a while now I thought he felt a bit odd right from the start, though I say it myself.' He took a large sip from his glass.

'So what's his name?' Wallin asked.

'I'm afraid I'm not supposed to tell you that,' Bäckström said. 'Not at this stage, anyway.'

'It won't go any further than this room,' Wallin said.

'Well, okay then,' Bäckström said, holding out his glass.

'He seems to have known most of the people in this town,' Bäckström concluded. 'Unfortunately he also seems to have been best friends with that damn idiot Bengt Olsson, so it was all a bit sensitive . . .'

'And he's also slept with my former wife,' Wallin interrupted, his face suddenly deep red. 'There's something I was going to give you,' he added, getting up.

A short while later he returned with one of the many photo albums in which he had documented large parties and other occasions since he had bought the manor.

'Here,' he said, passing Bäckström a photograph from the book. 'There are probably more if I look. That was taken on Midsummer Eve three years ago. Linda insisted on inviting her mother, and she brought her current boyfriend with her. Just one in what's bound to be a fairly long list, if you ask me.'

'I always suspected it was going to be something of this sort,' Bäckström said.

'You can keep it,' Wallin said. 'Just make sure you get that bitch. She and her so-called boyfriend have taken my only daughter from me.'

'I'm sure that can be arranged,' Bäckström said, putting the photograph in his inside pocket before his host had the chance to change his mind.

'I'll take that as a promise from the only person I can trust, evidently,' Henning Wallin said.

'Don't worry,' Bäckström said. 'Well, I'm afraid I should probably be thinking about getting going.'

'My man will drive you back,' Wallin said. 'One for the road?' he added in English, topping up Bäckström's glass.

While Bäckström was drinking expensive whisky, Rogersson had been handing over all his files and talking to Holt.

'I was thinking of heading back with Bäckström,' he said. 'Make sure the fat little sod gets home safely.'

'Well, I could certainly use you down here,' Holt said. 'For a few more days, at least.'

'The overtime ceiling,' Rogersson said, shrugging his shoulders apologetically.

'I was thinking that there's probably no need for overtime,' Holt said.

'Well, in that case I'm probably feeling a bit rough,' Rogersson said. 'I've been pushing things quite hard lately.'

'Drive carefully,' Holt said.

Very handy, having a man to drive you, Bäckström thought as he and Wallin were standing in the hall saying their goodbyes.

'This is for you,' Wallin said, handing over a box containing a bottle of the malt they had been drinking.

'I'm really not supposed to accept gifts,' Bäckström said as he took the bottle.

'I've no idea what you're talking about,' Wallin said with a wry smile. 'And I think you must have dropped this,' he added, pushing a thick brown envelope into the pocket of Bäckström's jacket.

Definitely no photos in that envelope, Bäckström thought as he sat in the back seat of Wallin's large black Range Rover, feeling inside the envelope in his pocket as discreetly as he could. I can feel it in my fingertips, he thought. Definitely not photographs.

'Can you stop at the police station on the way?' he asked. 'I need to pop in and pick up some things I forgot.'

No problem at all, according to the driver. From what his employer had said, he was at Bäckström's disposal for the rest of the evening. And probably longer than that if it proved necessary.

Bäckström left the envelope and box containing the whisky on the back seat while he went into the office one last time to say goodbye to all his incompetent fellow officers who were still sitting there, trying to work out which direction they were facing. He had his battered copy of the *Småland Post* in his pocket, and was thinking of giving it to Holt. If nothing else, then to thank her for her efforts the last time they had met, when she had almost managed to sabotage one of his old murder cases fifteen years ago. He had needed all his experience, all his guile and all his fingertip feeling before he had finally made any sense of it. Anna Holt was a prize example of a real cow, even though she was so damn scrawny, Bäckström thought.

But first he had dealt with that little poof Olsson. As a warm-up.

'See you, Olsson,' he said, with a broad grin. 'I don't know if you've heard, but I caught your perpetrator for you just before lunch.'

'Yes, I really must—'

'Bollocks to that, Olsson,' Bäckström interrupted in his most sympathetic way. 'Damn tragic story, seeing as it was one of your best mates, so you'll understand that I have to be a bit careful here. Considering your own involvement, I mean.'

'I don't quite understand what you mean,' Olsson replied, looking hurt but without any real anger. 'If you're referring to Månsson, I think I should point out that we only ever had any dealings on a purely professional level, because of our work, and—'

'Call it whatever you like, Olsson,' Bäckström interrupted, smiling even more cheerily now. 'But if I was creeping around in your shoes, I'd probably have a chat with my boss. To save him having to read about it in the papers, I mean.'

He headed towards Lewin. High time for the next poof in line, he thought. The man was sitting there as usual, trying to hide behind a mass of paper.

'Thanks for your help, Janne,' Bäckström said loudly. He knew Lewin hated it when people called him Janne.

'Don't mention it,' Lewin said.

'Okay. I won't bother. But at least you did what you could, and I'm grateful for that.'

Which left just the best, which of course he had saved till last. Anna Holt, who had had the nerve to take over his desk even though she'd only been in the building a couple of hours, timing her arrival carefully so that he had had time to make sure everything was already wrapped up.

'Having trouble letting go, Bäckström?' Holt said, giving him a neutral smile.

'Well, I've certainly had a fair bit of trouble,' Bäckström said. 'I thought I might give you a bit of advice before I go. There are still a couple of outstanding details.'

'And there was me thinking you weren't even on duty any more,' Holt said.

'Really?' Bäckström said amiably.

'For some reason I got it into my head that you'd already started celebrating,' she said with a shrug.

'Ah, bollocks. But if I were you I'd be pretty damn wary about our so-called colleague Olsson.' He handed her his copy of the *Småland Post*. 'If you take a look at the front page you'll see what I mean.'

'I'm sure it's not that bad,' Holt said, merely glancing at the paper. 'But thanks anyway. Your opinion is noted.'

'One more thing,' Bäckström said, having saved the very best till last. 'How are you getting on with establishing a link between the victim and the perpetrator?'

'Lewin and the others are working on it. I'm sure they'll find it in the end.'

'I suppose so. Only I've already done it.' He passed her the photograph he had been given by the victim's father. That made you sit up and take notice, you bitter little bitch, he thought with delight as he watched her stare at the picture in her hand.

'What's this?' she asked.

'The girl in the middle is our murder victim. To her left is her mum, and on the right is our perpetrator. The reason they all look so happy and relaxed is that the picture was taken at a midsummer party out at the victim's father's estate approximately three years ago. Apparently Månsson was getting his regular exercise on top of the victim's mother. Why he'd want to kill the daughter is still a bit hazy, but I'm sure her mother could help with the details if you bring her in.'

'You got this from Linda's father,' Holt said, more as a statement of fact than a question.

'I got it from an anonymous source. Well, if there's anything else you need any help with, just give me a call.'

'Thanks,' Holt said. 'I promise I'll be in touch if anything interesting comes up.'

As soon as Bäckström was safely concealed behind the door of his hotel room, he counted the contents of the brown envelope he had never received. The same result both times, so it was probably correct. The bastard must be rolling in money, he thought, once he had stopped counting.

Then he packed his belongings and put his three remaining chilled beers and the bottle of malt whisky in a little rucksack at the top, as a bit of simple sustenance on the journey for an exhausted police officer. When he handed his key in at reception he took the opportunity to pass on some thoughts about the service offered in the hotel.

'Try to sort out the people who do the laundry for you,' Bäckström said. 'And get the bar staff to speed up a bit. And fire the blind bastards working in the kitchen.'

The receptionist promised to have all this sorted before his next visit, and wished him and Rogersson a pleasant journey.

# 80

## *Stockholm, Monday 25 August*

On the way home Rogersson had sat behind the wheel taking care of the simple, manual tasks while Bäckström lay stretched out on the back seat, having drunk his beers while they were still chilled and then gone on to sample the fine malt whisky. Every so often he put his hand inside his jacket pocket and let his fingertips play over the contents of the brown envelope while he daydreamed about the newspaper headlines he could see in front of him. The man who solved the Linda murder, Bäckström thought with a deep sigh of contentment. Just before Nyköping he had switched to dreaming properly, enjoying the Warrior's Well-Deserved Rest until Rogersson pulled up outside the door of the building he lived in on Kungsholmen in Stockholm. As he had done so many times before after completing a mission, Detective Superintendent Bäckström of the National Crime Unit had returned home in triumph.

As a result, the following morning it was a good while before he realized that the bastard Lapp on the other side of the desk had entirely other ideas. No flowers, no cake, not even a basic cup of coffee, even though it was only eight o'clock in the morning and he had had to get up in the middle of the night to have time to shower, brush his teeth, buy throat sweets and prepare a suitable response to his supreme leader's heartfelt thanks for his efforts. What the hell's going on? What on earth is this police force coming to? he thought.

Johansson was entirely uninterested in the case. The murder of Linda Wallin and how Bäckström had managed to get all the pieces to slot into place, against all the odds, by using a tried and tested combination of routine, hard work, fingertip sensitivity and guile. Instead he had banged on about a load of mysterious expenses, cash withdrawals, porn films added to the bill for Rogersson's room, excessive overtime and all manner of irrelevancies which all the so-called experts around him had messed up, misunderstood and laid the blame for on him.

'You'll have to deal with this directly with the finance office,' Johansson concluded with a stormy expression. 'If you have a word with my secretary, she's arranged a time for you to see them straight away.'

'With all due respect, boss, I'm actually a policeman, not some number-cruncher,' Bäckström objected. 'And all those things that other people—'

'I was just getting to that,' Johansson interrupted, opening the next file on his vast desk. 'It's about the complaint that was filed against you last week.'

'Do you mean the complaint with no complainant, boss?' Bäckström said cunningly.

'I wasn't aware that there was more than one complaint,' Johansson said dryly. 'The case I'm thinking of concerns sexual harassment, and the complainant's name is Carin Ågren. She filed the complaint her-self. It was received on Thursday, and an interview was conducted with her that same day.'

'So how come I haven't seen it?' Bäckström said in an aggrieved tone.

'The simple explanation is probably that they haven't had time. There's no need to worry, Bäckström. I've spoken to them, and they've promised to get in touch with you some time today.'

'So what does she say?' Bäckström asked, glowering coldly at Johansson and the report he was holding in his hand.

'According to her, you're supposed to have waggled your little sausage at her. You can go through it in more detail with the internal investigation unit.'

What the hell's the man saying? Bäckström thought. What little sausage?

Apart from that, there wasn't much to add, according to Johansson. The finance department would talk to Bäckström about the expenses, their lawyer would talk to him about the legal aspects, the complaint against him would be dealt with in the usual manner, and Bäckström's immediate superior would take care of the practical details. As far as Bäckström himself was concerned, just one decision remained: whether or not he would prefer to be on holiday, on sick leave, or on leave of absence during the investigation into his conduct.

'Sick leave?' Bäckström said hotly. 'I'm not the slightest bit sick. I've never felt better. This sounds like something I should talk to the union about.'

'Good luck, Bäckström,' Johansson said.

# 81

Between Monday 25 August and Friday 12 September, Acting Detective Superintendent Anna Holt conducted a total of twelve interviews with Bengt Månsson, some long, some shorter. Deputy Chief District Prosecutor Katarina Wibom and Acting Detective Inspector Lisa Mattei took turns to sit in as the official witness. The first interview was the shortest, and Anna Holt was on her own with Bengt Månsson.

'My name is Anna Holt, and I'm a superintendent in the National Crime Unit,' Anna Holt said. And I'm forty-three years old, Holt thought. Single mother of Nicke, now twenty-one, fairly happy with life in general, even if a few things could be better, and the future will no doubt reveal whether there's any need to get into any of that.

'Then maybe you can explain to me how I come to be sitting here?' Månsson said.

'You're here because you're suspected of having murdered Linda Wallin.'

'Yes, that woman Wibom already told me that. That's what's so grotesque. I've got no idea what you're even talking about.'

'You don't remember?'

'Surely I ought to remember? If I'd murdered someone? Surely that's not the sort of thing that you can just forget?'

'I'm sure such things have happened,' Anna Holt said. 'Do you know what? I suggest we leave that bit for now.'

'So why else would we be sitting here?'

'Perhaps you could tell me how you got to know Linda,' Holt said. 'Start with the very first time you met her.'

'Sure,' Månsson said. 'If that will help. I'm happy to tell you how I got to know Linda. It's certainly not a secret.'

The interview was suspended after forty-three minutes, according to the protocol, and just half an hour later a curious Katarina Wibom just happened to be passing Holt's office.

'How's it going?' she asked.

'It's going exactly as I planned and completely according to my expectations,' Anna Holt said. 'He doesn't remember anything of the event itself, but considering what happened anything else would have been something of a surprise, to put it mildly. He's told me how he got to know Linda's mother and Linda. And he talks to me. He's even pleasant. Accommodating, considering the circumstances. Which is considerably more than one might usually expect. Perhaps you'd like to hear what he said?'

'If you've got time,' the prosecutor said.

The first time Månsson met Linda's mother was at a conference in May about three years ago. The subject of the meeting had been various projects with a social and cultural focus, managed by the local council and aimed primarily at young people from an immigrant background. Lotta Ericson was there in her capacity as a high-school teacher with a lot of non-Swedish pupils. He himself had been project manager on behalf of the cultural department of the council. They had evidently taken a liking to each other during the first coffee break. They went out for dinner together a couple of days later, and the evening had ended in Månsson's bed in his flat on Frövägen. Things had carried on in the usual way, and the first time he met Linda was at the midsummer celebrations out at her father's manor house outside Växjö about a month later.

'What happened after that?' the prosecutor asked eagerly.

'I don't actually know,' Anna Holt said. 'I suggested we might take a break there and continue tomorrow, and because he didn't object that's what we did.'

'That was smart.'

'I'm not so sure. I got the distinct impression that he prefers women who play hard to get. So I'm trying to appear slightly distant.'

'Is he hitting on you?'

'Well, he's certainly trying to make a case for himself. I dare say the future will reveal how our relationship develops.'

'Goodness, how exciting,' the prosecutor said, shivering in anticipation.

'Yes, it's always rather exciting,' Anna Holt agreed.

The day Anna Holt began her interviews with Månsson there was a press conference, one which turned out to be the most well attended in Växjö's history. At the centre of the platform sat the legal head of the preliminary investigation, Deputy Chief District Prosecutor Katarina Wibom, flanked by Detective Superintendent Bengt Olsson and the press officer of the Växjö Police. On the far left sat a reluctant Jan Lewin, who wasn't asked a single question but still ended up on television because of his expressive body language. He had been edited into a lengthy item on the main television news. Lewin had twisted his neck in a very odd way which suggested that he was extremely uncomfortable, and for some reason he had been used to illustrate Detective Superintendent Olsson's response to the only straight question Olsson had been asked.

First there had been a torrent of questions about their perpetrator, most of which the prosecutor had handled while the press officer did her best to maintain some sort of order among the journalists, and to pick questions as fairly as possible from the ones shouting loudest. Without going into any detail, the prosecutor anticipated that she would be able to charge him formally on grounds of reasonable suspicion the following day, or on Wednesday at the latest. They were still awaiting the results of certain forensic analysis, and beyond that she had no comment. And certainly not about the person who had been remanded in custody as a suspect.

After the routine follow-up questions about him and who he was, they had soon given up. There wasn't a journalist in the room who didn't already know his name, where he lived, and where he worked. His photograph, name and address had already been made public on the internet, and *Dagens Nyheter* and the four biggest evening papers would all be following suit the next day. The hunt was on for relatives, friends, acquaintances, neighbours and anyone and everyone who had anything at all to contribute, true or not, and no matter what.

So they had let go of the prosecutor and moved on to the police, going back to the beginning again. To start with, Bengt Olsson was asked to comment on the introductory phase of the investigation, but for some reason he had chosen to reply about something else. The question concerned the criticism that the Chancellor of Justice and the Justice Ombudsman had levelled at the decision to collect DNA samples from almost a thousand innocent Växjö citizens. According to Olsson, the recent reduction in the number of officers working on the case from approximately thirty to about a dozen illustrated that they had moved on to an entirely new phase of the investigation.

Was it the DNA samples that had led them to the perpetrator, the reporter from the main television news asked. No details there, either, but Detective Superintendent Olsson was at least able to say that DNA technology had played a decisive role in the final stages of their detective work. And it was here, for some reason, that Lewin and his skinny neck had made their appearance on television.

As soon as the press conference was over, Lewin returned to his office to try to forget what had just happened, and instead carry on with the hitherto fruitless search for the exclusive sweater that was the probable source of their blue fibres. Sandberg's idea of asking the retired pilot hadn't been entirely useless. Some years before he had actually bought just such a sweater in an airport terminal. A special offer, reduced price, and to top it all in Hong Kong of all places, where you could sometimes come across the most exclusive brands for next to nothing.

'If I remember rightly, it was reduced from nine hundred and ninety-nine dollars to ninety-nine,' he said.

Then he had been shown pictures of various sweaters, and had immediately picked out the pale blue one, V-necked and long-sleeved.

'It was just like that one. Brilliant quality. Cool in the summer, warm in the winter, my favourite sweater all year round,' the pilot said.

What had happened to it? One day he just couldn't find it, and that remained the case to this day.

Might he by any chance have given it to his younger daughter's boyfriend at the time? Definitely not, according to the pilot. The only thing he would have given him was a kick up the backside. And if he'd known then what he knew now, he'd have made a good job of it. As far as the rest of Bengt Månsson's dealings were concerned, he referred Sandberg to his daughter, although he would appreciate it if she could leave her alone for a couple of days, until she'd come to terms with what had happened. During the period they were talking about, he had tried to limit his own dealings with Månsson to the absolute minimum required by politeness. The great mystery, in the pilot's opinion, was that certain women, no matter how talented, beautiful or delightful they might be – like his younger daughter, for instance – still didn't seem to understand the first thing about certain men.

'Might Månsson have borrowed, or even ... well, stolen your sweater?' Sandberg had asked. She was already looking forward to meeting the pilot's daughter for a really long conversation about unfathomable men.

'I wouldn't be at all surprised,' the pilot snorted. 'I always thought he was capable of all manner of things.'

'How do you mean?' Anna Sandberg asked.

Well, not murder, exactly. When he and his family had been informed about the matter late the previous evening they had all been extremely shocked, and still were, but he had worked out what sort of person Månsson was fairly early on.

'Do you have anything in particular in mind?' Sandberg asked.

The first time he had realized what sort of man his daughter was living with was when she was seven months pregnant and he had bumped into Bengt Månsson with another woman in a restaurant in Växjö. Månsson had actually had the nerve to come over and introduce her as a colleague from work.

Utterly unreliable, notoriously unfaithful, told lies about absolutely everything, useless with money, made no distinction between what was his and what was other people's, was incapable of looking after his own child and showed no desire to do so, and seemed largely to use the pilot's daughter as an excuse to borrow her father's old Saab. The great mystery was still the fact that it had taken her two years to realize what he himself had started to suspect from day one.

'I'm sure he stole my sweater,' the pilot said. 'I've suspected him all along. And that was probably the least of it.'

However, the search of Bengt Månsson's flat that was currently under way had failed to find the sweater. If it had ever been there, then it wasn't there any more. Nor had they found much else that was of interest. Månsson's flat was surprisingly tidy. Considering the neighbours' unanimous testimony about the stream of young women that had passed through during the years he had been living there, they had left surprisingly few traces behind them. Most interesting were the things that weren't there. For instance, a month ago Månsson had thrown away the old hard drive in his computer and bought a new one.

'He must have got rid of the sweater already,' Enoksson said to Lewin. 'If you ask me, I reckon he ditched it when he was getting shot of the car.'

After the conversation Lewin made a note about the pay-as-you-go mobile phone that Månsson had called on the morning Linda was murdered. 'Who was the last call made to?' Lewin wrote on the to-do list on his computer.

# 82

'Tell me about the second time you met Linda.' It was the start of the second interview with Månsson. As Holt asked the question she leaned forward, resting her elbows on the table, with an interested smile, curious eyes . . .

'Well, the first time was at that midsummer party out at her dad's, when I was—'

'I know. You told me yesterday,' Holt interrupted. 'But what about the second time?'

The second time had been a complete coincidence, according to Månsson. It was a month later. They had bumped into each other in town. Not unusual if you lived in Växjö. They had started talking, and went to have a cup of coffee. Before they split up he had given Linda his phone number.

'What did you talk about?'

All the usual things you talk about when you bump into someone that way, if you'd only ever met once before. A nice, cheerful girl, funny too, with a slightly unusual sense of humour. A lot of under-statement, a lot of one-liners, which Månsson had liked because in his experience that was unusual in women. Still, it was really Linda's mother that he knew, and that had obviously affected the substance of their first conversation alone.

It was the opening Holt had been waiting for. 'So you talked about her as well?'

According to Månsson, it was Linda herself who had raised the subject, and he could still remember exactly what she had said. 'So tell me about my dear mother. Are you two still love's great dream, or what?'

At that point Månsson had chosen to be equally direct and honest. He had explained to Linda that there had never been any question of love's great dream. Naturally, he liked Linda's mother very much, she was a beautiful and talented woman. But definitely not love's great dream. Not on his side, nor on hers. Besides, they didn't have much in common. Lotta Ericson was considerably older than him, and lived a completely different, more middle-class life than his. Because they had both realized this without even having to talk about it, they had seen less and less of each other, and in recent weeks – since the midsummer party where he had met Linda – they had only spoken over the phone. The day before Lotta had gone abroad on holiday he had called to wish her a good trip. She had been fairly abrupt with him, so, if there had ever been anything between them, it was over now. That was certainly the impression he got from their last phone conversation.

'How did Linda react?' Anna Holt asked, still unswervingly curious.

In her usual straightforward, articulate way, which again was probably why he remembered it almost word for word. 'She said something like, "Lucky you. Mum's actually a right bitch." In English. She lived in the States when she was little, of course.'

On Tuesday two of Lewin's question marks resolved themselves in a way that a grizzled police officer such as himself could nowadays only dream of. First, a 27-year-old nurse from Kalmar called the Växjö Police to tell them things about the murder of Linda Wallin that she had only realized that morning when she read *Dagens Nyheter* at work and saw who Linda's killer was. After the usual preliminaries with the operator, Thorén took the call, and as soon as it was over he and Knutsson got in a car and headed off to Kalmar to question her.

On the morning of Friday 4 July, Bengt Månsson had called her on her mobile. He was in Kalmar, and was wondering if they could meet. All very spur of the moment, because he was going to the Gyllene Tider concert at Borgholm, over on Öland, that evening. After various practical details had been sorted out, including her having to cancel another date, Månsson had turned up at her home and within the space of ten minutes they were having sex. They had carried on with this pretty much all afternoon, and everything had been much the same as it had been on the three previous occasions she had met Månsson.

The first time was in the middle of May, when she and a group of friends from work had been to the theatre in Växjö, and Månsson had been their guide. After the performance, as soon as she managed to get away from her friends, they had gone to his flat and had sex, and to save time they had started the foreplay in the taxi on the way.

This time, though, things hadn't ended quite so well. That afternoon, during a pause in their sexual activities, Månsson had asked if he could borrow her washing machine to wash a sweater he was wearing. An expensive, pale blue sweater which he had managed to get rust stains on the previous day. He had been helping a neighbour repair his car, and had got his sweater dirty when he was lying under the engine. He had evidently also scratched his stomach as well, but when she pointed it out he had shrugged it off. Just a scratch.

She had explained to him that the sweater needed to be hand-washed, in as cold water as possible. Especially if he had managed to get blood on it. At any rate, the washing machine was out of the question, as any girl could have told him, but far too few men, unfortunately. Then she had washed it by hand for him and spread it out to dry while she got back to what she had been doing with its owner. That evening they had gone to the concert. The sweater was still damp, but that was no problem seeing as Månsson had a sports bag with him containing some clean clothes. Besides, that evening it had been about twenty degrees outside.

After the concert she had bumped into some old friends from Västervik, and while she was standing chatting to them Månsson had suddenly disappeared. Admittedly, there had been a lot of people milling about, but it was like he'd gone up in smoke. She had spent half an hour looking for him until she met a friend she worked with, someone who had actually been with her when she first met Månsson at the theatre in Växjö. Her friend told her she had seen Månsson quarter of an hour earlier, leaving the park with a young woman.

'So I dare say you weren't too happy?' Detective Inspector Thorén said in his most sympathetic voice.

Not too happy didn't even come close, but that wasn't actually what annoyed her most. Månsson wasn't exactly husband material, but he suited her purposes while she was waiting for Mr Right to turn up in her life. Since he presumably had the same purposes in mind, neither of them had anything to complain about on that score. What had made her most annoyed, 'completely fucking livid, actually', was the fact that he had got her to wash his sweater.

So the first thing she had done when she got home that night was grab his sweater, stuff it into the bag he had left behind, and throw the whole thing in the bin. She had spent the next few days hoping that he'd get in touch so she could tell him, but he never did. And she certainly wasn't going to call him.

'So you threw it all in the bin?' Thorén asked.

The sweater, a pair of worn underpants, maybe something else that she'd forgotten, as well as the bag they were in. They had all gone in the bin, but the bins of the building she lived in were emptied once a week and she didn't hold out much hope of anyone's finding them now.

'I'm sure it will be enough that we've spoken to you about it,' Thorén assured her, preferring to avoid the word testimony wherever possible. 'When you were with him that time, you mentioned that you noticed he'd scratched his stomach. You don't happen to remember what it looked like?'

Nothing special, according to the witness. Just an ordinary scratch. Ten centimetres or so above his navel.

How deep? Inflamed? Infected? How long? How old?

Not very deep, looked okay, ten or fifteen centimetres long, maybe a day old, just as he had said. It looked like he'd scratched himself on something sharp, and perhaps the easiest thing would be for Thorén to pull his shirt up so she could show him what she meant. Considering her profession, it would hardly be that unusual, she said.

'Thanks for the offer,' Thorén said with a smile. 'How about I draw a sketch on a piece of paper while you tell me what to draw?'

'That's it,' the witness said five minutes later, nodding at the sketch Thorén had just drawn. 'You never thought of becoming an artist instead of a policeman?'

'Actually no.' Thorén smiled. 'But I've always liked drawing.' A horizontal scratch about ten centimetres in length, and about ten centimetres above his navel, then some smaller scratches up towards his chest. And that was what it had looked like?

No doubt at all, according to the witness. And, as long as it didn't go any further than the three of them in the room, the reason she was so sure was that she had kissed it several times. She had suggested a bit of antiseptic, and then kissing it better. Månsson had declined the antiseptic, but she had kissed it better anyway.

'What a delightful young woman,' Thorén sighed happily once they were sitting in the car on their way back to Växjö.

'So why didn't you show her your washboard stomach?' Knutsson said, suddenly sounding rather cross.

'I was worried you might get embarrassed.'

'Little Månsson seems to have been pretty busy,' Knutsson said, to change the subject.

'Lucky for him he wasn't alive in Zorn's day,' Thorén said. Even though he was a police officer, he still had a genuine interest in art.

'Well, despite the minor disaster with the rubbish bin, I think we can be fairly pleased regardless,' Lewin declared a couple of hours later once he had heard what their witness had said. 'What did you mean about Zorn?'

Månsson's interest in women, Thorén explained. It was starting to look as though he'd slept with every girl in Småland. Or almost, anyway. Just like the artist Anders Zorn, who according to the stories managed to father fifty-five acknowledged but illegitimate children during the hours he didn't devote to painting.

'Fifty-five of them, in just two parishes, Orsa and Gagnef. So Månsson's lucky most girls are on the pill these days. Looks like he's only slipped up once.'

# 83

'What about the third time you met?' Holt said. Just as curious, still the same friendly interest as when she had started the interview more than an hour before. 'Tell me, how did that come about?'

According to Månsson, Linda had called him on the number he had given her. She had turned eighteen the day before, and her father had arranged a big party for her and all her friends out at his manor house. And now she was thinking of carrying on the party alone with Bengt Månsson.

'So what did you think?' Holt asked.

'To be honest, I was genuinely very surprised,' Månsson said. 'It had never even crossed my mind to call her, so the fact that she was calling me came as something of a shock.'

'What did she say?'

'That was one of the strangest things. She asked if she could take me to dinner. To celebrate the fact that she was now an adult.'

'How did you take that?'

'Well, I actually suggested that we could split the bill,' Månsson said.

'And what did she say?'

'That I didn't have to think about that at all, seeing as it wasn't her mother I would be going out with. That was what she was like. Very straightforward.'

'You were surprised?' Holt said.

'Well, it was a bit blunt, really,' Månsson said. 'Although of course I knew about her dad and all the money. Lotta had told me. So I knew about that already. And I'd seen where they lived, so I dare say I would have worked it out for myself.'

Then they had met. Had dinner at a restaurant in Växjö, chatting and joking.

'So who paid in the end?' Holt asked, maintaining the interested expression, though it was taking more and more effort on her part.

'Well, she did, of course,' Månsson said, still seeming surprised. 'I did actually offer to split it, but she had already made up her mind. It was like that was her thing, that she was a grown woman now and was perfectly entitled to invite someone like me to a meal if she felt like it. Besides, she said she thought she probably had more money than me, which of course was true, so I could only agree. And we're talking about a girl who'd just turned eighteen.'

'And then you went back to yours and spent some time together?' Holt said, not about to miss an open goal.

'Yes,' Månsson said. 'We went back to mine and made love, actually.'

'So tell me about the first time you were together,' Holt said.

Making love was exactly what they had done. Not just sex. They had made love to each other. Then Månsson had offered some wine, and they talked and slept together and had breakfast the next day. That was exactly how it had been, and the very thought that he was sitting here now, in a place like this, having to talk about it in this way, made him feel terrible. He had ended up in an inexplicable situation. He had never hurt Linda, and would never have dreamed of doing so.

'Do you know what?' Anna Holt said, looking at the time. 'I suggest we stop here and carry on tomorrow.'

'So he admits that he had sex with her?' the prosecutor said over lunch.

'He's not stupid,' Holt said.

'What about the rest? The memory loss covering Friday the fourth? He didn't try to talk about that?'

'He made a half-hearted attempt towards the end, but luckily I managed to stop him,' Holt said.

'You're going to wait with that?'

'I'm thinking of leaving it until I've got him to admit he was in the flat when it happened,' Holt said. 'When I know all about what else he got up to on the day he strangled her.'

'That's when it'll be time?'

'That's when it'll be time, and I was thinking you could sit in on that.'

'Have you any idea how this is going to end, then?'

'Sure,' Holt said. 'I know exactly how it's going to end.'

'Anything you feel like sharing?'

'I can write it down for you, if you promise not to read it before I'm finished with him.'

'It's probably best that you don't. I'd never manage that. I'm the sort who sneaks a look at the things people leave on their desks the minute they go out of the room.'

'Me too,' Anna Holt said. 'I reckon all proper police officers do. Nice to meet a prosecutor who does the same thing at last.'

# 84

On Wednesday morning Bengt Månsson was formally charged by the Växjö District Court on the suspicion of murdering Linda Wallin. The definitive report that it was his DNA that had been found at the crime scene had arrived from the National Forensics Lab the previous day. Despite this, Månsson vehemently denied through his lawyer that he had murdered her. He had no comment except that he was innocent and that the entire situation was completely incomprehensible to him. Anna Holt had consciously chosen to stay away from the legal proceedings. For her, it was all about not jeopardizing the trust that she was trying to establish. Månsson shouldn't have to see her in an uncomfortable setting. On the contrary, he should be free to think that she was staying away because she didn't quite believe what the others were saying about him. It was no more complicated than that.

'He asked about you, actually,' the prosecutor said afterwards.

'Good,' Holt said. 'I was hoping he might.'

After lunch she went up and collected him herself, and asked if he would mind a young female colleague of hers sitting in on the interview. 'But if you'd rather not, we can leave it,' she said quickly when she saw the flash of doubt in his eyes.

'No, it's fine,' Månsson said, shaking his head. 'If it's okay with you, it's okay with me.'

'Okay, that's that, then,' Holt said.

The session lasted three hours, and Lisa Mattei only said five sentences in all that time. Before the interview started Månsson had suddenly directed a question at her. 'This probably sounds really weird, but are you really a police officer?'

'Yes.' Lisa Mattei smiled even more warmly than Holt. 'But you're not the first person to ask.'

'You really don't look like a police officer, if you know what I mean.'

'I know. I think it's because I just sit and read loads of files all day. But sometimes I get to sit and listen as well.'

'Tell me about your relationship with Linda,' Anna Holt began. Linda Wallin had just turned eighteen, Bengt Månsson was thirty-two, but Holt had no intention of breathing a word about the age gap. Not yet. Next week, maybe, if things went the way she hoped.

He didn't really think you could call it a relationship. There were too many differences between them. They had just spent time together. Maybe twenty times in three years. More often at the start, less frequently later on. The last time he saw her was early in the spring when she called him to say she'd broken up with her boyfriend. But, sure, he had liked Linda. A lot, actually, and if he was completely honest, then he'd probably been a bit in love with her for a while. At least at the start, but what with one thing and another he'd never told her.

'I get the distinct impression that Linda must have been very fond of you as well,' Holt said.

That was doubtless the case, Månsson agreed, and it only made things more problematic given the circumstances. On one occasion she had even told him that she had written about him in her journal. He stopped speaking suddenly, and Holt saw the same flash in his eyes as when she had asked if Lisa Mattei could sit in on the interview.

'I know. I know how much she liked you, but there's something else I was wondering about,' Holt said, wanting to get away from the journal as quickly as possible. 'I've been a bit reluctant to mention it before, but I suppose the worst that can happen is that you object and we talk about something else instead.'

'Oh?' Månsson said. Hesitant and watchful, all of a sudden.

'Well, of course it isn't a secret exactly, but I get the impression that you're fairly experienced when it comes to women.' Holt shrugged her shoulders. 'Very experienced, even,' she said with a smile.

Månsson understood what Holt meant, but he didn't like the expression. Experienced was a hard, cynical word. To his ear, it was almost synonymous with worn out. Månsson liked women. He had always found it easy to talk to women, socialize with women, just be with women. In fact he had never had any close male friends, and he had never really missed them. But, yes. He had been with a number of women over the years, if that was what Holt was wondering. He liked women, he felt good when he was with women. Women made him happy, cheered him up and made him feel secure, basically, and that was pretty much all there was to it.

'I don't think it sounds the slightest bit odd,' Anna Holt agreed. 'I understand exactly what you mean, but I suppose I'm just wondering about Linda.'

'You mean that she couldn't have been particularly experienced at sex?' Månsson said.

'Exactly. It's the sex I'm after. I mean, when you had sex together, you and Linda.'

Entirely normal sex, according to Månsson, and that wasn't the slightest problem with someone like Linda, considering his feelings for her and hers for him.

'Normal, vanilla sex,' Holt summarized.

'When we were together, it was like when you're with someone you like a lot, someone you respect,' Månsson said. 'But sure, normal vanilla sex if you prefer to put it like that.'

What about all the others, Holt wondered. Everyone he'd been with, who'd been far more experienced than Linda Wallin – had that still just been normal vanilla sex?

Not always, according to Månsson, but as long as it was a matter of voluntary, mutually agreed behaviour between responsible adults, surely there was nothing wrong with that? Not if it was something they both wanted and as long as nobody got hurt. 'Take a look at any sexual advice column in any ordinary newspaper, and you'll see what I mean,' he said.

'I understand exactly,' Holt said. 'Besides, that isn't the reason why you're sitting here talking to me.'

'How do you mean?'

'What you just said, about mutually agreed behaviour between responsible adults. I agree with you entirely. What business is that of mine? After all, that's your private life. Look, why don't we stop now and carry on tomorrow? We've actually been sitting here more than three hours.'

'Thanks for letting me sit in,' Lisa Mattei said, smiling at Bengt Månsson. 'It was actually really interesting. I mean, what you said about being experienced and being worn out. I thought that was pretty well put, actually.'

'Well, thank you,' Månsson said.

'Well? What did you think about my little Bengt Axel, then?' Holt asked as soon as she and Mattei were alone.

'Not my type,' Lisa Mattei said. 'Mind you, I'm probably not his type either,' she added with a shrug of the shoulders.

'So who is his type?'

'Everyone, if we're to believe him.'

'But in your opinion?'

'No one apart from himself,' Lisa Mattei said, shaking her head. 'If you were to rewrite the interview and replace women with food, for instance, you'd see what I mean. A binge eater. That's what he is.'

'Anything else?'

'The journal,' Mattei said. 'The one that everyone seems to think Linda's dad is hiding.'

'So what do we do about that, assuming it's true?'

'Well, obviously Linda's dad has hidden it. We're never going to get hold of it, but Månsson evidently suspects that you've already read it – it was clever how you did that, by the way – so it might be just as well that we don't. His lawyer would want to look at it.'

'So what's he so worried about, then?'

'Anna,' Mattei said with a sigh. 'You know perfectly well what he's worried about.'

'That Linda's journal isn't just about vanilla sex,' Holt said.

'There, you see?' Mattei said. 'And you're talking to someone who's hardly even had vanilla sex. What do you need me for, really?'

# 85

By now, everyone knew who Linda's murderer was. And far too many people seemed to know him personally. The detectives were working a triple shift at full strength, and a torrent of tip-offs about Månsson was overwhelming the desks of the investigating team.

First Månsson's supplier got in touch with his confessor in the drugs squad of the district crime unit. He certainly wasn't the sort to shop his ordinary customers, but Månsson wasn't an ordinary customer any more. He had never been a particularly good customer either, come to that. Used to buy a couple of times a year, mostly cannabis. Now, seeing as he himself had just landed a two and a half year sentence, maybe he was due a favour in return?

More or less simultaneously Knutsson worked out how Månsson had learned to steal cars. A former classmate from Lund called to say that he and Månsson had spent several summers in a row working in a young offenders' institution in Skåne. Månsson had been practically minded and interested in mechanics, even though he almost made a virtue of the fact that his appearance suggested the opposite. But what he was undoubtedly best at was women. But of course they knew that already, didn't they?

Almost everyone who called in was a young woman. More than the detectives could have possibly wished for called to tell them about their experiences with Månsson. And even more to say that they had friends who had told them about him. One of the informants was particularly interesting. She had a friend who was now thanking her stars that she was still alive. According to what she was supposed to have told the friend who made the call, she had been with Månsson on the evening of Thursday 3 July. She had realized that something wasn't right and had left.

Two hours later she was interviewed by Knutsson and Sandberg, and, inevitably, the story she told them was rather different. But in all significant respects, and from the police's point of view, it was still extremely interesting. And it also fitted other information they had managed to gather.

At about ten o'clock on the Thursday evening she had gone round to see Månsson in his flat on Frövägen, out in Öster. She had been there on several occasions over the summer, and it had started the way it always did. On the sofa in Månsson's living room. But then she had suddenly put a stop to it.

'I don't actually know why,' she said, looking at Anna Sandberg. 'All of a sudden I just didn't want to any more.'

So what had he done then, Sandberg wondered.

First he had carried on as usual, but when she started to resist he had stopped.

Had he turned violent? Did he use force against her?

'No,' the witness said. 'He just got really angry. Like a little kid.'

And because the witness was just as angry herself, she had pulled her top back down, done up her trousers, grabbed her handbag and walked out.

'Thank God,' the witness said. 'If I'd stayed, he'd have strangled me too.'

In fact it was probably far worse than that, Anna Sandberg thought. If you'd done exactly what you usually did, then Linda Wallin would probably still be alive today. Then she had asked the obvious questions about Månsson's sexual preferences, and the witness had answered just like all the other women they had already spoken to.

A highly prized trophy among all the girls. Liked to take the initiative during sex. Handsome, strong, fit, a good fuck, a stallion who had mastered the various disciplines. Hard-handed if necessary and if she wanted it, open to most suggestions and ideas. But not violent, not out to hurt anyone, and certainly not trying to satisfy any sadistic tendencies of his own.

'That's what's so strange,' the witness said. 'I never realized he was a sadist. He was never like that with me.'

Because you always did what he wanted, so he never got frustrated enough when he was with you, Sandberg thought.

You were probably just the wrong type, Knutsson thought.

# 86

The fact that Lisa Mattei sat in on Anna Holt's fourth interview with Månsson was no coincidence. Holt was thinking of starting to twist the arm of their perpetrator, and needed Mattei there to ease the pain and make it less obvious to him. Mattei's friendly manner, her gentle appearance, her innocent exterior, made her entirely uninteresting to Månsson as a woman, and absolutely perfect for Holt.

'Yesterday you mentioned that Linda had written about the two of you in her journal.'

'Yes?' Månsson said with a wary look in his eyes.

'There's an exception to every rule,' Holt said. 'I know you and Linda usually had vanilla sex with each other, but what about the times when you didn't? The times when you played sex games, when you experimented with each other? I want you to tell me about that, and I don't think you'll find it very difficult.'

'No,' Månsson said. 'Why should it be? It was really nothing special. Just the sort of thing that perfectly normal people have done at least once when they're having sex.'

But it evidently wasn't entirely straightforward, since it took almost two hours for Anna Holt to get him to admit that on several occasions he had tied Linda's hands while he had sex with her. And it had been a long journey for his and Linda's sexual relationship as well, if he was to be believed.

Linda wasn't particularly experienced. Before she slept with Bengt Månsson the first time she had had four sexual partners. The very first time had been when she was fourteen years old, and she hadn't even been especially drunk. Just wanted to get it over and done with. All her previous partners had been the same age as her. She had never had an orgasm with any of them. But she did when she masturbated, the first time when she was sixteen, and carefully followed the instructions of the country's most famous sex therapist in a column in the Sunday supplement of the big evening paper. All of this she had told Bengt Månsson. The first proper lover in her life.

With Månsson she had always had an orgasm. Usually more than one each time they had sex. Only the second time they were together she had an orgasm from ordinary intercourse. Which was usually the hardest thing for most women, especially at the start, and that was when he made his discovery.

'I realized that she liked it when I held her tight when she was about to come,' Månsson said.

The first few times that was as far as things went. Then Linda herself had come up with the idea, without actually saying anything about it. She had been lying on her back on his bed. They had already had sex once. He was caressing and stroking her. Suddenly she had taken the cord of his dressing-gown and handed it to him, then held both her hands out in front of her, palms together. Very carefully he had tied them together, then tied her hands above her head to the top of the bed. In complete silence, in complete understanding, and with complete trust from Linda. And suddenly her lover, Bengt Månsson, had two hands free at the crucial moment.

'Obviously it makes a difference. If you're going to have an orgasm, then it's all about stimulation, physical and mental.'

Tied her up? Certainly. Hit her? Never. Tortured her without hitting her? Never. Not even harsh language, according to Månsson. Linda didn't like it, and she would lose interest. The path she enjoyed travelling was silent, enclosed, secret intimacy between just the two of them.

'Uncomplicated sex, basically,' Månsson said. 'If you do something you like, but don't dare to talk about it, then it wasn't really you who did it.'

'What do you think, then, Lisa?' Holt asked after the interview.

'Sigh,' Mattei said. 'Why ask someone who's practically a virgin about this sort of thing? Why do you think so many perfectly normal women run after dominant men? And almost always end up in bed with someone like Månsson. Anyway, Månsson's no man. He's probably not even human.'

'So what is he, then?' Holt asked.

'Some sort of sexual instrumentalist, if you ask me. I mean . . . how cool is it to hear that physical and mental stimulation are both important when you're having sex? How inexperienced do you have to be to realize that that's exactly what he's doing? And how turned on would you be when you realized that was what he was doing?'

'Doesn't sound much like fun,' Holt agreed.

'The interesting thing, if you ask me, and the only reason we're sitting in there listening to him at all, is what happens inside his head when he finds himself in a situation that he almost never ends up in, because almost all the girls have done exactly what he wanted the whole time.'

'And what situation is that?'

'When he's already frustrated right from the start. When he has just one thought in his head. Come and go, as so many blokes so romantically describe it. When the person he's with sees through him and refuses to join in. And when he realizes that she's seen through him. When he ends up feeling ridiculous.'

'And in that situation Bengt Månsson isn't much fun to be around any more.'

'And that's the situation where he strangles Linda Wallin, and he'll never admit that.'

'Not even to himself?'

'Not even to you or me,' Mattei said.

'Have you got any tips?' Holt asked.

'Rip him to shreds,' Mattei said with a gentle smile. 'Not because it'll make him confess, but because I'd like to see you do it. I don't think I've ever come across such a self-obsessed, long-winded and cretinous murderer before.'

# 87

Hard graft, conscientiousness and ingenuity were not only Lewin's defining characteristics, but also those of his closest colleagues. As a result, they had finished their preliminary profile of Bengt Månsson less than five days after he had been caught.

Thirty-five years old. Born in the General Hospital in Malmö on a fine Sunday morning in May, when summer had just arrived in Skåne for the first time that year. The first child of a single mother, thirty years old, father unknown. It was possible that he might have been able to explain the vague ethnic assumptions about the unknown perpetrator's DNA which had caused such problems for them, and were still lurking at the back of Lewin's mind.

There didn't seem to be much wrong with the mother. She came from a farming family near Ängelholm, and the relatives they had spoken to described her as beautiful and cheerful, a solid character, and enterprising with it. When she turned twenty she had moved to Malmö, and just ten years later she was a successful businesswoman with her own hair and beauty salon in the centre of town, in a prime location and with a growing number of employees. According to her older sister, she had met the unknown father on holiday to the Canary Islands, but Bengt Månsson's aunt was unable to provide any more precise details.

But she had shown a collection of photographs to the officers in Malmö who had questioned her. Of Bengt Månsson, from when he was a small and utterly enchanting little lad to when he graduated from high school some nineteen years later, by which time he had turned into an extremely handsome young man. More or less the way film stars used to look, only without the moustache. The aunt found everything that was happening quite incomprehensible, and her only consolation was that she was convinced the police would realize they had made a terrible mistake.

When Bengt was five years old his mum had met a new man. Fifteen years older than her. A relatively successful businessman and, oddly enough, still single. One year later the mother was married, and Bengt gained a half-brother, while his new dad had formally adopted him. The family had moved to a smart, expensive villa in Bellevue on the outskirts of Malmö. His mum had sold the salon for a healthy profit and switched to being a housewife, working part time from home as a representative for a German company selling hair-care products and cosmetics.

They seemed like decent, hard-working people. Respectably middle class. No negative comments from neighbours, schools, social services or the police. Neither against Bengt nor about anyone else in the family. Bengt had done well in primary school, and was just above average when he left high school. He had been physically fit, although not particularly interested in sport, and had been popular among his male classmates without having any close friends. And all the girls at school had started asking if they could go out with him back in primary school.

He hadn't had to do military service, being let off without having to take recourse to any bizarre medical excuses. After a year's sabbatical, which he seemed to have spent partying with his contemporaries, whilst earning a small monthly wage doing odd jobs in his dad's office, he had moved to Lund and started university. Four years later he graduated with a fairly soft degree in a combination of subjects. Film and theatre studies, philosophy, literature. He had been active within the university drama society and the student union, and various other of the less demanding clubs and societies on offer to students in Lund. And all the female students in his vicinity seemed to have fallen in love with him at first glance.

In the autumn of the year he graduated his mother died from cancer. In contrast to most cancer sufferers, she died within a month of receiving the diagnosis. The day before Christmas Eve that same year his adoptive father dropped dead of a massive heart attack somewhere between the twelfth and thirteenth holes on the still snow-free grass of Ljunghusen golf course.

He and his half-brother sold the villa and other assets. They buried their father, paid off any debts and divided what was left over. This was actually substantially less than they had evidently been expecting, and possibly a contributing factor to the reasons why the two half-brothers appeared to have had little contact with each other afterwards. As soon as the half-brother graduated as an economist he moved to Germany. For the past five years he had been working as the head of finance for a subsidiary of a Swedish forestry company. Married to a German woman, and living outside Stuttgart. He had refused to talk to the police when they called to ask him about his brother Bengt. Everyone in Bengt Månsson's family had either died or abandoned him.

At the age of twenty-five he got a job as administrator and project assistant at the cultural division of Malmö Council. That summer he had met the pilot's daughter, who was spending the summer working in customer relations at Sturup Airport. He applied for a new job as project manager within the cultural division of Växjö Council, and as soon as he got it he moved in with his girlfriend in a flat that his prospective father-in-law had arranged for them. About a year later their daughter had been born. And a year after that they had separated. He had got hold of a new flat on Frövägen, where he still lived.

Single, with access rights to a seven-year-old daughter whom he had seen less and less often over the years. A monthly income before tax of 25,000 kronor. A driving licence, but no car. No credit defaults or unpaid taxes. No notes in social service or police records. Not so much as a parking ticket, in fact. And all the young women who came near him seemed to fall in love with him.

At the age of thirty-five years and three months, he had raped and strangled Linda Wallin at home in her mother's flat in the centre of Växjö. And had thereby given the police a reason to summarize his known life up to his arrest and to compose the report known in police language and among officers of Jan Lewin's generation as the perpetrator's little biography.

*

Anna Sandberg had interviewed the pilot's daughter, who testified to Bengt Månsson's astonishing sexual appetite. But only at the start, when they used to spend pretty much every waking minute having sex. After they moved in together and she got pregnant, he had hardly touched her. Instead he had slept with everyone else, and as soon as she realized this she had ended the relationship.

In answer to a direct question: no, he had never been violent towards her. Apart from the frequency, they had indulged in ordinary, normal sex. Bengt Månsson was the 'most handsome man and the most charming slacker' that she'd met in her whole life, and she simply couldn't comprehend what he had done eight weeks ago. But she was primarily concerned about their seven-year-old daughter. They had already decided not to let her start school yet, and only the previous day she and her husband had made up their minds to move away from Växjö.

The evening papers had already offered her money and celebrity if she was willing to come forward and talk about her life with the murderer, and what it was like to be the mother of his only child, a little girl of seven. The bestial rapist and murderer who had a little daughter. What had finally persuaded her to leave Växjö, however, wasn't the male headline-hunters of the big evening papers, but the female editor of *Dagens Nyheter*'s family section. She had wanted to run a large, factual and sensitive article about that very subject. How she, her new husband and her daughter had become the victims of the media's news frenzy. About the daughter's postponed schooling, how it had influenced her emotionally when she had found out that her 'real daddy' was a murderer, their rumoured plans to move, maybe even change their names and apply for a protected identity. That was when she and her husband had made up their minds to go. They had turned the offer of an interview down flat.

On Friday Anna Sandberg and a female colleague from the Växjö Police went to question Linda's mother out at her summer house by Lake Åsnen.

It was a largely futile interview. Linda's mother was in crisis. The shock she had experienced when she found out that Linda had been murdered the previous month had developed into post-traumatic stress disorder just in time for the next shock, when the police had arrested her daughter's murderer and she had realized her own role in events. Now she was on open-ended sick leave, taking strong tranquillizers, seeing her psychiatrist pretty much every day, and under the constant supervision of her best friend.

She never wanted to set foot in the flat in Växjö again, but hadn't felt up to considering what on earth she was going to do with it. It wouldn't be particularly easy to sell, after all. It was now notorious as the 'murder flat' to anyone who read the papers, listened to the radio or watched television. The neighbours in the area where she was still registered were divided into two camps: those who tried to sneak a glance through the windows when they went past, and those who took detours to avoid the building altogether. She had already received one anonymous letter from a neighbour who was worried about the value of her own flat, and blaming her for it. But this was the very least of her worries.

It was more than three years since she had last spoken to Bengt Månsson. They hadn't had any contact since then. Basically, she didn't want to have any contact with him, and he hadn't made any attempt to contact her. She had stopped seeing him as soon as she realized that they didn't have much in common, and that he wasn't particularly interested in her. Her version of the story was the same as his. How they had met, how long they had seen each other, where they had rendezvoused. Anna Sandberg hadn't asked any intimate questions about their sexual relationship. She hadn't even considered doing so.

Linda herself had told her mother that she was also seeing Bengt Månsson. A year or so later, during the difficult period in their lives when Linda had moved back to 'the father she idolized', Linda had thrown it at her during one of their recurring arguments. Not that they had slept together, which her mum had suspected anyway, but just that she had met him. The following day Linda had phoned to apologize. According to Linda, it was the sort of thing you said when you were angry, and not meant seriously. Lotta had tried to put it out of her mind. Now she bitterly regretted not going straight round and beating him to death.

'It's my fault it happened,' she said, staring blankly ahead of her, nodding to underline what she had just said.

Anna Sandberg leaned over the table. Took a firm grip on her arms to get her attention.

'Listen to me, Lotta,' she said. 'Are you listening?'

'Yes.'

'Good,' Sandberg said, still looking into her eyes. 'What you just said is as stupid as if you had said it was Linda's fault that he murdered her. Do you hear what I'm saying?'

'Yes, I hear you. I hear you,' she repeated as Anna tightened her grasp.

'It was Bengt Månsson who murdered Linda. No one else, just him. It's his fault. And only his. No one else's. You and Linda are his victims.'

'I hear you,' Lotta Ericson repeated.

'Good,' Sandberg said. 'Make sure you understand it as well. Because it's true. That's what happened, and that's why it happened.'

After that Anna Sandberg and her colleague drove back to the police station in Växjö. Neither of them was feeling great. But compared to the woman they left behind, their lives were a dream.

'I could kill that bastard,' Sandberg said as she drove down into the garage.

'Let me know if you need any help,' her colleague said.

Knutsson and Thorén had continued the fruitless hunt for the journal and other similar details about the victim. They started by talking to her friends again, and got a bit of new information that way. Finally they went to see her father out in his manor house, and they managed pretty much as well as their colleagues had when they had spoken to him before on the same subject.

Henning Wallin had no knowledge of any journal. Naturally he had given the matter some thought – how could he avoid it when the police kept going on about it all the time – so the only thing he could offer were his own thoughts on the subject.

'If you wouldn't mind,' Knutsson said.

In Henning Wallin's opinion, a person's journal was the most private thing in that person's life. This was particularly true of young people, and even more so of young women. Like his daughter, for instance. If there had been a journal in her life, it would have been the place where she conducted the dialogue with herself that every sentient human being conducted with themselves about their own life, their feelings, their conscience. That would be where she would have confided her most private thoughts, and the only reason she would have done that was if she knew it would remain her private business.

'Can you understand that?' he asked, looking in turn at Knutsson and Thorén.

'I understand,' Knutsson said.

'Yes,' Thorén said.

'Good,' Wallin said. 'Well, if you'll excuse me, gentlemen.'

'I wonder if he's got rid of it, or just hidden it?' Thorén said in the car on their way back to the police station on Oxtorget.

'Either way, he's read it,' Knutsson said.

'To make sure there was nothing that identified the perpetrator,' Thorén said.

'And when he didn't find anything, he probably got rid of it. Or maybe burned it,' Knutsson said.

'I reckon he would have burned it,' Thorén said. 'He's not the sort to just throw something away. But I'm still inclined to think he's just hidden it somewhere safe.'

'Why do you think that?' Knutsson said.

'Because he's not the sort to get rid of things,' Thorén said. 'Although . . .'

'. . . we can't be sure,' Knutsson concluded.

# 88

Anna Holt's fifth interview with Bengt Månsson lasted almost the whole day. The witness was Lisa Mattei, and as before she had hardly opened her mouth. She just sat there listening with her gentle smile and kind eyes. As usual, Holt had begun with a different subject from the one Månsson was expecting. The truth was, there was no longer any great urgency regarding what they had discussed the day before. On the contrary, it was an excellent idea to let him have the whole weekend, all alone, to think about his contact with Linda Wallin.

'Tell me about yourself, Bengt,' she began, leaning forward on her elbows, smiling to show how interested she was.

'About myself?' Månsson said in surprise. 'What's that got to do with anything?'

'What were things like when you were growing up?'

'How do you mean?'

'Start at the beginning,' Holt suggested. 'Tell me about your very first memories.'

According to Bengt Månsson, his earliest childhood memories were from when he was seven, once he'd started school. Before that he didn't remember much. His mother and her family had often told him things he was supposed to have said and done when he was younger, but his own head was a blank.

His memories from the time he started school were nothing remarkable. Ordinary memories. Some good, and almost all of those uninteresting. Some less good, which he would rather not talk about.

Besides, he didn't understand the question. What did his childhood memories have to do with his current situation?

Nor did he want to talk about his parents. They had been dead for years now, and he had no intention of going into what had happened between him and them before that. But there was one thing that was worth pointing out. He only acknowledged one parent, his mother. He had no idea who his real father was, and he had realized early in life that there was no point asking his mother about that. He had had an adoptive father, but he didn't want to talk about him, and was trying hard to wipe him from his memory.

'You don't visit their graves?' Holt asked.

'My mum's grave, you mean,' Månsson corrected her.

'Your mum's grave?'

'Never.'

What about his adoptive father's grave, then?

'You mean I could have gone there to ease the pressure?' Månsson asked with a crooked smile.

'What do you mean by that?' Holt asked.

'To piss on his grave.'

'Tell me why you'd want to do a thing like that,' Holt said. 'Did he treat you that badly?'

Månsson had no intention of talking about that. Not to Holt, nor to anyone else either.

'Don't say that,' Holt said. 'Maybe I can help you.'

How could Holt help Månsson with his adoptive father? After all, he was already dead. What could Holt do to him? She could hardly lock him up, could she? He realized that Holt and her colleagues could tear him apart, but surely they had no jurisdiction over people who were already dead?

Anna Holt made three attempts. Approaching the subject from different angles. Taking her time. With the same result each time. Either he didn't have any memories, or he didn't want to talk.

'When you say that, I get the distinct impression that there's something you don't want to tell me about your parents, and your adoptive father in particular. Can I suggest that you give the matter some thought?' Holt said, and called the guard to take him back to his cell.

'So what did we get out of that?' she asked Mattei as soon as he had gone.

'He's using you to try out the story he's going to tell other people,' Mattei said, and went on to explain that after Holt's first question and Månsson's first answer, she had worked out what he would say three hours later when he was asked the last question.

'Good to know,' Anna Holt said. 'Maybe I should stick to talking to you from now on.'

'If I were you I'd be flattered,' Mattei said. 'Why would he risk you pulling it apart now? Better to save it for the men in white coats. He won't have to worry about them running round asking people who may have been there at the time if what he's saying is true.'

'You don't think you're crediting him with being more devious than he actually is?'

'He's not especially devious,' Mattei said. 'But he knows exactly how to lie to women. How to sell himself to a sceptical customer. That's what he's best at.'

'And I'm just an ordinary bimbo,' Holt said with a smile.

'Not to Bengt Månsson,' Mattei said, shaking her head. 'For him you're a smart bimbo. A dangerous bimbo.'

'But he's still going to get between my legs.'

'Don't say that, Anna,' Mattei said. 'You're way too good for that. What I mean is just that deep down he's absolutely convinced that he's eventually going to sweep you off your feet. Metaphorically, I mean.'

'So that's what he thinks, is it?'

'How could he think anything else?'


That afternoon Bengt Månsson sent Anna Holt a message via the custody officer. He had to talk to her again. It was important. Within fifteen minutes of receiving the message Holt was sitting in his cell. Månsson was feeling terrible. And he didn't understand why. Suddenly he felt a terrible angst, and he didn't understand what was going on inside his head. In the lavatory in the custody section just before Holt arrived, he had felt giddy and fallen over.

'I'll make sure a doctor comes to see you,' Holt said.

'Could you?' Månsson said.

On the way out Holt looked questioningly at the custody officer. 'How is Månsson, really?'

'What have you been doing to him?' the guard said with a broad grin. 'When he was going to the toilet just now he seemed completely gone. He was on the floor before I had time to grab him.'

'What do you think's happening, then?'

'He's better than anything I've seen before. Rule number one – feel bloody awful. Defend yourself with an Oscar for best male lead.'

Later, when she was about to head home to the hotel, she spotted something on the notice board which really had nothing to do with her investigation.

It was a page from the interview with the female journalist who had filed a complaint against Bäckström for sexual harassment.

The Växjö officer who had interviewed the complainant appeared to have handled similar cases before. Amongst other things, he seemed to be very aware of the significance that prosecutors and courts usually applied to the difference between careless or simply partial clothing, and the nakedness which could only be caused by sexual and indecent behaviour.

'Did you notice if he had an erection when he removed the towel?' the interviewer had asked.

She wasn't sure. She hadn't looked that closely. And she had been shouting at him to pull himself together.

'But you must have seen something?' the questioner persisted, aware that this was of decisive significance if he was to be able to manoeuvre this case through the eye of the needle that led to a courtroom.

'It looked like a little sausage,' the complainant said. 'An angry little sausage.'

Lucky Bäckström, Anna Holt thought, as she crumpled the sheet and tossed it in the bin for things that needed to be shredded.

'Serves him right,' Mattei giggled when she and Anna Holt were sitting in the hotel bar with a glass of wine each, talking over the week that had just ended.

'Yes,' Holt said with a sigh. 'Sometimes I wonder what's wrong with me. I actually felt a bit sorry for him. Imagine that, Lisa. I felt sorry for Bäckström.'

'You can get help for that sort of thing, Anna,' Mattei said, looking at her sternly. 'If you like, I could put the note back up again. If you give them so much as a millimetre, they've got you.'

'But not Johansson,' Holt said.

'Never my Lars Martin,' Mattei agreed.

# 89

Jan Lewin dreams every night now. Almost every night about that summer almost fifty years ago when he got his first proper bicycle and his dad taught him to ride it. But not about the bicycle, not about his red Crescent Valiant, but about that summer, and about the day when his dad suddenly had to go into town.

Daddy hadn't taken the bus like he usually did. Instead Grandad drove out in his car to pick him up. Daddy seemed tired. 'See you soon,' Daddy said, ruffling Jan's hair, but this time everything didn't go back to normal when he did so.

Then Grandad had ruffled Jan's hair as well, and that was strange because it was the first time in his whole life that Grandad had ever ruffled his hair.

'You'll have to take over, Jan, and be the man of the house and help Mummy while Daddy's in town,' Grandad said.

'I promise,' Jan said.

# 90

A never-ending summer. A landscape with as many lakes to swim in as stars in the Nordic night sky. That Sunday Anna Holt and Lisa Mattei packed a basket and headed out to one of them to recharge their batteries before the working week ahead.

First Anna had caught up on her neglected exercise regime. As soon as she had changed, she did her stretching exercises, then ran round the lake. No sooner had she got back, approximately ten kilometres and an hour later, than she had kicked off her running shoes and swum across the lake and back again. Then she had done two hundred sit-ups and the same number of push-ups. She finished by doing more stretches, slightly flushed, and caught her breath in the twenty-five-degree heat.

Lisa had found a spot in the shade to lie down and reread one of her favourite books from childhood, *Emil and the Detectives*, by Erich Kästner. The part where little Emil uses forensic evidence to catch the slimy crook – the holes made in the six stolen banknotes by a pin – in particular had left a lifelong impression on her soul, and even elevated Emil above master detective Ture Sventon with his more intuitive investigative technique. Lisa had been interested in forensics ever since she was a little girl.

After she had finished exercising, Anna had joined her in the shade to do some reading. With the help of telephone records, witness statements and various forensic information, Lewin had constructed a timeline covering the perpetrator's movements during the twenty-four hours in which he raped and strangled Linda Wallin. Anna needed it for her impending interviews, and she intended to learn every single time and every tiny detail by heart.

From about 18.00 on Thursday 3 July, Månsson had been at home in his flat on Frövägen in the district of Öster, approximately one kilometre from the centre of Växjö. Just after 22.00 he had been visited by their witness, who had refused to have sex. She had left him at half past ten in the evening, and as soon as she had walked out of the door Månsson had started making phone calls.

Between half past ten and midnight he had made a total of eleven calls from the landline in his flat. All of them to female acquaintances. Nine of them hadn't been home, and he didn't seem to have left any messages on any answering machines. One had spoken to him but couldn't see him because she was already busy. Another had answered but had slammed the phone down when she realized who it was.

Månsson had headed into town, and because the documentation of the next two hours was based upon various witness statements it was far from as solid and precise as the details gained from an ordinary landline, or even a mobile phone. Soon after midnight Månsson had said hello to one of the most common sort of witness at that time of day, a neighbour who was on his way back into the building after walking his dog. The witness was certain of the date, time and person in question. And that Månsson had been heading towards the centre of town on foot. Anna couldn't know it, but Lewin had sighed as he noted what the witness had said in his report.

After that there were two statements which indicated that Månsson had visited at least one pub in Växjö. The bartender who had served him a beer at about half past twelve, and again one and a half hours later, had recognized him from previous visits, and on this particular occasion he had noted that Månsson had no female company, and that he appeared 'agitated and wound up'. Lewin had sighed twice, and then noted the witness's information in his report. The next witness claimed to have observed Månsson at another watering-hole in the vicinity of the first some time between one o'clock and two o'clock in the morning. Because he had recognized Månsson in the pictures he had seen in the paper – 'I'm absolutely certain it was him' – Lewin had given an extra sigh this time.

At quarter past two things improved significantly. That was when Månsson had called Lotta Ericson's old number on his mobile from somewhere in the centre of Växjö. And because Lewin had both met and listened to the witness, and had seen the printout listing the calls with his own eyes, he hadn't needed to sigh at all.

Just after three o'clock in the morning, according to their own analysis of the murder of Linda Wallin, he had appeared at the building where Linda's mother lived. Linda's car was parked outside, and he must have recognized it. Månsson had probably acted on impulse and gone inside the building in the hope of being able to see Linda. Nothing odd about that, seeing as the coded lock had been broken for the past couple of days.

Then he had probably gone wrong, for the same reason as he rang the wrong number, and gone to the door of Linda's mother's old flat at the top of the building. He went downstairs again when the dogs started to bark, and carefully checked the list of occupants in the entrance hall. There he saw an *L. Ericson*, with the right initial and the right spelling, took a chance, rang the bell, and was let in by Linda, who had just got home.

The latter parts of this were all speculation, but seeing as they were Lewin's own speculations he had no problems with their credibility. On the contrary, his assumptions provided the basis for further conclusions which he had inserted into the log as notes. That Månsson hadn't visited Linda's mother since she had moved, three years before. That she probably hadn't informed him of that fact. That Linda didn't seem to have told him either, and that his visit to see Linda was spontaneous, not premeditated.

Between approximately quarter past three and five o'clock that morning Månsson had been with his victim at the scene of the crime. At approximately five o'clock he had jumped out of the bedroom window, and in all likelihood walked home on foot. He ought to have been back home before half past five.

Then he had packed a few essentials in a sports bag and decided to leave Växjö. Exactly why remained unclear. He already had tickets to see the Gyllene Tider concert on Öland that evening, but a great deal had happened since he got hold of them. A half-hearted attempt to flee? An attempt to get himself an alibi?

That was probably when he decided to steal the pilot's old Saab, Lewin thought. Taking the bus at such a sensitive time didn't seem terribly advisable. Better to travel independently.

So he sets off on foot from his home on Frövägen to the car park on Högtorpsvägen, one kilometre from his flat. At some time around six in the morning he is observed by the 92-year-old witness, steals the car and drives off. All entirely possible, since a brisk walk would get him from his flat to the car park in time.

At approximately quarter past six he sets off towards Kalmar, and some ten kilometres from the town he decides to get rid of the car. By then it ought to have been just before eight o'clock, assuming he stuck to the speed limit, Lewin thought.

Getting rid of the car shouldn't have taken long, and then he must have made his way to Kalmar on foot. No one had seen him catch a bus or said they had given him a lift. Then he spent the rest of Friday either in Kalmar with the nurse or on Öland at the concert, until midnight or just after. They hadn't managed to trace the young woman with whom he was believed to have left the concert, despite appeals in the media for her to contact them.

Where he spent the rest of the weekend was unclear. But on Monday morning he was back at work in Växjö.

'Jan Lewin is a very thorough man,' Anna declared once she had finished reading.

'A bit too long-winded for my taste,' Lisa retorted. 'And he has a terrible angsty way of conveying facts as well. I think he uses facts as a way of combating his own angst.'

'Unlike Johansson, with all his stories of his own triumphs and everyone else's idiotic failures?' Anna said, looking curiously at Lisa.

Not according to Lisa. Lars Martin Johansson wasn't remotely like Jan Lewin, even though they were a similar age. Quite the contrary. Lars Martin Johansson's stories had taught her more about police work than almost anything else she had done, read, seen or heard.

Besides, he was extremely entertaining, and there was always a pedagogical point to the stories he told.

'And of course they're all true as well,' Anna said, smiling in delight.

Completely true, according to Lisa, and quite remarkable, in the sense that Lars Martin Johansson was one of the few people who had realized that there was a way of seeking the truth by conducting an internal dialogue with yourself. Something which Skinner, of all people, had developed in his scientific essays about introspection as a way of finding the truth and the light. And which didn't have anything in common with our mundane and dull view of the difference between truth and lies.

'Because Johansson never lies, of course,' Anna teased.

'Not in the usual way,' Lisa said. 'He's not the sort. Johansson never lies to other people.'

'What sort is he, then?'

'Maybe he lies to himself,' Lisa said, her voice suddenly sounding rather abrupt.

'I can't think why you don't marry him, Lisa,' Anna said.

'He's already married. Besides, I don't think I'm his type,' Lisa concluded with a sigh.

# 91

On the Monday following that weekend, Anna Holt decided to go on the offensive and confront Bengt Månsson with Lewin's summary of what he had been up to. The friendly, listening Lisa Mattei was to be replaced by Anna Sandberg, if only to remind him of his great, and only, interest in life.

'How were you thinking of doing this, Anna?' Sandberg asked.

'I talk, you listen. If I want you to say something, you'll notice in advance.'

'Fine by me.'

'No threats, no promises, no rush. Otherwise you can be as bitchy as you like.'

'I don't think that last bit will be too much of a problem,' Anna Sandberg said.

'Seeing as I've tried to be honest with you all the way through, Bengt, I thought I should show you this summary,' Holt began, passing him a copy of Jan Lewin's timeline.

'Thanks, I appreciate that,' Månsson said politely.

'Good,' Anna Holt said with a friendly smile. 'Then I suggest you read it through quietly. Everything there is what we already know without having to ask you, but it would still be very interesting to hear your explanation.'

'Well, of course I can see what it says,' Månsson said five minutes later, when he had finished reading. 'And when I see it like that I remember that I probably did meet Linda that evening . . . that night,' he corrected. 'I remember that to start with we sat and talked, and then we had sex with each other, on a sofa, I think it was . . . but after that I don't remember a thing.'

'You don't remember a thing?' Holt repeated.

'It's like a black hole,' Månsson said.

'What's the next thing you do remember, then?' Holt asked.

Månsson remembered meeting an old girlfriend. In her home. She lived in Kalmar. They had spent the day having sex. They went to a concert that evening. Gyllene Tider. He remembered that. He had actually bought the tickets before midsummer, through a personal contact from work.

After that it was all black. All he knew was that he had felt a great sense of angst. He remembered that. And he had simply walked out. Left his friend there. Left the concert. And gone home to his flat. He seemed to remember catching the bus from Kalmar to Växjö. A black hole, terrible angst, home again. He didn't know when, but it must have been some time during the day because there were people about.

'So you got home again some time on Saturday, in the middle of the day?'

'If you say so.' Månsson shrugged. 'It's all just a black hole.'

'Is there anything you're wondering about, Anna?' Holt said, turning to her colleague.

'So all you can remember is that you can't remember?' Anna Sandberg said acidly.

'Yes,' Månsson said, looking at her as if he'd only just realized she was in the room.

'But you remember that you have a lapse in your memory, you're sure about that?'

'Yes. It's all just a black hole.'

'Between four o'clock on Friday morning and some time later that day, it's all just a black hole?'

'Yes,' Månsson said. 'Exactly. I can't explain it.'

'No, I don't suppose you can,' Sandberg agreed. 'I've never heard of such a precise memory lapse before. It's funny that you remember it so clearly, as well. That you remember what you don't remember, I mean, and that it just happens to cover the period when you raped and strangled Linda.'

'You can't think I'd sit here and lie about something like that?' Månsson protested.

'You probably daren't confess,' Sandberg said with a shrug of her shoulders. 'You're simply too much of a coward. I suppose you're the one we should all be feeling sorry for.'

'That black hole,' Holt said, changing the subject. 'You couldn't try to describe it? What does it look like?'

Like an ordinary hole. Which made him feel terrible angst without him knowing why.

'Terrible things seem to have happened when you were down in that hole,' Sandberg pointed out. 'How about trying to climb out of it?'

'How do you mean?' Månsson said.

'By telling us what you were doing down there. While you were down there.'

'I don't know,' Månsson said. 'I just found myself there.'

They didn't get any further than that, even though they carried on all day. Towards the end Månsson himself had several things that he wanted to say to them. Important things. It was important that they understood them. First, he hadn't killed Linda. They had had sex with each other. Entirely voluntarily. He hadn't harmed her in any way.

'How can you know that?' Sandberg interrupted. 'After all, you don't remember anything, do you?'

Månsson knew, even though he couldn't remember anything. He could never do anything like that. He couldn't even imagine contemplating anything like that.

'Well, give it some thought,' Holt suggested, and then she concluded the session.

'Okay, we've got him inside the flat now. We've got him on the sofa, having sex with Linda,' Anna Sandberg said, sounding precisely as bloodthirsty as she had been feeling all the way through.

'I suppose so,' Anna Holt said with a shrug. 'But we're not the ones he's telling.'

'I'm afraid I'm not with you,' Sandberg said.

'We're never going to get him any further than that,' Holt said, shaking her head. 'He just wanted to launch the idea of his black hole.'

'At least he's admitting that he doesn't remember.'

'He's not stupid. He'll have learned everything that Enoksson and his colleagues came up with off by heart. His lawyer will have seen to that.'

'There's one thing I've been wondering about,' Sandberg said. 'Why doesn't he try the other tactic? The sex game that got out of hand?'

'I expect his lawyer has advised him against that in no uncertain terms,' Holt said.

# 92

On his penultimate night in Växjö, Jan Lewin dreamed of that summer when his dad taught him to ride a bicycle. The summer he got his first proper bike, a red Crescent Valiant. The summer his dad died of cancer.

When he woke up, and emerged from the bathroom, he had to open the window to get some air. It was raining outside. A gentle rain under dark skies. And it had turned cold as well.

What am I doing here? he thought. It's over now. It's time to go home.

# 93

In the middle of the week Jan Lewin and Eva Svanström left them. They had done their bit and were no longer needed. Not in Växjö, anyway. On the way up to Stockholm Lewin sat there trying to summon the courage to suggest to Eva that it was high time they got their relationship sorted out. That he should divorce his wife and she her husband. That they should move in together. That they should start planning a future together. High time, at least for him, because his life was getting shorter quickly now.

It never got said, and considering what was going through Eva Svanström's head, perhaps that was just as well. As soon as she got back to Stockholm she was planning to make a real effort to sort out her marriage, and to thank Jan Lewin for their time together. In hindsight, it had gone on for far too many years, but each one of those days with him had made the years bearable. But how do you explain that? she thought. When your heart stops beating and all that's left in your chest is a black hole that you can't even bear to look into. Still less to talk about what you find there.

No memories before he started school. A mother he refused to talk about. An adoptive father resting under a gravestone that he didn't even think it worth paying a visit to in order to piss on it. An unshakeable conviction that he hadn't harmed Linda. The very thought that he might have done was unbearable, therefore he couldn't have done so.

Six more interviews on this subject, the last four of them attended by the prosecutor. On one occasion he had been surrounded by three women who took it in turns to talk to him: Katarina Wibom, Anna Holt, and Anna Sandberg.

'Three against one,' Månsson declared, even if his gallows humour and smile seemed extremely forced.

'We were under the impression that you preferred the company of women,' Katarina Wibom said. 'The more the merrier, we assumed.'

There was still the black hole, in which Bengt Månsson – according to their forensic evidence – must have spent the hour or so in which he raped, tortured and strangled Linda Wallin. And the car that he stole an hour or so later, to get away from there and leave it all behind him, was of limited judicial interest.

'A black hole,' Anna Holt summarized.

'Plus forensic evidence amount to something like a hundred and twenty per cent certainty,' Katarina Wibom added.

'If only he'd just denied it outright,' Holt said. 'Or at least tried the story of the sex game that got out of hand.' Well, you can't have everything, she thought.

On the afternoon of Friday 5 September Knutsson and Thorén left Växjö as well. Other murder victims were queuing up for their services. And the piles that were mounting up on their desks in Stockholm needed to be dealt with. Being both polite and well brought up, they said goodbye to Detective Superintendent Bengt Olsson before they left.

'Thanks for having us,' Knutsson said.

'If things go badly, we might meet again,' Thorén said. 'Well, you know what I mean, Bengt,' he added apologetically.

'I understand exactly,' Olsson said with a smile. 'Without you, I'm sure we'd have had trouble solving this one. Mind you, I suppose we'd have found him sooner or later thanks to his DNA.'

'Without us, Olsson and little Månsson would probably have moved in together,' Knutsson mused in the car on the way up to Stockholm.

'And lived happily ever after,' Thorén agreed.

'I wonder what's going to happen to Bäckström,' Knutsson said.

'Bäckström will manage. He always does,' Thorén said.

# 94

On Friday 12 September, Anna Holt and Lisa Mattei left Växjö and travelled home to Stockholm. Holt would be returning to her second-ment as superintendent of the national co-ordination office of the National Crime Unit. Johansson had already tried to lure her into his team by waving the newly instigated post of his staff officer, reporting directly to him. The thought of having to listen to all his stories wasn't exactly enticing, and she had turned the job down. Firmly, but obviously as amiably as she could. Johansson had reacted exactly as she had expected. He had sulked like a child for a few days, but just a week later he was back to normal, greeting her with almost demonstrative friendliness whenever they bumped into each other in the corridor.

He's like a child, Holt thought. I wonder what he's going to come up with next time.

Lisa Mattei would be going on leave to finish her studies at Stockholm University. She was hoping to be finished by the end of the year, when her leave ran out. But she was still worried. Every academic problem she solved seemed immediately to generate two new ones, usually more interesting than the one she had just solved, and the only appealing alternative she could see ahead of her was something like the job that Anna Holt had just turned down, which Johansson would never dream of offering her.

Funny that such a highly talented man doesn't realize what would be in his best interests, Mattei thought.

Before they left, Anna Holt had a lengthy meeting with Prosecutor Katarina Wibom, during which she handed over the hundreds of pages of interview protocols, all bar one in the form of a dialogue, and now neatly typed up and bound with the national coat of arms in blue and yellow on the cover, along with the logo of the Växjö Police. And prefaced by an introductory summary addressed to the prosecutor.

'I'm not going to get any further with this, so you can take over now,' she said, nodding towards the pile of files on the desk between them.

'Well, thank you very much indeed, Anna,' Katarina Wibom said. 'This is more than I have any right to ask for, and certainly more than I'd hoped for.'

'How's it going to go, then?' Holt asked. 'What's he going to get?'

'At a guess, life for murder,' the prosecutor said. 'The way I see it, Månsson and his lawyer have two possible defences.'

'And they are . . . ?'

The first was that he and his victim had been engaging in sexual games that had gone wrong. Voluntarily on her part, even enthusiastically, then an unfortunate accident, manslaughter and a few years in prison.

'And what do you think about that?' Holt asked.

'Forget it,' the prosecutor said, shaking her head. 'I wouldn't even have to come up with a charge of death through neglect. What we've got from forensics and the medical officer would be more than enough.'

'And you're sure about that?'

'Don't forget, we're talking about the District Court in Växjö here,' the prosecutor reminded her. 'Leaving aside the fact that it's simply not what happened, even if he tries to claim it was. Hopefully his lawyer is smart enough to advise him against even trying.'

'What else, then? What's the other option?'

The memory lapse, the prosecutor explained. If nothing else, then as a suitable marker to show how psychologically disturbed he is. To prepare the ground for all the sexual abuse and everything else that he was subjected to when he was little, which he'll talk about the minute he becomes the subject of a mental health examination alone with all those doctors who, unlike everyone else, can see inside people's heads.

'Since those nice people in white coats got the chance to add memory lapses to their box of tricks, there isn't a single criminal who can remember a thing any more,' the prosecutor sighed.

'Whatever happened to the good old pathological rush of blood to the head, a decent Swedish drunken rage?' Holt said, sighing as well.

'That disappeared when they started to sentence all the drunks to life imprisonment even though they had absolutely no idea that they had stabbed their best friend with their pocket knife the night before. Nowadays it's more complicated. Schnapps and vodka aren't enough any more. Not even if you've spent twenty years or so pickling your brain. Forensic psychiatry is always making new advances. The whole time. Leaving people like you and me standing where we were.'

'Will that get him off, then?'

'Never, not in Växjö District Court,' the prosecutor said. 'You can forget that. Mind you, I wouldn't want to bet on the Court of Appeal, because I'm sure that's where we're going to end up.'

'Found guilty of murder, and sentenced to a secure psychiatric unit with specific parole conditions,' Holt summarized.

'Possibly, maybe even probably,' the prosecutor said. 'The only consolation under the circumstances may well be that most lawyers have a very peculiar image of what secure psychiatric care is like these days.'

'Not exactly a bed of roses,' Holt said.

'Not exactly a bed of roses,' the prosecutor agreed.

# 95

On the second Monday in October the Swedish Newspapermen's Association in Stockholm held a large meeting where they discussed various matters of legal principle arising from the now notorious Linda murder. A number of the most elevated media figures in the country were on the panel, and the jewel in this media crown was naturally the editor-in-chief of *Dagens Nyheter*.

However, he was far from being the loftiest person present, if one were to try to arrange them in order of precedence at a state banquet, because the introductory speaker and guest of honour was none other than the Chancellor of Justice, CJ himself.

CJ expressed serious misgivings about the manner in which the police had investigated the Linda murder and other similar cases in recent years. According to the information he had requested, the police in Växjö, in collaboration with their colleagues from the National Crime Unit, had collected voluntary DNA samples from almost seven hundred people, samples which proved that their donors had absolutely nothing to do with the crime in question.

According to information that his investigators had gathered from the National Crime Unit, the crime had actually been solved in the traditional way, through a combination of information received, witness statements and detective work. The perpetrator's DNA had played a not insubstantial role in the evidence presented by the prosecutor in the preliminary investigation. That notwithstanding, and without prejudicing the outcome of the trial, CJ believed that the evidence gathered by more traditional means was more than sufficient to support the prosecutor's decision to bring the case to trial.

Speaking personally, CJ was strongly opposed to the use of the word voluntary in a context which actually concerned the ability of the police and prosecutors to employ so-called mandatory legal methods. As he saw it, these could not be reconciled, and so he welcomed the proposal of the so-called DNA inquiry to expand the judicial authorities' powers to gather DNA samples, conduct DNA analysis and record the results of these. The question of whether or not this was voluntary would soon be obsolete, and in the best of all worlds obviously everyone's DNA would be on file from birth in a comprehensive national database. For their own good, naturally.

In conclusion, he also took the opportunity to compliment the media for their scrutiny. With touching modesty, he declared that he couldn't be sure that he would have noticed the problem unless the media had alerted him in time.

The representatives of the media hadn't had any serious comments on CJ's analysis and conclusions. This was an important question, of decisive significance to every democracy under the rule of law, and, according to the editor-in-chief of *Dagens Nyheter*, it would be given even greater prominence in his own paper, if that were possible. From a personal point of view, he was both proud and happy that he and his talented colleagues had got the ball rolling.

The chair of the Swedish Newspapermen's Association, who was leading the debate, finally took the opportunity to ask the editor-in-chief of the *Småland Post* – since he was actually there, and because they didn't exactly meet every day – why one of the smaller regional papers had declined to publish an article which Sweden's largest morning paper had gone to press with immediately, following it up with numerous editorials and other reports in the news pages.

The editor-in-chief of the *Småland Post* thanked him for the question. Without going into detail, he felt he could none the less reveal that the decision had involved his personal knowledge of the author of the piece, knowledge which might not have been possessed by his colleagues at *Dagens Nyheter*, or which they might have chosen to disregard. What did he, a simple peasant from the provinces, know about the decision-making process at the country's finest paper?

Nevertheless, he had personally taken the decision to turn down the article by the librarian Marian Gross. He hadn't regretted the decision for a moment, and if he was presented with a similar choice in future, he was confident that he would make the same decision again.

After that they moved on to the Opera Bar, the veranda of the Grand Hotel, and other nearby watering-holes catering to a wealthier clientele, and, as usual, carried on the debate long into the night before the participants finally headed home to their families for a few hours of well-deserved rest.

# 96

On Monday 20 October, proceedings against Bengt Månsson began at the District Court in Växjö, and the judgement was made public almost three months later, on 19 January of the following year. The reason why it took so long was that the court had decided that Bengt Månsson should undergo an extensive psychological evaluation, to provide as thorough a foundation as possible for any potential verdict.

On 20 December a report was received from the forensic psychiatry clinic in Lund, but by then it was time to celebrate Christmas and the New Year and all the other holidays. And the court needed plenty of time to finesse its conclusions and generally to think things over.

It was clear from the non-confidential conclusion of the forensic psychiatric report that Månsson was severely psychologically disturbed, but that this disturbance was not sufficiently severe for him to require treatment in a secure psychiatric unit. So the District Court decided unanimously to accept the prosecutor's recommendation and sentenced Bengt Månsson to life imprisonment for murder.

The verdict was taken to the Court of Appeal, which requested a new forensic psychological evaluation, which this time was conducted at Sankt Sigfrid's Hospital in Växjö, under the leadership of Professor of Forensic Psychology Robert Brundin.

Brundin reached a completely different conclusion from that of his colleagues in Lund. It was his firm conviction that Månsson was suffering from a very serious psychological imbalance, and, in the Appeal Court's verdict at the end of March, he was found guilty of murder, and sentenced to a secure psychiatric unit with specific parole conditions.

The week after the verdict was announced, Professor Brundin took part in a lengthy television interview in one of the many social-programming strands of the state-run channels. What this was really about was an extremely disturbed perpetrator with severely chaotic aspects to his personality. These in turn could be traced back to seriously traumatic experiences in his childhood.

Admittedly, these weren't the sort of war experiences that traditionally chaotic perpetrators demonstrated, but their qualitative content and consequences were entirely comparable. And they were also covered by the laws of patient confidentiality, for which reason Brundin was unable to go into any more detail. But this certainly wasn't a question of a sexual sadist with clearly developed sexual fantasies. Nor a stereotypically chaotic personality. He was more of an interesting hybrid somewhere between a sexual sadist and a chaotic perpetrator.

'By which I mean that I have finally found the missing link between these two basic types, so to speak,' the eminently satisfied Brundin declared, simultaneously wishing himself and his new patient every success in the close contact that lay ahead of them.

'Do you think you'll ever be able to cure him?' the interviewer reporter asked him.

With all due respect to her and her programme, Brundin thought that the question was incorrectly framed.

'How do you mean?'

'This is really about how we can help future generations of people like him. But if you're referring to the length of time his treatment will take, I'm rather afraid that this patient belongs to what is already a lost generation,' Brundin said, because he also happened to be very well read.

Bäckström saw the programme on television. He was sitting at home in his cosy abode not far from police headquarters, with a beer, a small whisky, a sick note, an investigation into sexual harassment that would soon be dropped, and a fair amount left inside the brown envelope. Life could certainly have been a lot worse.

It would still have made more sense to boil the bastard down to make glue, Bäckström thought. For in spite of his many failings and shortcomings, he was still a man with a strong sense of basic justice.

# 97

On Friday 24 October, Linda Wallin's mother had been due to stand witness in the District Court in Växjö about her contact with the man who had murdered her daughter. The previous day she had spoken to Anna Sandberg over the phone, and they had agreed that Anna would collect her from her summer house the following morning. She was actually feeling better than she had for a long time, and was looking forward to putting this all behind her, so that she could start to deal with her grief at the loss of her daughter.

When Anna Sandberg arrived the next morning, the front door was wide open and blowing in the autumn wind. When she saw the gap in the neat row of polished rocks edging the raked gravel path she understood immediately what had happened. The divers found her that same day, four metres down. Before she jumped in the lake she had put on a winter coat with big pockets, and filled these with stones. Then she had tied a belt round her chest and upper arms, in case she changed her mind at the last minute.

In her top pocket she had a photograph taken at a midsummer party out at Linda's father's home some three years before. Linda in the middle, flanked by her mother and the perpetrator. Someone had circled the faces of Lotta Ericson and Bengt Månsson, and written the word *Murderers* above them. The envelope that the photograph had arrived in was on the kitchen floor, with no sender's address, and had been postmarked in Växjö on Wednesday.

The coroner's report into the death was finished long before the trial was over, and the conclusion had been clear from the moment the body was found. Linda's mother had committed suicide. Her grief at her daughter's death meant that she didn't need much of a push, and the identity of the person who had sent the photograph was never discovered. Linda's father had had no suggestions when the Växjö Police spoke to him about it, and he had already got over the loss of his former wife.

He was left to nurture the memory of his beloved only daughter.

# 98

In April the following year the CPR, committee for personal responsibility, of the National Police Authority finally concluded the case against Detective Superintendent Evert Bäckström. The reason why it had taken so long was that the prosecutor had only been able to drop the complaint against Bäckström for sexual harassment the previous week. Lack of evidence.

It had been a complex inquiry, in part because the evidence was unclear, since Bäckström had stubbornly stuck to his version of events. The complainant had more or less forced her way up to his room even though he had suggested that they meet in the hotel bar after he had taken a much-needed shower and changed into a fresh shirt. Towards the end of the investigation the complainant had also refused to cooperate, because she didn't think there was any point, and under the circumstances the prosecutor hadn't had any choice.

Which left the financial irregularities, amounting in total to some twenty thousand kronor. There were numerous mysterious cash withdrawals, one remarkable laundry bill, a strange list of materials detailed on an invoice for conference equipment which included, amongst other things, thirty-one whiteboard erasers at 96 kronor each, an invoice for porn films debited to one of his colleagues' rooms, and various other things. Most remarkable of all: on the day that the finance department brought all of this to Bäckström's attention, he had settled all their demands in cash. Considering his reputation, this was probably the biggest mystery of them all.

None the less, he was still reprimanded for a number of

transgressions against the rules and regulations governing members of the national police, and his union representative had to work hard to find a compromise solution that Bäckström's ultimate superior, HNC Lars Martin Johansson, could live with.

Bäckström had had to return to his original posting with regional crime in Stockholm, where they had placed him temporarily in the lost property office. Or Lost & Found, as every proper police officer, including Bäckström himself, called this final resting place for unclaimed bicycles and lost police souls.

He was, however, allowed to keep the rank of superintendent. Johansson wasn't the sort to bear a grudge, although Bäckström himself would happily have surrendered it if it meant he could escape sharing a workplace with his old brother-in-arms Wiijnbladh, who had worked part time in the same office since trying to poison his now ex-wife fifteen years before. Sadly, he had only succeeded in poisoning himself, which was why he had been transferred out of the forensics division and into the Stockholm Police's very own gulag archipelago.

# 99

In May that same year, during the now annual police conference in the Älvsjö exhibition centre on the outskirts of Stockholm, Detective Superintendent Bengt Olsson gave a well-received lecture on the main theme of the conference: conflicts between different cultures of policing. He took his illustrations from his experiences as head of the preliminary police investigation into the Linda murder.

On one side, he himself and his colleagues from the Växjö Police. They had limited resources, but a lot of local knowledge and a wealth of practical experience. On the other side, officers from the National Crime Unit, who never needed to worry about costs, and possibly as a result of this preferred to attack problems on as broad a front as possible.

Obviously, there had been certain tensions between these two groups. This was perfectly natural, and nobody's fault, according to Olsson, because they lived in different worlds and had been raised in different cultural traditions and beliefs. They had certainly been able to learn a great deal from each other, and he personally would like to point out the valuable contribution made to the work of the Växjö Police by the CP group, as well as National Crime's remarkable achievement when it came to registering the vast amount of paperwork generated by the case.

But in the end, Olsson remained firmly convinced that it was local knowledge that had been the decisive factor in the apprehension of the perpetrator. This needed to be taken into account in future, when consideration was given to how best to reinforce the resources of local and regional police authorities in connection with investigations into very serious violent crimes, and ought thus to form the basis for a new way of organizing things.

After the lecture Lars Martin Johansson had gone up and thanked Olsson. Not just on his own behalf, but on behalf of many other officers. Seldom had so many police officers had reason to thank one single fellow officer for talking so much shit in so short a space of time, Johansson declared in his very politest manner. And if Olsson ever needed help solving any more blindingly obvious crimes in future, he needn't bother to consider troubling Johansson and his colleagues.

On Friday 28 May, Lisa Mattei submitted her doctoral thesis at the Institute of Applied Philosophy at Stockholm University. Her dissertation was entitled *In Memory of the Victim?*, and that final question mark was what it was really about. The hidden messages concealed in the media's coverage of so-called sex killings of women, which the author had chosen to analyse from a gender perspective.

The classic semiotic connection between content and expression, and the remarkable fact that the first names of almost two hundred women had contributed the prefix to the sexual crimes that had ended their lives during the previous fifty years. From the Birgitta murder, the Gerd murder, the Kerstin murder and the Ulla murder, to mention just four nationally notorious and fifty-year-old examples, to the most recent cases of the new millennium: the Kajsa murder, the Petra murder, the Jenny murder . . . and the Linda murder.

That they had been quite simply transformed from women of flesh and blood into media messages. To symbols, according to conventional semiotic vocabulary. That the very best of the prefixes, from the media's point of view, could even be reused one last time if the police managed to catch the perpetrator.

From trainee police officer Linda Wallin, 20. To the Linda murder. To the Linda Man, at the end of the judicial sequence of events.

Symbols of what? What was there that united them, other than the manner in which they had been murdered, described in the media and finally dispatched to the relative amnesia of Swedish criminal history? Obviously, it couldn't be a simple question regardless of gender. After all, men's names were never used as prefixes to the word 'murder', and it made no difference whether the motives were sexual or merely unknown. Being a human being evidently wasn't enough. You had to be a woman, but simultaneously you couldn't be just any woman.

You had to be a woman of a certain age. The youngest of them might have been just five years old when she was raped and strangled, but with the exception of a dozen women working as prostitutes none of the others had been older than forty. The perpetrators' motives and methods provided no exhaustive explanation either. The number of women murdered during the same period because the perpetrators had a sexual motive, or where various things they had done to their victims suggested that was their motivation, was close to five hundred.

Lisa Mattei had asked the obvious follow-up question that would occur to every intelligent human being and female police officer. What was it that led the media to reject sixty per cent of the women who had been murdered for sexual reasons?

Many of them had been far too old. The eldest was actually over ninety when she was raped and beaten to death with the flat side of an ordinary axe. Many of them had lived in social circumstances that had been far too wretched. Had been with men who were far too socially excluded. Many of them had been murdered by perpetrators who had been arrested immediately or shortly after the murder, and their story wasn't good enough from a purely dramaturgical perspective.

In short, and in summary, they had lacked media value in the simple economic sense of selling more papers. The pictures weren't attractive enough. The text wasn't exciting enough. Their stories were too banal. They simply weren't good enough.

For some reason Lisa Mattei had chosen to dedicate her dissertation to almost two hundred women who were listed in Swedish alphabetical order, from A to Å, by their first name. The first was called Anna, the same Anna as in the Anna murder, and the last was called Åsa, the same Åsa as in the Åsa murder.

But my name is Lisa, Lisa as in Lisa Mattei, Lisa Mattei thought as she typed the last letter on her computer. I am thirty-two years old, I am a woman, a detective inspector, and soon a PhD.

# About the Author

**Leif G.W. Persson** is Scandinavia's most renowned criminologist and a leading psychological profiler. He has also served as an adviser to the Swedish Ministry of Justice. Since 1991, he has been Professor at the National Swedish Police Board and is regularly consulted by media as the country's foremost expert on crime. He is the author of nine best-selling novels including most recently *The Dying Detective*, which won both the Swedish Academy of Crime Writers' Award for Best Crime Novel of 2010 and The Glass Key for Best Scandinavian Crime Novel of 2010.